GHOSTS OF SEPTEMBER

MARC W.
SHAKO

This is a work of fiction. All characters and dialogue are products of the author's imagination and are not to be construed as real. The situations, incidents, and dialogues are entirely fictional and are not intended to depict actual events or to change the entirely fictional nature of the work. Any resemblance to actual persons, living or dead, events, or businesses is entirely coincidental.

Copyright © 2019 Marc Wobschall. All Rights Reserved.

For Dad
My hero. My best friend.

WEDNESDAY, SEPTEMBER 5, 2018

SIXTEEN YEARS, ELEVEN MONTHS, AND twenty-four days had passed since Ray Madison had killed his best friend. Now he awoke in the dimness of his grubby front room unsure if it was late evening or early morning, but sure he didn't give a shit which. His neck ached. Whoever designed the sofa clearly thought it best the armrests should be at an angle much better for breaking necks than for comfortable sleeping. The peeling plaster of the opposite wall blurred in and out of focus as his eyes settled on which of the three images was the right one. A groan escaped as he raised himself upright and let the build-up of stomach acid burn its way back down to where it belonged. This is not how a 39-year-old was supposed to feel. The empty bottle of cheap bourbon stared back at him from its place on the spindly coffee table with a shrug. *You did this to yourself, pal.* He glanced from his New Jersey window at the Lower

Manhattan skyline, and decided that the angle of shadows made it evening. It was a skyline he once loved, now it stared back at him vacantly like a stranger.

The hour meant that if he hadn't done it already, Joel would be calling soon. Great. Not that he didn't like Joel. Joel was a good guy, but he'd be pissed when he found out that he'd been drinking again.

Sponsors can be difficult that way.

He chuckled to himself as he shuffled into the messy kitchen, avoiding eye-contact with the dishes piled high in the sink and the letter on the table which was, in part, to blame for this latest lapse. He was feeling shitty enough without facing that. The horror show in the sink was the main reason he kept his bourbon in the cupboard by the fridge and not the one over the stacks of dirty plates.

The cool glass of the bottle felt good in his hand and, as always, the cap was unscrewed before he'd even contemplated closing the cupboard doors. The fiery liquid burned a path to his stomach making his eyes screw ever tighter as it went. Turns out Pepto Bismol is better for acid reflux. *Who'd have thunk it?* The bottle slammed to the counter and now it was time to close the cupboard doors. He grabbed the cap, a redundant act as he knew fine well that it wouldn't be going back on the bottle, and edged back towards the Ray-shaped dent in the sofa.

Ray lowered himself with the same groan as when he got up and slumped into his groove, and the moment his ass touched the seat, there was a noise. Nothing loud. Not scary or threatening. Obtrusive, yes. It sounded again. The vibrate

GHOSTS OF SEPTEMBER

of his cell phone.

'Hey, Joel. How are you pal?' he said aloud. Practicing to see exactly how much he was slurring.

'Not bad, Raymondo.'

Not bad. Not great either. He'd let it go to voicemail and fire off a quick text message. His appearance at a meeting with crusted saliva down one cheek and ruffled clothes he hadn't changed in a week would not go down well. Oh and the smell.

His cell finally stopped buzzing and he raised himself back up and started the hunt for his phone. He'd have to be fast. Joel would call back in a minute or so, he always did. It was after the second call that Ray would send the message. If he didn't do it quickly enough Joel would set off for his place. Joel might come anyway, he only lived in Hoboken. Fifteen minutes away; it might take longer if the traffic was on his side (and against Joel). But with the right message, he might dissuade Joel from coming at all and then he could get back to drinking, straighten himself up and tomorrow he'd come clean. Tell Joel that anniversaries were always the worst – as a recovering alcoholic himself that was something he'd understand – and start again.

Tomorrow.

Tomorrow was for fresh starts. Today was for drinking. He'd got a pretty good buzz going before he'd fallen asleep. That was rare when he started drinking. It was usually just drinking for the sake of drinking. Not for pleasure. Not so he felt a gentle, fuzzy warmth. Just so he didn't feel.

So he could escape this shitty apartment and the sad lonely existence it had come to represent.

He lifted a two-week-old copy of The Times from the armchair wishing he'd paid more attention to the buzzing and where it was coming from. Nothing there. He frisked himself, just in case, and came up empty. He hated this. He had to leave the fucking thing on, or Joel would invade his fortress of solitude, but it wasn't much use unless you knew where it was. And he'd be calling back in a moment.

Christ come on.

He turned a little too quickly and swooned. He lurched for the dining table and grabbed hold. Maybe it was amongst the pizza boxes and fast-food cartons stacked on the table... He gingerly moved them so as not to upset them, the smell was bad enough as it was; he could do without having to clean Lo Mein from the table, floor, dining chairs, whatever. Where is it?

The vibrating started again. Ray jumped, as much from eagerness as fright. The muffled buzz was coming from the sofa. It must have fallen from his pocket. Grabbing at the cushions, he threw them aside in turn until he found the right one. There it was. Joel calling. Naturally. Nobody else called these days. One by one, they'd all given up on him. Given up on him when he'd prioritized drinking over socializing. When he'd made excuses so he didn't have to leave the relative sanctity of his apartment. Didn't have to shower. Didn't have to shave. Didn't have to smile. Didn't have to pretend everything was okay.

None of them understood. They said they did, but they

GHOSTS OF SEPTEMBER

didn't. How could they? Being responsible for the death of another soul was a crushing weight. He knew a guy way back, older guy, one of his old man's friends (Jimmy or Jerry something), driving along, minding his own business and a kid ran out. From nowhere was what witnesses said. No way he could avoid it. He was only doing thirty. Less than the speed limit. Kid ran out from between two cars. He tried to brake. Tried to swerve. But he hit him. And while they were waiting for the ambulance to arrive, the kid died. Right there in his arms. Fucked him up. He was done after that. Went to therapy, but it didn't help. And this guy was in no way at fault. His old man had told him one afternoon, back in the days when they'd share a beer watching the football, that the guy saw this kid's body everywhere he looked. Not all the time. It would surprise him. Pop up at inopportune moments. He'd be shaving and the kid would just appear in the tub behind him. He'd open the closet to grab a shirt and look down and *boom!* The kid. Always the same. Dead. All folded up and crushed. Anyway, his old man's friend saw that kid every day, till he put a revolver in his mouth.

Not that he hadn't thought about suicide himself. Of course. Pills, maybe. He didn't have a gun. Never even fired one. His old man had been too drunk to show him how. Not that he cared about shooting. Pete was the all-action type. Pop took Pete shooting. Ray was too young. Well, he did go once. Didn't hit a thing all day. Pete hit everything. That was the first and last time Ray got invited. Not that he cared, he hated it. But it was just another thing for Pop to favor Pete for. So yeah, shooting was out. He'd probably miss anyway. Jumping was an option. His apartment was on the fourth floor. Maybe it would do it, maybe not. Might just leave him in a chair, eating through a tube or some shit. Like the dreams he used to have. Fucking wheelchair. Fuck that. Prisoner in your own body. The phone stopped ringing.

Focus Raymondo. No suicide tonight. More drinking to do. Send this text message and let's get on with it.

He dabbed through the cracked screen at the message icon. Of course Joel's name was the first to show. Nobody else texted.

- *Why would they? A screw up like me?*

- *Raymond?! Focus! Type a fuckin text message before he leaves his place.*

'Hey Joel, sorry I missed you. Just got out of the shower...'

He could see Joel now. Joel in his nice apartment, light shining off that round shaven head of his. Now he's picking up his keys to his nice car. Telling his nice girlfriend that he has to go out.

'I'm not feeling too good. I thought a shower might help...'

Putting on his shoes. Grabbing his jacket.

'I think it's best if I skip tonight's meeting...'

Reaching for the door handle.

And send.

Now he had to wait. See if it had the desired effect. He

GHOSTS OF SEPTEMBER

replaced the cushions on the sofa, slumped back into his groove, and waited. Joel was a prompt replier. Joel had just called so he already had his phone in his hand, how long could it take? A thin film of sweat had formed on his forehead. If Joel called again, Ray knew he was fucked. He'd have to answer and then Joel would hear the fuzziness in his voice and that would be that. Joel would come over and bust his balls until he let him in. A text message was the desired response. What the hell was taking so long? His phone buzzed. A text message. Ray allowed himself a little smile. He opened the message.

'I'll be right over. J'

Shit.

2

He slugged another mouthful of the cheap bourbon and surveyed the slum his apartment had become. Party's over, pal. Joel would eventually talk his way inside and that would be the end of this bottle. He didn't have long. This was the only bottle; no way was it going down the drain. He had to hide it before Joel was knocking on the door with one of those delicate, piano-playing hands of his. The problem was Joel had been his sponsor for so long that he knew all of his hiding places. Probably because when he was on the bottle, he'd used them all himself. Christ, he was like a bloodhound. He even found the emptied-out ketchup bottle filled with Jim Beam. That was a good one. The bourbon tasted a little tomato-ey, but he figured if he used it enough that would fade. But no. Joel had to ruin it. Like a goddam sniffer-dog.

He glanced down at his phone. Fifteen minutes wasted. How was that possible? He remembered the other, empty bottle on the coffee table. He lowered himself carefully onto the sofa, grabbed the empty and decanted a lousy half-mouthful into it. Now he could put the three-quarters of booze in a grade 2 hiding place.

The ketchup bottle was grade 4. Really creative. Like a bottle tied out of the window on a length of string. Grade 1 is the first place you'd look. Cupboards, cabinets, fridges; the places regular folks keep their booze. Grade 2 would be enough for this baby. Joel would presume that the decoy was responsible for his condition.

Ray jumped as there was a knock on his apartment door. Shit. Joel? Already? Who'd let him in the building? The cute Mexican chick from down the hall. She always smiled at Joel and had seen Ray and Joel together a couple of times. Another knock.

'Who is it?'

Like he had no idea.

'It's Joel. Open up.' For a small guy, he could sound like a tough nut when he wanted to.

Ray was frantically searching for the cap. Where the fuck had he put it? He scanned the room, head spinning a little as he did. It hadn't occurred to him until now that he was actually quite drunk.

'How did you get in the building?'

GHOSTS OF SEPTEMBER

'You gonna make me wait out here all night?'

There. The cap. Dining table. Smack in the middle of the empty pizza box. He'd treated himself when he wasn't drinking.

'Two seconds,' he shouted, trying to sound sober.

He grabbed the cap and twisted it on tight before staggering to the closet and stuffing the bottle into the inside pocket of his overcoat, then straightened out the coats so nobody could tell he'd been in there. Good enough.

He opened the door till the chain snapped tight, leaning forward to fill the gap with his face before Joel could do the same. Joel didn't say anything, but Ray caught the look in his eye. Not exactly disappointment. A sadness. Like Ray's drinking was somehow his own failure. Ray hated that look. It reminded him of his old man. That was probably the main reason he stopped visiting Pop.

He caved. He closed the door and slid off the lock. Without opening the door, he turned, knowing Joel would just follow him inside. It would just buy him enough time to take that last swig of whiskey from the decoy before Joel could take it away. When he drank it the whiskey tasted bad. Like Joel's disappointment had somehow tainted it.

'Jesus, Ray. When?'

'Three days ago, I guess.' Could have been four. He'd be hard-pressed to say what day it was.

'Today's Wednesday.'

'So four.'

No point lying now.

'Jesus, we spoke on Sunday. How come you didn't call me?'

Joel sounded wounded. He tried not to, but Ray could tell. After three years with Joel as his sponsor, Ray could tell. Their time together was probably the same reason they only spoke once a week, between meetings. In the beginning it was every day, but over time it had dropped off. By mutual agreement. That was the same reason they only hit the meetings once a week, just to show face.

'I let you down I guess.' Ray looked up at Joel, feeling pathetic and small.

'No it's my fault. I've been so busy. Crap. I just wish you'd called me,' he said taking the empty decoy.

Ray felt a sting of tears in the corner of his eyes.

Hold it in for crying out loud.

But he couldn't. A sob escaped. Real throaty.

'Hey, come on.' Joel sat beside him and put a hand on his shoulder. 'Let's get you straightened out. Come on. In the shower you go. I'll make coffee.' Joel motioned to stand.

Ray choked back his sobs, 'Wait.'

Joel stopped and sank back to the sofa.

'I fucked up, Joel, I'm sorry.'

'No need for that. It's done. It's in the past. I messed up too. Let's look forward.'

'It's an anniversary. You know how it is.'

'Tell me about it,' Joel said. But not like "I hear ya, pal." Like he really wanted to hear it.

Joel had heard his story at the meetings. More than once. Ray guessed that Joel sensed he needed to talk about it. Joel was an intuitive guy, but Ray could also tell that Joel blamed himself for this latest lapse.

'I let you down, Joel.'

'You already said that. I already forgave you. Stop apologizing.'

'It's just you know… Manny.'

Manny. To say his name hurt. He started sobbing again. Manny would still be alive if it weren't for him. 'I'd give anything to go back, you know.'

'You know how many times I've heard this story, Raymondo?'

'A lot?' Ray guessed.

'A lot. And no matter how many times I hear it, you know what it sounds like? It sounds like what it was - an accident. I know you feel responsible, but what happened - you didn't do it. And you can't go back. Think forwards. Right?'

That was the week when it all fell apart. His stomach tightened and lurched and he didn't want to talk about it anymore.

'You okay, pal?' Joel looked at him.

He could only nod.

'I'm gonna take a shower.'

'Good idea.'

Joel helped him to his feet and led him down the dark hallway to the bathroom. Joel reached for the light switch, but it just flipped back and forth in the dark.

'I'm gonna fix that.' Ray hated the way his own voice

sounded. Slurred with drink and thick with tears.

'You got a bulb out?'

'Nah it's the switch.'

'I'll take a look at it for you.'

'I want to do it.' He tried not to sound indignant but was unsure how well he'd done.

Joel smiled, 'Okay but not tonight.'

Ray smiled and his vision blurred with the old tears. 'Asshole.'

They both laughed as they turned into the bathroom. Ray hit the switch and the light came on, showing the mess inside. Black mold coated the corners, and the sink and bath looked more yellow than white. Damp dirty socks and underwear peppered the floor. Ray was embarrassed but it seemed not to bother Joel. That was impossible. He was just good at hiding it.

'You got it from here?'

'Yup.'

'I'll be down the hall, leave the door open.'

'Open?'

'Don't lock it.'

'Right.'

'Shout if you need me.'

Ray *mm-hhhm'd* and Joel disappeared back down the hall. Ray undressed and stood under the stream of hot water. He hadn't showered in days. It felt good. His stiff greasy hair took water and he shampooed. A few seconds in the hot, steamy water and he was starting to feel human again.

As he stood and dried the smell of coffee wafted along

GHOSTS OF SEPTEMBER

the hallway. It smelled good and nauseated him at the same time. Drinking it wouldn't keep him awake, but it would make tomorrow morning a little easier to deal with. These days, that was just about the best he could hope for.

'Ray?'

Joel's voice drifting from the living room. He shut off the water.

'What's this, Ray?'

The stashed bottle? Fucking bloodhound.

3

Ray sat opposite Joel in the living room, dressed in clean grey sweatpants and an old Strokes t-shirt. Both men were silent. Ray rubbed a hand across the stubble on his face and made a mental note to shave. Tomorrow. In the other hand the worn rabbit's foot keyring offered comfort as he rubbed at the balding patch that grew larger every time he had his struggles. The thought flashed through his mind that if he wasn't an alcoholic, he and Joel might actually be friends – that he might be more than just a sponsor, if he could ever get his act together. Every time Joel had to come round and do his rescue act, Ray got the same feeling. He scanned the room. It looked different. While he'd been in the shower Joel had tidied the crap from the dining table into black refuse bags and cleared the sofa and armchair of clutter. The bags sat by the door like unwelcome guests. Joel worked fast. He hadn't found the stash; he'd found the letter.

'Why didn't you tell me?'

Ray just stared at the rabbit's foot. 'I wanted it to be a surprise.'

'Well it is…'

'I fucked it up now.'

There was no way he'd be able to start a new job now he'd fallen off the wagon.

'Look at me, Ray.'

Joel's voice had hardened. Ray had no choice in the matter. He peered up.

Joel waved the letter. 'This is huge.'

'I blew it. Again.'

'Ray, you got yourself clean enough to actually make a positive step. You took a chance. So what it didn't work out this time. There'll be others.' Joel wasn't just cheerleading, that wasn't his style; he meant every word. 'Ray, if anything like what happened to you, happened to me? I don't know. You're going to meetings. Applying for jobs now… that takes balls. Huge balls. I'm fucking proud of you, man.'

Ray nodded, but had to look away, he didn't want to start crying again.

'Drink some coffee.'

The sweet coffee went down better than he expected.

'Feeling any better?'

'Much. Thanks. It gets too much sometimes. Then it gets away from me.' For a second, that heavy sob rose in him again, but somehow, he contained it.

'I know how that goes,' Joel replied.

Ray thought he did.

GHOSTS OF SEPTEMBER

'What do you think, could you sleep now?'

'Yeah, I'll get my sorry ass to bed.'

'I don't got to search the ketchup bottles, do I?'

Ray smiled, then thought of the bourbon in his coat pocket and his stomach turned. Guilt, most likely. He didn't want it.

'Ketchup bottles? No…' He paused. 'Overcoat. Closet. Inside pocket.'

'My man. I'll stay till you're asleep. Let myself out.'

'You don't have to,' he said.

Joel just stared.

'But thanks.'

He said goodnight to Joel and shuffled on unsteady feet into his bedroom. Joel had stayed even though Ray had said he didn't have to. Probably watching for the usual relapse. Or maybe he was just a good guy. The cool sheets enveloped him, and sleep was close. Joel had said he'd come by tomorrow. Just to check if he'd been drinking, he supposed. From Joel's point of view it made sense, but it was probably unnecessary. There again, tomorrow was another day. He closed his eyes and drifted into an uneasy sleep.

4

Ray jerked awake in bed. In the darkness the glowing green digits on the alarm flicked to 3AM. Dryness had taken over his mouth and his stomach churned through the spin cycle.

MARC W SHAKO

He settled his feet onto the cold floor and yawned. The quiet whoosh of cars passed outside on Newark Avenue at regular thirty-second intervals, but it was in the gaps of near New Jersey silence that he heard something else.

Voices. In the living room. Familiar, but he was certain neither voice belonged to Joel. A thin veil of sweat formed instantly on his back, sticking his shirt to his skin. He slowly raised himself up and reached for the baseball bat he kept beside his bed. It was gone. Laughter rose from the living room and was quickly shushed. His heart thudded heavily in his chest. His breath was short and he slumped to the floor and lifted the bed sheet with a clammy hand. He had to find that bat. He peered under the bed.

'Ray!'

A broken bloody hand grabbed him.

It was Manny.

Ray sat up in bed with a start, heart pounding in his chest. His eyes settled on the digital alarm, the clock flicked to 3AM. Air flooded his lungs in gasps until slowly, surely, his breathing came under control. Then, through the darkness, between his breaths, he heard something. Voices. In his living room. His heart was trip-hammering again. He reached out and put his hand on the solid wood of the baseball bat. He lowered a foot to the cool floor. There was laughter, but it was quickly shushed.

'What the…?'

The other foot caressed the floor and he raised himself up without a sound, shirt stuck to him, just as it was in the dream. The soft chatter of conversation drifted down the hallway, but again it wasn't Joel. He eased one foot in front of the other, bat raised, knuckles white. Just ahead, the soft glow of lamplight from the living room spilled into the hall. The voices lowered again to a whisper. His hand reached out for the light switch and pressed. Then again, and again.

'Still broken,' he said in a voice that sounded distant, disembodied.

He set off again, both hands gripping the welcome solidity of the bat. The shadows in the light at the edge of the hallway jerked, giving him pause as he edged to the doorway and prepared to strike. His stomach cartwheeled and the shirt tightened with each breath, sticking to his shoulders with sweat. The whispers quietened the closer he got to the living room, and then, the moment he reached the doorway, the whispering stopped.

Silence. Nausea pumped through him with each panicked heartbeat, then a voice called out.

'Raymond?'

Ray's grip on the bat loosened. It couldn't be…

'Pop?'

Ray peered around the corner to see his dead father sitting at the far end of the dining table. The only light in the room fell from above the table in a cone, like at one of his late-night poker games. His father eyed him with that famous Madison hardened stare. The swept-back hair was full and dark, his eyes keen.

Like before Pete died.

'Hello, Raymond.'

Ray shambled into the light and stood beside Pop. A beer sat in front of Pop on the table, perspiration coating the outside of the green bottle. The label was taped over, so the brand name wasn't visible, like on some cheap TV show. At least the table was clean. Thank God Joel had cleared the crap away.

'Who are you talking to, Pop?'

His father stared at him, and slowly reached out a hand to gesture at the opposite end of the table. 'Peter's here.'

Ray shifted his eyes, aware that he wanted to turn quicker, but was unable. When his eyes finally arrived at the opposite end, there, large as life, was Pete, smiling at him. An odd, robotic smile.

'What are you doing here, Pete?'

'Well, I'm pleased to see you too, baby brother.'

'Baby brother,' Ray repeated in a hollow, nervous laugh.

It was funny because he *was* Pete's baby brother, but Pete was still only eighteen years old here, the same age as when he died. He looked like Ray remembered, athletic and strong, hair hanging down almost covering one eye. It felt odd to look at him. Pete just stared and smiled that unnatural, mechanical smile.

'You'd better sit down.'

Ray's eyes traced back along the table to where his father was sitting. He pulled out a chair and with that slow robotic gesture invited Ray to sit.

'You're dead, too, Pop.'

GHOSTS OF SEPTEMBER

'Not now Raymond. Sit down.'

Before Ray knew what was happening, he was sitting at the table between his dead father and dead brother, a sweating green bottle of beer in front of him.

He cleared his throat to speak. 'Am I...'

His father and brother laughed aloud, a deep and hearty sound, just like they used to. Ray felt like an outsider all over again.

'Dead?' his father finished, suddenly not laughing at all.

'Not dead,' Pete said. 'We just wanted to talk to you.'

'About what?'

Ray didn't like this. It felt like an interrogation. Like the time he broke the neighbor's window with an apple. That doesn't sound right. An apple? Now he wasn't sure if that had happened at all.

'It was a softball, Ray. Mr. Zalewski's window. Remember?'

'Right. A softball.'

Pete spoke to him, 'Have a drink, Ray.'

Ray stared at the green bottle. Coolness issued from it as a bead of condensation traced a trail downward until it formed a tiny puddle on the table. His throat felt dry and tight. The bubbles floated in slow motion. Ray studied their journey and it was only then he noticed that the bubbles weren't floating at all. They were falling.

'I shouldn't. Joel would be upset.'

More booming laughter followed.

'Joel would be upset.' His father mocked.

Ray looked at eighteen-year-old Pete, wearing the Jets shirt and grey sweatpants he wore the last time Ray saw him alive.

'Relax, baby brother. Everything's going to be alright.'

Pete smiled again, but this time it wasn't robotic. It was natural and warm and charming, just like it used to be. Ray returned the smile as Pete raised his bottle and drank. Ray turned to his father who chugged on his beer, winking at Ray as he did so. Ray reached for the bottle and slowly tightened his hand round its cold wetness. It felt good. He raised the bottle to his lips and glanced at his brother. Pete nodded, still smiling. When he looked at his dad, he was smiling too. A warm smile that Ray hadn't seen since Pete died.

'Bottoms up.'

Ray closed his eyes tipped his head back and poured. The beer was cold and refreshing and the tiny bubbles burst as it slid easily down his throat. He emptied the bottle and set it back down on the table into the ring of water it had left when he raised it.

He smiled and turned to Pete. Pete stared back with empty, emotionless eyes. Ray looked at his father.

'What the hell are you doing, Raymond?' his eyes piercing, pupils shrunk to tiny dots.

'What?'

'Jesus, Ray,' Pete said.

Ray turned and looked at Pete. The bottle in front of him was open, but full. Ray turned to look at his father's

GHOSTS OF SEPTEMBER

bottle. It too was untouched.

'Jesus, Raymond.' His dad this time.

'What are you doing, Ray?'

He looked disbelieving at the three bottles, theirs full, his empty. Pop slammed his fist onto the table.

'What the hell's wrong with you? You drink all the time. Invite us here and look at you. You're a mess.'

'And a disappointment, Dad,' Pete chimed in.

'That's right, Peter, a fucking disappointment. Why can't you be more like your brother?'

Ray opened his mouth to argue, but the words were jammed. He hadn't invited them here, they'd arrived unannounced. But the argument was weak. They were right. He was a mess.

'Why can't you be more like me, Ray?'

'You used to be such a good boy. Look at your brother, Raymond. Look at him. Do you think he'd fall apart like you?'

Ray turned to see Pete, youthful, athletic, full of promise, still smiling that unnatural smile, but now tears streamed down his face.

'He's dead, Raymond. Dead. You're not. But you may as well be. Look at me Raymond goddamit!'

Ray turned back to his father feeling like a spectator at Arthur Ashe stadium.

'It should have been you, Raymond. It should have been you. You can't do anything right. My Peter was such a good boy.' His father sobbed.

'Look at what you've done, Ray.'

Ray looked back at Pete, who was still smiling, but at the same time tears streamed down his cheeks.

Pete spoke. 'You killed Manny, Ray. That was all your fault. You drove Kat away too. Remember? Sure you do.'

Ray felt his eyebrows draw together. Pete had died long before he'd ever met Kat. Kat who had loved him. He looked again at his dead brother. His heart hurt. He started to cry. Ray wanted to scream, but nothing came out. Pete grabbed his face and squeezed hard.

'Manny's dead because of you. Look at him.'

Pete turned Ray's head to the empty chair opposite. Only now it wasn't empty. Now it had Manny's broken body in it. All crushed and folded up, just like the visions he imagined his old man's friend having. Only Manny wasn't dead. He was alive. The skin dark red with blood, matted hair stuck to the left side of his face where the skull had been crushed. His hands folded on the table; arms broken at strange angles. Manny sobbed uncontrollably and the tears ran down his sunken, bloody cheek. One bloodshot eye peering through the wet, matted hair. Ray tried again to scream, but it was useless. He could hear his father but couldn't take his eyes away from Manny.

'Stop your drinking, Raymond. You've done enough damage. You're killing yourself. Can't you see it? When are you going to wake up?'

'Wake up, Ray.'

'Wake up, Raymond.'

'Wake up, Ray!'

Wake up.

THURSDAY

RAY GASPED FOR AIR AS he bolted upright in the pale morning light of his room. He glanced at the clock and fell back into bed. It was 8:12AM, not three. But his relief was short-lived as the rest of the dream filtered into memory. He propped himself up on his elbows and glanced around the room, checking for normality. Last night's dream was disturbing. Not because it had his dead father in it. Or his dead brother for that matter (not that it wasn't a factor). It was disturbing because it was a *new* dream. He'd had others, a series of different recurring dreams at various points in his life.

Before Pete died, he was awake at home (whichever home they were living in at the time) and everyone else was asleep, and the place was on fire. The roar of the inferno was deafening; thick smoke clung to the ceiling in boiling clouds, and the heat – heavy like a sodden cloak. So, half-blind with the smoke, and half-mute with the noise he'd have to alert the family. Save Mom. Save Pop. Save Pete. And, through the wavering lines of that savage heat, he saw the route to their rooms was clear, but he couldn't move. At first, he thought he was frozen in place by fear. Then he'd look down. He'd look down and see the wheelchair. Then he felt powerless. Arms leaden. Voice hoarse. All he could do was sit there, trying to scream loud enough over the roaring flames to wake the family. Sit there and watch as the fire crept closer with furious inevitability until it was at his feet. The air thick with the sickening stench of burning hair and flesh as his skin bubbled and popped. Then his legs were engulfed in flame and that fire rose until he awoke screaming.

In another dream he'd be outside his house as a fifteen-year-old kid, saying goodbye to his brother for the last time. Heart heavy with the knowledge they'll never speak again, but unable to do a damned thing about it. Pete is about to take off in his car for his friend's house and all he wants to do is say "don't go," or "drive safe," but nothing comes out. He just has to stand there tongue-tied, knowing his brother will never arrive. There's nothing he can do to warn him and the feeling inside him is one of overwhelming sorrow. That was the dream he had after Pete died, at least once a week, until fall of 2001.

After that a new dream took over.

He'd wake up and it would be the morning of September 11, 2001. The morning of the attacks. He'd be at home in his apartment, but instead of being ill and asleep like he had been originally, he was wide awake. Through the balcony window he'd look across the river into Manhattan and watch the whole thing unfold, knowing exactly what was going to happen, but powerless from doing a thing to warn those in the towers.

Each dream would end the same way: with him in the tightening grip of a panic attack. That constriction in his chest, the struggle for air, the darkening of his vision. From all his dreams, he'd wake up gasping for air. And crying. The strangest part was, outside of his dreams, he never actually had a real panic attack until after Pete died. From that point on they came all too often.

After this new dream he lay back down into the bed with a shiver and noticed something. His head felt clear. Not one hundred per cent, but way better than the Swiss-cheese dead weight he'd grown used to. But that wasn't all. There was something else. He sat up again, like a scientist performing an experiment, struck by how easy it was. Again, not perfect, but way better than he'd imagined.

'What the hell was in that coffee, Joel?'

He stood up. Something was wrong. No. Not wrong. It felt *good*. There was something – *off*. He rubbed his eyes and they settled into an image of his room. Only it wasn't his room. The dimensions were the same, the lines and angles were as he'd last seen them, as was the furniture; it was the same, but different. The same way a room appears different the first time you go there compared to the times you visit after. That wasn't it though. There was something else. It was cleaner. Brighter. It seemed strange to apply such a word to a room, but it felt *happier.*

Surely that's you *happier?*

'What the hell have I got to be happy about?' he said aloud.

His clothes, the Strokes shirt and sweatpants from the previous night, were gone. The clock flicked to 6:30AM and the radio burst into life. *Have a Nice Day* by the Stereophonics blasted into the room. Ray jumped at the sound. He smiled thinking he hadn't heard that song in years but remembered how he'd liked it in the past. With a shrug he shut the radio alarm off. Then stared. Coldness gripped him and questions flooded his mind. Why was there an alarm? Had Joel done it? Cleaned up in here and then set an alarm? Why would he do that? That's a weird sense of humor; Joel didn't seem the type.

From nowhere an invasive thought about the new dream pushed its way into his conscience. The dream last night: Pete died a long time before Kat was on the scene. There was no way he could have known she even existed.

'Fucking weird,' Ray muttered as he stumbled down the hallway.

Here he got the sense that this was somehow different too. It was difficult to pinpoint. The cloying sense of gloom was missing – like a cloud burned away by summer sun. He peered up at the naked bulb and reached for the switch. The light came on and flooded his tired eyes. He threw up an arm to protect them and hit the switch again, and this time, it went off. It hadn't worked in years. Joel must have fixed it.

GHOSTS OF SEPTEMBER

He tottered into the kitchen: a brighter, cleaner, happier kitchen. Joel had been here too. The bags full of crap by the doorway were gone, as was the pile of crap in the sink. He'd even taken the time to dry the dishes and put them away.

He turned quickly. A noise. From the direction of the hallway.

Someone else is here.

He froze. It was coming from the bathroom. The bathroom door was closed. He never closed it.

'Joel? That you in there?'

He stalked back down the hallway; his footfall silent. The strained whine of a hairdryer burst into life.

'Joel?'

Why would Joel use a hairdryer? New-born babies had more hair than he did. The hairdryer shut off and the door opened. A voice came from inside. A *female* voice.

'What did you say?'

Ray stood motionless, staring at the bathroom door, the morning light in his bedroom burning at the opposite end of the hallway. A head bobbed out of the door. Long flowing black hair cascading towards the floor. He recognized it immediately, but still, it made no sense. She turned to look at him and he saw her face.

'You say something?'

Kat. His ex-girlfriend Kat. Looking right at him, but it wasn't the dead-eyed doll's eye stare he'd got the last time he bumped into her. No; now those dark mischievous eyes twinkled with possibility – just like they used to. His head swirled as his mind was bombarded with memories. Mostly good. Not all. Towards the end he'd—

'Earth to Ray.'

His stomach fluttered and he felt the color drain from his face. His mind tried desperately to fill the gaps between whatever the fuck had happened last night and this moment. Her brow knotted and her eyes sharpened as she stared, baffled, at his silence.

Speak, Ray. Say something.

'Er… you want coffee?'

Her dark eyes softened. 'Thought you'd never ask.'

She retreated into the bathroom and Ray staggered into the kitchen. He leant against the counter and tried to arrange his scattered thoughts. What the fuck was this? The last time he'd seen her was an awkward meeting when he was in the Bronx. At Yankee Stadium what, five years ago? Six maybe. Christ, maybe it was ten.

YANKEE STADIUM - 2004

Andy stood grinning, his huge frame filling Ray's doorway, and in one of those meaty paws of his he was holding up two tickets for the Yankees. It was to be the day the Yanks clinched the AL East Division title, but that wasn't what made Ray glad to see him. Andy was the one person who up to this point hadn't given up on him. Rather than feeling outright gratitude, it came with a weight of responsibility. That his failings were letting someone else down hurt Ray. Himself, he didn't care about, his devotion to the bottle proved as much. The Friday night card games had stopped

GHOSTS OF SEPTEMBER

for a while after Manny's death, but when they did finally start up again, he couldn't face the guys. But Andy never gave up. The invites still came. Not only to the card games (not every time they played, but every now and then), but to birthdays, to Christmas and New Year. So letting Andy down after he'd reached out to him like this, three years after Manny's death, was not an option. Of course, when Andy had told him he'd got the tickets a week earlier, Ray had been on his way to being blind drunk. Luckily, he'd had the foresight to write a Post-It note and stick it to the booze cupboard door, so the reminder not to drink was staring at him the next day.

That week leading up to the day of the ballgame had been a toughie. The pressure of not only staying sober but preparing to go out in public built and grew day by day. He'd almost lapsed on the Thursday before, and he would have, if the bottle he'd grabbed wasn't half empty. Then it meant going out to get more. That was the only thing that had kept him sober. At the game they'd drink beer and talk shit about the old times, and all would be fine.

'You ready?'

It was a change seeing Andy wearing anything other than a Metallica or Iron Maiden shirt, standing there in his Yankees jersey.

'Let's go.'

They headed to the Port Authority Bus Terminal and took the "C" train to 145th Street. The train rattled along, and it wasn't long until conversation turned to the old days.

'You ever hear from Tony?' Ray asked.

'Yeah. Took Tina and the kids out to his place a few weeks back. Pretty good cannoli. He was asking about you.'

Ray felt his cheeks flush with embarrassment, what would Tony think if he saw what had become of Ray Madison? Andy filled the awkwardness of the momentary silence and pressed on.

'And the kids loved him.'

'Tony?'

Andy chuckled. 'Right? Big softy, man.'

'If only we knew.'

'Yeah. Ah but he was always a sweetheart. He'd bark at you, but he never bit.'

Ray smiled. 'True enough.'

'How would you know?'

Ray rolled his eyes theatrically. 'Here it comes.'

'Teacher's pet.' Andy broke into his Tony impression, 'Why can't you take a leaf from Ray's book? Three years, never had one sick day!'

'Always takin' leaves with Tony wasn't it?'

Somewhere behind Ray an old woman started a hacking cough which ended with her spitting whatever grossness she'd brought up to the floor. Ray felt sick.

'He'd bark at Manny plenty.' Andy laughed.

'What the *fuck* time is this?!' Ray said, in his best Tony voice.

Andy went into hysterics and Ray joined along.

Finally, Andy's laughter subsided. 'I miss it, you know?'

'The courier game?'

GHOSTS OF SEPTEMBER

'The laughs.'

'You miss the scooters?'

Andy grinned broadly. 'I could hardly sit on those fucking things.'

The image of six-foot-four Andy perched atop one of Tony's delivery scooters popped into Ray's head and he burst into laughter again.

'You imagining me on that scooter, you asshole?' Andy was trying to keep a straight face, but he was betrayed by his smiling eyes.

Ray couldn't answer for laughing. They laughed until the announcer said that 145th street was imminent and shuffled for the doors wiping their eyes.

They transferred to the "D" train on the Orange Line to Yankee Stadium but all the way to the game, since leaving his apartment, Ray had a feeling that something was going to happen that day. Not quite a premonition. And nothing bad. Just a gut feeling. Only when they were outside the stadium and Andy disappeared to buy hot dogs did it become clear what that was.

'Ray?'

Andy had been gone for less than a minute. The voice was female, and one he recognized straight away. He turned away. He couldn't let her see him like this.

'Ray!'

The second time was accompanied by a tap on the shoulder.

'Kat. Hi.' He smiled, trying to make it as natural as possible, hoping it would mask the embarrassment.

'What are you doing here?'

Ray threw a thumb over his shoulder at the stadium. 'Same as everyone else here, I guess.'

Kat laughed.

'How have you been, Kat?'

Ray wanted to get in first. He didn't want to talk about the past three miserable years, even though most of them were written on his face. But he wasn't the only one who'd aged prematurely in the intervening years.

'I have a daughter.'

It shouldn't have hurt him to hear that. But it did.

'That's great.'

Kat pulled her phone from her pocket and flipped it open, searching for a picture. Ray still didn't have a camera phone. There was nothing he wanted to document. The picture Kat revealed was of a blonde little girl with big dark eyes.

'Her hair is so blonde!' Ray said, enthusiastically.

Kat lifted a strand of her own dark hair, 'I know, right?'

'She's big.'

'Two years old. Her birthday was last week.'

That meant she'd had the kid with the guy she'd gone out with straight after Ray. Jason the asshole boss from the restaurant. Ray was surprised. Kat had come to see him after Manny died to make sure he was okay, but the visits stopped when things with Jason got serious. Jealous type, he guessed. It was a surprise that someone as strong as Kat had put up with his bullshit.

'So Jason...'

GHOSTS OF SEPTEMBER

Kat's face dropped and she shook her head. 'We broke up. Asshole started seeing someone else while I was pregnant.'

'Shit. I'm sorry.'

He was. All the joy vanished from her face and her mask slipped. Ray disliked what he saw. Her dark eyes were empty and sad and in that second Ray saw that she was as miserable as he was. Ray changed the subject.

'You still singing?'

But it only made it worse.

'No. I... I mean I could... There's just no time. My priorities changed I guess.'

Her face dropped, for a split second, and then she smiled again.

Somewhere between leaving him and now, Kat had lost sight of her dreams. Life had a different path for her. Life had taken them in opposite directions, but neither road led to happiness. Ray wished he could take it all back. His failure as a partner had led to this. In the moment that Kat's mask slipped, in that split second, she looked older. Ray hated himself. He wondered if they could get back together after all this time.

Ask for her number, you jackass.

'I was thinking—'

'Kat!'

A deep, ill-tempered shout came from within the crowds. Ray turned to see a man with a dark scowl moving towards them clutching two hotdogs.

'Where you been? I was looking everywhere for you.'

'Kevin, this is…'

Ray pulled a hand from his pocket in readiness to shake Kevin's, but when he handed the hotdog off to Kat, he pocketed his own hand. 'Yeah pleased to meet you. Let's go, Kat, we're gonna miss the start.'

'I should go,' Kat said.

Ray nodded. His eyes followed Kat as she walked away, hand in hand with her new man. He was waiting to see if she turned back.

'Ray!'

He turned to see Andy clutching their hot dogs. When he looked back, Kat was gone.

2

Ray stood in his kitchen; eyebrows drawn together in a knot. How in God's name did Kat get in here and where the hell was Joel? He reached for the kettle and flicked it on. Joel must have called her. Unless she dropped by because…

Ray froze. The kettle was different.

'The fuck?'

The electric tea kettle he'd had last night – for the past ten years – was gone. In its place was a new one. Well, new*er*. It looked familiar. He had to speak to Joel. He scanned the living room for his phone. He wanted an explanation and wanted it now. Joel called last night and then turned up almost straight after so the cell phone should still be in the living room. The arm of the sofa was empty. Of course, it wasn't there – why would *that* make sense out of all of today's bullshit? The arms of all the chairs were empty. Coffee table and dining table too. All the usual places he might leave his phone turned up nothing. There was no way he'd taken it to bed with him. That was something he'd stopped doing years ago. It was like the phone had never existed.

Kat's singing rose from the bathroom. Some song about being stuck in a moment that he'd completely forgotten about and hadn't heard in forever.

Like the Stereophonics.

He tramped back to the bedroom and saw the cell phone on his nightstand. Only it wasn't the cracked screen of his Sony smart phone looking back at him. It was a Nokia. A 3210. Almost mint condition. It must be fifteen years old. More. Plain black just like the one he'd had back in the day. He guessed it was the same one, even though he hadn't set eyes on it in years.

He snatched it up and navigated to the contacts quickly, like his mind was on autopilot. His eyebrows fell and his head jerked back.

How did you know to do that?

It was like he'd used it yesterday. He punched in Joel's name and hit search, but nothing came back. He typed Kat's name and her number showed. She spoke behind him and he nearly dropped the phone.

'Cancel the coffee,' in that thick Brooklyn accent, voice rich, soothing. 'I gotta bounce.'

He turned.

'Are you okay, Ray? You're acting weird...'

'Me?' he smiled. 'I'm fine.'

Her eyes narrowed; she hadn't believed a word of it. They stood for a moment, just looking at each other, then she darted over and kissed him full on the mouth. A long lingering kiss, every bit as good as he'd remembered. Almost like she'd forgotten the past seventeen years had ever happened.

'Don't forget about tonight,' she added. Eyes twinkling and that lop-sided smile. Christ, it drove him crazy even now.

Before he could say anything, she was gone. For a few moments, he stood silently in the cleaner, tidier bedroom before shouting, 'Okay what the fuck is going on here?'

Maybe it was in hope that some mysterious voice from the universe would answer. That's what he wanted: answers. Christ knew he had none. Trying and failing to fill the yawning gaps between his head hitting the pillow last night, and whatever the hell was going on in his apartment this morning was almost painful.

Despite Kat's random appearance in his bathroom, there was something about it that felt normal. Part of his mind accepted it as the status quo, even though she hadn't stayed over at his place since *that* week. The bell ringing in the back of his mind that something wasn't right wasn't just over the oddities occurring in his apartment. Not the fresh feeling of brightness and replacement of old gadgets with new. It was something else. Something about Kat.

It was her all right, no doubt about it. But it was an odd version of her. She was acting like their past together had never happened. Her demeanor had the same outlook that

GHOSTS OF SEPTEMBER

his place had. Fresh, bright, hopeful. Not only that but she looked good. *Really* good. Better than when he'd seen her at the Yanks years back. Now she looked better still.

The kettle clicked in the kitchen and snapped him back to this strange new reality. As he padded down the hallway, he realized that he really did feel better than he had in a long time. That awful feeling of heaviness and lethargy that accompanied his drinking bouts was gone. His mind felt clear, alert, the images sharper than they had in a long time. In months. In years.

It was then he stepped into his living room and, from the corner of his eye, noticed something out of the window. Again familiar but somehow different. The hairs on the back of his neck raised and he fought the urge to look. He stood frozen like someone had hit pause on reality, knowing precisely what was about to happen, but trying with everything he had to fight it; as if he'd spotted a huge spider on the wall that wouldn't be real until he looked at it. His stomach tightened, and, with his eyes screwed shut, he slowly turned to face the window.

He peeled back his eyelids and, as he cast his eyes from his fourth story window across the Hudson and into downtown Manhattan, he felt the color drain from his face. The sound of his heartbeat in his ears rose in a deafening crescendo as his eyes settled on the impossible.

Rising from the dead center of the skyline were the shiny concrete and steel ghosts of the World Trade Center's Twin Towers.

3

He grabbed the counter to steady himself and squeezed his eyes closed. The counter swayed with the room and sickness rose in him. That was why everything felt different. It was another dream.

He retraced the steps he'd taken from the bedroom to the hallway to the kitchen. He recalled the cold linoleum of the carpet-less hallway under his feet. He hadn't just teleported from the bedroom to the kitchen, like in all the other dreams. The level of detail was incredible. The sights, sounds, and smells of his flat as it was before the attack were all around him. He opened his eyes again and stared at those twin columns. Buildings etched deeply into the memory of anyone who had been close to a television on that dreadful, haunting September morning.

His dreams of that awful day were never this vivid, despite the timeline of his nightmare playing out in what felt like a play-by-play, minute-by-minute reconstruction. The main events were always painted in meticulous detail. Every sense amplified at the moment of the inevitable. Any time now, as with all the other dreams, he expected to see a Boeing 767 slam into the upper reaches of the North Tower.

He hopped down from the stool, unable to remember the moment he'd sat, and as his feet touched the floor his knees buckled. The counter was close enough for him to reach out and keep his feet. The counter that felt so real. His disbelieving fingertips traced along the cool surface as he staggered to the window and took in that bluest of skies. Scanning the skyline, he waited for the screaming engines of the plane to fade in, just as they always did. His hands trembled as he braced for the feelings of impotence and horror to flood his senses. In his dreams he always knew that the first plane was no accident and that the second plane was close behind. The endless horror of trying and failing, trying and failing, trying and failing to contact those in the South Tower so that they could evacuate before the second plane came roaring into the steel belly of the building.

He turned away. This was his dream and he was in control. He didn't have to watch this. He could wake himself up whenever he wanted. All he would have to deal with is the loss of Kat. His heart was heavy at the thought of dealing with losing her all over again, but it would be infinitely better than the other option of watching and living through the heart-rending trauma of that horrific day.

He had to wake himself up, but no matter how he grabbed and pinched and twisted, whenever he glanced at the window, there they were, the Twin Towers staring back defiantly. A dream this deep – this real – would take something more. It would need blunt force. Or... his eyes fell to the stove. He marched over and lit the gas. The hypnotic blue fire drew him in and for a moment all he could do was stare. Then he looked at his hands. He'd need a sacrifice. As a southpaw, the decision came easy. The blue flame hissed as he lowered his left hand to his side and pushed the right hand forward, stopping inches from the hissing fire. Air entered his lungs in deep controlled breaths. He closed his eyes and plunged his hand into the heat. The temperature soared from his immediate surroundings to Hell. He screamed and withdrew his hand. He opened his eyes and…

Nothing. Still here.

Same clean, happy apartment. Same old/new kettle. The low hiss of blue fire challenged him to try again. His red palm stared back at him pleadingly, but he ignored it and turned it back over. The previous attempt was too short, that was all. A longer spell in the fire would work. It had to. He held his breath and thrust his hand back in. The flames licked the palm of his hand, and pain exploded. Fighting with everything he had he held his hand in place, in spite of the searing heat. It would wake him, if he could just hold it for… A loud, guttural scream burst out and he quickly withdrew his hand, plunging it under soothing cold water.

'Why isn't this working?' The pain from his hand and confusion at his situation made the words come out in a whine he cared little for.

The cool water soothed the searing heat of his hand, but all the same… Nothing had changed. Nothing but the glass-shard agony of his ravaged palm. Could this really be a dream? There were no jumps in time or location or logic. The water soothed his hand, returning it to a natural temperature, then colder still as he let the icy water ease the stinging.

The chill of the tiled floor contrasted with the sting of stabbing agony as he stumbled into the bathroom. Steam billowed into the hallway and the residual heat from Kat's shower made him feel sick: the only benefit being the fog on the mirror. At least he could avoid his own reflection. If he looked in the mirror now and saw what he was expecting to see, he wasn't sure his mind could handle it. He splashed cold water onto his face and a nebulous idea was forming as to what was going on; a look in that mirror and a twenty-something version of himself staring back at him would confirm it. He snatched the towel and patted his face dry. The rough fibers stung his palm as he dabbed at his cheeks and came to terms with the idea that he couldn't hold the towel there forever. He had to prepare for what was coming: the sight of his younger self. Prepare for a face not ravaged by years of alcohol abuse or aged by the stress of losing everything within the space of a few brutal days. He took a deep breath, raised the towel, and wiped the mist from the mirror.

An excited giggle escaped as he caught sight of his 22-year-old self. The hair was full, and black. The sick grey pallor of his skin had been replaced by a vibrant glow and the face had a healthy weight to it. This wasn't the sad, drawn mask that his face had become over the wasteland years that had followed that week, set in motion from the very second that first plane tore a hole in the side of the steel and concrete monolith that now stood like a phantom across the water between here and downtown. The most startling difference was in the eyes. They were bright. Full of enthusiasm and hope. Not the empty pits of despair they became after Manny had died. After Kat had left. After turning to the bottle for comfort. Ray felt a sob rise in his throat. He tried to swallow it, but it was too strong. He collapsed to the cold tiled floor of his Jersey apartment and wept.

4

Consciousness swirled around Ray and seeped into his aching body, the cold tile of his bathroom floor offering little comfort. He'd been gripped by a dream. A nightmare. In the dream it was before that awful Tuesday morning and he couldn't wake himself up. It had been so realistic; the clean fresh smell of his flat before he'd let it go to hell; the bright, hopeful naïveté of that world – whether perceived or real – that existed before that day; the stinging pain of the burn in his hand he'd used to wake himself up.

Then, suddenly, from that addled state between sleep and wake two things became obvious: somewhere in his flat a mobile phone was ringing; and there was a terrible sharpness in his hand, the kind of stinging throb that only comes from a burn. His eyes sprang open. How long had he been there? The phone rang again. Not the Strokes - his current ringtone - but the tinny twang of a monophonic reproduction. An old Radiohead tune. *No Surprises.*

It wasn't a dream. He was still there.

No. It was impossible. Maybe he'd been sleepwalking. Wasn't that much more plausible? Yes. He'd imagined it. All of it. All of it except the part where he'd tried to set fire to his hand.

His sponsor had cleaned up a little. Hadn't he said he was going to? What was his name? *Joel.* They'd talked about fixing the light. Maybe he'd done these things and Ray had somehow sensed a return to the old days. In his sleep he'd dug out his old phone. Dreaming about the past. The good life where he'd longed to be. He looked down at the red palm of his right hand. What an idiot. At least as a lefty he burned the right hand. His head hurt.

Reality washed over him. Kat was still gone. Manny, Pete and Pop were still dead. And he still had his shitty 2018 life to live. Sure, the place looked better now Joel had cleaned up, and he didn't want to sound ungrateful, but it was simply polishing the turd that represented his sorry existence.

The monophonic ringtone finally stopped. Thank Christ. Whoever was on the phone could wait. He had 2018 shit to deal with and he was surprised with the clarity of the awareness of that fact. Maybe Joel's cleaning trick had worked on him. Like some nature/nurture Jedi mind trick, his improved surroundings had brought about a better, refreshed feeling in himself. That felt like it should make sense. And yet, how many of his thoughts followed such a lucid path these days?

He sat up. Again the movement was smooth, easy. Whenever he sat up, it was a struggle, impossible without an accompanying groan. He peered down and saw the trim figure of a man planted firmly in his early twenties, not the pudgy sadness of a drunk approaching forty. Nothing made sense.

Was he in that time before the fall of 2001? Before the shell-shocked aftermath brought about by the rapid onset of terror. Isn't that what this felt like? Before the anger, and overwhelming feeling for the need of reprisals and vengeance. Before the paranoia. That time when you weren't looking over your shoulder, or casting an eye of mistrust over some suspicious looking guy: the guy who's nervous for no reason other than everyone looking at him in a way like he's done, or is about to do, something terrible, when all he really wants is to go back to a time before, the same as you do. A time when he wasn't viewed with suspicion. When he was just a New-Yorker. Nothing more. A New-Yorker like you or me and life was hopeful, and people weren't willing to kill themselves to make a point. That future felt so far away that all the negative emotions were distant and remote, too. He felt young and hopeful and positive in a way that he hadn't felt since forever. The colors here were sharper, brighter. A 4K rendering of an SD world. It was beautiful.

That other, suspicious world now felt a long way away. Almost like a memory. A memory of a future yet to unfold. Ray focused his thoughts on that future. He gasped and winced and reached for his temples, bending double at the pain. It started small; like searching out a word evading the tip of his tongue, but it quickly bloomed, like the dead spot was growing, cannibalizing other memories at pace until it exploded and that emptiness was vast, rapping on the inside of his skull, then collapsing in on itself, pulling invisible ropes from his temples until he thought his head might implode.

He jumped to his feet and stared at his reflection, agog. Now the eyes were puffy and red from the sobbing preceding his deep sleep. He struggled to take in a breath through his swollen sinuses, but there was no doubt – this was early twenties Ray. His hand stung from the burn and he ran it

GHOSTS OF SEPTEMBER

under the cold water.

The refreshing water cooled his hand and a revelation hit him. This really was sometime before September 2001. That's why everything looked cleaner. That's why his modern gadgets and equipment was replaced by older stuff in better condition. It *was* newer. That's why Kat was here. That's why she wasn't pissed at him. She was still his girlfriend. Because she was here, that meant it was sometime after February 2000.

'No. That's horseshit, Ray. Think.'

It couldn't be. It was impossible. He had no idea how he got here, yet here he was.

'Wait a minute.'

There was an easy way to prove it. Two easy ways. Both stood one hundred and ten stories tall in the view from his window in downtown Manhattan. All he had to do was to go to his living room and stare through the large double doors that opened onto his tiny balcony. There he'd either see the shining steel of the Twin Towers, or he wouldn't. That would confirm if he'd been sleepwalking or not.

Something about the idea of this being a dream didn't ring true. Young Ray Madison stared at him from the mirror. He *did* look younger. He *felt* younger. Better. The urge to drink was gone, because this *was* 2001, maybe 2000, and he was yet to fall into the all-consuming grip of alcoholism.

From his bathroom, into the hallway, heading for the living room, he was sure that he'd see the Towers. With each step the feelings of positivity and hope returned. He flicked the light switch. Light. Freshness hit him as he entered the living room. Ray stood for a moment and took in that iconic skyline. His eyes teared a little before he snapped back to the new-old reality when the pain from his hand pulsed and throbbed with his heartbeat. The sooner he took care of his hand the better.

He staggered back into the kitchen and turned on the radio, hoping to get a hint as to the date while he fished the first-aid box from under the sink. The radio announcers were waxing lyrical about Pete Sampras and Andre Agassi.

'Man, what a game. It should have been the final.'

'Right. But it was only the quarter final and you have to wonder how much it took out of Pete Sampras, he and Agassi two of the oldest players in the tournament.'

'It sure didn't look that way last night. They seemed ageless.'

'And what about that ovation? Twenty-three thousand people clapping and cheering for three solid minutes. In case you haven't heard, they played on past midnight...'

'They say you could see the stadium lights from Queens to Manhattan.'

'That's right, playing past midnight, it's Pete Sampras who goes into the U.S. Open semi-final...'

Ray was trying to recall the moment, wiping soothing lotion into the stinging red rawness of his right palm. The U.S. Open quarters meant it was late August maybe. That's what the weather looked like. Then the announcement was over and some song that he didn't recognize started. He wrapped a bandage around the hand and went back to the living room, thinking how much easier life was with the

GHOSTS OF SEPTEMBER

Internet. All the information he could ever need at the touch of a button. Now he couldn't even use his shitty cell...

The thought stopped him dead. He bolted along the corridor to the bedroom. His shitty old cell might not have Internet access, but it sure as shit had a calendar. He snatched the phone up with his left hand and pressed the unlock key. As if on autopilot, he remembered how to find the calendar without hesitation.

He wished he hadn't.

He slumped to the bed and stared at the green hue of the tiny monochrome screen. The tiny black pixels had arranged themselves into the impossible. He stared at the date.

THURSDAY, SEPTEMBER 6, 2001

9:29AM

DAZED AND CONFUSED RAY SAT at the dining room table staring at a blank sheet of paper with a pencil in his good hand. He scribbled the word 'Possibilities'. Despite all his tests, the likeliest, most obvious answer was that this really was a dream. But even as he wrote it, it didn't feel right. The most obvious wasn't always the correct, his burned hand was testament to that. He decided to move on and come back to that idea. So, other, less obvious, more crazy options: It might be 2001. The original 2001. He had slipped backwards somehow on the original timeline. If that were true it meant that in five days' time, the unthinkable was about to change his and countless other New-Yorkers' – Americans' – lives.

Perhaps it was an alternate timeline. Maybe in this time, in five days, nothing happens. Nothing at all. Life plays out in the normality of those days before the attacks. Innocent. Carefree.

He remembered reading after the attacks that the Feds or CIA or somebody like that knew what was coming. Some foreign version of those guys - maybe in France - had heard something and tipped them off but for some reason or other the memo never got high enough up the chain of command for it to be taken seriously. Maybe this time it had. Maybe he'll turn on the news in the next couple of days and hear about how the biggest attack since Pearl Harbor has been foiled.

Another possibility was that the attack would happen, but not on the same day. Maybe sooner, maybe later. Or that something would happen, but it would be slightly different somehow. More planes or something. Or bombs.

Then there was another thing: if he really was in the past, how long would he stay here? Days? Months? Maybe he'd go to bed tonight and wake up back in 2018. That idea comforted him. This new-old reality could be for a few hours, days, weeks, years even, but he had the feeling that somehow, he'd end up back in the old life. Or new life from this perspective. He couldn't pinpoint why he felt that, but the idea had a ring of truth to it. And with that came the reality that whatever he did here would have some bearing on that future.

The Butterfly Effect. He had to tread carefully. The pencil scratched furiously on the notepad and he double

GHOSTS OF SEPTEMBER

underlined what he'd written:
DO NOT INITIATE CONTACT!

As long as he was here in this alternate reality, he had to maintain some sort of status quo that jibed with what had gone before. One misstep could have dire repercussions, and there were two equally unsavory ideas that accompanied the thought: One, that when he went back to 2018 the new reality he'd created would be unrecognizable, worse perhaps than the original waking nightmare that followed the attacks; Two, and this was much worse, that he didn't go directly back to 2018. Instead, he had to live through a terrifying new reality of his own creation.

A shrill chirping came from the bedroom. His cell. He didn't want to answer it. The confusion of the morning had him way off kilter. Somewhere inside he wanted this to all be a dream. One with insane levels of detail, no skips in logic, where he could injure himself and not wake up, and where he could sleep and still wake up trapped inside. It couldn't be, and yet he'd never be able to explain what was going on or how it was happening otherwise.

The phone was still ringing. He sprang to his feet and bound through the hallway hoping to reach it before the caller rang off. If he was to beware the butterfly effect, he could ill afford to ignore it. He snatched up the phone, his thumb hovering over the answer key. Had he taken this call originally the first time around? He had to be careful what he said. The caller was Tony. Instantly he knew who it was, even if it was someone he hadn't spoken to for almost seventeen years. He pressed accept.

'Yeah, hello?' Ray flinched at how his voice sounded. Thin and sinussy from his crying earlier.

'Ray? That you? You sound like shit.'

Tony was a blue-collar guy about the same age as his dad. Overweight from sitting in the office all day. Tough, brutally honest, a great guy to have on your side and overall, a pretty good boss.

'I'll be honest Tony I don't feel too sharp.'

'Shit, I was gonna rip you a new asshole, now I almost feel bad.'

He sounded genuine, but Ray had a feeling that there was more than sympathy in his voice. Disappointment. Like Ray's absence from work would affect Tony and the business. There were other couriers, though. How bad could it be? Still, he didn't really want to go in.

'Why? What time is it?'

'It's almost ten. I've been calling all morning.'

Almost ten? It was almost nine-thirty last time he checked. Time flies. Shit. So much for butterflies. It hadn't occurred to him that he had to be at work.

He loved his old job. Strange to say it, because it was nothing glamorous and the other guys saw it just as *work*, but being a courier got him out and about in the city. He loved New York. He might live in Jersey now, but he was born and raised in Queens. They'd only moved to Jersey so his ma could be closer to her folks. But did he love New York City. The sights, the sounds. The smells. Most of the smells. Today...? He really didn't feel like going, but that

GHOSTS OF SEPTEMBER

little voice whispering about butterflies made him think twice.

'You okay to come in? I can spread your deliveries around; you know if you don't feel up to it. You're my best guy, kid, I can't lie.'

Tony was being so cool about it. He'd expected more resistance. Sure, he was always a fair guy, and in the three years he worked for Tony *that* week was the only time off work he had through sickness but… Fuck. This was bad.

'Ray? You there?'

'Er, yeah.'

Butterflies, Raymond.

'Yeah I'll be there. I need about an hour.'

'Great. Thank you. See you soon.'

This was so bad. In one sweeping wave it hit why Tony was being so cool about his being late. Like some cosmic gears had turned, 2018 clicked into 2001 and Ray's memory wasn't from the future, but from the very recent past of 2001. His crying made it sound like he had a cold. A cold like half of the guys had. A heavy one, too. It had spread through the office like wildfire. Almost everybody had it and it kept them from work for a good few days. Tony stopped the guys meeting for cigarettes it got so bad. It was the reason Ray had missed work the first time around. That was the reason Manny took his deliveries. Including the one that got him killed. The fucking flu. Manny got it first, he gave it to Andy; it went from there… Today was Thursday. Manny was coming back to work today. How did he know that?

Because you spoke to him about it yesterday.

All his thoughts about the butterfly effect and he was over two hours late for work. Maybe there would be no knock-on from this. He could ill afford to waste more time thinking about it. He wanted – no *needed* – some sense of routine, normality, to perhaps restore some inner equilibrium. He went two the bedroom and opened the wardrobe. There it was. His old uniform. Thoughts of the butterfly effect drifted to the back of his mind. All he could wish for now is that they stayed there, but he knew that couldn't last.

10:17AM

He grabbed a duffel bag and stuffed in the chocolate brown uniform, which he actually liked (he looked good in earthy colors, at least that's what Kat told him). For the first time that morning he stopped thinking about butterflies and timelines and consequences and focused on the routine. And it felt good. The less attention he paid to the outside effects of his being here and just savored the moment the better he felt. Bit by bit, those feelings of hope and peace and happiness returned.

By the time he'd dressed and turned everything off in his apartment he was feeling *good* about being here. After all, this was the good time. (Or the closest it got to that since Pete died. That was a weight he'd always carry. The day his brother died a big piece of him died too.) He closed and locked the door to his apartment and headed downstairs in

GHOSTS OF SEPTEMBER

the cool stairway of his building. A bright rectangle of light burned in the front door, he grabbed the handle and pushed it open.

The sounds of that New Jersey morning amplified as he stepped outdoors. Cars going by on the nearby Newark Avenue, the gentle twitter of birdsong. The sounds of normality. He'd forgotten these sounds, or at least to enjoy them, since that week. He ventured outdoors less and less and when he did the sounds were muffled, muted. Like he was numb to them. Like the morning after a concert. Before they were amplified. Clearer.

For Ray there was no *during* the attack. Just a *before* and *after*. He'd taken to his bed, ill on the Monday night. The night of the tenth. He'd cried himself to sleep after hearing about Manny. The first thing he'd done was contact Kat who was by that time his ex, and, to her credit, she'd come to visit him. She stayed the night, though of course nothing happened. He'd fallen asleep and the next morning Kat left for work. Ray went back to bed, his phone on silent from the night before, and by the time he woke up, the Twin Towers were two piles of steaming rubble and dust in the heart of Manhattan. He woke in the middle of a nightmare and lived it for the next seventeen plus years. Over the following weeks Kat's visits tailed off. Ray pushed her away. She probably couldn't stand the bitterness and anger and self-pity.

None of the bitterness and anger were here now. They were distant, as if they'd happened to another person. Ray walked a few paces with his car key in his hand and his brain whispered a question. *How do you know where you parked?*

He answered it aloud, 'Because I only parked yesterday,' and smiled.

The smile widened as he saw the British racing green paintwork of his front fender, the way a stranger smiles in the street upon seeing a friend. This really was an old friend. The 1991 Chevrolet Lumina Z34. His heart smiled. He'd forgotten about this. How he loved this car. He'd had to sell it to raise money but now, as he traced a hand over the cool metal, it was almost like he'd just bought the car himself. This really was like a dream. He shook his head before unlocking the door and climbing in.

He slid into the seat and shut the door and, for the first time since he'd woken on this strangest of days, he felt at home. Everything felt right. He motioned to adjust the seat and mirrors then stopped himself, like The Fonz going to do his hair before realizing it was already perfect. He grinned as he reached over to the glove box. A satisfying metal clink revealed CDs by the Strokes, the White Stripes, and the Boss. The Boss. That disc must have had a thousand miles on the clock, but he never wanted to hear it as much as he did right now. This was going to be a good day. He gleefully opened the Springsteen CD case like a kid on Christmas morning. He felt his face drop. It was empty.

'Son of a bitch.'

Some Christmas morning. Like that huge box under the tree he'd been eyeing all December wasn't a slot car

GHOSTS OF SEPTEMBER

racing game, but *clothes*. Shoulders slumped, he turned the key in the ignition and the car roared to life and something beautiful happened. A glorious noise blasted from the speakers. Not loud enough to deafen, but loud enough to invoke a primal cheer. The wail of Clarence's sax. The Boss was already in the CD player. He wound the window down and headed for the city.

Maybe it was going to be a good day after all.

10:46AM

The swelling sounds of Clarence's sax warmed him as the city stared back: a friendly face that he'd not seen for the longest time. A face touched by innocence that mirrored the naivety peering back at him in the rear-view. This was what he'd missed. This was *his* New York. The growing sounds of traffic that refused to be drowned out by the Boss; the wail of sirens that for a split second seemed to harmonize with the sweet ache of saxophone; the shouts of cabbies echoed by the crowds lauding Bruce. In front of him, across the bay, Manhattan rose from the island like something from a monster movie: an army of steel giants, all dwarfed by the Twin Towers. But they weren't threatening. Not to Ray. To him they were like old friends, maybe they'd been away, but now they were back, and it was fucking great to see them.

He was a few minutes away from seeing Manny. His stomach cartwheeled like a teenager's rushing to a first date.

What if Manny sensed there was something wrong? Or the emotion of seeing him after all these years was too much? Both were a possibility.

It nibbled away at him and the closer he got to midtown, the less friendly it felt. Less and less did the sounds ring of voices past. They started to sound more like a warning. Stay away. Don't get involved up here. You might think you belong, but you're way off, pal. You haven't belonged here for a fuckin' crow's age. His head ached and each glance up at the towers was met with a flash into the future. Gaping holes, billowing blackness, for less than a split second, but more than enough to register. Enough to knock him off kilter. The sound of blaring horns transformed into screaming jet engines and back again. He blinked and the lively street before him became the ash-coated wasteland of the post-apocalypse.

A loud horn blasted, snapping him from his trance. Reality surged back and Ray screamed out, staring down oncoming traffic. He slammed on the brake and yanked the wheel, clothes stuck to him with sweat, the front end quickly crossing back into lane.

As Ray moved through the light traffic for West 47th Street one thing was clear to him: he didn't want to see Manny. Not yet. The raw emotion of it all would be an overdose. It was better to wait outside and see if he could spot him before going in. Screw the extra few minutes he'd be late. Fifty yards from the entrance into the yard, he drew to a stop. This would be close enough. The yard stretched back, fenced off at the end of the block at the opposite side

GHOSTS OF SEPTEMBER

of the crossroad. The entrance in the side of the building revealed the garage space inside. The usual hustle was absent at this time of day and Ray sat in silence for a few minutes scanning what little movement there was inside, waiting to see if he could spot Manny's shoulder length black hair. Nobody came in or out. If he waited too long, there was a chance Manny was already out and would come back in.

'Shit.'

Duffel bag slung over a shoulder, he got out and locked up and paced tentatively towards the main building. A gentle stream of cars passed by and Ray kept checking back, expecting to see Manny coming up behind him, but there was nothing there but West 47th. Before him, fleeting views of the garage opened up between the pedestrians and he bobbed and weaved trying to get a glimpse inside. At the yard entrance, the tinny sound of a radio rose between the whoosh of passing cars. There was no high-pitched engine of scooters though, which meant no Manny, and he went straight into the building.

Tony brought in these custom scooters; 125cc 4-stroke hairdryers, they got great mileage and they were great for dealing with traffic. Tony wanted to stand out from the crowd because a lot of the other companies just used regular bicycles: heavy on the legwork but not sacrificing too much on delivery times, mostly because those crazy bastards ignored the crossing signals and just went. But Tony said the scooters made us look more professional, and business was booming, so maybe he was right.

Tony supplied everything for the guys too. All the other companies he knew made couriers pay for safety gear and locks for the bikes; they even made them pay for their own uniforms! Not Tony. A real pro. Sad for him, most of their work was documents. A pick up here, drop off there. Then email came along. Between that and the anthrax scare after the attacks they just about finished him off. Tony was sharp though. He saw the iceberg on the horizon and sold up. Opened a restaurant out in Secaucus, where his family was from. Ray quickly diverted his thoughts as that blooming void spread through his mind.

He edged into the garage almost like an intruder, his eyes automatically scanning for Manny. The shop floor was empty of all but five scooters, one for him and each of the guys that was sick, and another two out of commission in what they called "sick-bay". The office and kitchen doors were open as usual, and now he could hear the song on the radio clearly. One he'd already heard that morning: Bono singing a song about getting yourself together. Ray had given up on U2 after *Zooropa*. That album just didn't make sense. It was Smashing Pumpkins and Radiohead from there. That was the year *Siamese Dream* and *Pablo Honey* came out.

'Ray!'

Tony was leaning sideways, his head appearing at a comical angle through the doorway to his office.

'Come in here!'

He was waving one of those big meat-paws at him.

GHOSTS OF SEPTEMBER

Tony called, you moved. He stepped into the office, peering back over a shoulder into the shop as he did, certain that Manny would be standing there waiting for him.

'Thank Christ you made it. Half the fuckin guys are sick, I got two bikes down,' he waved a dismissive, disgusted hand towards the scooters quarantined in their own sick-bay, 'and of course one of the guys I got out is Leroy.'

Leroy fixed all the bikes. Scooters. Tony called them bikes. They were not bikes.

'Here's your list. Good to see you.'

Ray took the piece of paper thrust at him with a list of pick-ups and drop-offs. A lot in the financial district. No real surprise. That's where the bulk of their jobs came from. At least before email took over. And the anthrax thing. He went to the changing room, and after glancing in the mirror, decided that he did look good in the uniform.

His focus shifted from avoiding his dead best friend to getting his work done. A welcome distraction. He'd managed to avoid Manny: for now.

11:00AM

Ray had been out in the city less than a minute since he'd gotten his list from Tony. When he set off, a strange feeling came over him, one that had been there in the flat that morning. Then it had been mingled with him freaking out for it to fully register, but now it was back, and without the distraction of trying to fathom what the hell was going on, it became clear to him what the feeling was. Déjà vu. Mild, but nagging. Stranger than he'd experienced before because of how long the feeling dragged out.

Normally it was fleeting, a confluence of events, images, sounds that came together as if being tuned on a radio, and vanishing as soon as they were recognized, now the feeling lingered. Ray wondered if it was because the events of this version of 2001 and the original were in alignment.

The further he got from the office, the lower the odds of bumping into Manny, which meant the more he could enjoy old New York. He picked out the places he'd always recognize as he went by, some of them now gone forever, lost to the ticking hands of time. Like Lutèce on the East Side. It was a big deal when the French restaurant closed in 2004 and it felt like that place had been around forever: even though it had always been too fancy for Ray's wallet, to see it back where it belonged gave him a smile.

As the shadows grew longer and morning turned into afternoon the déjà vu came and went, but when it came it seemed to stick around, and the longer the day went on, he became numb to it, the same way your nose tunes out the stench of piss and sweat when you're riding the Union Line, or like that one time he and Manny walked into Sonny's Bar after someone had thrown up, and everyone was just sitting there like the place didn't stink of vomit.

At intervals he'd remind himself not to think too much and just enjoy the day until eventually the feeling of déjà vu faded. Ray settled deeper and deeper into the past, just like he'd settled into the groove of the couch, and it felt

GHOSTS OF SEPTEMBER

more and more like home. This is the time where he belonged. 2018 New York wasn't for him. It didn't want him; the feeling was mutual.

As the list of jobs shrank and the shadows lengthened, the warm feeling of familiarity and welcome dissipated. A sour taste in his mouth grew as the hours ticked by and his breathing became shorter.

You need to get a hold of that, Ray.

The last place he wanted to be was New York traffic with a panic attack. It was as if the car horns and shouts were just that little bit louder the closer he got back to the office. Not many would feel this approaching the end of the workday, but today it meant so much more. He'd be facing a demon much bigger than him. Guilt.

No matter how many times he'd heard he was blameless in Manny's death, he would never accept it as truth. After all, Manny had died because he was covering *his* jobs. Killed by a hit and run driver of a stolen car, just because he'd done the right thing and gone to work when Ray was too fucking weak to do it.

Ideas and possibilities danced around his head. The main one in the form of a question: If I do bump into Manny today, do I tell him about his future? Which was swiftly followed by two other thoughts.

His possible *future.*

and

Butterflies, Ray. Butterflies.

The idea that Manny would somehow know exactly

how his future would unfold remained. Like he'd be pissed at Ray for calling in sick and blame Ray for his death.

It should be me. I should have gone to work that day. This had nothing to do with Manny.

Hadn't you covered for him all week?

He was doing the right thing. I screwed up. I wasn't so sick. I could have gone to work.

And you'd be dead.

Maybe I would and maybe I wouldn't. And so what? A waste of a life. A life given up to the bottle because once again, Ray Madison was weak.

That's Pop talking.

Maybe Pop was right. I was too weak to go to work. Too weak to face the reality of what I'd done.

What had you done? Got sick?

I didn't have to just give up.

Blazing horns dragged him back to the present. For the second time today he'd crossed into the wrong lane. If he didn't watch himself, he wouldn't have to worry about Tuesday; *today* was going to develop into a nightmare. He looked up to see he was almost back to the garage.

It was time to meet Manny.

4:07PM

The lengthening shadows had turned the day cooler and as Ray drew nearer to the depot, the thought of seeing Manny after all this time left him shaking. The depression; the sadness; the fucking guilt, they were forcing themselves to the

GHOSTS OF SEPTEMBER

front of his mind. 2018 emotions overwhelming the 2001 joy of seeing his friend alive. The general 2001 happiness of the moment. That 2001 lightness where terrorism wasn't a thing yet. Where people don't go out of their way to maim and kill others.

Ray pulled over and let the late afternoon traffic glide past him as he stared into the workshop. From this angle he saw a lot of what was going on inside, saw the guys milling about. All the guys. Wesley, the small quiet guy who looked like The Proclaimers, with his John Lennon glasses and tall hair. Andy the Viking - built like a wardrobe with his long flowing locks. Helluva card player. Andy hosted the Friday night poker games he and Manny loved (even though they usually lost). It was just a great time. Andy and Wesley were people he hadn't seen in years, but who he recognized instantly, as if he'd only seen them last week, because of course, as far as his mind knew, he had. For a moment he felt a heaviness that he'd fallen out of touch with them – a moment that faded quickly when 2001 jostled its way back to the front of his mind and that expanding void bled into his memories. Staring back into the shop he saw everyone. Everyone that is, except Manny.

After ten minutes he realized that Manny was still out. He could make it into the shop, drop off his bike (screw getting changed) and escape back to the sanctuary of his car unseen. All he had to do was to move fast. A few yards back a gap in the flow of traffic appeared and he pulled away from the curb. Cars rushed by in a heavy metal stream and his plan went through his mind.

Get in, get out. Eyes to the floor. Put your day clothes in your bag. It's not like you want to talk to anyone anyway. The more you talk to people you know, the more chance there is that they'll see you're acting fucked up. They'll ask too many questions, maybe put two and two together. Maybe come up with four. The smallest thing could trigger a butterfly effect.

The gap in traffic came and he twisted the throttle and lurched over the road and into the alley alongside the shop.

Get in. Get out. Don't get caught.

He pulled into the shop and parked alongside the other bikes against the wall. Tinny music echoed in the shop, but the usual laughter was thin on the ground. Illness levels high = morale, low. The sounds swelled as he took off his helmet and swung his leg over the bike. Paranoia had him sure that all eyes would be on him, but when he turned, it came as a pleasant surprise that nobody was paying him any attention.

If Tony saw him trying to get out of here in uniform, he'd give him all hell. He hated the idea of the guys going out to bars in uniform, made the company look bad. Unprofessional.

If you get caught, that draws attention. He'll just make you get changed anyway. Cross to the lockers, get changed. And do it fast.

Wesley nodded and gave his weird smile as he went past (always the quiet one). Andy the Viking smiled and gave a high-five.

GHOSTS OF SEPTEMBER

Smile back. Make it natural.

It crossed his mind to talk about the ball game that day they watched the Yanks win the AL East Division, until that instant nip of tension in his temples reminded him it hadn't happened yet.

Christ, Ray. Focus.

Andy went on his way without saying a word and Ray stared down at the cold grey smoothness of the shop floor.

Look alive, Raymondo. The clock's ticking.

Inside the locker room, Hughie was getting changed. Hughie was a Scottish guy, from Glasgow, or somewhere close. Skinny. Pale. A bit like Rod Stewart. But maybe that was just because he was Scottish. His accent was completely indecipherable, but he was a good guy. Didn't have Wesley's serial-killer vibe. He mumbled a greeting as he stepped into his jeans. Ray replied and opened the battered green door to his locker, shirt already open. He reached down to untie his laces and watched in horror as they twisted themselves into the kind of knot an Eagle-scout would get badges for. Trying to undo the damage only made it worse. He slid his foot out.

Fuck it. Deal with it tomorrow. Just get out of here.

He dropped his pants and stepped out of them, grabbing his jeans with the other hand as he did.

Faster. Must go faster.

He swam into his T-shirt as Hughie said something about a beer. He fastened half of the buttons on his fly, then just did up the top one.

'Sounds good. Remind me tomorrow though, right?'

Hughie muttered a reply in the affirmative. Ray wasn't listening.

Sneakers. Go.

Then a noise in the shop set his heart fluttering.

A bike entering. He knew who it was. There was only one person it could be. Manny was the only guy not here. He heard the others greeting Manny with the enthusiasm reserved only for the most popular guy at work.

'Where is he?' Manny shouted. 'Tell me!'

Ray knew straight away who he meant. Wesley's high voice saying to try the changing room confirmed it. He sure as shit wasn't looking for Hughie; those two couldn't understand each other without subtitles. He was looking for Ray, and Ray was cornered with nowhere to go.

This is it.

4:25PM

Ray swooned and steadied himself. A giddy lightness exploded within him but was quickly clouded by the idea that Manny would be pissed at him. Angry for something that in this timeline was still to happen. It was like he'd told a lie and Manny could find out any minute. It was ridiculous. It gnawed at his insides and brought out that cold sweat.

Nice deep breaths, Ray. Not now.

All he'd wished for the last seventeen years was to meet his old buddy one last time. Shoot the shit over a couple of cold ones. And laugh. Laugh till he cried, and it hurt

GHOSTS OF SEPTEMBER

his ribs. Now the moment was really here, he wanted to run.

The first time around, this meeting in 2001, might have been the last time he saw Manny alive. Sounds faded around him. Manny pulled off his helmet in the shop and Ray saw his smile. The sob sank back down his throat and his own smile warmed his face, a warm tear spilling down his cheek. It felt like an airport reunion, which would sound crazy to Manny. After all, in this world they had only spoken yesterday.

He wiped the tear away and Manny turned presenting his wide grin in all its glory. Ray always thought Manny looked like a young Lou Diamond Phillips. Manny always said otherwise and called Ray a racist piece of shit. He smiled. 2018 sorrow had tried to force itself front and center, but it had failed, overpowered by 2001 joy. Manny raised a hand for a handshake, but Ray bypassed it and squeezed his friend.

'Holy shit, man, easy!'

Manny gave his buddy the double tap on the shoulder, like a wrestler tapping out of a grasp. It was that 2018 sadness stepping forward that made him let go. If he started to cry now, he'd be powerless to stop.

Manny smiled, 'I don't see you for three whole days, man, and you turn queer?'

Ray remembered the sickness Manny had recovered from and used it as cover for his over-enthusiasm. 'Fuck you! How you feeling, buddy?'

'Ah okay. Still not a hundred percent but close

enough.' His features clouded. 'How the fuck are you? You don't look so good yourself, man.'

I woke up this morning and found out I was seventeen years in the past for no fucking reason whatsoever.

Probably not the answer Manny was looking for.

'I think I'm coming down with something.'

'Fuck, man, we still going to Sonny's?'

Sonny's. There was a name he hadn't heard in a lifetime. That was the place they used to go. All the time. It was a dive, but it was *their* dive. And they loved it. The bartenders all knew them by name, what they drank at what point in the evening, and as the night went on, they would no doubt be able to predict which songs they'd play on the jukebox. He wanted to say "yes" but there was something niggling in a corner of his mind. Maybe it was the delicate flap of the wings of a butterfly. Ray ignored it. Here was a guy he hadn't seen in years and he was thinking about the butterfly effect.

Fuck butterflies.

'What?' Manny asked, a baffled look on his face.

'You're damn right we're still going.' Ray grinned and ignored the gut feeling that there was something wrong.

That was his first mistake in 2001.

4:43PM

They took Ray's car. Manny didn't drive. Not outside of work. Always insisted that you didn't need a set of wheels in New York City, or Jersey for that matter, more trouble

GHOSTS OF SEPTEMBER

than it was worth. Maybe he was right. Tony let him use the work scooter too. So long as he filled her up when he was through, Tony didn't mind.

That's what he was riding when the car hit him.

'You okay, man? You're quiet.'

'Sure. Sorry. Just thinking.'

'What happened to your hand?'

Ray glanced, embarrassed at the bandaged right hand that gripped the wheel.

'Latest Playboy that good?'

Ray smiled, 'Fuck you.'

He was trying not to chuckle, 'I thought you'd leave it to Kat these days. Who is it this month? In Playboy.'

Ray was trying his hardest not to laugh, 'I burned the fucking thing, making breakfast.'

Manny grinned. 'That's what I'd tell people.'

Driving through Jersey Ray spotted The Bottom of the Barrel, a big old barn of a bar, and wondered how many of the other places that had gone would still be round now. Like Grillo's Italian Ice stand out in Plainfield. He loved going there as a kid, when mom and Pete were still around. But it was more than just places. Channel 9 seemed to be better back in the day. Fuck knows, probably just rose-tinted nostalgia, but Lindsey Lloyd Young doing the weather, like Robin Williams in *Good Morning Vietnam*, 'Heeeellllooooo, East Hanover!' it just seemed to be more of a local thing. That was gone now.

'You see that new Britney Spears' video? Holy Shit.

I'd fucking destroy that chick.'

Ray thought the idea of him having feelings towards a nineteen-year-old girl as a thirty-nine-year-old might be weird, but judging by the stirring in his loins, his 22-year-old mind was fine with it.

'Totally. That's the best midriff of all time.'

'Oh, man. Don't fucking start me.'

It was then that it struck him how *young* Manny was. His own mind seemed to flit between 22-year-old enthusiasm and exuberance, and 39-year-old seriousness. It felt to him like he'd aged 10 years in *that* week anyway. In being killed, Manny had dodged that particular bullet, and Ray thought again that it was lucky for him for that to have happened. The only silver lining to the shittiest of clouds. That wasn't just him trying to rationalize and minimize the shroud of guilt that hung over him. Him and Manny were so similar that he was certain what happened that Tuesday morning would have hit Manny just as hard as it hit him.

'Don't go quiet on me, man. Thinking about Britney. You've done enough damage to yourself.'

The two laughed loudly as they pulled up to Sonny's. it was good being back here. Like he'd never been away, though Ray couldn't shake the feeling he shouldn't be here. Nothing to do with the fucking butterfly effect or 2018. This was a 2001 feeling.

8:21PM

'How about this one,' Manny started, speech slurred but still clearer than Ray's.

Ray and Manny were in the middle of a round of *What if?* questions. Manny had started asking who would win a fight between prime Tyson and prime Ali. Ray had hedged by saying that Tyson would probably win sixty out of a hundred, but Manny was convinced the champ would be Tyson. Fourth round K.O. after hunting down Ali and killing the body. Manny had then answered Ray's question about fantasy dinner party guests with Hendrix, John Lennon, and his dad.

Ernesto Torres was working his second job, late-night in a 7-Eleven, when two guys came in to stick up the place. Ernesto argued when he should have agreed. That night he never came home. Manny was six years old. He never let his dad's death get him down. Sure it affected him, how could it not? But he never used it as an excuse. To him it was more of a spur. In fact, he was easily the most positive guy Ray knew. Manny was ambitious too. He always wanted to set up his own business. A sports bar. Decorated with a boxing theme, with pictures of all the greats on the walls. He was sure that Manny could make it work. The guy could start a party at a funeral.

Manny finished his question, 'If you could go back in time to when Hitler was a baby, would you kill him?'

The room spun and darkness bled into Ray's vision in a vignette.

'Whoa, you okay man?'

Ray nodded and drank his beer, shaking consciousness

back into his head and trying to play it off as normal.

'Good question... what would you do?'

Ray was deflecting. It felt like an answer to that question had gravity. And someone was listening.

'I don't know if I could kill him...' Manny drained his glass and slammed it to the table and started to smile. 'But I'd definitely punch him.'

Ray and Manny exploded in laughter.

'You'd punch a baby?'

Ray could barely breathe.

'Not any baby, just baby Hitler.'

Ray straightened his face.

Manny's smile fell away too. 'What is it, man?'

'What if,' Ray whispered conspiratorially, 'he only turned out to be such an asshole because some bastard with a time machine punched him when he was a baby.'

Manny started to laugh again and picked up Ray's glass, holding it up to the light, 'Whoa! What is in this?'

Ray burst into laughter again.

'It's your round,' Manny said, after the laughter had subsided.

'What? No,' Ray challenged.

Manny stared, straight-faced. Then Ray saw the smile creep into his eyes.

'Fuck! I almost had you!'

Ray's ribs were hurting, 'No you most definitely did not.'

Manny's face changed, like he'd smelled a pungent fart. He sneezed violently.

GHOSTS OF SEPTEMBER

'Whoa! Right in my beer!'

'Sorry, man, but you really should have finished by now.'

Ray remembered reading somewhere that if unimpeded, the germs from a sneeze could travel seventeen feet. Then he read somewhere else that it was way farther than that.

'Come on, drink up.'

Ray emptied his glass and Manny started toward the bar.

'Think of a new question while I'm gone.'

Ray had a question all right. He just wasn't sure he wanted the answer. Before he knew it, Manny was dancing back from the bar, shimmying with Suzie the waitress en route.

'You think of one?'

'Hmm?'

'A question.'

Ray started but paused, like he was about to break all Ten Commandments at once and God was watching. Manny just stared at him. He wasn't sure if he heard it for real or if he was imagining it, but he thought he heard a fluttering.

'If you only had a week to live, would you want to know?'

Manny's eyes widened, then he burst out laughing. 'Fuck, man, we had four beers and you throw this shit at me?'

'We had eight. And I'm fuckin serious.'

'I know you are. That's what worries me. Jesus. I don't know. I never thought about it.' He paused, thinking for about half a second, then said, very definitely, 'Yes.'

Ray was surprised. Even at his lowest, the thought of his own mortality scared him. It was the one thing that stopped him from offing himself. He'd decided to take the slow route with it in the end. The bottle would do it, but it would take its sweet time. He was certain his dad would say it was more evidence of his cowardice, despite the fact that he'd taken to drink himself for a while after Pete died. That's how Pop liked his double standards.

'You would?'

'You wouldn't?' Manny said. 'That way I get to get as much in as possible. Girls, drugs, all that shit. Go out with a bang, man.'

Shit. Now what? Tell him that in four days a stolen car would hit him doing fifty and break his neck?

'Wouldn't you?' Manny asked.

'Hmm?'

'Would you want to know?'

Ray thought about it. Before his answer would have been a quick one. No. No way. Blissful ignorance was the way forward. Knowing is death row. A ticking clock. Pressure. Old Ray didn't want any of that. Now? His mind hurt thinking about it. This was probably one of the few points he and Manny disagreed on. It should have been obvious that Manny would want to know.

So tell him. If you told him he could stop it. Avoid it.

GHOSTS OF SEPTEMBER

And what if he couldn't? What if death had to have his man? Maybe he'd make it worse. Manny had died quickly, instantly they said. The idea of Manny cheating death and then being hunted down after chilled him to his core. Like in that movie where a bunch of kids are thrown off of a plane just before take-off then the plane crashes and death follows them, picking them off one by one.

He heard a story once of a parachutist who jumped out of a plane at 13,000 feet and pulled the cord. Nothing happens. Experience and training kick in and the parachutist calmly pulls the reserve. Again nothing. Now the parachutist is falling towards the earth at terminal velocity and making his peace with God. As the ground looms he sees the countryside below getting more and more detailed, instead of fields he can see blades of grass; instead of bales of hay, he sees the individual straws; the greenness of the trees, becomes hundreds of individual leaves, until – contact. The parachutist lay there wondering why nothing had happened. No pain, no bright white light, no life flashing before his eyes, then he realizes: he's alive. He's landed in the only pile of hay in the field yet to be baled and survived without a scratch. He gets up and walks away, dazed, amazed, and sure he's cheated death.

Later that same day, in his bathroom at home, the parachutist steps in a puddle of water, slips and falls. Where the water came from, who the fuck knows? Anyway, on the way down he hits his head on the bathtub. He dies instantly. Those who do cheat death eventually get caught by time.

You can cheat death, but not forever. You might get one over on death; time is undefeated.

'Oh Raymond...'

Ray was spared from answering when *No Surprises* piped from his pocket. As it did the strange familiarity of déjà vu clouded around him. Something weird was going on. He looked down at the name.

Kat.

Fuck.

That's what was wrong. Kat's last words from that morning:

Don't forget about tonight.

Of course he had. He couldn't blame himself with the fucked-up morning he'd had. This was the niggling 2001 problem that had been gnawing at him all afternoon since he'd met Manny. Nothing to do with saying the wrong thing to his best friend. It was Kat. The problem was that second time around he'd made exactly the same decision now as his idiot-self had when he was twenty-two: to come drinking with Manny instead of meeting Kat at the restaurant where she worked. This time around he didn't know. He'd forgotten. He'd got excited when he saw his friend and made plans when he already had them. It was something he used to do a lot. It would infuriate Kat who read it as Ray not wanting to spend time with her, which wasn't true. Either way, Ray now had a problem.

'I've got to take this.'

GHOSTS OF SEPTEMBER
9:38PM

Manny nodded and checked out a group of hot young things at the bar while Ray prepared to take Kat's call. An emptiness took over the fluttery nostalgia in his stomach. Kat would be fuming. Now he'd been thrown a lifeline, a second chance, and he'd still got it wrong. The worst part wasn't about him, it was Kat. The humiliation. All her co-workers would be there giving her sympathetic looks. Fuck. He took the call.

'Kat, hi. I'm so sorry.'

There was a silence. His hand reached and rubbed his neck, but before he could start his weak excuse, she spoke.

'You're sorry? Fucking sorry? Let me guess, you forgot.'

'Wait I can explain…'

More silence from the other end of the line.

'No. You know what Ray? You can't. And even if you could, I don't want to hear it. It's the same old tired bullshit. Are you drinking?'

The jukebox was blaring and the guys shooting pool weren't exactly being quiet.

'I've had a couple, with Manny. I haven't seen him…'

'For three days. You haven't seen him for three days! What the hell is it with you?'

'I'll make it up to you… Kat?'

The line was dead. What had just happened? History repeated itself, and he couldn't be sure, but it felt like the conversation was word for word the same one he'd had originally. Like it was a script. You can live it again, but here's how it goes. No improv just read. His hand started to hurt, and when he looked down, he noticed it was balled into a tight fist. Blood filled the white knuckles as he opened his hand and that percussive throb settled back into the burn on his palm.

A hand grabbed his shoulder. 'You okay, man?'

Ray almost jumped out of his body. The fun had left him. He felt sick. He'd been screwing around here, drinking, and having fun, when there was more serious business to take care of. A chance to make a difference had fallen into his lap, and here he was, typical Ray Madison, fucking it up. All the bitterness he'd felt towards Pop, but in the end, Pop was right.

And now what? Do you tell Manny? What if you go to bed tonight and wake up back in 2018?

Manny eyeballed him over the threshold and the air inside suddenly seemed thick, stifling. He didn't want to spend another second in there.

'Manny I gotta go.'

'Go where? You ain't driving nothin. You look like shit.'

An odd sensation swept down his face where the sick whiteness was being quickly flushed with crimson. Even though there was no way she would answer his calls now, he had to talk to Kat. But Manny was right. Driving after beer while he was so pissed at himself was dumber than making toast in the bath. He had to get away from the bar.

GHOSTS OF SEPTEMBER

It felt suddenly alien. Like an old friend had betrayed him.

But what about Manny?

He could send him a text message as soon as he got back home. Home. He had to go.

'Manny, I feel weird, I think I need to go.'

'You want me to call you a cab? You don't look so hot.'

'I need the fresh air I think.'

'Fresh air?' Manny frowned. 'This is Jersey!'

They both smiled, but Ray's was heavy. The point at which he should go was well behind him.

'I'll come with you, man.'

'You know, I need a little time to think.'

Manny's smile faded.

'I'll see you again before...' Ray stopped himself.

'Before what?'

'Nothing. I mean I'll see you at work. Tomorrow.' But that was a lie. He didn't know if he would.

Manny nodded and they gave each other a quick hug. Ray wanted to hold on for longer, but he felt 2018 barging its way to the front of his mind and he let go. He turned and headed for home and didn't look back. Outside, in the cool breeze that carried the music and laughter away from the bar, another sensation took over. Not guilt. Not anger. And not déjà vu. This was the feeling that someone was watching from the sidelines. Watching and taking notes. If he was to stay here in 2001, it was a feeling he'd have to get used to.

MARC W SHAKO
9:47PM

Heat flushed through his body and his fists were balled into tight knots. History repeating itself. It was like a cruel trick. He snatched as much Cool New Jersey air as his tight chest would allow at a time, sure hyperventilation was coming any minute. He stood still, threw his shoulders back and closed his mouth, drawing in a deep breath through his nose. His heart rate slowed almost instantly, and slowly, the grip around his chest loosened until it was gone. The anxiety had passed, but that feeling of being watched lingered as he faced the direction of home and set off, playing what had happened over in his mind.

"Here's a second chance, kid, but I'm gonna make sure you screw it up exactly like the first time."

All he could think of was calling Kat, but he knew better than anyone that the smart move was to give her space. She was so pissed tonight that there was no way she'd listen to a word he said. She was as stubborn and headstrong as he was, and the combination wasn't always a good one. Old Ray would have just called and called. Sent a stream of text messages. That was why she'd left him. One of the reasons. The friction at times like this was enough to start a forest fire. It wasn't the main reason though: He'd spent so much time wallowing in self-pity that he'd started to believe his own victim bullshit. If he saw a future like the one old Ray was offering, he'd run like quicksilver in the opposite direction, too. He'd been such an asshole. Even if he went to bed tonight and woke up in 2018, not calling now was the best thing to do. And the hardest. He sent a simple apology text message and left it at that. If he was still here, he'd call tomorrow, see if he could patch things up. Maybe take her to Winnie's in Chinatown, she always liked it there (more for the karaoke than the food).

By the time he turned into Elizabeth Street, with its one-story houses and chain-link fences, his pulse rate had steadied, like his breathing. This place felt like home to him at any time and the light September breeze in his hair had a soothing influence. What Manny had said about wanting to know if he was going to die haunted him. The words echoed around his mind over and over.

Ideas on how to save Manny dominated his thoughts. Telling Manny that he should avoid Upper Manhattan first thing on Monday wasn't enough. That was something he had no control over. The way things were going, Manny's jobs on Monday morning would *all* be in that part of town. Then what would he do? Take those jobs himself; maybe even trade Manny for them. Manny wouldn't know why; he was so laid back he would switch just because Ray asked him to. All he had to do was make sure he was at work on Monday morning. It might mean he was killed instead. The thought didn't scare him as much as he expected. Manny would do more with his life than he ever had. Maybe death would leave Manny alone then. It filled its quota. One dead guy. Who cares who it is?

What if you're not here, Einstein?

From nowhere a gust of wind kicked dust up into his

face and sent a garbage can rattling along the street. He shielded his eyes from the wind and whipped round, sure that he would see a shadow following him. The burning feeling of eyes on him was back, stronger than ever. The trash can clanged along the sidewalk, empty and hollow, and tumbled into the gutter. It rocked and settled as the breeze died down. His pulse beat in his ears. The street was empty, but looking back it seemed darker. The shadows were longer, like hands reaching out to take him. The welcoming feeling he'd got when he entered Elizabeth Street was long gone.

It's just the angle you're looking at. It's fine. Go home.

He turned back and started for home again. But after a few yards, he stopped.

Up ahead, in the shadows, he spotted something. A new shape that wasn't there before. It was there now, plain as the Twin Towers were through his window that morning. A figure. Huddled up against a wall. Like a mirage. He'd never seen a ghost before, but he imagined this was how it would feel. The guy was halfway between him and his apartment building at the end of the street, like he'd dropped out of the sky. Ray set off again, trying to keep an even pace, hoping to hide how afraid he really was. As he got closer, he saw it was a man. A black guy in his sixties, sitting cross-legged and leaning against the wall, his long greying dreadlocks tied up in a red bandana and, despite the darkness outside, rocking black Ray-Bans. Slanted against the wall beside him was a white cane. A distinctive character, even by New Jersey standards, but one Ray had never

GHOSTS OF SEPTEMBER

seen before - in this time or the other. As Ray approached, without turning his head, the man spoke in a soothing voice touched with a hint of Caribbean accent.

'Evenin'.'

Ray was the only other person on the street, so he must have been talking to him.

'Evenin'.' He replied as he walked past.

'You okay, brother? You look like somethin's troubling you.'

Ray stopped.

'*Look* like?'

'Your voice. It's sad.'

Ray turned.

The man stood and without hesitation or faltering grabbed the cane at the first attempt. He took a few steps toward Ray with his head cocked oh so slightly at an angle but stopped before he got too close and invaded his space. 'You from round here? I ain't seen you before.'

Ray wanted to question his use of the word *seen* but didn't for fear of being offensive.

'Figure of speech,' the man said, smiling.

Confused but not wanting to appear rude Ray answered. 'I've lived here twenty-two years.'

'Twenty-two?' The man sounded surprised.

'Four. I mean. Four years.'

'That's better,' said the old man. 'Name's Charles. Most folks call me Charlie.'

Ray was sure he'd never seen or met this guy before

but felt a calm in his presence that he hadn't felt all day. For a long time for that matter.

'Do I know you?'

'You didn't. Now you do.' He smiled. It was as perfect a set of teeth as Ray had seen.

'Nice to meet you Charles. I'm Ray.'

'Sure you are. Tell me Ray, what's troubling you?'

This is the point where he would normally feel uneasy talking to somebody he hardly knew, but Charlie seemed to pre-empt the discomfort with another smile and before Ray knew it, he was answering.

'Got a friend in trouble. Not sure how to help.'

'Sure you are.'

The old man said it with a confidence and surety that left him shocked.

'Catching flies ain't goan help nobody.'

Ray closed his mouth, only now realizing it had dropped open in surprise.

'Problem is, Ray, that plan you've got? It won't work.'

'What? What plan?'

'The plan you came up with to save Manny. It won't work. Not that it ain't a good plan. It is. The problem is that between then and now things are gonna change. The past is set. I know, I know, this is the past, but not now it ain't. Now it's now. Now it's now and the past is set. But the future? That's slippery. Like liquid. It moves. A good plan today is a bad plan tomorrow. Don't worry. You'll come up with another.'

Ray wasn't so sure. 'I wish I shared your confidence.'

GHOSTS OF SEPTEMBER

'What the hell kinda talk is that?'

Ray stepped back involuntarily, again surprised by the old man's conviction. The breeze whipped up again, rocking the empty garbage pail in the gutter.

'You got a girl, Ray?'

Ray nodded, not wanting to give too much away.

'Describe her to me. In a few words.'

For the first time Ray was hit by a hint of discomfort.

'Go on. What is she like?'

'She's awesome.'

Too awesome for a loser asshole like me.

'Go on.'

'She's cool. She's strong. Independent. Knows her own mind.'

Charlie was smiling, 'And do you think a cool, strong, independent woman would be with someone she thought was an asshole? A loser?'

Ray shook his head.

'If you're such an asshole, why does Andy not give up on you? Why does Tony think you're his best guy? How comes Manny likes you?'

'How the fuck do you know all this? How do you know Manny?'

Charlie flashed that set of perfect teeth once more. 'Everybody needs a boot in the ass every once in a while, Ray.'

'And you're the boot?'

'Something like that.'

Ray took a step closer, 'You grifting me old timer?'

Charlie didn't flinch. 'What's wrong Ray? You think I see?'

'I fucking know it.'

Charlie tipped his head back and laughed a rich, throaty chuckle. He took a small step towards Ray and whispered, conspiratorially. 'I do,' he said, grabbing the rim of his glasses and lifting them, 'but not with these.'

They were standing close now, but Ray felt no threat. Ray was staring into the milky white of Charlie's eyes. Charlie lowered the glasses and Ray felt unease tickle the back of his neck.

'Don't worry, brother. I'm on your side.'

'Am I dreaming again?'

'You'll wish you were. But look at your hand. Is it not burned? Look at your face. Is it not young? And your friend, he lives, yes?'

Ray just nodded.

'This is real, Ray. Did the other guy find you?'

'Other guy?'

'Mean old bastard. With a beard. Crazy eyes. White guy. No offence.'

Ray shrugged.

'He looks a lot like Charles Manson, but maybe that's more of a vibe. You will. See him I mean. He'll try to stop you. Not physically. But he's a stubborn old fucker who doesn't like guys like you coming back here and moving shit around.'

Ray was more convinced now than ever that this was

a dream. That he'd fallen asleep and the next time he woke up it would be 2018 and he'd be back in his dingy apartment. Older. Alcohol ravaged. No Kat. No Manny. Sad and alone, but somehow relieved that this was all over.

Charles grabbed his burned hand and squeezed. The pain surged up his arm and he pulled it back with a scream. 'Fuck!'

'Still think you're sleepin'?'

Ray shook his head. Deep down, maybe he wanted it to be a dream. Now he was back, it wasn't everything he'd dreamed or remembered. It was good to see Manny and good for him and Kat to still be together, however thin a thread that was hanging by at the moment, but he'd remembered this as a simpler time. A more innocent time. And for a few hours this morning, when he slipped back into his old life like it was a comfortable shoe, that's how it felt. Now that the novelty had worn off, it felt different: serious; dangerous; threatening.

'Don't worry, Ray. You have the answers. You know when you'll wake up don't you?'

Ray hadn't thought about it, except for a second this morning, but now he thought he knew the answer. 'After?'

Charlie nodded. 'You got things to do here Ray. Before you go.'

'Do you mean...'

Charlie shook his head, 'I don't have the answers, brother. Just the questions.'

'I need to go home.'

Ray looked at his watch, it was twenty after ten.

'Jesus, it's late. Where'd the time go?'

Charlie just smiled. 'That's the other guy. He does that.' The smile dissolved. 'Watch out for him, Ray. Mean old bastard.'

Ray watched as Charlie turned and ambled away, white cane sweeping lazily before him. He stopped, broke into a tap dance, swinging the cane and tapping it on the floor like Fred Astaire might, then stood still again. Then, like the tap dance never happened, he continued walking - cane sweeping before him like a radar beam - and started to sing. *Just a Closer, Walk with Thee.* After a few seconds a window opened and a fat guy in a grubby white T-shirt leaned out.

'Shut the hell up, you crazy old fuck.'

Charlie sang louder and without turning his head aimed a middle finger at the man. Without a word of protest, the man slid back inside and closed the window. Ray grinned.

Without turning, Charlie shouted back. 'Oh, Ray?'

'Yeah?' he yelled back.

'That feeling you were being watched?'

'Yeah.'

'Wasn't me.'

Charlie set off again.

Ray frowned, turned and walked. He didn't stop until he got home.

GHOSTS OF SEPTEMBER

10:26PM

Back in his apartment, Ray drew the curtains. He couldn't bring himself to look at the Towers. Things had changed. This was no longer a return to more innocent times. Those Towers now meant responsibility. Huge responsibility.

He noticed his hand had reached into his pocket on autopilot, toying with the rabbit's foot keyring for comfort. He surveyed his new, old apartment. Nothing made sense. The meeting with Charlie seemed real enough, but while they were talking, it was like time around them had stopped. His thoughts were clear. Now, back in his place, he felt drunk again.

He filled the kettle and prepared a mug of coffee, sugar and freeze-dried grains sprayed across the counter like modern art. He stumbled to the bureau in the living room and slid out the bottom drawer. A notepad and pencils stared back at him. He was supposed to be using them to write songs. The guitar Kat had bought him as a birthday gift was gathering dust in the corner of the bedroom.

'Another failure.'

Focus, Ray.

He grabbed the pad and pencil and sat at the dining table. If he was going to make his time here count, he needed a plan. He scribbled down three bullet points and tried to develop each into a workable plan of action, to put right what had once gone so terribly wrong. In this drunken state, coherent thoughts were hard to come by. He folded his arms and placed his head there hoping the thoughts would somehow come quicker, rubbing the bare patch on his rabbit's foot keyring, like it was a genie's lamp, wishing for inspiration. The last thing he heard was the bubble and click from the kettle before he fell asleep.

FRIDAY

AIR BRAKES HISSED AS THE bus pulled to the curb and the doors swung open. Ray stepped aboard and took an empty seat by the window, bathing in the sunshine which shone brightly outside. A perfect day. He gazed out of the window at the grey concrete and green bushes then beyond, across the gently rippled surface of the Hudson, at their destination. The doors hissed closed and with a jerk the bus set off. Across from him, in a backwards facing seat, a pretty, dark-haired woman about his age smiled back. Ray held eye-contact for a second, before looking back out of the window as the road swept down into the cool darkness of the Holland Tunnel.

Ray looked down at his hands in the orange glow of the tunnel light and smiled. The right hand unbandaged. He flexed it and turned it over to examine the palm. The redness and stinging were both gone, and relief flowed through him in a soothing wave. This was going to be a good day. He looked back up at the girl, who was now sitting in glorious sunshine, having already emerged from the tunnel wall. But something was wrong. The smile had vanished. Her wrinkled brow had drawn over her dark eyes. A chill shuddered through him and he leaned forward to see what had caused her worry, but his view was blocked by the tunnel walls. He turned back to the woman and as he watched, her eyes widened with shock. She clutched at her throat, lower jaw trembling. Ray shivered and his breath ballooned before him in a cloud. Then, finally, as the bus emerged from the tunnel, he finally saw the source of her distress.

The street was lined with people, all staring into Manhattan. At the World Trade Center. A tall woman in a business suit pointed and Ray traced the line from her finger all the way to the top of the North Tower. Thick smoke billowed from a wound in the building and into the clear sky like ink in water. He felt cold and alone and longed for human contact, but when he turned back to the girl she was looking away, her face contorted into a grief-stricken silent scream. It was then that Ray noticed the other passengers on the bus.

Not every seat was taken, but in the ones that were, each passenger sobbed. Middle-aged women, old men, firefighters. One group in business suits, a man in a wheelchair surrounded by colleagues, a tall handsome man their leader.

Now Ray's coldness and loneliness became something else. His hands trembled uncontrollably, and it took everything he had not to scream aloud. His eyes scanned the bus looking for someone, anyone to give him a sense of calm.

They settled on a man who didn't cry. The woman next to him sobbed silently: make-up running from her eyes in black rivers, her long flowing hair wild. In contrast to her good looks, the man was tall, gaunt, his hair was thin, his white shirt stuck to his chest with sweat. Black expressionless eyes peered from his angular face through horn-rimmed glasses. His tie *cornflower blue* was loose, and he'd rolled up his sleeves, but he looked as far from casual as Ray could imagine. The man stood and stared at the floor of the bus; his gaze seemed to stare through it. His tie fluttered gently in a breeze that wasn't there. For a moment Ray got an X-ray snapshot of the man's face and the perfect outline of his skull. Some of the other passengers turned to look at the man and as they did, he removed his glasses and slid them into his shirt pocket, then, he took a step forward.

He lifted off the floor and the woman beside him screamed a piercing, uncomprehending scream. His arms flailed and his clothes fluttered. Others now screamed. Men and women both. Ray watched helplessly as the man levitated, arms flailing, clothes fluttering, his face a peaceful mask. Ray was overpowered by the urge to look away. Anywhere, just not at the man. He raised an arm over his eyes and turned just as a sickening thud resonated, the amplified sound of Rocky hitting raw meat in Paulie's refrigerated locker.

Another male passenger cried out in shock. 'Oh, God.' Two simple words, but he'd never heard anyone talk that way before. Two simple words saturated with fear. With disbelief. With horror. He never wanted to hear it again.

The bell rang and the bus jerked to a stop. Ray looked out of the window to see where they were and his eye was drawn to another hole, this one in the South Tower. The inky black smoke from this one merged with that from the North Tower and Ray was hit with realization of where they were going. The last place he wanted to be. He jumped from his seat. Now the other passengers had stopped crying. They stared at him. Like they knew. Knew that he didn't belong here. That he was an anachronism, an impostor from the future.

He had to get off. The doors opened and he made his move. As he reached the doors, he was hit with a surge of people rushing in the opposite direction. Most dressed in office attire, and just like the man some of their clothes fluttered. Amid the office workers were security guards. Police officers. Firefighters. All panicking. Bloodied. Bruised. Screaming in horror. Covered in dust. All pushing against Ray to climb aboard.

He screamed out. 'Let me off. I want to get off!'

Above the commotion he heard laughter from the front of the bus. Ray turned and looked at the mirror and into the driver's seat. It was a hunched old man. Wild hair. Crazy eyes. Shrieking with laughter. Ray threw a panicked look back out of the window at the line of people trying to board. Thousands stretching out as far as the eye could see. Ray was getting closer to the doors when there was another

GHOSTS OF SEPTEMBER

surge. He was pushed backwards into the bus and he fell.

'Help me!'

Hard-soled shoes stood on his hand, his arm, his legs. The young woman he'd seen in the seat opposite his leaned down. Ray thrust a hand towards her as more and more people stood on him to board the bus. A bone in his leg snapped. The pain surged through his shin along to his knee, the shattered edges of bone grinding sickeningly against one another under the weight of a dozen feet. He reached out for the girl, noticing now the bandage was back on his hand.

'Please help me!'

She scowled, 'Help *you*?'

As she said it the scrambling stopped. The screaming stopped. Now it was silent. One by one the passengers, and by now there were hundreds, turned and looked down at him. Black looks. Cold stares. Teeth bared like wild dogs.

A middle-aged woman in a dirty, purple, smoke-stained business suit scowled, '*You* should help *us*!'

One by one they spoke. Voices drenched in fear. Jagged with horror. Hollow with despair.

'Please help us.'

'Why won't you help us?'

'We need help.'

'Help!'

Ray screamed as they closed on him. Clawing at him with bloody, dusty hands. Drawing closer until the shrinking gaps of daylight vanished. Darker and darker. Until he saw nothing.

8:21AM

He screamed himself awake and by the time his eyes opened he was sitting upright. But he wasn't sitting at the dining table. He was in bed. Undressed. He panted for air. Tightness gripped his hand. The bandage. He'd never done gone walkabout in his sleep before. *First time for everything.* He surveyed the bedroom; it still held the same brightness it had from the dream. Like he was still in 2001. So weird. His head felt clear. Clearer than when he was drinking at least. He swung his feet to the floor and stood. It too was easier than when he was drinking. *What if it wasn't a dream?* As he ambled along the hallway his eyes were drawn to the broken light switch.

In 2018 it's broken. It works in 2001…

He held his breath and reached out, praying that it wouldn't work. That the light wouldn't come on. That when he pressed the button, the same cool darkness would fill the hall. His Adam's Apple bobbed, and he hit the switch and broke out in a cold sweat.

Shit.

'Maybe Joel fixed it.'

In the living room he saw a lined notepad on the table. Written at the top of the notepad in bold capital letters, in his own unmistakable handwriting – *SAVE MANNY*. Circled and double-underlined.

It still doesn't prove a thing. It could all be explained

GHOSTS OF SEPTEMBER

away. Joel – he came and tidied and cleaned the place. It was him who fixed the light. He went away and Ray dragged all the things out onto the table. Burned his hand. While he was sleepwalking.

There was only one way to prove it was all a dream definitively. He eyed the curtains, heart beating a little faster as he did so. Beyond lay the answer. Like in the *Wizard of Oz* - all the answers are behind the curtain.

His eyes were already squeezed closed as he approached the window and grabbed handfuls of the thin, scratchy curtains. With a flick of his arms he flung them back. If he opened his eyes and saw the towers, that would settle it - it was real. Air washed into his lungs in shallow waves and he peeled back his eyelids. They settled on Lower Manhattan captured in the optimistic glow not long after sunrise. For a second it wasn't clear. Then the blurriness came into focus and settled on the Twin Towers. It was real. And he had to do something about it.

He spun his head round to the clock on the wall. The second hand jerked to the 12 and the minute hand clicked into place in the opposite direction. He couldn't exactly recall the time the first plane hit the North Tower, but he knew it was close to half past and there was a little voice in his head repeating the same four words over and over.

What if it's today? What if it's today?

It felt as if his stomach had been stolen, numb like an arm that he'd fallen asleep on. Is this what the other dream had been about all along? It wasn't a memory, because he hadn't been there to remember. So maybe it's this. A premonition. A premonition of something that he's about to experience. All he can do is stand here and watch. Maybe a phone call will do it. If he calls right now, they could clear the buildings.

And what do you tell them, Raymondo?

The same feeling of impotence hit him, like a fly writhing in the sticky web of a spider. The worst part was, it felt *exactly* like the dream. This is what the dream had been about all the time. Only a couple of minutes had passed since the last time he looked at the clock, but that second hand swept on, indefatigable. He scanned the skies. Miles of open, pure blue stretched out to the horizon in all directions, empty of clouds and aircraft, and he fixed eyes on the North Tower. His eyes drew lines outwards to where a plane might come from, and there, heading northward, he spotted something. A black speck. With both JFK and La Guardia in Queens, air traffic was a common sight in the skies over New York City.

But this was different. A little too low. A little too fast.

He stared, transfixed, those same feelings from his dream engulfing him in a fog of déjà vu. He glanced back at the clock. The hands crawling inevitably to twenty to 9. Something about that time seemed to fit. Yes, that was around the time of the attacks. A spray of ice-water washed over his neck. He screamed as the plane neared its target.

He pounded the window with his fists, 'No! God, no!'

He waited for the inevitable; caught in the grip of the panic attack that was sure to follow. Waited for the orange fireball to explode into the sky. His heart pounded in his ears.

Suddenly he was inside the Tower. Staring in disbelief as the screaming engines of the 767 sent the aluminum aircraft, laden with jet fuel, into the building and just as it was about to hit, he was back in the silence of his apartment.

Nothing.

No explosion. No fireball. A silhouette appeared at the other side of the South Tower and kept going on the same route.

He went to the kitchen, made coffee, and returned to the living room. He sat as he had the night before, with the notepad. He tore off the top sheet, wrote at the top of the clean page

STOP THE ATTACKS

and paused. He had to think of as much detail as he could remember. In 2001, because of the illness that had kept him in bed, he slept through the attacks. The only information he had was from the news reports that came in the following days – played on a loop searing certain details into his memory. Now as he searched for them it hurt.

That empty space where the info should be, expanding, corroding the memories around it, spreading like a virus, like they were some sort of glitch that the matrix had to erase. What he could have told you with certainty two days ago was either gone or disappearing fast.

He fought through the pain and the fog and scribbled whatever he could recall before it was gone forever. The North Tower was struck first, sometime around a quarter to nine. He remembered that from his dreams. Those belonged to him, not the matrix. United Airlines? That rang a bell. The plane struck somewhere close to the top of the building – he sketched the Tower and the damage. *90th floor?* Around a half hour later an American Airlines flight struck the other tower near the middle - somewhere around the 60th floor. He drew again.

Where did those flights take off from?

He squeezed the rabbit's foot and screamed out, wincing, and flinching at the flare of agony the attempt at recollection brought.

That information is important. He doesn't want you to have it.

What did he have? Not much. Maybe the airlines were the wrong way around, but the times felt right. Close at least. And that was it. That was everything. Getting as little as he had hurt like hell. A stabbing ache filling the gaps in a memory that was yet to be formed.

There was more. He knew more and couldn't recall it. Something about the flights. The dull ache behind his eyes had become a sharp stabbing at the temples. He had to stop. He would come back to it later. Staring at the information he had, he realized that he didn't have much at all. He turned his gaze to the Towers. As he stared, his vision blurred, and it became clear that if he was to get more information, something he could use, he would have to visit the World

GHOSTS OF SEPTEMBER

Trade Center. He'd have to go to the Twin Towers.

9:15AM

Ray gazed out of the window at the Towers. They were gargantuan, as if to emphasize the scale of the task he was facing. What if the attacks didn't happen here? Maybe this is an alternate timeline. Maybe he wouldn't have to do anything at all. Maybe the eleventh would come and go without incident.

Now you really are *dreaming, Raymondo.*

Despite the last seventeen or so years of barely leaving the apartment, he had never felt so alone. He was about to do the one thing that he hadn't done since that week. Take a chance. Twist when it was easier to stick. Act when it was easier to refrain. And he would have to do it alone. There was no one he could turn to for help. He supposed in times like this a guy would normally turn to his father.

Fat fucking chance of that happening for him. He wanted to speak to his father now, but not for advice. Just to say some things that he'd never got chance to before Pop died. He should know that he pushed his only living son away. And that, in small part, contributed to his alcoholism. Why should he die and get to just fuck off without that guilt? Ray heard the pencil snap.

'Pushing your buttons from beyond the gra...'

It's 2001. Pop. He's still alive.

There you go, kid. Something else to feel like shit

about.

Christ, with everything that was going on he hadn't realized. It would have been obvious to anyone else from the beginning. He and Pop barely spoke, but he was still his father, for crying out loud. Would he even help? Pete was always the favorite. Pop was never the one Ray turned to for advice. That was always mom. Until cancer stepped in and made that impossible. In fact the only time that he went out of his way to meet Pop was to watch the odd ball game and Ray realized that for all the shit and resentment and pain there would be nothing he'd like more than to have one last beer with Pop and watch the Jets.

The sound of a tear hitting the notepad dragged Ray back to the present. He wiped at his face. He would try to arrange a meeting with Pop, but that would have to wait. He had to visit the Towers and he had to do it soon. That would be impossible if he had to go to work.

9:29AM

He paced the bedroom, cell phone in hand, preparing what he would say. The contacts in his phone slid past until he landed on Tony and hit the green button. It rang a couple of times before Tony answered.

'Tony?'

'What's happening, Ray?'

'Tony, I don't feel so hot. I won't make it in today.'

'You sound a lot better than yesterday…' Tony said, almost a question.

GHOSTS OF SEPTEMBER

That's because I haven't been crying.

'I feel a lot worse.'

'Christ, you're putting me in a tight spot here, kid.'

'Sorry, T. I just think if I take the day off today, I'll be okay for Monday.'

'What's so special about Monday?' he asked.

I want to make sure I'm able to work so that Manny doesn't get hit and killed by a stolen car.

'Nothing, it's just... I don't feel so hot. I think if I can rest a few days, I'll make it through the next week is all.'

'Well, Christ, I can't force you kid, if you don't feel good, you don't feel good.'

'I really don't, T.' That part was true enough.

'Okay, kid. Rest up. Let me know how you're doing on Sunday.'

Relief, 'Thanks a lot, T, I really appreciate it.'

'No problem. You covered for Manny all week. Now he can cover for you.'

Ray was dumbstruck. He stood motionless until Tony ended the call, his words ringing in his ears.

Now he can cover for you.

Like it was a warning. Not from Tony. From *him*. The crazy old bastard driving the bus in his dream. It hadn't occurred to him that Manny could be killed today. Was it possible? A pre-emptive strike from death. Father Time gets his hits in early. No. Surely not. He hadn't done anything yet. Manny was supposed to die on the tenth. The Monday morning. That was still on the cards. He hadn't stopped it yet, hadn't even tried, so there was no need for plans to change. Christ, he felt sick. He wasn't prepared for this. Every decision a potential domino that could fall in the wrong place and do untold damage.

He dressed in his work uniform, thinking that once inside the towers, it might give him better access to places a civilian wouldn't have. If he needed to go and explore, he could say he got lost and it was his first time at the WTC. Having not visited for over seventeen years, it would be like viewing them for the first time. Almost. Any notes, he would have to take mentally - it would attract too much attention if he carried his notepad around.

He stepped into the hallway and noticed that something had changed. Yesterday it felt good to be in 2001 New York. Today it felt strange, as if the very fabric of the walls knew he was plotting against the past. Like the passengers on that bus, they knew he was an anachronism. Yesterday was liberating. Like the old days. New York like it used to be. Now he was looking over both shoulders, like he was hiding some big secret. In a way, he was. He felt like this and he hadn't even left the building. He was too distracted to drive to the Towers so rather than walk back to Sonny's to pick up his car, he would take the PATH train.

He stepped from the shadow of his apartment building into the warmth of the morning.

'Morning, Ray.'

His heart leapt in his chest. He turned. It was Charlie.
Charlie's real?

He hadn't given Charlie a thought since last night.

GHOSTS OF SEPTEMBER

Truth be told, he thought he'd dreamt him up. But here he was, large as life. Last night he seemed cheery. Now he was somber.

'You felt it, didn't you?'

Ray just nodded. It was the change. That's what he was talking about.

'Good. It's important you realize. He'll come after you.'

Ray knew exactly who he was talking about. 'I saw him last night,' said Ray, 'in a dream.'

'He won't do it himself. You'll see him, but it won't *be* him. You'll be okay for now. You're here, not doing too much damage. You start trying to make changes, you'll see. Lines forming in front of you. Traffic lights will be red. It'll look like coincidence, but you'll know better. The more you try to change, the more you'll piss him off.'

'I can't let Manny die.'

'Good. But just be careful. You talk like that; the old fucker *feels* it. He don't think you'll do much of anything. Not in your nature.'

Ray stared at Charlie's feet and nodded.

'Try not to worry, Ray. Whatever happens is going to happen. You can't worry about it now. You do what you can. Now. Everybody is busy regretting their past or worrying about the future. I'll tell you what I'd tell them, if I thought they'd take a blind bit of notice: You need to take care of now.'

Ray looked up at Charlie, 'Who are you, Charlie?'

'Everybody needs a friend.'

'Or a boot in their ass.'

'Or a boot in their ass,' Charlie repeated with a soft smile.

'Are you like him? His opposite or something?'

Charlie smiled again, the smile you'd give a kid who questions everything, brimming with curiosity. It could have come off as condescending, but it didn't. It was nothing but charm.

'Or something is right. Go on. Get going. Time's a wastin. You'll get to noticin it does that.'

'Will I see you again?'

'You will, that I promise. Now get gone, Raymondo.'

Ray wanted to ask something else, but the question vanished as quickly as it came. Charlie turned and sauntered back along the street. After a few paces he threw a hand up in a wave, as if he knew Ray was still watching. Ray turned in the opposite direction and went to the PATH train. From there, it would be less than forty-five minutes before he was at the Towers.

9:56AM

The Port Authority train ran from Grove Street directly to the Towers. In less than twenty minutes he'd be at the World Trade Center. Now that he had strayed from the path of his previous 2001 actions, he was no longer followed by that cloying fog of déjà vu. He ignored the scrutiny of surrounding onlookers and instead stared into the black eye of

GHOSTS OF SEPTEMBER

the tunnel. The smell of stagnant water accompanied the constant drip of water coming from somewhere unseen, an offbeat percussion that amplified Ray's growing sense of claustrophobia. He stepped back from the tracks and leaned against a pillar for comfort. If this is what it was going to be like working to change the past, it was going to be a long few days indeed.

Right then, bright light shone at the far end of the tunnel, making it appear wider. Musty warm air caressed his face as the squealing brake of the shiny blue and silver PATH train slid by endlessly, before finally lurching to a halt. A robotic female voice announced that the train would stop at Exchange Place before a male trust-me-I'm-a-salesman voice asked passengers to clear the closing doors. He was already seated by the time the PATH pulled him towards what was feeling more and more like a date with destiny.

The rhythmic rattle of train on tracks rocked him gently, but the feeling did little to soothe him. It suddenly felt like one of his dreams. Not the dreams of 2018: not the burning house that he can't escape because he's stuck in a wheelchair; not saying goodbye to Pete one last time. No, this was more like the ominous terror of another September nightmare.

The cold clutches of that morning's dream gripped him forcing a shudder. If he closed his eyes he could have been back on that bus, heading for disaster. All eyes on him. Accusing.

MARC W SHAKO

You shouldn't be here.
Why don't you want to help us?

The air in the train grew thinner. He grabbed at the collar of his coffee colored uniform and undid another button. The shiny-headed businessman opposite peered over his newspaper. Ray stared back and the businessman turned his focus back to the sports pages, but when Ray looked at the next passenger, an overweight young woman, she immediately averted her gaze too. Ray closed his eyes and leaned back, resting his head on the cool glass. A wave of nausea swept through him. Maybe this was what it was like for someone with the "wrong" skin tone after the attacks. All eyes on you, waiting for you to make a move that you hadn't even thought of. The closest thing he could equate it to was the feeling he got when he had to speak to authority figures: nervous without ever having done anything to be nervous about. The eyes that ate into you full of mistrust and doubt. The train rocked and the sickness rose in his throat, he opened his eyes to check out the map. Only two stops to go, but he imagined looking up at the sign to see a whole bunch of extra stations thrown into the mix by Charlie's crazy adversary. Or that the WTC stop would somehow be gone altogether.

The tug of gravity took hold again as they arrived at Exchange Place. The doors opened to allow another blast of that warm, dry air into the train. He'd be getting off in a few minutes and it couldn't come soon enough.

The metal of the handrail cooled his sticky palm as he pulled himself to his feet, lurching this way and that with

GHOSTS OF SEPTEMBER

the camber of the tracks. He tottered along to the doors and wiped the sweat from his brow, pretending to gaze through the windows but actually noting in the reflection that the other passengers were still studying with uneasy eyes.

The PATH jerked to a halt and the doors slid open to blast a welcome breeze, still warm, but one that now cooled his face.

He'd arrived. He was at the World Trade Center.

10:19AM

Crowds jostled him along the platform as he followed the signs and the rush up the escalators; into the World Trade Center. The throng was made up of a mixture of business suits and casual clothes, peppered with a smattering of trench coats. The trench coats belonged to the Wall Street crowd avatars; same trench coats, same suits. A computer simulation crowd. The odd one here or there in running shoes for extra comfort.

The huge hallway was cooler than below ground and he felt lighter as he entered the tower lobby. The last time he'd seen this was in a documentary about the attacks: the reality of what he was faced with flickered back and forth; the pristine marble and solid glass which carried an air of almost palatial grandeur switching to the crumbling, shattered, post-attack disarray. Unaware of the forthcoming horror, civilians chatted and laughed, an ease which Ray knew he'd be unable to relate to for some time. The occasional chirp of a cell phone cut through the noise, after all, this was a time when people used phones for talking. Muffled announcements came from above and the clack of heels on tile went by somewhere, possibly carrying the coffee he could smell.

He rode the escalator, being bumped by those in way too much of a hurry to just stand there. The tightness in his throat had loosened and the nausea he'd felt was slowly sinking back down to his knotted gut. He was trying to act like he fit in here, like he belonged. The Chinese couple in front were gasping and gaping at everything, pointing out insignificant features that would be nothing more than rubble in a few days' time.

He finally got off and stumbled towards the bank of elevators, avoiding eye contact with the stocky guard that faced him up.

'Help you pal?'

The voice was cheerful but didn't match the demeanor.

'Got a pick up. On 84.' He pointed to the company logo on his shirt, then at the signs which listed the businesses and the floors they occupied, relieved to see that the 84th floor wasn't vacant.

The guard just looked back at him. Ray was wearing his work uniform, but the guard's face was saying that it wasn't going to be enough. Ray's vision blurred briefly before refocusing.

'You okay?'

As Ray looked at the smooth marble on the wall, his whole field of vision flickered and when it did, he was transported to the morning of the attack. The crowds were gone. The walls looked like a set from the Matrix movie - smashed and crumbling marble, clinging desperately to the wall. A cool breeze blew in from the plaza through the shattered windows, carrying with it a faint wail of sirens and the thick smell of pulverized concrete. His head felt light like he was nodding off in front of the late-night movie.

'Pal?'

The guard's voice snapped the scene back to reality and the crowd noise filtered back in.

'Er, yeah, I'm good,' Ray lied. 'Think I ate some bad seafood.'

The guard stood aside to give Ray access to the elevators. 'Take it easy.'

Ray nodded thanks and went. That was it. That was how easy it was to gain access into the building. A uniform. No ID. It made him feel sicker as a fresh wave washed over him.

A half-dozen suits filed into the elevator as he approached, and he reached the back of the line. He stepped inside and about faced, turning to the doors in time to see them close. He swayed gently and there was a sound he recognized. Faint, distant, echoey. No Surprises. He reached into his pocket to retrieve his cell phone. He looked at the caller ID window. Again his vision blurred, and the image drifted apart into two. He tried to focus, but the two images came together and kept going. As they passed each other he saw the name.

MARC W SHAKO

Pop.

His father was calling. The man who had been dead for seventeen years. Ray felt the blood draining from his head until he was under a cloak of blackness.

The murmur of activity faded in, as distant and echoey as when it faded out, but when Ray came to, he found himself not in the elevator, but lying on plush carpet. The high ceilings were the real reason for the echo, not some unconscious wooliness. He peered up into the kind eyes of a white-haired security guard.

'Welcome back, chief.'

'Where am I?' said Ray, propping himself up on his elbows, confused not to be at home.

'One World Trade Center. Sky Lobby, to be exact.'

Sky Lobby. Of course. The Twin Towers had Sky Lobbies. If you wanted to go to the top floor, you had to change elevators here. There were only service elevators that ran the full height of the towers. He read somewhere it was a safety feature, something about stopping the elevator shafts acting as a giant chimney.

Ray turned to face the windows. Blue skies stretched out to the horizon, but Ray found no comfort in them. His eyes immediately picked out aircraft gliding along, and his backbone tensed instantly. The longer he looked the more planes he saw, each one increasing the possibility that they could be heading right here. Right now.

The genial guard helped Ray to his feet. 'Musta clocked your head when you fell. You've been out a while.

GHOSTS OF SEPTEMBER

Where were you going, before you blacked out?'

He didn't really know. Now he didn't care. He had to get out of here. All he remembered was something about Pop and suddenly the image of the forlorn Lobby downstairs flashed into his mind and when it did, he looked around him at the Sky Lobby and it was transformed into a similar horror.

Thin fingers of smoke clawed at the ceiling around light fixtures which flickered from swinging damaged light fixtures.

'I've gotta go… I've…' he paused, unsure of what he wanted to say and repeated, 'I've gotta go.'

Ray stumbled to the elevator, jabbing at the button with a bandaged hand that trembled wildly. The Sky Lobby had a gentle, reassuring buzz of activity. Reassuring, until he realized that the buzz was coming from hundreds of employees, guests, and visitors whose lives would all be in grave danger when the attack started in earnest. An attack that could already be underway. Sickness rose in him and he tried to focus on the lit floor numbers above the elevator. The lights blinked on and off with terrific speed. 90th, 80th, 70th. Ten floors every few seconds. A small crowd had gathered around him awaiting the arrival of the elevator and it felt as though they were stealing his air. The arrival of each new person made it harder and harder to fill his lungs. He slowed his breathing, sucking longer draughts of air in more slowly, stepping forward to give himself more air, but as he did those behind just shuffled that same couple of inches filling the void he'd vacated. The ping marked the elevator's arrival, but his leaden legs kept him from moving. The crowd pushed past him and into the car. The occupants all about faced and stared as if challenging him to enter that cramped space. Ray saw the lights flicker in the foggy car and took a half step back. The doors closed and Ray turned and headed for the stairs.

The door swung open and as the overhead door-closer dragged it shut that buzz of activity disappeared. Instead of helping Ray's nerves it served only to heighten them further. The stairwell was lonely and unwelcoming. Soon there would be people crowded in here, filing down the stairs, not quite in a state of panic, more in a stunned disquiet at horrors unknown which unfolded on the upper reaches of this stricken tower. Ray sucked in another deep breath to calm himself. He checked his watch. Charlie was right. The "other guy" had stolen a lot of time. It was somehow after eleven.

11:16AM

It seemed impossible that his journey had started a few hours ago. How long had he been out for?

He peered over the edge of the railing to see how close he was to escape and was assaulted by dizzying vertigo. He leapt back against the wall, wishing more than ever that he was at home, with a cold beer in his hand. The sheer scale of these buildings terrified him, not to mention the scale of the task he faced. *Potentially faced.* The task of guiding just short of three thousand souls down this concrete tomb to safety.

What was he doing here? Saving his relationship with Kat was one thing. As far as the crazy old guy who looked like Charles Manson went? He wouldn't give a fuck. And saving Manny? That was just one guy. But this? It seemed ridiculous to him that he'd even contemplated it. Ray darted down the lonely staircase, barely in control of his feet as they tried to take two, three steps at a time. Stopping the attacks was too much. He couldn't do much of anything from in here. Maybe clear out the odd office. Help somebody downstairs if they couldn't do it alone. But three thousand souls? Not from in here. He'd need to do something else. He just didn't know what.

The floor numbers diminished and with them, Ray's feelings of dread. But the lower he got the bigger the feelings of ineptitude and incompatibility of the task he faced. It had taken thirty minutes to come down fifty floors. He tried to calculate the time needed to get from the floors above the impact zones to the floors below, which should have been simple enough, but again, he found that thinking about it made his head hurt.

'Just get the fuck out of here, Ray,' he muttered.

He reached the lobby level and left the oppressive stairwell for open spaces. The noise grew as he approached the lobby and doubled when he pushed the door open. Voices echoed from the marble tiled walls as visitors chatted about the routine, the minutia, the unimportant as they went about their business.

Soon all of this would be chaos. The floor underfoot went from plush carpet to hard marble as he hurried for the square of light from the Plaza that represented escape. Security guards and suits alike cast odd looks at him as he stumbled for the doors, sure that the moment freedom was within reach, a savage explosion would ring out and snatch it away. His knees were giving way. He tried to go faster, but each step felt less certain than the last, the square of light burning so brightly now that he saw nothing of what lay beyond.

He stumbled and fell into a tall man in a suit. A man in his early thirties. Slender. With thinning hair and horn-rimmed glasses. Electricity surged into him on contact. He turned to see the man looking back at him scowling, and Ray's mouth dropped open. His face. Long, thin, hawkish. It was the man from his dream on the bus. The clothes were different but... The falling man. *He's real.* The lady with the long golden hair beside him was real too. For a horrific second Ray got an X-ray snapshot of the man's face and saw the smashed bones within. Ray screamed, and he scrambled to his feet, lurching out into the Plaza.

He ran for the closest flowerbed and vomited. Gasping for air, he collapsed onto his back and closed his eyes against the two steel giants which loomed above him into that endless blue. He couldn't do it. The task was too great, and he, too small. In the darkness behind his closed eyes he saw the man tumbling, clothes pressed against his skin at one side, billowing out behind him on the other. Ray

GHOSTS OF SEPTEMBER

opened his eyes and turned onto one side, before raising himself up on all fours, still sucking in huge breaths of air.

Yesterday, New York felt like a reunion with an old friend. Now he felt that the city, *his* city, was against him. That it was in league with Charlie's "other guy", the guy who took time away never to be returned. Pint-sized, stooping, but inexplicably powerful. Ray felt small, alone, vulnerable. Like it was *his* face on an FBI wanted poster. Like every pair of eyes was on him. Like they *knew*. They knew he didn't belong here, and whatever his intentions, they wouldn't let it happen.

He lurched to his feet and away from the towers. Throngs of people parted around him as he stumbled through the Plaza, as if he were a leper. He had to get home. Home was the only place he would feel safe. Staggering onto West Street, the sound switched from the echoes of the Plaza to the regular hustle and bustle of New York City. Business suits now mixed with Regular Joes, cops, homeless guys, and hustlers. All going about their business, some without a care in the world, most like they were late for something or another, none aware that, potentially at least, in four days' time, all of their important duties would be thrust into awful perspective that would cast a long, growing shadow into their futures.

He ran along the road as quickly as his rubbery legs would allow, trying and failing to hail a cab that he wasn't even sure he could afford. He shrank at every blaring horn and wailing siren that burst or rose in the air. All sounds that served as a reminder of the looming terror which grew closer with each passing second. He ran north along West Street desperately searching for a cab without a fare. It felt wrong to stop running. He'd made it past Pier 25 and had almost reached Hubert Street. At this rate he would end up walking through the Holland Tunnel for home; a trip that would take the best part of two hours. Old Man Time stealing more precious minutes.

No sooner had he finished the thought than he saw the potential haven of a cab, light glowing, two lanes over. He used all the wind he had left to whistle through his fingers and surprised himself with the volume he mustered. The young black driver waved acknowledgement and weaved toward the curb. Ray trotted the few steps to where the cab was waiting and fell inside.

'Jersey City,' was all he could say as he gasped for air in the back of the cab.

Now, twenty minutes was all that stood between him and home. A small victory. Small but meaningless. Hollow, unless he could come up with another way of changing the future and stopping the attacks without setting foot in the towers. He sank back into his seat and closed his eyes.

He felt each red light like a dog on a leash. Restraining his progress with frustrating ease. *Traffic lights will be red.* He opened his eyes and watched as the passing buildings shrunk in the number of stories until they reached the darkness of the Holland Tunnel. Fluorescent strip lights bled through the darkness and bounced off the dirty tile, tile which had probably once been white. The smell of car

GHOSTS OF SEPTEMBER

fumes filled the tunnel, which seemed to go on forever, but rather than feeling claustrophobic and endangered, here Ray felt a peace and calm that was missing outside. As if the tunnel walls were a shield from danger. From his seat he could see the red taillights of the cars ahead reflecting from the ceiling and thought that it was like glimpsing back in time for a matter of milliseconds, like seeing the light from the sun as it was eight minutes ago. It was just then that the eight-minute-old sunlight from the Newport Parkway burst through the end of the tunnel. He was almost home.

Five minutes later the cab pulled over outside Ray's building.

'That's twenty-five on the nose,' the driver said, in a calm, soothing voice.

Ray frisked himself and remembered he'd deliberately left his wallet. The harder he was to identify the better, he thought, not really knowing why. He felt some bills in his pocket and hoped it was enough. He pulled a ten, a five, and three singles out of his pocket.

'Shit.'

'You short?'

'I got it,' he said, fishing a limp ten from his back pocket.

He wanted to do more than leave the three-dollar tip the extra ten bucks afforded him. Warn this guy somehow. Maybe he knew somebody who worked at the Towers. Some regular fare or friend or family member. How would he even word something like that?

In the end, all he could do was hand over the extra ten dollars, force a ragged, tired smile, and thank the guy. And that's exactly what he did before turning for the sanctuary of home.

1:34PM

Back in the calm of his flat Ray sat on one of the dining chairs, head in hands, body tensed. He wanted to scream. He'd wasted the best part of a day; gone to the towers in the hope of getting something he could actually use and come back with nothing. Although, it wasn't a completely wasted trip. He knew something now he didn't before he went - This task was too much. Too big. All he'd thought about, prayed for (though he was nobody's description of religious), for the last seventeen years was this moment. To come back to the time when his life wasn't fucked. The time when the *world* wasn't fucked. He didn't care if that sounded schmaltzy, that was how he felt.

Even if it didn't change the world, the day those towers fell changed him. Before then anything seemed possible. Anything in a good way. He believed that generally people were good. That they looked out for one another, even in New York where nobody's got time to shit. After, the opposite seemed true. Sure, the city had pulled together to clean up and get through the mess and the shit and the horror, and there were stories like the town in Canada who took in people from grounded flights, but all that aside, that was

GHOSTS OF SEPTEMBER

a dark time. The darkest. He hadn't been an idealist; losing your hero when he's two weeks after his eighteenth birthday will do that for you, let alone watching your parents pull themselves apart and seemingly forget they had another kid to take care of, but before that day the world was brighter, more innocent. So was he. After it he was tired. Numb. It all went to shit from there. Maybe he'd stopped caring after that point. Sure he'd heard about man's inhumanity to man, but this was the first time he'd seen it. Felt it. That day, it landed right at his door.

He'd woken up to that wounded skyline and it was like something from *Invasion of the Body Snatchers*. Something that looked like a loved one, but there was something wrong: an impostor where a familiar sight once stood. He just thought that skyline would last forever. But nothing did. Him and Kat hadn't. Or Manny. Or Pete. He'd gone to bed with an aching head and fever and woken up to another world. Like a nightmare. Much worse than the one he was trapped in now. He looked down at his burned, bandaged hand.

It's not a dream, remember?

How could he forget? Now he had the chance to do something about it. Didn't he? It was only now that he thought about what the real reality of what this was.

Despite the panic that overcame him at the towers earlier, the only thing that felt right was that he'd been given an opportunity to fix everything. By who? That was another question. Maybe it was a sick joke played on him by the universe. Give the one chance to put it all right to the person worst equipped to do so. A guy who took zero risks just to avoid the panic attacks that came ever since Pete had gone. A guy who quit at the first sign of danger or difficulty. This is a job too big. Too overwhelming. He couldn't do it. His dad was right. Pete was the one. He was a loser.

So that's it? You gave up. Without even a hint of fight. Threw in the towel before the ring walk.

'Fuck you!' he screamed at the ceiling. 'Damn you to hell! You sick fuck! I didn't ask for this and I don't want it!'

He ignored the screaming pain from his balled fist.

'You're fucking with me! Why? Because you know you can, and I just gotta sit here and take it!'

Ray sank to his knees. His voice came out hoarse and throaty and he spat bitter words to the floor of his kitchen.

'I didn't ask for this.'

Yes. You did. And even if you didn't, you've got it. Do you know what other people would give for this opportunity you've got? It's a shitty deal, but Christ and Sonny Jesus it could be a damned sight worse. Three thousand people are depending on you. They have it much worse. They are going to die. In ways you can't begin to fathom. They might be the lucky ones. Thousands more are going to breathe in that dust and shit. People whose only goal is to help drag this city from its knees. They have a death sentence that will last for YEARS. Every single day of their lives, every time they take a breath, *they'll be reminded of that nightmare. Nobody's going to help them. You've already quit? Get off your knees and at least* try. *Do* something.

GHOSTS OF SEPTEMBER

Get off your knees and do something.

Ray nodded and wiped his nose on his sleeve. Surveying his apartment, the optimistic brightness had faded. The corners now touched by shadow. Just a hint, but enough for him to notice. *It only gets darker from here.* He planted his good hand onto the floor and raised himself up onto his haunches. He inhaled a deep haltering breath and stood full length before moving across to one of the dining chairs and sank onto it. On the table before him, the notepad and pencil awaited. He took the pad and started a fresh page, writing at the top:

STOP THE ATTACKS

2:16PM

Ray stared at the message he'd received from Manny. He must have sent it around the time Ray was out cold on the floor in the Sky Lobby of the North Tower.

>*Drinks! Tonight! Sonny's at 8?*<

It was taking everything he had not to accept.

>*I can't man. Got shit to take care of.*<

He stared back at the notepad. If he really was going to do something about this, he needed to settle on a date. He had to focus his energy on one time. There was no way he could do anything wondering, dreading that it could happen at any time. The worst part of that was, it *could* happen at any time, but if he was to deal with it – or at least try to –

then he had to focus all of his energy on the original timeline. The morning of September the 11th, 2001. Yes, there were hundreds of possibilities. But only one seemed – *felt* – right. He was reliving it. He didn't know why, and he didn't care.

His phone buzzed again. It was Manny.

>Everything OK?<

Manny had picked up on him acting weird. Hard not to. Maybe the way he left Sonny's last night; Manny would just put it down to woman trouble.

Ray stared at the sketch he'd made of the towers. He shuddered.

>I'll be fine. I'll be in touch.<

Spending all weekend drinking and laughing with Manny in Sonny's. Just the thought of it…

Save him, you can do that all you like…

His phone buzzed.

>If you need anything, shout me.<

Manny was always there for him. And he would repay that favor.

First all he had to do was to figure out how to stop terrorists without setting foot in the towers. Simple.

The one thing he'd really learned from inside the Towers was that being in there on Tuesday morning was halfway to a death sentence. Anyone at the top would need the best part of an hour to get down if the elevators were out of commission. Going to the Towers was a huge no-no. He needed to do something else. To prevent the attacks from happening in the first place. Would a phone call be enough?

GHOSTS OF SEPTEMBER

He could call the FBI and warn them that something was going to happen. If he provided enough detail, it would be hard for them to dismiss him as a crank. They'd have to look into it. He had to give them something from before the towers were hit.

He started a list and rubbed the rabbit's foot for luck.

The Towers: he knew where they would be hit, give or take, and when. A date, and times...

The pain in his head started.

Empty space. Growing...

The Hijackers: nineteen men. From Saudi Arabia. Mostly. One face stood out of the group. Their sneering leader.

The emptiness, spreading. A computer virus multiplying, deleting files...

Ray winced and rubbed at his temples. His name... Moha—

Pulling. Tearing...

Ray screamed aloud. He wiped at the wetness below his nose, not surprised to see blood. That information was not for him. He simply wrote "ringleader", then crossed it out, rewriting it with a capital letter.

No, thinking up new info wasn't going to work. If he was going to do this, it needed to be information he already had.

He stroked the rabbit's foot with his thumb. 'Come on, Pete. Help me out...'

The flights.

If he could remember enough detail about the flights, then the feds could check out the details and stop those planes from ever taking off. If that happened everything would be okay. No attacks. No plane crashes. No Pentagon fire. No collapsing towers. No office workers standing where the windows used to be and staring into the void, deciding between sickening drop or hellish inferno. One phone call. One phone call and the authorities could stop it. And maybe, just maybe, the close call of it will give them the kick in the ass they needed to stop something like this, or worse, from happening again in the future. It would give him time to fix things with Kat. Fix things with Kat and save Manny.

One phone call. He shivered deep down, and in the same place that shiver came from, he knew it wasn't going to be that simple.

4:05PM

Ray sat at the table staring at the notes he'd made, a half-eaten ham and cheese sandwich beside him. The notes were of what he could remember about the flights that crashed into the Twin Towers. If there was enough detail here, the FBI would be able to ground all flights. The flight which crashed into the field in (where was it? Pennsylvania?) and the one which struck the Pentagon included. The FBI would ground all flights and stop the whole fucking shitshow.

The only problem was, he had nothing like enough information. Thinking about the eleventh from the point of view of the past hurt. He was pretty sure that the first flight was American Airlines. That was the first flight which struck the North Tower at some time shortly after 8:45.

He tore off the top page and put it with his other notes and drew a vertical line down the next sheet of paper. At one side he wrote Pros and at the other Cons. He left the Pros side blank and went straight to the Cons. He felt that this list would be more forthcoming. He was correct.

CALL IT IN

He listed the reasons he thought that calling the FBI would be a bad idea. They might think it's a hoax; they must get hoax calls all the time. They'd ask for his name and he'd have to give it, or they'd trace the call back to him and think there was something fishy about the whole thing. Through some sick mix-up they might believe that he is in some way involved in the attacks. That was an idea that wouldn't go away, lingering like the smell of horse shit in Central Park. The thought that he could be trying to stop this thing from happening and through a depraved twist of fate it would be his face plastered all over the news. Not Bin Laden. Ray Madison. One false move and you could end up being blamed for the whole fucking thing. Have your name spat out in bars, at dinner parties, on the news, in the history books. It made him want to throw up.

His eyes burned and his head ached. He hadn't slept well the night before and with the tiredness came a strange light-headed feeling. Different from what he'd felt in the Towers earlier. A dryness sat at the back of his mouth where the nasal passage entered, but that was so subtle he wasn't even sure it was there and the moment he acknowledged it, the thought was gone. He rose to go to the bathroom. Maybe splashing water on his face would help. On his way past the door, he double checked the lock and slid the chain into place.

As he shuffled along the hallway he glanced at the once-broken-now-working light switch but avoided touching the damned thing. He entered his now tidy bathroom and it took him back through time to when it really looked this bright. This clean. A gentle warmth stole into him and comforted him like the sun breaking the clouds and just as it did, there was a knock at the door.

The jump at the sudden sound knocked the comfort out of him. His heart raced. This was supposed to be his sanctity, like "base" in a childhood game of chase, but now he was afraid. His dry mouth confirmed it. Ideas, thoughts, imagination all pumped through him riding a wave of adrenaline. Who the hell was it? The police maybe. Somebody knew what was going on and had reported him. The game was up. Without saying a word he moved back along the hall and approached the door like it was a venomous snake. More banging. He leaned toward the peephole. It wasn't the police. When he saw who it was, part of him wished that it *was* the cops.

He slid the chain back off and unlocked the door, drawing a deep breath before he opened it.

GHOSTS OF SEPTEMBER

'Hi,' he said, mouth still dry.

'Hey,' replied Kat. 'We should talk.'

Ray's heart thumped in his chest and butterflies frolicked in his stomach. He should have expected this. Kat was never one to leave anything up in the air. She always faced whatever was thrown at her full on, always spoke her mind, and never gave up. Even if the outcome wasn't what she hoped it would be. Ray always gave advice that fell short of a resolution. "Wait and see" wasn't in Kat's vocabulary. If the result was feeling shitty, she dealt with it head on and moved forward. He stepped aside and she breezed into the flat, bringing with her the déjà vu memory of what had happened the first time they broke up.

THE BREAK-UP

Ray fell through the door to his apartment. His fingers caught the door frame at the last moment, and he swung around, almost hitting the wall until a hand slapped against it. A throaty chuckle escaped, and he realized it sounded like Beavis from MTV, which just made him giggle more. He had no idea what time it was and cared less. If they hadn't told him and Manny to clear out of there, the two of them would still be tearing it up at Sonny's. He was allowed to be drunk. Kat was pissed with him. Again.

Ah fuck it.

'She's always pissed at me.'

It seemed a lifetime ago that they'd met at the karaoke

bar that sat exactly halfway between Cusato Couriers and Dino's Restaurant where Kat worked. A happy coincidence of two random office nights out colliding. He'd already sung *Dancing in the Dark*, which just happened to be one of her favorites. Manny had done *Runaway Train*. He always did a good job of that one. She sang Alanis Morissette - *You Oughta Know*. By the time she took the stage, Ray's interest was already piqued at someone who chose such a ballsy tune. Manny said she'd been smiling at Ray from afar ever since he'd sung the Boss, but he was sure that he was just fucking with him. When it got to the line in the song with the cuss word, Kat removed all doubt. She looked straight at Ray with a gleam in her eye. He thought he'd pass out. The guys fucking loved that.

Ray shook the memory from his head and stumbled past the dining table. The notes about the road trip he and Manny were planning to Florida were sprawled across it – something else for Kat to complain about no doubt. He kept on and into the kitchen and fumbled at the switch for the radio. An excited announcer faded in, cheering fans in the background.

'Well, the lights are back on now and this game is still officially too close to call. We're now into the sixth hour and, if good omens are your thing, the last time a game went on this long between these two teams, the Yanks beat the Red Sox 4 to 3. That game was over 20 innings all the way back in the summer of love, August 29th, 1967.'

'Shit,' was all he could say. Disbelief that the game was still on. He stumbled across to the TV and found the game there before turning off the radio. Before he could sit there was a knock at the door.

'Now?'

He staggered back across to the door and opened it. Kat stood there, fuming.

'Hi,' Ray tried to hide that dopey, wasted smile he had after this much beer.

She sighed. 'Jesus, Ray. You're wasted.'

'No I'm not.'

'I had hoped we could talk but…'

'I'm fine. Come in.'

She paused, probably weighing up whether coming in with him this drunk was a total waste of time. He opened the door wider and stood aside. From behind, a *thwonk!* of ball-on-bat was followed by a loud cheer from the crowd. He craned his neck to see what was going on.

'Ray? I thought we should talk.'

He spun round a little too quickly and thought he might vomit. Kat approached the table and looked at the notes.

'What's this?'

'Hmm? Oh. Road trip. Florida. Manny says…'

'Manny, Manny, Manny.'

Ray scowled, 'What's that supposed to mean?'

'Just when I think we're getting somewhere. Just when I think I can count on you; you fuck up and let me down. It's like you're doing it deliberately. You let me get so close then you do something dumb and push me away. It's screwing with my head and I'm not sure how much more of it I can take.'

'I'm screwing with *your* head? I go for a couple of beers…'

'A couple! Christ, Ray, you can barely speak.'

Another *thwonk!* on TV and Ray wanted to turn to see what was going on but knew that doing so would just piss Kat off even more.

'I told you I'm fine.' He edged round the back of the sofa so the TV would be in his peripheral.

'Jesus, Ray. I've come all the way over here to talk to you and you're trying to watch the damn ball game.'

'No I'm not,' he moved on unsteady legs to the table and gathered the papers into as neat a pile as he could manage. 'Let's sit here and talk.'

The look in her eyes was one of regret, but he couldn't work out if it was regret at coming in even after she'd seen how drunk he was, regret at wasting her time coming over here in the first place, or regret that their relationship was hanging by a thread. But they'd work it out. They always did. She was just right for him and that was that. There was no denying he pushed her to the limits, but that was just how it was between them. He thought about turning the TV off but didn't want to miss anything.

Shit. She's mid-sentence you fucking idiot.

'…and I don't think you realize how much it hurts me. I'm not needy or clingy. God knows I don't ask much from you Ray. But you keep putting everything, everyone, above me.'

She was right. He had no arguments there. It wasn't

GHOSTS OF SEPTEMBER

something he meant to do; he was just...

An ass, Raymondo. You're an ass.

His eyes drifted out of focus on his apartment key as it flipped over and over against the table between Kat's delicate fingers. Watching the twirls made him feel sick. Now he was into the territory where he didn't know what to say that wouldn't just dig a deeper hole. That regret in her eyes. He was starting to feel that it was more serious. He had to tread carefully now or...

Thwonk!

For less than a second, his eyes flickered instinctively towards the cheering coming from the TV. He hoped that it had gone unnoticed, but the key stopped twirling and was slammed flat against the table and sliding its way across to him.

Kat was already standing up. 'You know what, Ray? Forget it. Enjoy your game.'

She kissed him on the cheek and for a second, his stupid mind thought all was well. She was out the door before he realized it was goodbye. He tried to stand, but his chair was pulled too close to the table. He almost fell before he wiggled himself free. By the time he had, the door to his apartment had already slammed shut. Kat was gone.

4:06PM

Kat stepped away from the front door and toward the table. Ray glanced where she was headed and saw his notes. He blocked her path and turned to gather the papers.

'What's that?'

His heart leapt. The scattered pages had names and dates and his rough sketch of the towers after they'd been struck. He wasn't sure how much she'd seen but quickly stacked the papers as best he could and turned them over.

'Nothing. It's just… nothing.'

'Didn't look like nothing.'

'I was just looking at maybe taking a trip somewhere.'

It was lame and he had no idea where it came from, but it was all he could think of. He'd always been a terrible liar. Manny could talk his way into (or out of) any situation. Ray remembered he talked a bouncer out of charging six guys from work a cover charge to a club where The Strokes was playing before they hit the big time. Ray had no idea what he said to the guy, but every time that guy worked the door when they went back, they never paid. That guy was always pleased to see him, too. Pop always told Ray, "Tell the truth, it's easier to remember," and that had worked pretty well for him so far. It was a theory that was going to be stretched to the limit over the coming days. Ray just hoped that his bullshit was enough to deter Kat from pressing him on the issue. He stuffed the notes into the drawer.

'Oh yeah?'

Kat's tone was pissed. Jesus, what now? She must think that you're taking a trip, running away from your problems. Like you always do. He was fucking this up without even trying. Now he wanted to tell her what was going on. Maybe it would be enough to convince her that he

GHOSTS OF SEPTEMBER

wasn't running from his problems like he had in the past. Now he was taking a stand. It would explain his weird behavior and give him the freedom to take care of saving Manny, then he could focus on saving their relationship.

That, of course, would be too easy. If Kat knew that something terrible was going to happen, she would call the authorities straight away. She'd tell him he *had* to act. There would be no convincing her that he was just one guy and that he was too small in the grand scheme of things.

'Nothing concrete. I probably won't go.'

She nodded, but it was sharp. Like the intake of breath that came with it. She was still pissed.

He added, 'Besides, I can't go now. Not with things not being right with us.'

Better Raymondo. Much better.

'Please, take a seat. Can I get you a coffee?'

Kat always liked to drink coffee, even at night. If he had a coffee now, he'd be awake all hours. It wasn't a big deal, tomorrow was Saturday, but he was far too wired for sleep anyway. Caffeine was the last thing he needed. What he needed now was to fix his relationship with Kat. Then he could focus on saving Manny.

Kat smiled. 'Sure.'

Ray hoped that Kat would start humming a tune or tapping a beat out on the table - signs that she was relaxed. She did neither. Instead she sat in awkward silence. At the dining table. He was hoping that she'd take one of the comfy seats in the living room. That would have been a good sign too. He wanted to talk while he prepared the coffee, but just hid in the kitchen, repeating to himself over and over: *Don't fuck this up. Don't fuck this up.* He carried the coffee slowly to the table with trembling hand, careful not to spill any.

'What happened to your hand?' Kat said, nodding at the bandage.

Ray felt his face flush the rouge of embarrassment. 'Aw, I burned it. Making breakfast.'

Kat smiled and shook her head as if to say, "Typical Ray". She was warming. Slowly. Very slowly.

Ray's eyes burned a hole in the floor. He saw a pattern in the linoleum, kind of like an hourglass. He remembered it from the point of view of the future and how he hadn't seen it for years, recalling a moment in the past when he saw it for the first time. Maybe that was now.

'Listen, Kat, I'm really sorry about last night. I feel like such an asshole.'

'You should. You *are*.'

I wanted to see my best friend I hadn't seen for seventeen years. The guy who died because I took a sick day at work. The guy who'd still be walking around and making a better go of his life than either of us ended up doing, if it wasn't for my dumb ass.

'It was Manny. I hadn't seen him...'

He stopped mid-sentence and remembered how, at the beginning of his relationship, he'd played Kat and Manny against each other. Using one as an excuse to do whatever he wanted. He wanted to see a ball game? "Sorry Kat, I'm meeting Manny." He felt like a quiet night in? "Manny, dude, Kat's breaking my balls." This was the first time since Manny's death that he'd thought about it. Maybe he hadn't even noticed it before, like he was doing it subconsciously. Truth was, after Pete died, Manny and Kat were the only people who acted like he was important, and he got a kick out of the attention. Either way, the result was Manny and Kat did not get along. That embarrassed him. They would have been good friends. It was strange looking at things with hindsight that were happening in the moment. Either way, he'd been an idiot and liked himself less for the fact.

She scowled. 'Manny, Manny, Manny. That's all I hear out of your dumb mouth.'

'You know, you're right. I'm sorry. It's not Manny. It's me. I fucked up.'

'You always fuck up, Ray.'

His father's words coming from his girlfriend's mouth. That hurt.

'I'm sorry, Ray, but you need to hear this.'

Here it comes. Keep your idiot mouth shut and listen.

That was where he'd screwed up (one of the places he'd screwed up) in the past. His twenty-something self had been more interested in winning the argument than learning anything.

'Just when I think we're getting somewhere. Just when I think I can count on you; you fuck up and let me down. It's like you're doing it deliberately. You let me get so close then you do something dumb and push me away. It's screwing with my head and I'm not sure how much more of it I can take.'

Then he saw something that crushed him. Nothing huge, a fleeting moment, but the gravity of it hit him hard like an unexpected gut-shot. A look in her eyes. Dead. Like she had given up on him - on *them* - already. The old feelings of their break-up flooded back. The shock of the break-up he hadn't been able to process under the tidal wave of negative emotion that had swept him away as a twenty-two-year-old. Now he wondered how he'd been so blind to it the first time round and wondered how much else he'd missed. He was losing her all over again. A car honked its horn somewhere in the distance. Another honked back. Back in his apartment, he could see her slipping away but this time he knew what was at stake. It was more than his own selfish happiness. For a split second he saw her as he did that day at the ball game. Her sparkle gone. That aura dulled and faded. Like an evil spell cast to remove her beauty. The heaviness of futility pressed on his heart. He was watching her heart break before his very eyes. She stared at him, tears welling and giving her eyes a false sparkle that made him want to cry. He couldn't look at her.

What he had to do was say something. Anything.

Speak, Ray, goddamit.

'You're right. You deserve better. I'm sorry. I'm… sorry.'

It killed him to think of the way he'd hurt her. He hoped that being open and upfront with her would maybe prove to her that he had changed, because Christ knew *that* was true.

GHOSTS OF SEPTEMBER

He looked up from the hourglass on the floor and into her eyes. They'd changed. The dull had gone. She'd been expecting the *old* version of Ray to answer. To argue. To drive his point home and ignore everything that she'd said. In that second, he knew, balls to bones he just knew that if he had argued, that would have been it. Their relationship would have been over. She'd have slid the key to the apartment across the table, stood, kissed him on the cheek, and walked out of his life forever. Just like she did the first time.

'I've been so stupid. I've had the best thing in my life right in front of me and not seen the real value of it. I've taken you for granted instead of making you what you really are. The number one thing in my life. I'm so sorry. Please forgive me.'

She coughed out something halfway between a laugh and a sob.

He gazed at her, 'I miss you so much.'

She jumped to her feet and shot around the table, sat on Ray's lap and hugged him so tight he found it hard to breathe. That was just fine with him. He squeezed her back just as hard, like he had already lost her and won her back again. Who knew? Maybe he had.

'I love you,' she whispered.

Ray embraced her tighter and, over her shoulder, saw the hourglass on the floor blur through his tears. They held each other for the longest time.

11:09PM

MARC W SHAKO

The end of Friday approached unnoticed. It was like crazy-eyes Manson was stealing seconds from under Ray's nose, just like Charlie had said he would. Ray thought that Manson could actually be Father Time. Syphoning sand from the hourglass grain by grain. Stealing handfuls while Ray wasn't looking, the same way he added it when you were stuck in traffic or waiting in line someplace. Now he was stealing sands not by the grain but by the bucket.

Ray and Kat had moved from the dining table to the sofa and talk had moved from their faltering relationship to more frivolous themes. Pop culture mostly, as Ray threw his favorite bar room questions at Kat, getting to know her all over again. Favorite cover song (Nirvana's version of *The Man Who Sold the World*), best album (Modest Mouse, *The Lonesome Crowded West*. I mean, it's great, but best ever?), The Kat Ballion awards live from Jersey City. He had to be careful not to mention anything from after 2001, but the couple of times he did draw a blank look from Kat, he was able to pass his mistakes off as bootlegs Manny had played for him, "The album will be out soon, wait till you hear it". To Ray life had almost stopped in 2001 so his slips were few and far between.

Kat didn't seem to mind, as far as Ray could tell she loved this bonding time they were having. She would even laugh off his slips, 'Lemme guess, bootleg from Manny?' every time Ray made one. They got closer and closer until they were kissing, which felt as good as Ray remembered, but at the same time felt *wrong*. She wasn't really kissing who she thought she was. She thought she was kissing her twenty-two-year-old boyfriend, not a version of the same from seventeen years down the line.

While he was enjoying their chat, Ray couldn't help but feel the whole thing was a little manipulative. Unnatural. In his mind he was scoring points against the younger version of himself, picking his words carefully. He drifted away for a second and thought about it, rationalizing that anyone else in his position would do exactly the same. Whether or not they pretended to be doing it for *her* was another thing entirely.

'Stop.' He said.

Kat pulled back, just a little too far for Ray's liking. 'What's wrong?'

'Nothing, I just feel weird.'

'Because of kissing me?'

He pictured himself on a huge chessboard, trying to maneuver, a white pawn, toward Kat's black queen through a series of eggshells.

'No, no! I mean, I think I'm coming down with something.'

Kat's eyebrows drew together, a tiny micro expression that he was all too used to seeing, when from nowhere, he sneezed violently.

She leaned around him, raising up onto one knee, lifting cushions and throwing them back into place.

'What are you looking for?' Ray asked, baffled.

She smiled, 'The pepper.'

Ray laughed, 'I'm serious!'

'You look it.'

Ray frowned, 'I'd hate for you to catch something.'

'Very sweet,' she was smiling again, 'but I can't help thinking you're allergic to me.'

When she did smile Ray forgot about everything, just like he always had. It only lasted for a second. His mind's eye envisioned the chess board again, him being backed into a corner by fate as the seconds ticked by on the clock.

'I have to get up early tomorrow,' Ray said choosing his words like the accused in an interrogation, 'but I'd really like for you to stay the night. No funny business.'

Kat scowled that fake scowl of hers that only ever lasted for a second before it cracked into that pretty, wide smile.

'Where do you have to be on Saturday morning?'

'I gotta drive up to see my old man.' Ray replied, only half-lying. 'Shit.'

He grabbed his phone from his pocket.

'What is it?'

'I meant to call him back before. I lost track of time.'

It was late now. But perfect. The machine would take the call and Ray could pretend it was casual.

'Hey, Pop. I'll be dropping in for a visit on Sunday for the game and a beer. See you then.'

He ended the call.

'Sorry about that.'

Kat stood. 'Okay. But don't think you're off the hook mister.'

Ray held up his hands gesturing that he understood

GHOSTS OF SEPTEMBER

perfectly, but inside he was trembling. For once he thought his poker face had held, but depending on what Kat said next, he wasn't sure how long it would last.

Kat's face grew serious and her brow drew oh-so-slightly. 'I need you to take me, take us, more seriously. I need for you to prioritize our relationship.'

Ray held his breath. Tomorrow morning was trying to figure out where those flights had come from, and maybe a road trip. A trip to any airport was placing himself on Old Man Time's radar, and the harder he was to locate, the better. He had to visit his old man's place for Sunday afternoon, which meant a few cold ones, then make sure he was back in New York for Monday morning, or Manny was a dead man. Anything after Tuesday might mean that the opportunity had passed altogether. He had a feeling that whatever happened, and *whenever* that was, the second it was over, so was his moment in the past; with that came those same feelings of impotence that his recurring nightmare gave him.

All of this plus the sneeze that had just escaped meant that he'd be feeling worse by the day, almost the moment, if his memory of the illness served him well. Kat must have seen the change in his face because hers reflected it, and in his mind a big hand reached for the black queen and placed it directly in his line of sight. Check.

'I couldn't agree more.' He said.

She smiled. 'Good. So I want you to take me to Roselli's. Sunday night. 8 o'clock.'

His mind raced. He could meet Pop first thing, come back to New York, go to the restaurant and be here ready to go to work on Monday morning. That gave him all day tomorrow to work on the plan.

'Sounds perfect.'

She smiled and leaned in for another one of those kisses. Ray kissed her back for a moment before his conscience stopped him and he broke the embrace.

'Germs, remember.'

She smiled and gently took his burned hand. He'd almost forgotten about it. 'You are in the wars. Come on. Bed. No funny business.'

They went to bed and Ray held her until she fell asleep in his arms. Ray didn't sleep. Not straight away. His mind raced at the host of options awaiting him. The wheels were turning, like the cogs in the back of a grandfather clock. He could feel them, almost certain that they were turning against him. At least tonight felt like a small victory. He wasn't sure how long it would last, and he wanted to savor the feeling, aware now more than ever of the fragility of it all. After a few hours his tired body succumbed to a deep, disturbed sleep.

SATURDAY, SEPTEMBER 8, 2001

RAY OPENED HIS EYES TO the darkness of his bedroom and decided that Kat's gentle snoring must have woke him. It was 3AM. Sleep had been hard to come by. His mind was racing, flitting from one thought to another, trying to fill the gaps in his knowledge of how everything had unfolded that Tuesday morning in 2001. He'd narrowed down the rough times the flights had hit, airlines, ideas of flight numbers, just not the originating airport. It frustrated him, because he knew at some point, the info had been there. He had managed to get an image in his head of the Ringleader of the hijackers too. No name to go with it and not enough to describe to someone else, but enough for him to recognize. He might just have enough information to make a call to the FBI and—

Ray froze and an icy sweat broke out across his body. Just as in his dream a few nights ago, he heard voices coming from his living room. His heart raced. He glanced to his right, happy to see the baseball bat propped in the corner. Slowly, he rose from the bed and gripped the bat tightly, raising it high, ready to strike. The voices drifted along the hallway, faint, conspiratorial. He stepped into the hall and crept along, dreading the creak in the floor that might give him away. The far end of the hall was colored by the gentle light from a lamp. As he got closer it was clear that the voices weren't the whisper of collusion, but the TV.

I definitely didn't leave that on.

Ray reached the end of the hall expecting to find his dead father watching the tube, but when he got there, the room was empty.

Ray lowered the bat and entered the room, but as he rounded the couch and reached for the remote, the TV ads ended, and a gameshow appeared. One he'd never seen before.

'Dilemma?' Ray said, staring at the title written in the same font as *Jeopardy*. 'What a rip off.'

He stood upright, remote in hand, and waited to see if Alex Trebek would appear. When the host did appear, Ray fell back on his ass onto the couch.

It was a man he'd only seen before in dreams. A small, stooping man with wild hair and wilder eyes. Now he wasn't dressed in vagrant clothing but a shiny blue sequined tux. The audience applauded enthusiastically.

'Welcome back!' he shouted as the applause died down. 'Now, before the break, our contestant Ray from Noo Joisey was faced with a…' he stopped and swept his hand

GHOSTS OF SEPTEMBER

up towards the ceiling.

'Dilemma!' the audience shouted.

The host laughed, 'Never get tired of that!'

The audience chuckled with him.

'Ray had to decide if he was going to take action himself and try to stop the worst attack on the mainland United States since Pearl Harbor…'

The camera panned across to the contestant. Ray was looking at himself. Dressed in a suit, sweating under the studio lights and smiling at the host like nothing was going on.

'Or gather as much information as possible, and call the eff-bee-eye, and hope they'd do all of the hard work for him.'

The camera was back on the host who lowered the prompt card with the *Dilemma* logo on the back, and with a serious face, asked Ray, 'Have you made a decision?'

The camera switched to Ray, who nodded, 'I have.'

'Any last-minute advice?' the host shouted to the audience.

The audience screamed back, their responses an even split between the two choices. The host gestured for them to quiet down, and the studio fell into a tense silence.

'What have you decided?'

'Well, I've given this a lot of thought…' he took a deep breath and for a second the camera cut to the studio audience, on the edge of their seats. '…but I've decided that going into the Towers is a suicide mission so… I'm going to call the Feds.'

A ripple of audience applause was peppered with the odd gasp. The host again gestured for silence.

'And is that your final answer?'

Ray just nodded.

'You said call the FBI, the correct decision was…'

Silence hung and Ray sat unable to tear his eyes away from the image of himself on screen.

'Call the FBI!'

Cheesy music and audience jubilation blasted out as balloons and confetti rained from above. Kat, Manny and Pop all ran onto the set and bounced up and down with joy, hugging contestant Ray.

'Johnny, tell him what he's won!

A smooth voice-over oozed out over the celebrations, 'The FBI storm into the departures lounge of Boston's Logan International Airport on Tuesday morning to find… absolutely nothing!'

The audience went wild as the voice-over continued.

'Ray Madison is arrested for wasting the time of a Federal Agency and our host takes him out of the picture without lifting a finger.'

The audience continued their delighted celebrations, but now Ray and the others were standing agog, listening to the nightmare unfold.

'Meanwhile, Ray is sitting in a cell thinking of what an idiot he's been and two fully loaded jets slam into the Twin Towers just as he said they would, only on a different day, or at another time. Now he's not a nut; he's an orchestrator.

GHOSTS OF SEPTEMBER

Not a prank caller; a terrorist.'

The host applauded, smiling and shaking his head, unable to believe the good-news story being told.

'Our winner tonight gets flown directly to the tropical climes of Cuba. There he spends two excruciating weeks of torture and waterboarding for information in sunny Guantanamo Bay. After giving up all of the information, because, by God he knows everything, he's fast-tracked through the criminal justice system and injected with a barbiturate, paralytic, and potassium solution until he suffers respiratory failure, which will bring about muscle paralysis, and then he can look forward to agonizing heart failure.'

Ray cut the audience joy to silence with a click of the remote. A chill gripped him as the words of the voiceover rang in his ears. The picture shrank to a dot and left Ray staring into the reflection of his living room.

That's when he saw it.

In the armchair beside him. A figure.

His stomach rolled and the second he spotted it in the reflection of his TV screen was the same moment that figure popped into his peripheral vision. Before he turned, he knew who he was going to see.

'Is that what you want?' he shrieked.

He leapt at Ray who scrambled to his feet and away from the man he'd just seen on TV.

'You can't do it! You can't stop shit!'

He jabbed at Ray's chest with a bony finger and Ray wasn't staring at a crazy old man in vagrant clothes, but his father. Ray squeezed his eyes shut and shook his head. When he reopened them, the crazy old man was back, jabbing at him, forcing him backwards against the door of his apartment.

'Get out of here, go on!'

He pushed Ray aside and yanked the door to his apartment open. But instead of seeing the darkness of the hallway, what Ray saw was an empty, mirror-image of his apartment. But this wasn't the clean, bright 2001 version of his home. It was the dim, sad 2018 version.

'Go on. Get out of here.'

Ray stood staring into the future.

The past is set in stone. The future is liquid.

Charlie's words. It wasn't the future. Not anymore. It was one possible future. If Ray accepted it.

'Get out!'

Ray realized that for all of his screaming, the old man couldn't *make* him go. Or he would have already done it. The sight of the future awaiting him made him sick. He was staring into a future with no Kat. No Manny. He didn't want it.

The old man screamed, 'GET OUT!'

Ray screamed back 'NO!' He snatched the door and with everything he had slammed it shut.

7:30AM

Ray awoke with a start just as the radio alarm kicked in.

The guys - the way-too-enthusiastic guys - talked

GHOSTS OF SEPTEMBER

about a marathon ball game the night before. The Red Sox beat the Yankees after nineteen innings in a game lasting almost seven hours. He vaguely recalled that the game was important somehow somewhere but then the thought was gone like the foggy recollection of a dream. Mr. Enthusiastic also said that Michael Jackson's show the night before in Madison Square Garden was a success, despite MJ looking a little foggy onstage. MJ had been dead for years. His rejection of 2018 in his dream had worked, but it gave him no joy. It meant that his recurring nightmare was an approaching reality. This was still 2001.

The good news was, while his subconscious had been raising red flags about all the things that could go wrong, it had also filled in one of the blanks for him. Before, he couldn't think where the planes were taking off from. His dream had given him the answer. Logan International Airport. Boston. It was a clue. He just had to work out how to use it.

'Good morning,' Kat rolled onto her back and stretched, making the sweetest groan Ray had heard in a lifetime. 'How are you feeling?'

He hadn't even thought about it. The burn on his hand felt better, that was for sure. The throb had gone and last night it didn't wake him up, if he had turned onto it in his sleep. The dryness in the back of his mouth had a heavy feeling to it now, it felt laden with bacteria, as if he could feel the individual germs partying like it was 1999. The shirt he'd slept in clung to him gently, a thin film of sweat holding it in place.

'A little better,' he lied, not sure why he'd done so.

Maybe it was just his mind, but this morning had the feel of a one-night stand. Each pause felt like a lifetime; the whole thing somehow aggravated by the lack of sex the night before. Part of him was now pissed at his conscience, as he lay looking at her svelte form in the Strokes T-shirt she'd spent the night in. An opportunity missed, so what if it was wrong. This whole fucking thing would probably kill him anyway, it would have been his last chance. A little voice spoke up:

She's still he-re.

No. It still wouldn't be right. It would be creepy. The guilt he'd carry for sleeping with her now would far outweigh the satisfaction of it, and that satisfaction would be oh so sweet.

You did the right thing once. Now just do it again.

She looked into his eyes, making his resistance all the more difficult.

She wants you to do it. What are you waiting for? You're going to blow this thing. This could be your chance at happiness, you're going to regret it.

'Lemme make you pancakes,' he said jumping out of bed.

Kat gestured to move, and Ray held up an objecting hand.

'Please, Madame, I shall bring them to you,' in the terrible French accent which never failed to raise a smile.

She giggled. He turned and entered the hallway and

GHOSTS OF SEPTEMBER

wondered if he hadn't slept with her because it was the right thing or if he was scared of under-performing (or worse, not performing at all). He tried to shake the thought from his head and get back to planning his day, and it was going to be a long one.

8:45AM

Ray lifted the tray from Kat's lap and kissed her on the forehead, still longing to do much more. He dropped the dishes into the sink and tidied the kitchen as Kat got dressed and ready for her morning shift at Dino's restaurant. She had a double shift today, lunch and evening. It gave Ray the freedom to take care of his business guilt-free and come back tomorrow night.

Now all you need to do is make a plan, genius.

Things were still a little stilted between them, though the chat they'd had over pancakes and coffee had gone some way to relieving the tension. Ray had done something his twenty-two-year-old self rarely did; ask Kat about her day, about her plans. She'd taken the opportunity to remind Ray about Sunday night, but some of his optimism had waned. He was certain that between now and then a proverbial spanner would be thrown into the cosmic works, and he surprised himself by thinking that now wasn't the time to worry. That he'd cross that bridge if and when.

He kissed Kat goodbye, a long lingering one (maybe this *was* the last chance) but felt no guilt. The moment she left he dashed into the bedroom, dressed in the recently vacated Strokes shirt (he loved the way it smelled after Kat had worn it), rushed into the living room to fish his notes from the drawer. As he did a wave of panic washed over him, like he'd lost his wallet or phone. The sense that the notes would be missing gnawed at him and the hallway seemed to stretch out to lengthen the time it would take for him to find out the truth. Or that when he got to them, the info he'd recalled last night before he fell asleep would vanish. He ended up in a run and yanked the drawer open. It squealed in opposition.

He lay his notes on the table and added the bits and pieces he'd pulled together from the night before. He had to plan quickly. Something that would keep him away from the Towers,

because going in there is a suicide mission,

but stop the whole horror show from unfolding.

Logan.

He could go to the airport and intercept the Ringleader there. He was sure he'd know him if he saw him. All he'd have to do was stop him getting on the plane. To do that, it would help if he had an idea of the layout of the place. See what security was like. He could go today. Check it out, take a detour to visit Pop. He'd be back in time to take Kat out tomorrow night. And go to work on Monday, and make sure Manny didn't go near Manhattan. It wasn't much, but it was a start. A plan.

The notes stared up at him, showing everything he could remember about *that* day, and nerves ate away at his gut. It was too open. Too revealing. He had to get something to keep them in. *Hide* them in. He went back to the drawers and tugged the next one open. He wasn't sure if it was memory or something else that told him the folder with his tax returns would be in there, God knew they weren't there in 2018, but it was just the latest in a string of such events that he'd stopped worrying about the "how" and grabbed that too, slamming the drawer shut. Tax papers emptied from the plain manila folder onto the table and Ray stuffed his all-important notes inside.

That was it. He was going to Boston. All he had to do now was to get cash and go.

10:19AM

Ray cruised through New York City heading for an ATM, warm September sun shining into his lap. Ray flexed his hand, the burn now down to an uncomfortable sting but the new dressing a little too tight. The sports guys on the radio talked about the marathon ball game some more before moving on to the US Open final scheduled for tonight between the Williams sisters. Apparently the first Grand Slam final between siblings for 117 years. He found himself listening constantly, waiting for the moment to come when he least expected it. That awful moment that the broadcast would be interrupted to bring bad tidings of an "accident" at the Twin Towers.

Tall monuments to capitalism went past in procession,

casting large, intermittent shadows into the sanctum of his Chevy. Where Walker Street opened into Church street, he found a parking space close to a place he wasn't sure was even there anymore.

Ray turned off the radio, stepped out of his car and into the buzz of New York City. His autopilot had worked. It had guided him to a nearby bank which had an ATM (he'd had to walk for a couple of minutes, but still, not bad). When he saw it, it was empty, but as he neared, a line formed. *Lines forming in front of you.* The shade of the building made it colder than the car ride, but the smart business lady with the tight-fitting navy skirt was a nice distraction. She finished her transaction and strode away, drawing the eyes of the line with her. The scruffy kid in an oversized leather jacket went next and took way longer than Ray hoped or expected. Ray glanced at his watch and when he looked back up the kid had vanished. The mid-aged businessman, who last time Ray saw was also checking his watch, had taken up his position at the machine. A female voice behind him cleared her throat and Ray took the single step forward that politeness allowed. Then he heard a noise that unsettled him.

Through the traffic noise and machine-gun rattle of a distant jackhammer, the beep of the balding businessman's PIN being entered into the machine cut through. Ray glanced down at his card. He didn't remember owning the card, let alone the PIN he'd need to actually withdraw money. Shit, what was it? He hadn't changed the number for years, but seventeen years? Surely, he'd changed it once

GHOSTS OF SEPTEMBER

in that time. Maybe he'd changed it and changed it back. His 2001 PIN could be the same as the 2018 one. The wail of a passing siren was mixed with the shuffling sound of cash being counted. Baldy collected his bounty and strode away with the same assuredness of the slender businesswoman moments before - though Ray was pretty sure that now, nobody was watching. Ray was up.

You'll remember, just like how you remembered how to navigate your old cell phone. Don't overthink it...

He slid his card into the slot and waited for the prompt to insert his PIN. He tapped in the digits. An age went by before a message appeared. They were the wrong digits. He tried a different combo. Wrong again. He had wanted to avoid going into the bank if at all possible. The next incorrect answer would mean that his card would be swallowed by the machine anyway, leaving him no choice. He withdrew the card and headed for the bank entrance.

10:28AM

Inside the unnecessary air-conditioning of the bank, the sounds of the world faded against the hum and chatter of tellers and riffle counting of hard-earned green. A cough echoed through the cavernous space, and he eyed the tellers perched behind Perspex windows along the far wall. He crossed the marble floor in the warm September sun that poured through the huge windows and joined the line for the tellers, hoping to pick out the weakest of the bunch like a predatory lion.

His gaze settled upon a twenty-something girl, all eyes and teeth, with a lights-are-on-but-nobody's-home look about her. As far as she could tell, Ray was twenty-something himself, so maybe he could flirt his way out of trouble. Where was Manny when he needed him?

He got to the front of the line and the austere matron lookalike called him forward. A glance at the young teller showed the sweet old lady she was serving was almost done.

'Hey, pal. Let's go,' came a voice from behind.

Ray stepped aside and let the tough-looking Italian past. The little old lady shuffled away, and the pretty young teller called him forward.

'Welcome to Bank of America, how may I help you?'

Ray mirrored the girl's smile and hoped his wasn't quite so absent, 'Hi,' he glanced at her name tag, 'Taylor. I got a kinda embarrassing situation, I hoped you could help me out.'

The teller's brow knotted, and her head tilted theatrically to one side, 'What seems to be the problem?'

'I, er, I forgot my PIN number. I kinda need cash, I'm in a bit of a jam.'

'Oh dear. I see.' She flushed and looked flustered, glancing left and right to those either side of her. 'Just one moment.' She stood.

'No, wait!'

But she had already gone. She walked hesitantly to the austere matron.

GHOSTS OF SEPTEMBER

Shit.

Matron served her customer and the young teller smiled at Ray and held up a finger to signal how long she'd be. Ray nodded and smiled. Should he just go? He looked into the teller's hand and saw his card. Fucking noob. She wasn't supposed to take his card; now he had no choice. He had to wait.

Okay, Raymondo. This is a test. Breathe.

Ray turned back to see if as many people were watching him as he thought. Nobody was. Then he saw something, *someone*, in the corner. Was it? It couldn't be. What the hell would he be doing in a bank anyway? He tried to rationalize it, but as much as he tried, he couldn't explain away the fact that the guy in the corner rifling through the leaflets on loans and high-interest accounts looked for all the world like the Ringleader.

He looked a little different from the photo Ray had seen so many times. The one that looked like a mug shot from a police station. With the sneer and heavy eyelids that spoke of arrogance and hatred. Almost cartoonish in its villainy. Surely Ray's eyes were playing tricks. This was too much like a killer revisiting the scene of a crime, Ray thought, before remembering that the crime was yet to be committed.

'Sir.'

A stern female voice from behind. It was not the soothing sweetness of the twenty-something.

'Sir!'

Ray turned and came face to face with the snooty looking matron, her tall hair solid with lacquer of some sort.

'Yeah, sorry. I'm sorry.'

'How can I help you?'

Ray turned back. Whoever the man was, he was gone. What if that was him? What would he do anyway?

'Mr. Madison.'

'I'm sorry,' Ray replied turning back, 'I forgot my PIN.'

'My colleague informed me. Would you like to withdraw some money?'

'I need some cash to visit my old man, er, my father.'

She stared through Ray, but he surprised himself by staring back. Before he would have probably folded, given up, and disappeared back the way he came and cancelled the whole thing. Not now. He stared. Another cough echoed somewhere behind him.

Matron's stare softened. 'May I see some identification?'

Ray handed across his driver's license and gave a winning smile. Susan returned the smile and tapped Ray's information into the system. She looked at the screen.

'How much money is in the account, sir?'

Shit.

'Sir?'

'Lemme think.' Ray tried not to snap.

The account had never held a fortune. He tried to think and the sharp pain in his temples returned. The account had held about two and a half grand at its fullest, that was before the attacks. After that he'd pissed it away. Drinking the money until he had to claim welfare, and if his old man hadn't shuffled off when he did, Ray would probably be out on the streets. The pain swelled and moved behind his eyes, but that could have been the flu that was slowly taking over his system.

'Around two thousand five hundred.'

Susan looked back at him for a second before turning back to the screen. Taylor smiled that pretty, vacant smile at Ray as Susan's fingers tip-tapped the keyboard some more. What was taking so long? Was she making a note on the account? His mouth was a dry mix of nerves and flu onset. Finally she looked back.

'Your mother's maiden name?'

'Kennedy.'

Susan smiled and to Ray's amazement her smile was as pretty as Taylor's.

'The nature of this transaction means the limit on the amount you can withdraw today is two thousand dollars.'

He played with the pen held captive on its chain, trying to work out how much he might need in taking down a terror plot. Fuck it.

'I'd better take the full two thousand.'

Susan smiled and handed back Ray's card and driver's license, before bidding Ray farewell and telling him she'd leave him in the capable hands of Taylor.

Ray sighed a breath of relief. When Susan got back to her window, Taylor leaned forward and whispered, 'I've never seen her smile before.'

Test passed.

He grabbed the envelope Taylor slid under the partition.

'Can we do anything else for you today?'

'Thank you. No.'

Ray turned and headed for the exit, forgetting that he'd seen the man that looked like the Ringleader at all.

11:56AM

Five lanes of grey Connecticut Turnpike flew by. Ray had decided to take the I-95 to Boston and was already tired of it. He still had three hours on the road. Soon he'd pass through 'The Park City' of Bridgeport and get a welcome change from grey to green. He had been thinking about a short break a couple of hours up the road, maybe in New Haven, but on his current trajectory he wouldn't hit Logan till after 4pm, and that was if he didn't look for a motel first. The radio announced the Yankees loss for the third time and Ray decided that was the last time he wanted to hear about that today. If the attacks did happen before Tuesday, he'd hear about it soon enough. He reached into the glovebox and pulled out a copied CD with *White Stripes* scrawled on it in Manny's unruly hand. This album had always reminded him of his friend.

There was one thing about the trip he was enjoying. This new route he was taking, this deviation from the original past, freed him from the nagging sense of déjà vu that

GHOSTS OF SEPTEMBER

loomed over his time in NYC. Every time he did something differently in this time, the déjà vu vanished. It was odd to him that he'd just noticed. The idea that Old Man Time also noticed the feeling of déjà vu was missing entered Ray's head. What if the crazy old fucker felt the difference too? The thought was like an ex-partner that crashed this date Ray was having with uncharted territory.

Dead Leaves and the Dirty Ground filtered from the speakers and he glanced at the manila folder on the passenger seat. The fleeting sense of optimism at his minor success with Kat evaporated. The folder, or more specifically its contents, cast a shadow over him, and the niggling doubt of his time here resurfaced. Like that feeling he hadn't locked the door as soon as he left the apartment building. The tiny victory at the bank of not turning and running at the first sign of adversity shrank at the scale of what he could face. And even though Tuesday morning loomed large on the horizon, he couldn't get Manny out of his mind. Selfishness ate away it him for prioritizing saving his friend, but that bigger problem (he dared not think the words "terror attack") wasn't his fault. Manny's death was.

Thinking about that bigger problem sickened him to his stomach. That so much rode on his shoulders was responsibility like he'd never felt. His breathing quickened and he realized how shallow the breaths were. He drew a deep, considered breath and flexed his hands, hoping to rid them of trembling. The tiniest of excuses now would surely force him to throw in the towel. His father's voice berating him for doing so screamed in his head.

So much for changing. It was enough to drive him to drink.

His mind flashed back to the sighting in the bank. It was a strange mix of certainty that the man he'd seen was the Ringleader and being somehow convinced at the same time that it wasn't him. That it *couldn't* have been him. In the moments where he'd tried to recall the details of 2001, he had the impression that before the attacks the Ringleader and his cronies were spotted in Florida, in a bar, drunk and loud. Like he was *trying* to be spotted. And there was something about him being in Portland and flying to Logan on the morning of the eleventh. These were the things that told him that it couldn't have been him. It was Old Man Time, fucking with him.

All these "memories" could be half-truths mixed in with some of Andy's conspiracy theories. Andy had told Ray on one of their meetings after the attack that some of the hijackers were found alive, victims of identity theft. He'd also said something was wrong with the speed of the planes that hit the towers. Like they were going too fast. And something about another building which fell. The more Ray thought about this the less certain he felt. What of his recollections was Andy, what was truth? He could go crazy just trying to separate the two.

Ray tried to change his thinking but didn't get far. The idea came he'd probably see "the Ringleader" a lot now, now he was thinking of him. Like that song you haven't heard for years and then you hear it three times in a week for no reason. He was pretty sure he'd read somewhere that that was a thing. The idea that Old Man Time might be planting Ringleader-lookalikes everywhere to screw with him was something that he was acutely aware of, even if it didn't sound so likely.

He was bored with the I-95. Just like he was bored with 2001. In 2018, every time he went to bed, he wished more than anything that he could wake up here. That he could hit rewind and return to the carefree days and pause a while. Now that he was here in 2001, the opposite was true. But now deep down he knew that whatever was going on, it wouldn't be over until Ray lived through the moment he'd slept through all those years ago. He had to live through the nightmare. Then he could go home.

2:07PM

Ray had passed through the pleasant greens of West Haven and enjoyed snapshots of leafy Middletown. He had passed through Hartford (his view from the road was nothing special) and was making good time. The best course of action, he'd told himself in a serious voice, was to find a half decent motel, check in, go over the notes one last time, then hit Logan. After the airport he'd have more info to flesh out the scant notes he already had.

He glanced at the manila folder. The details he had so far were pretty good. The headaches had tried to prevent him from getting too much on paper, Old Man Time's safeguard, he supposed. Nonetheless, he'd got a pretty detailed timeline, starting with the first Tower being hit, and ending with the collapse of the same tower some ninety minutes later. Somewhere in between he had the Pentagon being struck, and Flight 93 (which was the only flight number he could remember for sure) crashing in a field somewhere in Pennsylvania. The finer details on those he couldn't remember, but he was pretty sure both events came after the second plane slammed into Tower 2. He'd sketched where the planes hit the towers, and although he was using the imagery from his dream for that, it seemed to ring true to his actual memory and all the other dreams he'd had, but he couldn't help wondering if there was some kind of Mandela Effect thing going on.

Andy said the Mandela Effect came from a time some writer was chatting to a friend about the South African civil rights guy Nelson Mandela and how the friend was convinced he'd died in prison, even though he was released and had enough time left over to be elected South Africa's Prime Minister. Now the Mandela Effect manifested in different, less obvious ways. People claiming stuff like car logos and cartoon theme songs had changed from when they were a kid. They were blaming the guys out at Cern in Switzerland who'd built some kind of particle collider. The collider had opened up wormholes or some other scientific mumbo-jumbo and the men in white coats out at Cern were screwing with people just to see how much they could alter before they tried something huge. The irony that he was trying to do something huge now to the past hadn't escaped him. He heard somewhere that memories were tricky little buggers - to the extent that police found them consistently unreliable. He heard that every time we remember something that the first time was a true memory. After that, we just remember the last memory. Until it becomes a copy of a copy of a copy.

Mandela effect or no, there was no way that folder could go with him to Logan. Job number one after checking in would be to find a fucking good hiding place. The contents of that folder were enough to get him into a *lot* of trouble for a *long* time. Which is why when Ray heard the police siren and snapped out of his dream to see a motorcycle cop telling him to pull over, he knew he was in trouble.

2:16PM

The cop was just sitting there. Ray stared into his mirror watching the cop filling in paperwork astride his bike. The blue and red flashing lights were quick to give him a headache, so he couldn't look for too long, but it seemed every time Ray stretched a hand across to the passenger seat for the folder, the cop would glance upward, mouth something, and look back down to his notebook.

He was probably radioing the dispatcher, getting them to run a check on his plates. Whatever was going on, Ray knew that if the cop saw him trying to hide the folder, all it would do is draw more attention to the damned thing. He turned the White Stripes off and waited.

The cop swung a leg off his bike and started the slow, deliberate, stress inducing mosey to Ray's window. Ray rolled the window down, in readiness. The rising sound of speeding cars and stink of pollution drifted into the car. Sweat prickled his back like tiny glass shards. He felt bad. In fact, he felt like shit. His eyes ached when he tried to move them, and his headache had settled into a steady thudding rhythm to mirror his rising heartbeat.

Relax. Maybe he doesn't care what the folder is. It's probably a routine traffic stop.

Ray checked his mirror and saw how pale and sweaty he was. The face that stared back looked more like alcoholic, 2018 Ray. Like a travesty wax model of his younger self.

'How are we doing today, sir?'

From the angle Ray had the cop look imposing, statuesque, and he wondered if it could all be the work of perspective alone.

'Good,' was all Ray could manage. He looked away; the stern look on the cop's smooth features making him nervous.

'You don't look *good*. You had a drink today?'

'I wish.'

'Come again?'

'I said I wish I'd had a drink,' he replied looking up at the cop. The cop was far from impressed. Ray folded. 'No, sir. Not a drop.'

The cop ducked down a little to breathe into the car. Behind the mirrored aviator sunglasses, Ray was certain the

GHOSTS OF SEPTEMBER

cop's eyes had fallen straight onto the file. Ray froze.

'What's wrong with your hand?'

'I burned it. On the stove. It's almost better n...'

'What's that in the folder?'

Fuck.

Ray's heart trip-hammered in his chest. How the fuck did this escalate so quickly? This was it. Jail. Gitmo. Notoriety. What the fuck was he going to do now? A rolodex of thoughts fluttered through his mind.

One phone call.

You'll get one phone call.

Pop.

Call Pop.

Tell him you're sorry and that he should call Manny and Kat.

Explain what's going on.

Get a lawyer.

'Sir?'

'Sorry?'

'I aksed you a question.'

I know you did. You wanted to see inside the folder.

'Do you know why I pulled you over?'

His head swirled. Was that the question? Was it possible he'd misheard the cop? Was that all?

'No, officer. I don't.'

'You were weaving pretty bad. You crossed the lanes a couple times. Nobody was near you, but it did not look natural. And now I get a look at you, you look like you've had a drink...'

'I swear...'

'Don't interrupt me. Do you have license and registration for this vehicle?'

Ray passed them over. A layer of sweat had filmed on his face again and a bead traced over a temple down his cheek. The cop stared at his license and glanced up at Ray intermittently, like he was playing spot-the-difference. Ray felt each grain of sand whirlpool through the hourglass and as they went, so grew the certainty the cop was going to ask to see inside the file.

'I was just driving to Boston. I'm going to surprise my dad. I haven't seen him...'

The cop held up a hand, he wasn't in the mood for small talk. He passed Ray's paperwork back to him.

'Step out of the vehicle for me sir.'

'I haven't been feeling—'

'Step out of the vehicle.'

An involuntary sigh escaped as he leaned forward to grab the handle. The cop let him. He was observing. Maybe Ray would do something to give away his "drunkenness". That's what he's thinking. Everything from here is a sobriety test. Ray opened the door and stepped out. The cars flew by and Ray felt a creeping sense of danger. How easy it would be for one of them to lose concentration, maybe rubbernecking to see what was going on with him, perhaps looking at a text message. Then have to take evasive action to avoid smashing into the car in front. They'd plough straight into—

GHOSTS OF SEPTEMBER

'Sir.'

'Sorry, yes.'

Please don't ask about the folder please don't ask about the folder please don't ask

'Can you…'

This is it. He's going to say it.

Images of himself tied up somewhere in some grey-walled nondescript space, the result of a photo opportunity like those at Abu-Ghraib flashed into his mind, the point-of-view switching with the flash of the camera; inside the cloth bag that was over his head, and the bag reeked of vomit and the stench of other foulness crept in through the pores of the bag while the tortured screams of the other inmates bounced from the bare stone wall and he knew that aside from the cloth bag he was naked, exposed, and—

'…walk in a straight line for me?'

His legs nearly gave out from relief. 'Yes! No problem.'

But as soon as he said it, he felt regret at his hubris. The headaches and the flu kicking in meant he was prone to bouts of dizziness. Dizziness that might easily be interpreted as drunkenness by an over-eager cop.

'I've been feeling ill and I get dizzy, but it isn't a problem.'

The cop said nothing and moved a few yards ahead, his boots clipping off the tarmac. He turned to face Ray and the onrush of traffic and waved Ray forward. Ray stepped slowly and (he hoped) steadily towards the cop and when he reached him, the cop gestured to turn around and walk back. He did, and on the way back felt more sure of his footing.

'Stop!'

Ray turned to face the cop who was already behind him.

'You said you're feeling sick?' The cop asked, a hint of concern on his face.

Ray nodded.

'The flu, I think. It's just starting. It's been going around the guys at work.'

'You mind telling me where you're going today?'

'Boston, to surprise my old man. I think I said already.'

The cop's radio squawked, and Ray jumped. The cop just stared.

'I was thinking about going to a motel, taking a nap,' Ray offered.

'That mightn't be a bad idea.'

The cop was going to let him go. There was not going to be any arrest.

'You mind telling me what's in the folder on the front seat of your car there?'

He hoped his poker face was holding out. Just go for it. Shoot for the stars. Hope he buys it.

'Just some holiday plans. Wanted to maybe get a flight, from Logan. Hit L.A. Maybe Vegas.'

The cop nodded, completely void of emotion. 'Sir, I'd advise you to get off the road at the earliest convenience if you're feeling unwell. Just pull into the shoulder if you feel you can't make it to a motel.'

Ray nodded, trying not to make his movements exaggerated.

'Don't be trying that windows down, radio up nonsense either. It only works for so long. And watch your driving.'

The cop nodded and touched a finger of farewell off his helmet.

'Have a nice day, sir.'

'Thank you.'

Ray waited for the cop to walk past him and bolted for his car. He sat counting seconds as hot air flowed into him, trying not to go into a full-blown panic attack, waiting for the cop to go by. A vignette of darkness crept into Ray's peripheral vision. If he passed out now and the cop saw him, he was screwed.

Breathe Ray. Slowly. Imagine a bag inflating. Slowly. Slowly.

The darkness retreated and the cop passed, and as he did, he gave that same farewell gesture. Ray sank further down into his seat as every muscle relaxed at once.

He glanced at the folder.

'Motel. And you're getting hidden.'

4:34PM

Tired and still edgy from his run in with the traffic cop, Ray pulled into the lot of the Bluebird Motel. From the road grass ran up to the flat wall of the main single-story building, part hidden by overgrown hedges. He liked how the lot was unseen from the road, with the rooms sheltering it in a shallow and squared off 'U' shape. He liked how it was close to Logan, about forty minutes' drive, but that there would be others closer. If the worst did come to the worst, it wouldn't be the first place the cops checked. He also liked that the lot already had two cars in it. If it were only his car, it would stand out, exposed. He swung into a space close to the reception area, tucked the folder under his arm and stepped out.

The building muted the noise of traffic. At night it would be quieter still as the number of cars decreased, not that he expected the coming days to bring much sleep. He walked to the reception in a half stumble, legs still unsteady from his run in with the law. Now that a cop had reported his vehicle, he weighed up the pros and cons of taking a rental car. He filed it in his mind in a drawer marked "later". First, he had to get a room without making a show of himself.

He pushed the door open and overhead, where the gentle tinkle of bell should ring, there was a dull *clunk*. A small silver-colored bell hung over the door with the clapper removed. Dusty air hung thick and the place looked like it hadn't seen fresh paint since Reagan was in the White House. A burst of applause exploded from somewhere in the back - a TV with the volume set somewhere near deafening. He moved to the desk and saw a small room in the back, where an old geezer sat in a worn mustard-yellow wing-back armchair, eyes glued to Wheel of Fortune.

GHOSTS OF SEPTEMBER

Smoke snaked from a two-inch-long growth of ash at the end of a self-rolled cigarette gripped loosely between the old timer's crooked fingers. Here was the man responsible for the clapperectomy.

He looked down at the reception bell on the desk and held no expectations as he brought a hand down upon it. He was almost surprised at the satisfying *ping!* produced. The old man grumbled without looking up. Or getting up. Ray hit the bell again. The old guy muttered and groaned as he rose. He shuffled from in front of the TV into reception slower than Ray thought humanly possible.

The journey ended at the desk in front of Ray. The old man stared. Ray waited for him to speak, but nothing happened.

Ray smiled. 'Hi. I need a room for a couple days.'

'Cash or card?'

'Cash.'

'Good. Cause we don't take card.'

He turned the registration book around and tapped it with a crooked finger.

'Sign here.'

Ray looked down at the book and the headers at the top of the page. Name, date, room number, number of nights, car license plate. He didn't want to fill it out. All information could be incriminating.

'You need all this?'

The geezer looked up and said nothing for the longest time then said: 'Yes.'

Ray picked up the pen.

The gruff, smoke-soaked voice came again. 'Bath or shower?'

'Shower's fine.'

'Good. Cause we don't got baths.'

Ray studied the signing-in book and raised his eyebrows. Name. He would have to use his first name or remember the fake one. He scrawled Ray into the box, then put his mother's maiden name after it. Should be easy to remember. He put yesterday's date.

'Room 11.' The old geezer wheezed and took a long drag from the cigarette which, somewhere between the TV and here, had lost the surreal length of ash.

'Eleven, of course,' Ray said, pen hovering over the section in the book.

There was an electronic *bzzzt!!* from the TV followed by a burst of enthusiastic applause and the old geezer turned his head to the back room, grumbling again. Ray wrote a one in the space marked room number. The entry for room one, he altered to eleven. He scrawled his license plate into the book, thought about exchanging a couple of digits, then thought against it. How dumb/careless could one guy be? There and then, the decision to rent a car was made for him.

'Okay, that's me.'

The old guy finally turned back.

'If I need to stay extra nights can I just arrange that with you?'

'Uh-huh.'

They stood looking at each other for a moment.

GHOSTS OF SEPTEMBER

'Er... my key?'

The old man's eyebrows climbed his forehead and a surprised grunt escaped as his slid the key across the desk to Ray then turned and shuffled back to the TV at twice the speed he'd left it, leaving Ray alone.

'Thanks.'

Ray trod along the wooden boards outside until he reached room eleven. His paranoid mind questioned why the old timer had made him walk past at least eight empty rooms to get to his, but he was glad of the privacy the distance offered and ignored it. He slid the key into the lock and looked back instinctively to reception, checking he wasn't being observed. Nothing doing. He turned the key.

The door squealed open and Ray was hit with the same dusty smell as in reception. The room was clean, but somehow grubby at the same time. What had once been whites were now greys and the yellows, brown. The lumpy bed sat against the left wall and a dresser and a foggy mirror opposite. On the cigarette burned dresser sat a small TV and across from it the door to the bathroom.

Ray closed the outside world away and sat on the bed, surprised at how comfortable it was. It might look lumpy and sunken, but it felt as good as the one he had at home. He lay back, closed his eyes for a moment. Just a moment.

The clouds of sleep drifted away, and Ray lay, eyes closed, enjoying the refreshed feeling. Taking shuteye always gave him a boost, but he was unsure how long he'd been out. He reached into a pocket and grabbed his phone. He peeled an eye and squinted at the clock, bolting upright.

An hour and a half had passed. He still had to get to Logan. Shit, he still had to hide the folder. The unfamiliar room greeted him, and he scanned for prospective hiding places for the notes. Then a horrible feeling came, crawling up the back of his head in a cold sweat.

What folder?

6:05PM

Panic gripped him as he jumped to his feet, spinning back to face the bed in the hope he'd been sleeping on the folder.

'Where the fuck is the folder, Ray?' he said, voice shaking.

The empty bed stared back. Icy coldness washed over him afresh accompanied by a familiar tightness in his throat.

'Stay calm.'

He threw back the bedsheets before running to the dresser. He was sure he'd taken it from the car.

'Where the fuck is it then?'

Did he hide it when he came in? He didn't remember hiding it before sleeping. He had it at the reception, he was certain. Or maybe it was still on the front seat of his car for all the world to see.

Check it's not outside. If not, search here. For fuck's sake do it quickly.

He frisked himself for his car keys, felt them in his

GHOSTS OF SEPTEMBER

pocket and burst from the room. The sky was a shade darker and the traffic a touch lighter as he sprinted towards the car, fumbling for his keys all the while. The folder was nowhere in sight. He ducked down to look through the windows. He opened the door and dropped to his knees, searching under the seat. He had taken the folder from the car. It was in his hand when he went to reception. He'd put it down to sign the register. When he picked up the key, he must have forgotten it.

He slammed the car door shut and sprinted to the reception. He flung the door open and stopped dead when he saw the cops.

6:12PM

The cops stood at the desk, talking to the old man. Both turned to face him. One black, with a moustache. The other white and the cleanest shave he'd ever seen. He must have been younger than Ray was now. The old geezer turned, too. Ray glanced at the register, and next to it, sat the folder. The ribbon was still tied, but it looked different. Like it had been opened and retied.

Could have just worked itself loose. Breathe.

Shallower and shallower breaths came, his field of vision now dotted with stars. The cops stood between him and the folder, which meant if he was to get it back, they'd have to pass it to him. They'd have to *touch* it. He felt sick.

'Yeah?' The old geezer barked in that half cough of his.

Ray peered up from the folder to see the cops were still looking at him. His gaze turned to the old timer and he drew in a deep, deliberate breath, 'Er, I forgot my folder.'

He pointed at the manila file. The old guy and the cops both turned. The black cop reached over. Everything happened in slow motion as the cop picked up the folder and swung it in Ray's direction. A white corner of paper poked from the top and grew as the folder got closer and closer and Ray wasn't sure if the folder would reach him before the page came out completely.

He broke the slow-mo spell and stepped closer. He grabbed the folder, poking the half page back in.

He smiled, 'Thanks.'

The black cop nodded, and his colleague was staring at Ray. The old man was looking at the cops. Ray stood still, his heart pounding in his ears. He could feel the folder dampening from his sweaty hand.

'Can we hurry this along?' The old guy asked the cops.

The cops both turned back to him and he asked them about finding the guy who'd trashed his room. Ray turned and pulled the door open, hearing the bell *clunk* overhead. He walked out as calmly as possible and stepped outside, the breeze chilling the sweat against his forehead. All the way back to his room he felt the cops' eyes burning the back of his head.

How could he have been so stupid? So careless? It was something like this that would land him in Guantanamo. His stomach shrank and he felt the guilt and fear balled up there, cold and heavy.

GHOSTS OF SEPTEMBER

He grabbed the cold metal of the doorknob, and his curiosity got the better of him. He glanced back at reception, but nobody was watching. He entered the room and slammed the door behind him, and his eyes scanned the room for a hiding place.

6:50PM

Ray swung into the huge lot at Logan and began searching for a space close to the entrance. Endless rows of cars lay in front of him, but there were plenty of spaces too. Over the terminal B building a 747 soared skyward at a steep angle and a shiver crawled down his back. On the way here he'd thought about the incident with the folder and how it felt like something more than a coincidence. More like a warning. Charlie's words about the crazy old man screwing with him while he was in this place rang in his ears. Charlie saying he was powerful and not to be trifled with, felt like he wasn't a man: He was an idea. Or even some kind of god. The way he was watching, or could at least feel, every move that Ray made when he was back here in 2001 made him *sound* like a god. Like he oversaw this time. Maybe of all time.

His headache settled in whenever Ray thought about it. Heavy and strong behind his eyes. He put it from his mind and tried to focus more on the job in hand: he had to get information on the flights and come up with a way of stopping what was coming from here: three thousand souls depended on it. He swung into a vacant parking space around fifty yards from the entrance to terminal B and locked up.

On the way to the building his mind drifted again to the sighting (*potential* sighting) of the Ringleader at the bank that morning and proceeded to flick through a raft of examples of what he should have done, if he weren't such a pussy. What Pete would have done, in the same scenario. There wasn't a lot he *could* have done, short of killing the guy, and he was no killer. Besides, how could he kill someone who he wasn't even sure was the same guy he was looking for. Worse than that, at the moment, he hadn't killed anyone. It would be like…

Killing baby Hitler? That's the pussy talking. What about intent*? The guy* wants *to murder thousands of people, isn't that enough?*

'No. It's not,' he mumbled as he passed into the building, all the while knowing he had to do something. He imagined coming back through those same doors, hands cuffed behind his back, dragged by large police officers as the press snapped pictures of him. Murderer of an innocent man.

Harried passengers dragged suitcases through the busy terminal building, rushing this way and that as unintelligible announcements hissed through the PA system. All unaware of the approaching horror. Unaware that the way air travel is done is about to change forever. He stood watching as crowds moved in clusters towards flights, holiday destinations, reunions. Tracking down lost luggage. Searching

GHOSTS OF SEPTEMBER

for rental cars. Heads craned upward at ceiling signs. It dawned that he didn't have a plan. Not even the beginnings of one. He was supposed to come up with something on the way here. (He'd wanted to do it at the motel, but of course, he'd missed that particular boat through over-sleeping.) A short checklist had formed in his mind. Renting a new car and so on, but before that he needed to buy a ticket. He wasn't planning to take the flight, but he thought that the ticket might be a useful (if expensive) prop. Plus he wanted to see the layout of this place and get his bearings before Tuesday morning.

Tuesday morning.

A shudder stole through him. A group of men would pass through this airport and board a plane with the intention of hijacking it and crashing it like a missile into a building at 500mph.

The departures board would help fill gaps in his knowledge. The flight he wanted was an American or United Airlines, he needed to check if this was the correct terminal for domestic flights, and which gates the flights departed from. He didn't want any surprises on… Now the word 'Tuesday' was loaded for him. His breath quickened.

Keep it together, Ray, for fuck's sake.

He stood below the board and peered upward. This was the terminal. Flights to Miami, and Detroit, and Los Angeles. The little yellow dots that made up the words blurred and merged as he stared. Just looking at Los Angeles, something resonated. Like the tumblers in a lock falling into place. That was it. Two hundred percent. That's where both flights were going.

He turned and scanned for a ticketing desk, seeing everything but. Currency exchange, lost and found, restrooms. Then he spotted it and weaved through the crowds. There was no line, only a pretty lady with intelligent eyes and too much make-up waiting for him.

'Hi.'

'How can I help you?' All eyes and teeth, as his old man used to say.

'I need a little information. I'm looking for a flight to Los Angeles,' he paused, bracing for the inevitable nausea, 'on Tuesday morning.'

'Okay, let's see what we have.'

She tip-tapped the keyboard hidden behind the bulky computer monitor and without looking up asked, 'Is there any time in particular you were looking for?'

Ray thought. He didn't really have specifics. He just wanted to hear flight numbers, hoping to hear the one that would jog his memory. And turn his stomach.

'Early. Anything before nine.'

'Okay… we have…'

'You have anything with United Airlines?'

'Yes we do. There's a flight at 8am.'

Nothing stirred. He had hoped that hearing the time would resonate just like seeing LA on the departures board had. He needed more. 'What flight number is that?'

'Sorry?'

It was a weird request. He smiled and repeated the

question. 'The flight number?'

'Uhhh... that would be... flight one-seven-five.'

Nausea crashed through him.

Bingo.

Ray patted himself down looking for a pen. The lady smiled and slid a pen and small notepad across to him. He smiled back and scribbled the information down quickly, like it would escape if he didn't.

'That's great. Just out of interest, do you have anything with American Airlines?'

'Yup, we do. We have one that takes off at a quarter to eight.'

'And the number?'

'That one is... flight 11.'

His mouth watered with sour saliva. He felt like vomiting. While unpleasant, he couldn't help but feel this information gathering was almost too easy. He scribbled the number and tore off the note, folding it once and slipping it into the back pocket of his jeans.

'That's great.'

'Would you like to purchase a ticket today?'

He suddenly felt cold. Like someone was watching him. And he knew exactly who it was.

'Yes. Yes I would. A single.' He fought to smile.

After a few seconds' thought, he plumped for the early flight. That was the one most likely for the Ringleader to take. He wanted a good excuse to be as close as possible to that bastard before he got anywhere near a plane. Again he thought of ways of stopping him. Telling security he'd overheard something, or saying he'd seen something. Or following him to the men's room. The idea of killing him popped into his head, only this time he wasn't so quick to dismiss it. The thought was black and heavy, and he hated himself for it.

'Sir? Are you okay?'

Ray looked up, startled.

'Your nose.' She pointed.

Ray traced a finger below his nose and felt the wetness and familiar copper smell of blood. Two tissues were grabbed from a box somewhere out of sight like a magic trick and thrust across the desk at him. He snatched them and nodded thanks.

'How much for the ticket?'

She tried to smile but Ray could see she was disconcerted at the amount of blood his nose was producing.

'It's fine. Happens all the time. The ticket. How much was that?'

She forced a smile. 'That'll be a hundred ninety dollars. Your name, sir?'

The idea of using his mother's maiden name came to him again but then he thought about security. He didn't want any reasons for his background to be brought into question.

'It's Ray. Ray Madison.'

She smiled a little more naturally and her fingers lightly tapped the info into the keyboard, the sounds drifting over the buzz and background chatter of the crowds. He

GHOSTS OF SEPTEMBER

showed his driving license over the counter at her.

She barely looked at it.

There was an electronic buzz behind her as the ticket printed. She turned, grabbed it, turned back, handed it to Ray, and that was that. That's how easy it was.

'What gate will that be leaving from?'

'Well I can't say for certain, but that one usually leaves from B12.'

Ray stuffed the bloody tissue into the inside pocket of his jacket.

'I need to rent a car, while I'm here in Boston,' he lied, surprised at how easily the lies came.

She pointed, none the wiser, 'It's just past the baggage claim, on the left.'

Ray smiled. 'Thanks very much.'

He was enjoying how people reacted to him in this time. They responded to his youth and confidence in a way he didn't appreciate the first time around. He fleetingly wondered how many people were aware of the value of that.

Renting a car was more difficult than buying an airline ticket. Not that it was problematic, but the ease with which he obtained the ticket made him think of the changes brought in after the attacks and again he questioned how many lives that had saved, which was a roundabout way of his brain to question the logic of his whole endeavor. He was torn, but in his mind his father's voice echoed.

Don't be a faggot, Ray. Why can't you be more like your brother?

He was told where to collect his car by a woman strikingly similar to the one he bought the ticket from. Another one of society's invisibles. Someone you met and forgot. Like a street cleaner. Like a pizza delivery guy. Like a courier.

How he would have enjoyed the anonymity of his uniform now.

He'd done almost everything he came to do. He didn't like the idea of abandoning his car here, but after the traffic stop, he had little choice. It was just one more shred of comfort he'd have to do without. Now he just wanted to find the gate he'd be using on Tuesday. Check out what kind of security there was. If there were guards around. Where the restrooms were. Again the image of him kicking the Ringleader around the wet floor of the men's room came, and again, he let it stay. He walked slowly, seemingly without purpose, wanting to soak up as much of his surroundings as possible.

The weight of someone struck his shoulder as they brushed past. The man turned back, whether to apologize or just to see who had inconvenienced him, and time slowed. Ray fixed eyes on the man who hit him. It was the Ringleader.

7:20PM

Ray froze as the Ringleader went by. He could only watch as four more men strolled past, time slowing to a crawl, the sounds of Logan Airport fading to silence. The Ringleader

GHOSTS OF SEPTEMBER

was wearing a different shirt from the one he'd been wearing that morning.

If it was him this morning.

Sickness rose in him, and his legs weakened. The men were laughing together. Ray wanted to follow but he was frozen. His legs were weak and leaden. Time sped up again and the airport chatter and buzz faded in as the men dissolved into the crowds. Ray's legs shook uncontrollably as he watched them get further away.

Not now. Get it together.

They were heading to the gates.

Was it time? Were they doing this now? Fuck.

He finally stepped forward and started to follow. People walked by him and towards him and in front of him, all in his way, none stopping to let him go first, all expecting him to be the one to give way and move. The back of the Ringleader's head fleetingly came into view and disappeared behind those of his colleagues. Ray tailed them and sped up, gaining ground.

The group marched ahead, others splitting around them; the same people who Ray had to move around like a salmon heading for breeding ground. They were looking at gate numbers and pointing and Ray realized that he'd got to the gates without passing through a single metal detector. They stopped twenty yards ahead. This was his chance. He was going to catch them and…

And what?

They'd stopped at gate B12 and an announcement for

a flight to LA rang out overhead. Ray scanned the background for a security guard. There was not a single one. He'd have to deal with it himself.

Now only 20 yards of empty floor separated them. Ray had a clear view of all five men, the Ringleader's face was obscured by the back of another guy's head, but Ray was sure it was him. He said a silent prayer for an answer to his problem. That was the moment the Ringleader said something to his friends and turned to walk away. Ray followed. The others gabbled loudly, excitedly as Ray walked past. He put a hand up to the left side of his face, pretending to scratch his head. The Ringleader was walking faster than Ray, getting farther and farther away with each step, until he suddenly slowed, and turned. He'd gone into the men's room.

Ray stopped in the middle of the hall, in disbelief. He walked more slowly now, weighing his possibilities, his father's voice berating him for doing so. He'd have to follow him. And what then? Could he really kill a man? But that wasn't really the question. The real question was: could he kill a man in a busy international airport, and get out without being spotted? Again the thought of violence nauseated him. He got to the men's room and went to place a tentative hand on the door to push it open, when it suddenly swung away from him. A long-haired kid in his late teens stood there, his face an explosion of acne. Ray stepped aside and the kid left, shaking his head.

The entrance to the john had a wall that stopped a few feet to the right as the room opened into the bathroom itself.

GHOSTS OF SEPTEMBER

Ray stepped in and turned right, stopping before the end of the wall. The door swung closed behind him and the chattering and announcements faded into the echoes of urinals squirting cleaning water. The lemon smell of cleaning products was overwhelming, and sickness rose again in Ray's throat. Somewhere around the wall, tuneless whistling echoed. Ray edged around the corner and into the bright white fluorescence of the bathroom. The Ringleader was nowhere in sight.

Ray turned to the row of stalls and ducked down. Of the ten stalls, just two were taken. One pair of shoes faced the john, the other faced the door. The outward facing pair was nearest and as Ray crept past, the sound of straining and waft of foulness rose. The second stall from the end was where the Ringleader must be. There wasn't time for the Ringleader to drop his pants. Ray drew nearer, wondering what he was going to do when he got there.

He waited, expecting to hear the flush of the toilet, but there was no sound. He edged along, and the urinals flushed again. Ray jumped and stopped, using a hand to clamp the startled scream in his throat. He set off again and the squirting sound of water stopped to his left, he heard muttering coming from the Ringleader's stall. He stopped again, one door along, and listened.

The words were unclear, but the muttering went on. The moment it stopped the toilet five doors back flushed. His heart leapt. Ray had to make his move now. Trap the Ringleader in the cubicle and beat him senseless. He rushed to the stall door and went to throw it open. Again it disappeared before he could place a hand on it. This time there was no pimply teenager. Now the Ringleader stood in his way. Ray shrank back as if expecting attack, but the Ringleader burst past him, again barging into him like he wasn't there. Ray scurried to the back wall and watched the Ringleader, walking with the same urgency, as he left the bathroom.

His heart thumped in his chest and his breaths became ever shallower, the darkness creeping into his peripheral vision. Stars formed over the growing dark, then at once vanished, until there was nothing. In the black, the room swirled. Ray gasped for air and his sight came back, bright, overexposed. The other occupied stall opened and a forty-something guy in a sharp suit left and walked straight across to the mirrors. He checked his hair, before looking at Ray, then shook his head and turned from the bathroom without a word. His hard-soled shoes echoed and as he went, their sound became deeper. The room blurred, then went black.

8:21PM

The nauseating smell of lemon-fresh cleaner faded in first. Ray opened his eyes to the men's room at Logan. He'd blacked out. A fat guy with a wispy beard and AC/DC shirt entered. He regarded Ray, who was still slumped and sweaty, and stopped dead.

'Er, are you okay?'

Ray felt shame wash over him and gingerly raised

GHOSTS OF SEPTEMBER

himself to his feet. He nodded and wondered what was going on.

The Ringleader. The attacks.

He ran for the exit past the bewildered Samaritan and out into the terminal building. He scanned left and right. Crowds of people filed past, but the Ringleader was nowhere to be seen. As far as Ray knew, he was on board a plane headed for L.A. A plane that would be diverting to Manhattan. He felt the shameful guilt of failure heavy in the pit of his stomach again. He looked at the clock. 8:24pm. He'd been passed out on a men's room floor for almost two hours. Nobody had reported him. Nobody had checked on him. Probably thought it was just some loser too afraid to fly who'd got wasted before take-off. In that time, if the Ringleader and company had taken a flight, it would already be too late. He couldn't report it. And he certainly couldn't stop them. The sense of failure was crushing. The feeling that he was standing with his nose pressed against the glass of his apartment window screaming at a plane as it vanished into the towers was complete.

9:20PM

He tried to fight it. At least, that's what he told himself. For the first time since he woke up in 2001, he wanted a drink. *Needed* a drink. Today had been the worst since his return to the past. He'd slipped back into his old ways so easily. Like it had always been a part of him. Even in 2001 his alcoholism had lain dormant, waiting to be aroused. Now, it slept no more. The night he'd gone for beers with Manny, he hadn't given his alcoholism a second thought. It was fun. Drinking for enjoyment. Now he wanted to hurt himself. He'd found himself the dirtiest, dingiest bar and parked his rent-a-car outside. The broken neon sign, which could muster not even a flicker, hung over the door, as empty and dead as he felt.

The incident at the airport had left him shaken, way beyond anything he'd anticipated. If he'd had any doubts about the difficulty of his mission before, they were well and truly dead. Old Man Time was watching, and he wasn't about to let some chicken-shit upstart change anything lightly. This was an opponent Pete would struggle to overcome. An adversary much too strong, and more than the lack of will to fight, it was now the fear which rendered Ray impotent.

The dive bar door stared back at him.

Go in now and what? You've proved nothing. You're no better than that fuck up you left in 2018. This is what he'd do. The going gets tough, the weak get drinking.

Loud rock music poured from within like siren song as a drunk staggered from the dim interior into the shadowy lot. The bar door slammed shut and the music was again a muffled series of thuds and beats. Ray watched as the drunk staggered away, giving Ray a cursory glance as he went.

Go in now and you might as well go back to your apartment with a bottle of that piss you buy from the liquor store and just relive the nightmare that's approaching.

GHOSTS OF SEPTEMBER

Stumble through that sorry existence you call a life and commit a slow suicide with a bottle of cheap bourbon stuck to your hand. How long would it take? 17 years at the last count. Seventeen fucking years. Sure, your liver is shot, and your kidneys aren't in much better shape, but you're not actually that close. It could take another ten to finish the job.

The drunk had now vanished, and it was just him and the bar, beating like a heart in the dead night.

That guy was hammered. Is that really what you want?

Ray flung the door open and stepped into the chill night. It had taken so long to drink himself to death because he couldn't even bring himself to doing that properly. Now he could. Escalate things. Could probably do it in five years, if he set his mind to it.

The closer he got the muffled sounds became recognizable as the Rolling Stones. He placed a hand on the cold, heavy metal of the door and paused.

This is stupid. It was a minor setback. You knew it wasn't going to be easy. You've dealt with panic attacks from the time Pete died. Avoiding those is one of the reasons you've played it safe ever since. It doesn't have to be like this.

But it did. And he knew it.

9:27PM

The music blasted as Ray shoved open the door. Before it could swing shut he stepped into the dimness of the bar.

MARC W SHAKO

The smell of stale beer instantly hit him and the twenty or so customers stared at him, as if they'd never seen one like him before. One by one they went back to their drunken conversations as Ray entered further into the dark energy of the bar. The long rectangular room opened to his right, an odd mix of neon and shadows. Laughter rose and fell around the clack of pool balls from the far end of the room and before him, a series of booths ran the length of the wall, a guy slept with his head folded in his arms on the table in front of him. Ray turned and approached the bar.

The bartender was surprisingly slight, and Ray feared that if a fight did break out, it might go on forever with no-one here to stop it.

'What'll it be?'

The loud voice didn't match the timid, ratty features and took Ray by surprise.

'Bourbon. Double. Neat.'

'What kind?'

'Whatever's cheapest.'

The barman was effortlessly efficient like he'd been born behind a bar. Ray broke a twenty and grabbed his drink. He stared into it like a diver on the high board. His eyes came back into focus and he slammed the fiery bourbon down and slid the glass back across the beer-soaked bar. The rat-faced bartender looked up from the glass to Ray.

'Again.'

The bartender took the glass without saying a word and poured the same. Ray paid, nodded thanks and about faced.

GHOSTS OF SEPTEMBER

The booth next to Sleeping Beauty was a forest of empty bottles, but the third was vacant; he slid inside, wanting to keep his distance from the meatheads shooting pool. The Stones were still singing about rape and murder and right now that suited Ray just fine. He eyed the bourbon. This time he sipped.

Ray discovered that he liked this shit hole. In the time since he'd arrived, nobody had bothered him, and the bourbon had settled his nerves to the extent that he was able to enjoy the jukebox without ever playing it himself. It had taken five bourbons to calm him and now he'd switched for beer, wanting to prolong the buzz without passing out.

The table was ringed with water where his beers had sat. The third was going down just swell. His mind was occupied with where he went from here. Tomorrow would probably hurt. And if the hangover was too strong it would render him useless for at least half the day. He was supposed to be taking Kat out. And visiting his old man. That left him no time for the folder.

He'd gone from the airport to the motel, stashed the tickets and his cash, before finally turning on the TV, praying that no night-time disaster had been visited upon New York. After a (very) short wait he'd decided enough was enough. Nothing was going to happen – not at night – and it was time for him to get drunk. He'd retrieved a chunk of the cash and come here, planning to sleep in the car and get a head start first thing. He might not be able to stop the attacks, but he'd be fucked if he was going to let his best friend and relationship die. It just meant that the folder would have to stay in his motel room. If somebody found it…

'Fuck the folder.'

Ray raised his glass and drained it of beer. He rose on unsteady legs and went back to the bar. From the relative privacy of his booth he'd lost himself. The bar was busier now. Twenty odd patrons (some very odd, ha ha). He chuckled to himself. The rat-faced barman poured him another beer and he tottered back to his table. The moment he sat, the record on the jukebox finished and for a second, between the clack of pool balls and drunken laughter there was a silence so complete it made the skin on his forearms break out in gooseflesh. The calm before the storm. Something was coming. And sure enough, right on cue, that split second of perfect silence was broken when the door swung open and five loud men spilled in. So loud that all eyes in the bar turned to them. Including Ray's. What he saw was this: five men, Middle Eastern in appearance, and, as his eyes adjusted in the darkness, he saw a familiar face. The first of the men looked exactly like the Ringleader.

10:37PM

Ray looked away, frozen in horror as the man led his cronies to the bar. They crowded round him and chattered excitedly, laughing as if they had not a care in the world. Ray's stomach somersaulted. For the third time today he'd seen him.

GHOSTS OF SEPTEMBER

If it is him. You're wasted. The lights in here. It's too dark. And you got a fleeting glance. It might not be him.

Ray didn't want to look to confirm. If it was him, the run in at Logan airport would make him suspicious. This time he'd do more than barge past. Old Man Time would feel this ripple for sure. He had to get out of there. His blurry eyes scanned the bar. The only exit was the way in, and that would mean walking directly past the one person he hoped to avoid. The only other way was the bathroom. If that had a window. It was a door that didn't quite fit the jamb properly, harsh light glowing ethereally around it in the corner – just past the meathead pool sharks.

He lurched to his feet, and almost fell. Young Ray wasn't the drinker Old Ray was. Between him and the pool table, the small jazz club tables surrounded by stools seemed to move, to dance, blocking his path. He traversed the floor, weaving through the obstacles and grabbing an empty bottle from a puddle of beer on the table closest to the john. The meatheads screamed hysterically at a friend's Tina Turner impersonation as he mimed his way through *Nutbush City Limits*. Ray bumped into Tina, and expected the worst, but all he got was derisory laughter at his drunkenness.

The men's room door slammed aside, and he raced for one of the two stalls inside the wet bathroom. Inside the stall, the front of the cracked toilet bowl was caked with vomit, the only dry thing in this whole place it seemed. The stall door banged shut behind him and he backed against it, fighting his own urge to spew. He drew deep gasping breaths and threw his head back. The empty Bud bottle felt heavier than a tire iron.

He ran through his mind the conversation he'd had with himself after the run in at the bank. What would you do if...? Now was his chance to answer. This could end here. Now. Tonight. Tuesday would be a distant dream. If he killed the Ringleader now, he could focus all his efforts on saving Manny. Rebuilding what he had with Kat.

What if that's not him?

'What if it is?' he murmured.

He stepped to the cistern, raised the bottle, and smashed it. It broke in half, leaving a threatening jagged mouth, perfect for causing mortal damage. *Worse than a box-cutter* he thought from nowhere, and shuddered.

If he made his move in the barroom, his cronies would make sure whatever happened to their friend, something much worse happened to him. Which meant waiting until he came in here. Him being the leader on a job like this, chances were he wouldn't come in alone, especially after Logan; he'd be too exposed. Meaning he'd have to attack two people.

Attack? That's no good, Ray. You'll have to kill *these fuckers.*

His stomach turned again, a bitter mouthful of saliva rising up the back of his throat. He hadn't been in a fight since high school. And then Robbie Brady had dished out a merciless beating. Pete and him used to play fight, but it was just that – playing. Here he'd have to kill two guys and

GHOSTS OF SEPTEMBER

make it out without rousing the others. Then he'd have to drive. He could barely walk. He looked down at the bottle. His knuckles were alabaster white, and the bottle trembled uncontrollably. His stomach convulsed and Ray hurled bourbon and beer into the cracked bowl.

Then, the outer door to the men's room squeaked open. Ray turned to the stall door and peered through the crack. It was him. Six feet away, probably unaware of Ray even being there. And he was alone. Ray peered back down at the bottle. Now it was motionless in his hand. No tremble. Not a flicker. He'd washed over in a perfect serenity, the likes of which he'd never felt.

Do it now.

The bottle gripped in his left hand, he folded his bandaged right around the door handle and prepared to pull.

10:55PM

The sound of music swelled. For a moment Ray thought it was in his head, but unintelligible chatter rose and fell, echoing from the wet tile. He released the door handle. Through the crack in the door, he saw another man had entered. A friend of the first. Ray held back, still tightly gripping the neck of the ragged bottle. He froze. If they looked under the door to the stall, they'd see a pair of feet standing, waiting, listening. If he moved, he'd draw attention to his own position, and then his hand would be forced. He'd *have* to attack. If he moved now, it would be two against one.

One who hadn't been in a fight since high school.

But if he did strike now, if he killed this man, they'd have to call off the attack. They'd have to postpone.

Postpone. That's all.

They'd wait. Get someone else to fill his role and wait. It would be nothing more than prolonging the inevitable. Thousands would still die, only difference being, he'd be in no position to do a damned thing about it.

He shifted his weight and his foot scraped on the floor. The excited chatter of harsh Arabic stopped. A bang resonated from the stall beside his. Boot-on-door, shortly followed by the slam of door-on-wall. Ray waited for the inevitable. He'd backed himself into a corner. When these guys came through the stall door, he wouldn't be able to do a thing. Just accept whatever they laid on him. He cursed under his breath. His hand felt sweaty on the bottle neck and a burst of numbness spread through him, preparing for the beating that was coming.

'Wait.' He shouted.

Silence.

He moved back now, to leave room for the door if – *when* – it did come flying in.

But it did not. Instead a harsh Middle Eastern voice shouted. 'Come out. Slowly.'

Ray placed the bottle on the cistern. If he was going to face these guys, he wanted to talk his way out of trouble, not seem a threat.

'Okay.'

He edged to the door and prepared to open it. Doubt

GHOSTS OF SEPTEMBER

filled him that the man on the other side of the door was the Ringleader. It could just be a guy who thinks he has someone following him. Ray was about to find out. He reached for the door and noticed his hand was shaking. Another wave of nausea flushed, and he swallowed it hard.

The sound of music rose, and a loud bang followed. The sound of door handle on tile.

'Get the fuck out of here.'

A deep voice.

Silence.

'Get the fuck out of here, NOW.'

There came no resistance from the other side of the stall door. Just shuffling feet barely audible past the strains of Led Zeppelin. Ray noticed for the first time the absence of clacking pool balls. It was the meatheads. The music faded as the door swung shut. The guy who looked like the Ringleader was gone. Ray peered out from the cubicle and saw two of the meatheads. The tallest standing in a sleeveless denim jacket, the other in black, a short haired biker. No Tina Turner. Ray stepped out.

'Thanks, guys. I think those fuckers were going to—'

The meatheads rushed him, the smaller landing a punch flush on his jaw. Ray fell to the wet floor, a flash of pain firing up one side of his face and on his back where he hit the wall. The biker dragged him to his feet effortlessly and gut-punched him. Ray felt his internal organs distort and squash and he instantly doubled over, only the biker's grip stopped him falling.

MARC W SHAKO

'Money.'

Ray coughed, 'What?'

This time the punch came from the taller thug. The blow was heavier, this time to the face, Ray felt the double pain of the punch to his cheek, then the flush of numbness at the back of his head as it collided with the cold tile. The lights darkened, his knees buckled, and the music faded to nothing.

For the second time that day, Ray was out cold.

A vast expanse of arid desert unfolded before him. He was already in motion. Ray stumbled across the rocky terrain under a blanket of crushing heat. He wasn't sure how long he'd been walking, but the blisters inside his shoes were wet and angry, like walking on glass shards. In the angular yellow mountains beneath the clear blue sky was cool black shade, respite from the savage desert heat. The powerful sun pressed onto his burnt shoulders and he knew he had to make it to the caves that lined the horizon.

The feeling that he was being followed was still with him, but he was certain that turning to check now would present the same as last time: endless desert backed by ragged mountains and not a soul in sight. Somewhere in his mind, in the corners where the light of knowledge cannot touch, where instinct and doubt and truth all hide in the shadows, somewhere there, he knew there was more to reaching the caves than just escaping the crippling heat. All ahead were colors. Pale blue sky. Bright yellow desert. Deep black caves. And then, something new: a speck of

GHOSTS OF SEPTEMBER

white. Waving. A man in robes. Too far to see, but he was sure it was a young man. He was sure it was Pete.

He redoubled his efforts, stumbling on jagged rock as he did so. Ignoring the pain of his feet. Ignoring the blast of heat that invaded his lungs with each gasping breath. Almost running now to where Pete was waiting, at the squat opening of the smallest cave. He had to make it. It felt as if invisible sands were disappearing through an impossibly huge hourglass topped with a radio mast.

Pete waved a slow, endless wave, "over here". His young face clouded with concern. Ray sped up. Blood squelched inside his shoes and light desert dust climbed the dark brown of his uniform trousers. The first step into the shade and the temperature dropped instantly, like he was immersed into cool water. But still that sweltering summer sun lurked over the mountain tops, pouring its heat into the desert below.

Pete smiled, and suddenly his feet stopped hurting and his skin stopped burning.

'You made it,' Pete said.

'Why wouldn't I?'

Because he's out there?

Ray frowned and nodded.

'Why am I here, Pete?'

'It feels like a test, doesn't it, baby brother?'

An eighteen-year-old kid calling him that should have felt strange. It did not.

'It does. But a test of what?' Ray asked.

Pete never said a word, but the answer still came.
Faith.

Faith in what? Ray wanted to ask but didn't. Pete walked the few feet to the cave entrance. It rose twice Pete's height and offered welcoming coolness. Ray followed until Pete stopped and only now Ray saw that beneath the folds of his robes, he was wearing an Iron Maiden shirt.

'I can't go in, baby brother. You have to go alone.'

Ray understood. He hugged his eighteen-year-old big brother and stepped into the cool damp of the cave.

Inside it was dark and widened into a long tunnel, the end of which curved out of sight into the black abyss. Ray turned back, but Pete was gone. All he saw was that burning patch of light from the outside. A drip of water echoed from somewhere around the corner and the laughter and chatter of voices followed.

Ray edged along, harried by the stabbing agony of his blisters. He traced a hand along the slimy wet rock to steady himself on the uneven floor until he reached the corner. The corner from where the voices and laughter came. He stopped and turned back. The square of burning light was cut in half by the cave wall beside him. Another step and he'd be inside. The sound of chatter started again, too low for him to make out a single word; loud enough to pique his curiosity.

Curiosity won out and he ventured onward, leaving the safety of that bright square behind. Around the corner there wasn't a soul. The cave narrowed and the ceiling lowered: not enough for him to touch both of those slippery walls at

GHOSTS OF SEPTEMBER

once, and the jagged ceiling was out of reach to all but a giant. The cave seemed to go on forever, narrowing and lowering as it went, but, at the far end where the voices echoed and drifted through the dark, the warm welcoming glow of fire danced on the walls. He sped up a little, aware it was a dream, yet certain he would be free of it sooner if he did speed up, and as he got closer to the voices, he started to pick out words. The voices were English, but with an accent. Something Middle Eastern. He was now ducking into the cave; blind save for that orange glow that reflected dimly from the walls ahead. He squeezed through, jagged rock sticking hard into his chest and back at once. He was stuck. The echo grew louder, and he knew that around the next corner, where the fire crackled and spat, the cave opened into a giant chamber. His heavy breathing hurt. Each breath forced his expanding ribcage into the rough cave walls. Panic gripped him and laughter grew from around the corner mocking him. He planted a leg and hand behind him and pushed with everything he had. He was stuck fast. Now he couldn't be sure if the wetness on his chest and back was water or blood. He readied himself to push again, this time exhaling everything in his lungs.

He burst through the crack and landed hard on the cave floor, gasping for air. Ray was suddenly aware of how small he was. He'd been tracing his hand along the wall where the 'S' bent into the chamber and the opposite wall was suddenly half a football field away. He looked up and saw that the ceiling was just as far, the constant drip louder here. He edged along to the corner facing the wall and stopped. From here he could go no further without blowing his cover. A fizzling sound overhead drew his eyes upward. A pink neon sign which flickered in the dark read *Time Can Not Save You*. It fizzed again before blinking out. The words he heard from the voices around the corner were now full sentences. Sentences; ideas. He listened over the dripping water and crackling fire.

'But surely the Americans will have protocols. Surely they will know that their planes have been taken and blow us out of the sky.'

The voice was harsh, angry. Not one he was familiar with. A softer voice spoke in reply.

'That is why, when we take their planes, we shall strike all of our targets at once. Then there is no way for them to react in time.'

The softer voice was that of Osama Bin Laden. It dawned on Ray he'd never heard him speak, but here in this dream he was sure of it. A third voice spoke, equally soft, identical to the second in almost every way, yet Ray was certain it came from another mouth.

'And when the targets have been struck, the world will watch as our plans are fulfilled, and the towers fall.'

A fourth voice now, higher pitched than the others, but again not one Ray knew.

'But the buildings are built to withstand such destruction. They will not fall.'

'Do you know what temperature the fuel from a plane burns at?' a soft voice replied.

GHOSTS OF SEPTEMBER

'Yes. No higher than fifteen hundred degrees Fahrenheit.'

'And at what temperature does steel melt?'

'No lower than twenty-five hundred degrees Fahrenheit.'

'Exactly.'

The other, younger Bin Laden spoke. 'You know that the plane has operational limits?'

'Yes. Of course. We have planned very carefully. The maximum speed at sea level is 330 miles per hour.'

'And what will happen if you fly at speeds above this? Like the speeds used at thirty thousand feet.'

'The air at sea level is much thicker. The engines lack the power to propel the craft at such speeds at lower altitude. Not only that, any attempt to fly above such speeds would cause massive structural damage. The plane will break up and crash…'

'Fly at the higher speed.'

'I will.'

Ray's flesh crawled as he listened. Nothing of what he heard made sense. His heart was already hammering, but it was about to go up a notch.

Another voice spoke. This one harsher in tone than the others. It was the Ringleader. 'What about *him*?'

'The one who listens?'

At that moment Ray felt strong hands grab his shirt at the shoulders and thrust him into the cavern. The four figures huddled around the fire turned at once. It took a few seconds for his eyes to adjust to the light, and when they did, he knew the faces staring at him. Manny, Pop, Kat, and crazy Old Man Time all staring, murder and hatred burning in their eyes. Manny opened his mouth and Bin Laden's voice spilled out.

'Kill him.'

11:36PM

Ray jolted awake and winced at the bright lights. The left eye didn't open fully. The skin around it was raw and tight. His head throbbed with dull pain that reminded him of the throb in his hand a few days before and he pulled himself inward to protect his aching ribs. He opened one eye and peered down. He was on a bed with a flimsy green curtain pulled around it. Beside the bed was a chair. And in the chair, a figure.

'Sir?'

Ray turned his head and saw the light and dark blue of a state police uniform.

Fuck.

According to his name badge, his name was officer Shaw.

'How are you feeling, sir?'

'Like shit…' He scanned the area within the curtain. 'Where am I?'

'Saint Florian hospital. Somebody dropped you off outside. Any idea who that might have been?'

Those fuckers had a conscience? Who'd have thought?

GHOSTS OF SEPTEMBER

'I don't even know what day it is.'

He glanced at his watch. 'It's Saturday. Just. You've been roughed up a little. Any idea who might have done that?'

Ray reached into his pocket. The roll of twenties was gone. And his wallet.

'Shit.'

The cop sounded genuinely concerned, 'What is it?'

'My wallet. My money.' He checked for the motel key. Nothing. 'And my motel key.'

Officer Shaw raised a hand, opened it and something jingled, a high-pitched sound that Ray cared little for. He looked up to see his motel key and for a second, he was relieved. Then a chill swept through him as it dawned that it would have been far better if the meatheads had taken it. Jesus. Is that why the cop was here? Had they been to the motel and found the folder? No. He'd hidden it. Hidden it well. He looked at the key fob.

'We took the liberty of emptying your pockets. I just wondered if you had any information on how you got here. You were dropped off by somebody. Were you doing something you shouldn't have been?'

'No. I was drinking. At a bar. Some dive I found.'

'And you were attacked?'

That's right. He started to put two and two together. The rat-faced barman must have tipped off his Village People buddies about the stranger's roll of twenties. And he'd been worried about the Ringleader and his pals. Great.

'I guess. I don't remember much.'

'What's missing? Physically, I mean.'

'I had some cash on me. Couple hundred bucks. My driver's license was in my wallet.'

'What's your name?'

He doesn't know. Good. Give him a fake. The one you signed in the guest book at the motel. What was it?

'Ray.'

'Ray?'

Ray frowned, feigning confusion. The cop raised his eyebrows, as if it were obvious.

'Your last name?'

'Kennedy.'

'Ray Kennedy.'

Ray smiled sheepishly, 'That's me.'

'Okay Ray Kennedy. Tell me about the attack.'

Attack? Fuck. He found the folder.

Ray's heart rate took off like a triphammer and he wondered if he could outrun the cop. Shaw was young and in shape. No dice.

The cop spoke again. 'Did you get a look at who attacked you?'

Christ, Ray. Take it easy. He knows nothing.

This was a complication he could do without. Now he knew that Old Man Time was serious about protecting his precious past. It's not just the main players you gotta watch, no sir. Anyone can turn at any time. Was that true, or just paranoia? The bar was a dive and he could have been more careful with his money that was for sure. He was alone and

GHOSTS OF SEPTEMBER

carrying way more cash than was necessary. But at the same time, he had the feeling that if he wasn't where he was, contemplating what he was, that this would not have happened. Got to step away from this.

'No. They jumped me. From behind. In the men's room.'

Ray sat up and a boa constrictor of pain wrapped itself around his ribcage, snatching his breath from him. He winced.

'Easy there.'

Shaw was being nice to him, but Ray could tell that he was sizing him up. Something about this didn't fit. Guys who are shot during robberies are dropped off outside hospitals, not guys roughed up during muggings: That's what the cop was thinking. Who the hell *had* dropped him off? And why?

If Ray had questions of his own, Shaw must be bursting with them.

'You said you were at a bar? Which one?'

'I don't want to go back.'

'Nobody said you have to.'

Easy Ray. Don't fuck this up.

The cop spoke again, 'You don't seem too drunk. Why is that?'

'I drank a little too much. I got sick, just before those assholes jumped me.'

'Assholes?' Shaw asked. 'Plural?'

Careful Raymondo.

'I heard two voices.'

'How did you get to…'

Have to tell him the name of the bar.

'Joey's.' Ray finished.

'So how did you get to Joey's?'

'I took a cab,' he lied.

'You were drinking heavily enough to get sick.'

Where is he going with this? Watch yourself, Ray.

'Rough day.'

The cop was young, but just like in his dream, he envisioned him reaching to the corner of his jawline and pulling off a mask, like a Scooby-Doo villain. Of course the villain this time would be that stooping, crazy old bastard who'd been watching his every step since he'd set foot back in 2001.

'I'd had enough to drink. You know, getting sick and all I was about to take a taxi home. Back to the motel,' he corrected. 'It was pretty close by.'

Fuck.

Shaw didn't flinch, but Ray knew this was what he was hoping for. He was young, but he was nobody's fool. 'I was hoping that this key would give me some clues as to where you're staying. The name of the motel isn't on there. The closest ones to Joey's are The Jack of Hearts, but it doesn't look like one of theirs, and the Bluebird…'

He trailed off. They both knew he'd just named the right one. *Great job, Poker Face.* Now this fucker wants to see where you're staying. You may as well tell him that you hired the car you drove to the bar in. Just fill in any blanks he might be struggling with. Shit, just show him the folder, get it over with.

'While I was going through your pockets, I found this.'

He pulled a folded piece of note paper from his top pocket. Ray didn't know what it was until the cop opened it and he saw his own handwriting. It was a note: Flight 175, 8AM.

'What's this?'

His heart leapt and he felt the color drain from his face.

Shaw stood. 'Whoa, are you feeling okay?'

He reached up and steadied his head in both hands. 'Yeah. Just a little dizzy. My head. It's killing me… It'll pass.'

Shaw sat and waited for Ray to lower his hands before speaking again.

'So… the flights? You going somewhere?'

His policy of telling the truth because it was easier to remember than a lie wasn't going to work here.

'L.A. Tuesday. Need some sunshine. Maybe take in a ball game.'

'Lakers fan?'

'God no,' he blurted, then, 'no offence.'

The cop smiled, 'None taken. I'm a football man. Patriots.'

Ray nodded. 'Just wanted the chance to see Kobe in his prime,' he smiled and hoped it didn't look too forced.

'Was the ticket expensive? For the Lakers?'

Ray put on a coy smile, 'Honestly, I was hoping to

scalp one.'

'I appreciate your honesty.' The cop smiled too. 'So you got your ticket? For the flight.'

Checkmate.

'Yeah. I have.'

It's in the folder I have hidden in my hotel room. The folder where I have detailed information on a terrorist attack that hasn't happened yet. So detailed, in fact, that it looks like I'm part of it. Perhaps even chief orchestrator.

Shaw went on. 'You feeling well enough for a drive? I thought I'd give you a ride home, you can show me your ticket.'

'Great'.

11:54PM

A cool breeze whispered through the trees as he crossed from the hospital entrance to the black and white that was waiting for him. Shaw moved quickly and silently, and Ray struggled to keep up. Running was out of the question. Now *thinking* about walking hurt, let alone the act of walking itself. Running was a distant dream. He'd just have to take the ride from the cop, get back to the motel, do whatever he could from being arrested. He'd made too many waves, drawn too much attention. If he got out of this, his focus would be on seeing Pop, rescuing whatever he could from his relationship with Kat, and saving Manny. His eyes ached and he wasn't sure if it was from the beating or from the flu which had been tightening its grip on him all week.

GHOSTS OF SEPTEMBER

Shaw reached his car and opened the passenger door for Ray. Ray was surprised he wasn't going in the back, and it must have shown.

'I can trust you,' Shaw said. 'Can't I?'

Ray smiled again hoping that it looked natural. 'Sure.'

He eased himself into the seat with a pained moan, thinking he'd sat too quickly, though it probably wasn't humanly possible to move any slower. He felt like warmed up shit. Shaw moved around the car and slid into his seat, reminding Ray to fasten his seatbelt before they set off.

Ray's hope that the journey would be silent evaporated quickly. Seems Shaw wasn't as trusting as he made out.

'So how long are you staying in the area?'

'Till Tuesday.'

'Why the motel? You're not from around here?'

'New York City, originally. Jersey now.'

'They don't have flights from JFK?'

Shit Ray, can you keep all these strands together?

'I'm planning to visit my old man. I don't see him too often. He lives close by. In Enfield. He prefers the quiet, now.'

'I get that… You can't stay at his place?'

Ray smiled again, sheepishly, staring ahead. Shaw glanced at him.

'We, uh, we don't get along so good.'

'I hear you loud and clear on that one. Me and my old man got our differences.'

Thank Christ. A break.

'I think staying with him would be too much. Small doses, you know?'

'You got that right.'

Shaw fell silent for a moment. Ray stared ahead, awaiting the next question, going over a replay of the dive bar bathroom. The Ringleader escaping. He tensed and his breathing sped with his pulse. He'd never get a better chance. If those guys hadn't come in—

What? You wouldn't have done anything. Your bruises would have different boot prints is all.

Maybe that was true. He couldn't afford any hesitation at Logan. It was a line he'd *have* to cross.

Shaw's next question never came. Instead came a small, satisfied nod. He was happy with his answers. For now.

SUNDAY, SEPTEMBER 9, 2001

THE COP SWUNG OFF THE road onto the driveway, rounded the corner into the lot and slant parked in front of room 11. He turned off the engine and it quietly ticked to itself for a moment. Shaw paused as if readying himself before taking the keys out of the ignition and unfastening his seatbelt. He paused again, then opened the door and stepped out into the lot. Ray watched in the mirror as the young officer came around the back of the car and opened his door.

'Need a hand?'

Ray shook his head and raised himself out of the car. Shaw grabbed his arm and helped him upright without a word. Ray turned to look at Shaw who opened his hand and from it dropped the room key, dangling from the ring on his finger and swinging gently in the breeze. Ray took the keys and stepped towards the door.

Just before he put the key in the lock, Shaw tapped his

shoulder with one hand and reached for his firearm with the other. He pulled the gun from its holster and tapped on the door with his other hand.

He whispered, 'Say, "it's Ray," and step back.'

'It's Ray,' he said in a tone louder than usual.

After a few seconds of silence, Shaw nodded. 'Open up.'

Ray twisted the key and they stepped into the motel room. Ray flicked on the light, and the bulb glowed dimly overhead. Shaw holstered his piece.

'Okay Ray Kennedy, let's see this ticket then we can go our separate ways.'

Ray nodded, then looked at Shaw.

'I hid it. This place don't look too safe.'

The cop glanced at the surroundings, 'Smart move.'

Ray knew the cop was just doing his job, but he could do without this. He was already struggling to keep his eyes open and he wanted to get an early start. The coming twenty-four hours would be busy by any standards. He had to visit Pop, nice and early, that way he could spend a few hours with him before patching things up with Kat, spending time with her so that he could free himself up to somehow save Manny. He had problems. Bruised ribs and an increasingly worse dose of the shit that swept through the office would make it unbearable.

Ray went over to the bed and reached up to the natty painting of sunflowers that hung above it. He took it down and laid it on the bed back-side-up, trying as best he could to act naturally. If Shaw got a hint of something off, this could be curtains and for a moment his head was inside the cloth bag and his nostrils burned with the thick stench of vomit. He removed the back of the painting and took out the folder, placing it next to the picture frame, away from the cop.

The cop asks to see the folder now you're fucked.

But Shaw was eyeing different corners of the room and checking the bathroom. Ray opened the folder, using the gatefold to obscure the contents, and took out his flight tickets. Shaw emerged from the bathroom. 'What's in the folder?'

Ray looked at the sheet of notepaper sitting atop the pile. A drawing of the Twin Towers, damaged and smoking, stared back. He reached below for the second sheet. No pictures, just words. A timeline, leading up to the eleventh. Ray felt sick as he touched it and flashed it at the cop. Long enough to reveal times, but not to read details. Long enough for him to feel uncomfortable. He just hoped it was enough to satisfy the young officer.

'Holiday plans,' he put it back, trying to make it look casual, and grabbed the rest of his cash which now looked like a pittance, 'Spending money.'

'Lemme see that.'

Ray's throat instantly tightened, and air entered his lungs in tiny snatches. Sickness washed through him.

'The money?' Ray said hopefully, thrusting the cash forward.

'The paper.'

Ray swallowed and reached back down for the to-do list. It felt so heavy he could barely lift it.

Shaw grabbed it.

'It's nothing interesting, just a list of stuff I need to do.'

'Get motel… Visit Logan… Buy tickets…'

Ray wanted to reach out and snatch it back. If he read much farther he'd be looking at words like "Ringleader" and "attack". If he took it now, the cop would know he didn't want him reading. All Ray could do was stand there.

'… Check layout… What does that mean? "Check layout"?'

Ray swallowed the saliva in his mouth before replying. Shaw was staring.

'I don't fly often. I like to know where the gate is, check in desk. Stuff like that. Reduce the stress.'

The cop nodded and glanced back at the sheet and continued reading. It took all Ray had to stay conscious. Shaw nodded and gave Ray the paper back.

'Tickets?'

Ray hid the list before handing them over.

Shaw inspected them, again reading aloud. 'Ray Madison.' He looked up at Ray, eyes staring.

Was this it? Was this the moment it all crashed down around him?

'Sorry. I panicked back there at the hospital.'

Shaw just stared.

'I don't have much to do with the cops.' Ray said.

Shaw reached around his back to where he kept his cuffs and Ray's stomach dropped. A lunge at the cop and

GHOSTS OF SEPTEMBER

he might be able to reach him before he can grab his gun.

And you'll have to grab it. What then? He knows your name already. Are you going to shoot a police officer?

When Shaw brought his hand back around, what was in it wasn't the shiny chrome of handcuffs.

Ray's eyes widened. 'My wallet.'

The cop nodded. 'Your wallet, minus the money. But the documents... all there.'

Ray felt his cheeks flush hot with embarrassment and hoped that the cop wouldn't be able to see it in the dim light of the naked bulb.

'I wanted to come here because I knew you were lying to me back at the hospital.'

The paper-thin walls of the room were closing in, his breaths once again became shallow. His heart thumped in his ears.

For Christ's sake Ray, don't. You pass out now and he's in that folder like it's nobody's business.

'You got a phone number? For your dad?' The cop handed his small spiral bound notepad with the pencil thrust in the top.

Ray nodded and scribbled the number and put the pencil back in its wire home.

'So now, if I call this number, and ask for...'

'Mike.'

'Mike Madison, that's who'll answer, and he'll be able to verify your story?'

Ray nodded. 'That's right.'

'Got a cell?'

Ray grabbed his cell from the drawer in the nightstand and passed it to Shaw. Before he was glad he'd left it here, now he thought it would have been better if the Village People back at the dive bar had taken the damned thing. The cop stared at Ray. Ray just looked back, watching his future tumble away before him.

Shaw nodded. 'Good.'

He handed the phone back to Ray.

'A word to the wise. Next time, tell the truth,' he said, placing the notepad back in his pocket, and handing Ray his wallet. 'It's easier to remember.'

'That's it?'

Shaw shrugged. 'The rest of your story seems to check out. Get to bed, get some rest.'

He opened the door to the lot, stopped and turned back.

'I have all of your details, Ray. I'll call this number at a reasonable hour. If I don't speak to Mike Madison, you'll be seeing me again. Either way, I'll be back here on Tuesday afternoon. You'd better be gone.'

Ray nodded. Shaw disappeared outside and closed the door. Ray crossed the room and locked it behind him, before turning back to the bed and collapsing. Now he didn't bother hiding the tickets or the folder. Now he just wanted to sleep. He set an alarm for 8AM before quickly falling into a deep slumber.

GHOSTS OF SEPTEMBER
11:45AM

A car door slammed outside. Ray propped himself up in bed on his elbows and squinted through one eye at the flimsy curtains. His ribs ached and he winced, intensifying the tightness around his swollen eye, but neither of these dominated his pain this morning. It was his headache. Part beating, part hangover, part flu. His eyes ached as he glanced at the radio alarm. His stomach fell away. It was late. Much later than he'd hoped. That ding on the head must have been a beauty.

'Fuck.'

He swung his legs out of the bed and reached up to touch the eye that caused him so much discomfort. Sharp pangs of pain radiated through the tender flesh. He stumbled into the bathroom to check the damage. The light came on harsh and glaring and he flicked it straight off again - it was too much for his head this morning. The bruising of his eye wasn't anything like the shiners he and Pete used to exchange every few months in their playful rough housing, he'd been expecting it to be darker. The swelling and tightness felt worse than it looked. His ribs hurt badly though. Every breath came with a sharpness, and he prayed that the bruising there faded double-quick.

The flu had really jumped up a notch overnight. His eyes ached; his head throbbed. He'd have to find a pharmacy, if they opened on Sundays. Usually, he never bothered with meds, just waited the illness out, but now he couldn't afford not to be at his best. His head was light, his throat sore.

Today he didn't have time to screw around. He had to visit his old man, meet with Kat and fix the smoldering remains of their relationship, and then figure out some way to save Manny. All that and he'd already lost four hours. He got dressed and ready to go.

He held few expectations of his meeting with Pop. They were never big talkers, mostly because they had little in common, besides sports. And Pete. Ray couldn't recall a time they just shot the shit over a cold one. That was something he regretted. Pop would be his first port of call; now he'd only have time to stay for an hour. Then he'd have to say his goodbyes. That gave him pause. This wasn't some see-you-next-week situation. Pop would be dead in a few months. "Goodbye" wasn't going to cut it. Christ. Even if everything did work out at Logan as he hoped, he'd have a handful more meetings with Pop, best-case scenario.

The more time he spent back in 2001, the less he expected best-case scenarios.

Right now, he needed to hit the ground running. He pulled the car keys from his pocket, grateful that the assholes at the bar who'd put him in hospital were only interested in money. Outside, the weather was mild again: Another day of Indian summer. He wondered again who'd taken him to the hospital. It wasn't the Ringleader that's for sure. That would be a twist more than he could take. The car key was already in his hand, as he stepped outside. He stopped dead.

GHOSTS OF SEPTEMBER

'Oh no.'

The parking lot outside the motel was empty.

12:08PM

The empty bell clicked overhead as Ray burst into the stuffy reception. Wheel of Fortune blared from the back room and Ray wasn't surprised to see the scruffy old guy glued to the TV. He rang the reception bell twice. The old boy muttered before turning to see Ray.

'Yuh?' He shouted from the worn armchair.

'Need a taxi.' Ray shouted back.

The old timer turned back to the screen, surveyed what he'd potentially be missing if he got up right now, and decided that the timing was fine. He shuffled into the reception wearing what looked like the same dirty clothes as yesterday, moving at a rate so slow Ray felt it was deliberate. He was tempted to reach over the counter and grab the old guy by the face, pulling at a mask that would reveal Crazy Ol' Father Time. The visual was so strong that it chilled him. He flinched and stepped back.

Without a word to Ray the old man picked up the phone and dialed. Ray waited as the old boy coughed into the receiver before telling whoever had answered that he wanted a taxi. He finally looked up at Ray.

'Where to?'

'Joey's.'

His thick eyebrows raised. 'The bar?'

'That's right.'

'Uh?'

'Yes. The bar.'

He grunted and relayed the info, waited a few seconds and silently put the receiver back into the cradle. He turned and started back into the TV room, just before he reached the doorway he said, 'Half an hour,' without looking back.

'Half an hour?'

'What are ya? Hard o' hearin'?'

'Fuck!'

Ray stepped back into the lot. He sucked a deep breath of fresh air as he stepped outside, before smarting as his ribs forced the air out. He grimaced and treaded the wooden boards back to his room, fighting the shortening breaths and rising heartbeat as he went.

This was it. Old Father Time had beaten him. There was no way he could do everything now. He'd go to Joey's, pick up the rental. On the way he'd ask the cab driver about local pharmacies that might open on Sunday. He'd buy drugs and get to Pop's. That would take him to two-thirty. Maybe 3 o'clock. There he'd stay an hour, before heading back to New York to meet Kat and straightening everything out with her. He'd be there for 8, if he drove fast. There he had a problem. He had to figure out how to tell the girl he's just committed to putting above all else that he had to leave. Leave to meet the best friend that caused so much friction between them. Once he'd done that, he had to come up with a plan to make sure Manny didn't go to work tomorrow morning.

GHOSTS OF SEPTEMBER

This was how it was going to be. Right up until it happened, it was going to be against the clock. After the business with the cop last night where he'd come so close to blowing the whole thing, more doubts fogged his thoughts than ever. Now he just wanted to call the FBI and be done with the whole thing.

Just call them. Tell them about Logan. Four or five Middle Eastern men with box cutters. The Towers. Everything. Tell them and be done with it. Get your own house in order.

Back in his room he turned on the radio. The habit of listening for news of the attacks was one he'd be happy to see the back of. Before any of that other shit on today's to-do list, he had to make a decision on the folder. Whether or not he did call the Feds, this was the one thing that could get him put away. For that reason, he'd normally be against taking it with him, but after last night and the business with the cop, he had second thoughts. If he left it here and the cop decided to drop in for some reason…

The pitiful pile of cash he had left sat atop the notes. It wasn't much, but at least he wasn't in the position where he had to beg from Pop. The last thing he wanted today was for it to look like he had ulterior motives. This was purely a social visit. This was about Pop. He didn't want his old man reading anything else into this.

His cell phone buzzed. He picked it up and saw that there were 3 missed calls and one text message. The missed calls were all from Kat. He checked the message. That too was her.

>*Are we still on for tonight? xx<*

'Fuck.'

So much for cancelling with her and meeting Manny. He typed out a reply.

>*Of course! Can't wait! See you at 8. X<* and hit send.

He took half of the cash, enough to buy meds, pay for the cab, and have enough left over for emergencies. He stared at the folder. It was decision time: Hide it in another place or take the bastard thing with him. Fucking nosey cop. Leaving it here was risky, taking it with him was a big mistake. But that was a chance he'd have to take.

1:19PM

The cab driver pulled to a stop and Ray paid up. He was almost sixty, a black guy with a friendly face that reminded Ray a little of Charlie. He wasn't so talkative, perhaps freaked out by Ray's black-and-blue appearance, but he had been able to tell Ray where he could get cold and flu meds. Joey's was barely recognizable in broad daylight. A sad, squat building bereft of any rough-diamond charm it might have held the night before and Ray wondered how many folks had met someone in the dim light of that same bar and got a shock the next morning in the cold, cruel light of day; looking at Joey's now, he knew how they felt. He stepped out making sure he was clutching the folder (no more mistakes today) and left the guy counting his fare.

The rental car was still there, at least, sitting lonely in

the back of the lot. Relief coursed through him to see the car unmarked. Windshield intact, headlights unbroken. But something was wrong. He hurried across the glass strewn carpark, noticing tufts of grass sporadically sprouting through the tarmac. He strode past the low building of the bar, shattered glass and small stones crunching underfoot, and noticed that the bar wasn't open yet, or at least if it was, nobody had found their way to the jukebox. As he got closer, he noticed the car sitting lower than usual. His voice came out in a whine. 'No, no, please God no.' He went straight for the nearest tire. 'Fuck!'

There was a long gash along the flat edge that hugged the floor. He turned quickly for the cab, just in time to see it pull away. He ran after it, shouting, but it was no good.

He marched back to the car. The other tires too were slashed. No fucking way he could drive it like this, and it would take at least an hour to get to Pop's place on four inflated wheels. He checked his watch, his heart thumping against his aching ribs and, from somewhere behind him, the shrill crashing of glass upon glass resounded. The rat-faced bartender from the night before was emptying bottles into bins.

'Hey!'

The barman turned and his face drained to a shade paler when he saw Ray. He tried to turn and head back into the bar. Ray hurried over, dropping the folder to the tarmac.

'Hey! Don't walk away from me.'

The guy stopped and turned. Ray got closer and saw

that in the broad light of day this guy was even uglier than he'd first thought. The guy slumped with a lack of confidence that upset Ray. This guy looked to Ray like he had less confidence than his 2018 self. Ray felt a pang of sympathy as he tried to imagine what it was like to live like he was living, embarrassed, low, lonely.

'You. You know what happened to me don't you?'

The guy said nothing. Just shook his head. Ray could tell that this guy was afraid of him. Scared that if he said the wrong thing, he be on the receiving end of a beating himself. Ray never looked like the intimidating type, but with the bruises and scruffy appearance, he could pass for crazy.

'You told those assholes I was carrying a lot of money. What was your cut? Twenty percent?'

He shifted uneasily, looking at his own feet. Ray took a step towards him, like he might rush the guy.

He shrank back and spat the words out in a panic. 'Ten! Ten! It was ten!'

'Ten percent. I hope it was worth it, you piece of shit. They cut my fucking tires too, you know. Now I'm fucked.'

'I can call you a cab.'

'A fucking cab! It'll cost me every penny I've got.'

He mumbled something under his breath. Ray took a step closer.

'What did you say?'

'I said I stopped them.'

Ray grabbed a handful of his shirt, 'You *stopped* them? Look at my fucking face.'

GHOSTS OF SEPTEMBER

Finally he looked up, small eyes watery with tears, 'Yeah. They were going too far. So…'

'You. It was you who took me to the hospital?'

He looked away again. 'I'm sorry.'

Christ, the poor bastard was even a lousy crook. Ray let him go and felt the weight shift as he lowered his heels to the ground.

'Why? Why did you help me?'

'I dunno. I felt bad I guess.'

'Well, I'm still screwed, and you still owe me.'

'I can call a cab I said.'

'And my fucking tires?' Nothing. 'Huh? I gotta be in New York City at eight.'

'I know a guy,' he blurted. 'Owes me a favor. My cousin. But he won't be able to do it today. Tomorrow maybe.'

Christ. He felt the threads unravelling as he wasted time arguing with the little rat who'd screwed him over. The whole day was fucked. Tension pulsed in his arms. He rushed forward and grabbed the barman, smashing him to the floor. He curled his good hand into a fist and brought it down on the runt's face.

'You fucked my whole day. My whole life.'

He brought his fist down hard again and again. The rat begging for forgiveness. Ray stopped, chest heaving. He stood, dragging the bartender up with him, and threw him backwards into the stack of crates which leaned impossibly before falling completely, bottles crashing to the floor.

'How did you get me to the hospital? Do you drive?'

He looked back at Ray and wiped his bloodied nose, 'I used your car. That's probably the only reason you still have the keys.'

'Then how the fuck did you get the car back?'

'Huh?'

'I said, if I still have the keys, how did you get the car back here, ya fuckin moron?'

'Okay, Okay. I used my car.'

'So where is it now?'

'I can't give you a ride. I gotta open the bar for Joey. He'll be by later an' if it's closed, I'm fucked. You ain't the only one with problems you know?' He was shouting, his voice high and nasal.

Ray believed him. He nodded.

The guy looked at Ray. 'I'll call you the cab. I'll give you the money for it. The ten percent. You wanna wait inside?'

Ray thought twice about trusting this guy. He seemed on the level now there were no meatheads around, that's usually how these guys operated, he thought. But a tiny alarm bell was still ringing in the back of his mind.

'I want to make sure you don't call your asshole friends.'

The guy nodded and shuffled inside. Ray went back to pick up the folder and followed the guy into the bar.

Joey's in the daytime looked grim. Tiny windows let in minimal light and without the neon glow the place just looked sad and his mind drifted to Kat and their accidental meeting at Yankee Stadium, seeing her minus her glow.

'Want anything? A drink or something.'

Ray shook his head. 'Just a cab.'

Ray eavesdropped on the phone conversation the guy was having. If this prick was calling his buddies, Ray would put his sympathies aside and hand out another beating without a second thought. Not that he wanted to. The scuffle outside was the first time he'd raised his hands in anger since high school. It was a feeling he cared little for. After a moment he decided that the call was just to a cab company. It came as a relief.

The skinny bartender hung up the phone. 'It'll be fifteen minutes.' The guy wandered over to the register and reached underneath. Ray wondered if the next thing he saw would be a gun.

'Here.' He handed Ray a roll of tens. Fifty bucks. 'I'll get your tires fixed too.'

He hoped that part was true. What he really expected was to come back tomorrow to either find the car smashed to pieces or gone altogether. If that did turn out to be the case, he'd be relying on skills he hadn't used in a lifetime. Pete's friend Liam Whitney had taught them how to hotwire a car when Ray was fourteen years old. He wondered if he'd still be able to do it and thought that, if pressed, yes, he could. Though he'd much prefer not to.

'What happened? Last night.'

The barman shrank back a little.

'Your pals beat the shit out of me and then what?'

He wiped his nose across his sleeve and checked to see if it was blood. It wasn't. 'Everybody heard the fight and scrambled. I just closed the place up. I dropped you at the hospital when I saw what they'd done.'

'What about the Arabs?'

His pronounced brow drew down over his eyes.

'There were five guys. Foreign. They came in just before...' Ray pointed at the bruising around his eye.

He shrugged. 'I don't know if they were Arabs, but I came out from the john and everyone was gone.'

'What's your name?'

'Corey.'

'Corey, does that TV work?' Ray pointed to the TV suspended over the register. It was small and too high to watch unless you were sitting at the bar. Joey's was not a sports venue.

Corey nodded. He turned it on. 'What station?'

'News. Doesn't matter which.'

'Takes a second for the tube to warm up.'

Corey turned on the TV and started putting clean glasses on shelves. By now Ray was 99% sure that whatever was going to happen was coming on Tuesday but keeping his eyes and ears to the ground via the news was a new habit he'd find hard to break until this was all over. Every time he was at this stage, after clicking the TV on – before the picture came, he expected the worst. The sickening feelings of the day flooding back. But when the tube finally warmed up, the pictures were of Venus Williams. She had beaten her sister in the US Open final.

GHOSTS OF SEPTEMBER

'How long you been running your little side business on outsiders, Corey?'

Corey stopped stacking the shelves and without looking at Ray said, 'I said I was sorry. I gave you the money. You beat the shit out of me. Maybe it'd be better if you waited outside for your cab.' He waited for a reply before carrying on with his job.

Ray had become the bully. Probably everybody Corey knew was a bully. 'You're right. But you did leave me in deep shit.'

Corey turned, 'Look, I feel bad mister, I really do. I fucked up. I'll speak to my cousin, see if he can take care of your car today. I don't know what else to say.'

Ray nodded and the barman shuffled back to the bar, shoulders slumped, head down. Ray almost felt sorry for him. Then he remembered his plans, as bruised and battered as he was the night before, and his sympathies shifted back to himself. He checked his watch. He didn't like how quickly today was going. Not one bit.

2:43PM

The cab snaked around the winding roads that led to Pop's place, nerves twisting Ray's stomach as it went. It wasn't just that he was meeting Pop, as if that weren't enough. It was his plan for the night. Getting back to New York for 8 o'clock now would be almost impossible. Kat would be so pissed. He'd still have to figure out a way to save Manny.

He glanced down at his hands. One bandaged, tightly gripping the folder, the other balled into a fist, knuckles bruised from beating Corey.

Even if he didn't have so much shit going on, meeting Pop was usually a tense affair. It was ridiculous that he'd be so nervous visiting his own father. As he neared the house, he felt his defenses going up, one by one. In preparation for the cheap digs, the snide remarks. That was the worst part. Outside of the dreams, Pop was never open in his criticism. It was never "Why can't you be more like your brother?" It was masked beneath a loaded question. "How is the courier life treating you?" or a snarky comment, "Pete was always the athletic one."

He sneezed, violent and wet, managing to catch it in the crook of his elbow, and drawing a "Gawd bless you" from the near silent cabbie. He thanked him and peered into the bag of meds they'd picked up en-route. The contents of this bag and the cab ride were going to break him financially. He'd bought a bottle of water to wash down as much medication as possible, the headache was now a manageable throb, and the congestion was gone completely. It was easy to take breathing for granted.

The taxi drew to a halt in a pleasant leafy suburb. Plush lawns and picket fences. It had been over twenty years since he'd come here and now it felt smaller. Whether that was because he'd grown, or if he was comparing it to New York, he didn't know. Likely a combination of the two. Now it didn't matter. It was early afternoon but now things had a sort of inevitability to them. Whatever was coming was unstoppable. An iceberg on the horizon and nobody in the crow's nest. No, not nobody. *Him.* He'd never felt so small or insignificant.

The cabbie took the crumpled notes Corey had given to him and he stepped into the street, amazed at how quiet it was. No sirens, no constant hum of traffic. It was a quiet so complete it was almost spooky. The second hand of his watch forged relentlessly onward, he could only stop and admire its ability to keep going before heading up the drive. It was a little after a quarter to three in the afternoon and he still had to meet Kat, and of course there was the whole Manny situation. He'd have to hit the road by 4. A little over an hour was the most he'd be able to stay. *Jesus. A fucking hour.* That sounded terrible. It was the last time he was going to see his father alive, and all he could afford him was one lousy hour? They'd never had a close relationship, but sixty minutes?

At least it'll be easier to stay civilized.

His stride became a shuffle as he got closer to the door, and somebody watching might think they were looking at a reverse of Charles Darwin's evolution of man. He raised his hand to knock and held it there. The one hour he'd sacrifice brought home how quickly time was moving. He looked down at the folder, and it made him feel sick. Time was going way too quickly.

This is it Raymond. The last time you're going to see him. Try to be nice. No, not nice. Civilized. *Don't let his last memory of you be a bad one. Ignore the comments about*

MARC W SHAKO

Pete.

He knocked and waited. His mouth had never been drier, his stomach lurching that hangover washing machine feel. The desire to be here with Pop for the last time was equaled by his desire to be elsewhere. The urge to turn and run was overwhelming. What if it descended into the usual shouting match? No memory at all would be better than a bad one. The sound of a key turning inside the door came.

Too late.

He forced a smile as the gap in the door widened and Pop's face appeared.

'You missed the first half, damned Colts…' his voice tailed off when he looked up. 'Jesus, Ray. What the hell happened?'

'Ah, nothing Pop. I got in a fight is all.'

He waved him inside, 'Come on in.'

He led Ray into the living room, his limp worse than Ray remembered. Like the house, the living room was smaller than he recalled, but every other aspect remained identical. Touches of mom's decorative style shone through. After all this time, Pop still held on.

'Take a seat, kid. Can I get you a beer?'

After last night, even though his hangover wasn't a killer, Ray didn't feel like beer. The bunged-up feeling in his head had worsened since yesterday, and he wouldn't enjoy the beer even if he had one.

'Can I just have coffee? I don't feel so good.' He raised the bag of meds to add credence to his story.

Ray watched as the enthusiasm drained from Pop's

face. He recovered in less than a second, but Ray had seen it all the same.

'I bought 'em special, but… Coffee. Sure.'

'I have a pretty bad cold, you know…' His voice trailed off.

Pop nodded, then forced a wan smile. 'Sure. Beer doesn't taste so good when you feel like that.'

He disappeared into the kitchen and Ray felt his face redden. He'd just stepped through the door and he'd already managed to disappoint Pop. *Do not fuck this up, Ray.*

He put the folder down beside the armchair and leaned the bag of meds against it. Nausea flushed through him. That damned folder. If Pop could see what was inside that thing… He checked his watch.

Fifty-three minutes.

Pop came back in and pointed at the TV. 'Damned Colts are up 31-14 at halftime.'

Ray wanted to say he wouldn't have time to watch till the end but thought better of it. Try not to kill the afternoon before it's even started. On the TV the commentators were going through the key plays of the first half, saying how well it had started for the Jets with Coles' touchdown before the Colts came into life.

Pop limped back into the room, carefully carrying two cups of coffee.

'You're not having a beer?'

Pop lowered himself into his armchair and without looking said, 'Not if you're not having one.' He turned to

Ray. 'What was this fight?'

'Ah it was nothing, Pop.'

'Really? 'Cause a cop called here this morning.'

Ray's grip on the handle of the mug relaxed. He jarred his arm forward to address the spilling liquid and felt a pang of pain snatch all the air from him.

'A cop?'

'That's right. Are you in some kind of trouble, son?'

Tell him. Tell him everything.

No. He'll tell me to stay out of it. To call the Feds.

So call the fucking Feds. Is it so wrong to take care of your own shit? Deal with your problems. This is too much for you. Just tell him.

Ray looked up and for the first time in his life saw concern in the lines of Pop's face. He was only fifty-five, but he looked old and fragile, the result of a life of struggle, and Pop's own ticking clock became obvious now.

'It's nothing Pop. I just went to a bar in the wrong side of town. Got mugged. Two guys jumped me in the men's room is all.'

Pop shook his head, 'Christ. You know, I don't know what this world is coming to.'

Ray's eyes were drawn down toward the folder.

You don't know the half of it.

When it did happen the first time around, he remembered the effect if had on Pop, and he was sure it helped hurry the process of his dad's death along.

'They slashed the tires on my car too. That's why I had to take a cab.'

GHOSTS OF SEPTEMBER

Pop's mouth dropped into the shape of a small *o*. 'Raymond, it must have cost you a small fortune. You feel terrible. You look awful. You should have postponed.'

'No.' Ray snapped. He calmed himself, 'It's fine Pop. I wanted to see you.'

Pop smiled as if he were taken aback by the sentiment. Ray had never expressed anything like that to his father.

'I'm glad you came.'

Ray wanted to move the conversation on, fast. 'How's your leg doin?'

He cringed a little inside. Pop's old war wound, something he didn't like to talk about. More the circumstances of the injury, than the wound itself. He always changed the subject quickly whenever it was brought up. The leg had forced him to quit the military. Stopped him from working. Stopped him from doing a lot of things. He could still drive, and that was something. Pop loved to drive.

'It's playing up a little,' he offered. 'Maybe we're finally gonna get some rain.'

Ray nodded.

'Anyway. Enough about my dumb leg. What about you?' Pop looked concerned.

'I know I look like crap, but I'm fine, I promise.'

His mind drifted to the folder. The plane tickets. The plans. Tuesday. He felt sick again.

Pop nodded. Ray turned to the TV. He felt the tears coming. Whatever had gone between them, the man was his father, and he was going to miss him. Pete was Pop's favorite, that was for sure, but Ray had thought about it a lot. Pete would have been his favorite too. Especially after Pop injured his leg: he lived vicariously through Pete's sporting achievements. Pete was the better scholar too. When the car accident took Pete, he was on his way to meet his friends. A celebration of the exam results that were to take him to Syracuse, where he'd no doubt become their hero quarterback. Ray couldn't live up to that. He was the journeyman. Pete was a superstar. When Pete died, all Pop was left with was the disappointment.

They chatted about the game, and even shared a joke. The coffee was good and the more he drank, the better he felt. (Pop always made better coffee than Mom did.) Ray checked the time and when he saw that thirty minutes had already passed, a heavy sadness clouded over him. He still had to meet Kat and save Manny.

'You got somewhere you gotta be?' Pop asked.

'No. Why?'

'You haven't stopped checking that damn watch of yours. You're making me nervous.' He smiled.

Ray smiled too. They were actually getting along. Maybe it was because he was the only link Pop had left to Pete.

That was a mean thought. Just enjoy it. Don't fuck this up.

'Listen Ray.'

"Ray" now?

'I want you to take some money.'

'What? No. I couldn't.'

GHOSTS OF SEPTEMBER

'You said those guys cleaned you out. You had to take a cab to get here—'

'It's fine.'

'Ah!' he barked, finger raised into the air, the way he always did to signal that the discussion was closed. 'So you'll borrow it. Pay it back whenever you can.'

'You don't need to.'

'You'll take my car too.' As if it were already a foregone conclusion.

'No, I couldn't.' He thought about his own car, abandoned in the lot at Logan.

'So long as you bring it back without a scratch.'

'Pop.' Ray said pleadingly.

'End of discussion.'

End of discussion. Since he'd arrived here, an awful thought crept into Ray's mind and as much as he tried to dismiss it, it kept creeping back in. *What if all those times where Pop was being an asshole about Pete and you being a failure, weren't Pop at all? What if they were you being defensive about your own failures? Your own shortcomings. God knew there were enough of them. What if Pop wasn't the monster after all. Maybe it was you Ray, you fucking screw-up. Guy gives you his car and his money. Why? To make you feel like shit about not being able to provide for yourself? What the fuck kind of twisted logic is that?*

Ray's phone buzzed. Another text message from Kat.
>Can't wait for tonight. I love you x <

MARC W SHAKO

Four hours till he was due to meet her. Ray fixed things with her, and that was it – happy for life. No pressure. Sure it wasn't always going to be sunshine and rainbows, he wasn't a total idiot. But that feeling that however shitty your day is, there's someone waiting for you at home. That was something sorely lacking in 2018.

'Is that that girl of yours?'

Ray looked up, 'How did you know?'

Pop smiled. 'Stupid grin all over your face.'

Ray threw his head back and laughed. Pop too. Pop went back to watching the game. The Colts were up 38-17, and it was another game all about Peyton Manning. Ray glanced across at Pop. The clock on the phone said that he had fifteen minutes left with him. Fifteen minutes, then Pop would be alone. Ray would leave him, just like Pete had. Like Mom had. But they'd already gone. Ray was the one who'd be leaving him alone. Alone to look at reminders of his failed marriage to an alcoholic wife, and two kids who'd left him.

The Jets had crept up to the 18-yard line, and Vinnie Testaverde threw to Richie Anderson, who got as far as the 6.

'Pete had an arm like that.' Ray said, unsure of where it came from. He was worried that it might sound like a lame attempt to curry favor, but he needn't have worried.

Pop smiled to himself. A sad, regretful smile. 'Yeah he did.'

The Jets gained another yard before Richie Anderson made it over the line and the crowd went nuts. Just a

GHOSTS OF SEPTEMBER

consolation, but Pop and Ray got swept up in it too. Pop was on his feet. Ray looked down to see that he'd been playing with his keys. Something he always did when he watched football. He turned the keys over and stroked the rabbit's foot and before he knew it, he was back there.

The gentle breeze caressed his face as Pop watered the lawn, the lawn in their old place back in East Hanover. Pete glanced over as he opened his car door, a strange look on his face. Instead of climbing into the car, he lowered his foot back to the road and closed the door and jogged over to where he stood. He fumbled at his keys and thrust his hand out, closed, palm facing down, and Ray held his own hand underneath. Pete opened his hand and Ray felt something small, soft, light, drop into his palm.

Ray looked up, surprised. 'I can't.'

Pete just smiled, but it never reached his eyes and Ray wondered if it was part of the memory or reality. 'Sure you can, baby brother. I hope it brings you more luck than it did me.'

And the feeling of confusion came back at the strange statement from the guy who had the world at his feet. Ray watched as his big brother, his hero, jogged back to the car, light catching the flowing material of his Jets shirt. And Pete looked across from the driver's seat but this time he didn't smile. Not this time.

'I still miss him, Dad.'

Pop turned and smiled, his eyes damp with tears. 'Me too, son.'

In that single moment his father looked sadder and smaller and lonelier than he'd ever seen him before. And he was going to leave him like this. He'd never see him again. Tuesday would be Tuesday. If it didn't happen sooner. And whatever happened to Ray, he knew in his gut that he wouldn't spend any more time in 2001. That would be it.

'I love you, Dad.'

Pop was trying more than ever to control himself, and for a minute he just stared at the TV in silence.

'I love you too, son.'

Ray glanced down at his watch.

Five minutes. Then he'd have to leave.

Pop stood and lifted his empty mug. 'How about more coffee?'

Ray thought about Kat and their date. Their future. It was clear to him now that their breakup had done almost as much damage to him as Manny's death, and he instantly felt sick and cowardly and selfish at the thought. Kat was the Yin to his Yang all right. That would have been it, he was sure. But when he glanced up at Pop, a thought entered his head that scared him. He could postpone.

No, Ray. You can't.

He could kiss goodbye to any future with her. She'd probably end it on the spot. It would be a bridge too far. She would be so disappointed. Crushed.

She'd be alive, *Ray.*

Pop repeated his question. 'Ray? Coffee?'

GHOSTS OF SEPTEMBER

Ray smiled at his father, 'How about a beer?'

Pop smiled back, 'One. Only one. You're borrowing my goddam car.'

They both laughed.

Ray stood and headed to the bathroom. 'I gotta go make a phone call.'

4:24PM

Like the rest of the house, the bathroom at Pop's place now felt too small for him, but he still managed to find room to pace. Kat's phone was ringing in his ear, while he played over in his mind what he was going to say. He was flipping a mental coin to see if he should tell her the truth, that he doesn't want to leave his old man alone - or lie and say that he's having car trouble. That's when she answered.

'Yeah?'

Inquisitive, not accusatory. Cautious, not hopeful. She was setting herself up for a disappointment and Ray knew it. He knew then that the right move would be the truth.

'I'm at Pop's. My car broke down.' He heard the sigh and what may have been crying but carried on. 'So I won't make it tonight. I'm so sorry, Kat. Kat?' There was nothing but silence at the other end, like time had stopped. 'Honey?'

He heard a deep breath being inhaled at the other end, and he was just about to say that he'd make it up to her, take her someplace really fancy, when she spoke.

'Goodbye, Ray.'

That was all. Even if there was time for him to say anything else before she put the phone down, he couldn't speak. That was that. It was over. He felt a sense of loss that he hadn't felt since…

Maybe it wasn't the end. Maybe he could fix it. It was Old Man Time up to his tricks. Forcing him to say things he didn't want to. Things that he knew were wrong. That was how it was going to be. Walking into Logan Airport on Tuesday morning was a death trap. Whatever he wanted to do, for all his well laid plans and best intentions, something would go horribly, terribly wrong.

'Fuck it.'

He dialed the number for the operator.

'Give me the number for the FBI.'

This is it. Tell them. Tell them everything you know. Focus on your own shit. Tell them, wash your hands of the whole ugly mess and get on with your life.

'Which office?'

'What sorry?'

'Which office would you like to speak to? Boston? New York?'

'Boston. Gimme Boston.'

She went and there was silence and Ray prepared his speech.

Do it fast, like ripping off a Band-Aid. As soon as you hear that voice in the Boston branch office, you speak.

'Hello?'

Without hesitating he launched into it. 'Hello, my name is Ray Madison.'

GHOSTS OF SEPTEMBER

The operator replied. 'I'm connecting you now.'
Shit.
'Thank you,' Ray muttered.

But the operator had already gone, and the phone was already ringing. The tone of the ring lower, shorter. More serious. Now he felt like an idiot.

'Hello, you're through to—'

Ray ended the call.

6:39PM

For the first time in, maybe ever, Ray was enjoying his old man's company. There was no animosity between them. Maybe because Pop wasn't comparing him to Pete every two minutes. Maybe because Ray wasn't on the defensive. For all he knew, this was going to be the last time he saw his old man alive – anything could happen at Logan on Tuesday morning, and that included something he might not walk away from.

The beer didn't taste great. In fact, it didn't taste of much at all, like a bottle of alcoholic soda water. He wasn't sure if it was the illness or mixing his drink with the meds, but his head was in the clouds.

The Jets had lost to the Colts and now, as the game highlights played out on TV his mind drifted back to Thursday morning, when he'd first arrived back in 2001. His ideas that perhaps this was an alternate timeline and that maybe in this time, when the big day rolls around, nothing happens. Nothing at all. Life plays out in the normality of those days before the attacks. Innocent. Carefree.

After everything that had happened so far, today especially, that idea seemed fanciful at best. Idiotic at worst. That was the scenario he wanted to believe more than anything, but he just couldn't bring himself to accept it.

The other possibility he'd entertained was that the attack would happen, but not on the same day. Maybe sooner, maybe later. Again, with an inexplicable sense of knowing, the idea felt wrong; more plausible than the attack not taking place at all, but wrong all the same. If it didn't happen today (he did think it would happen during business hours), then realistically it only left tomorrow. Monday.

It won't be Monday. It will be Tuesday. Like it was the first time.

He'd almost forgotten about the Butterfly Effect entirely. He recalled thinking that as long as he was here in this alternate reality, he had to maintain some sort of status quo that jibed with what had gone before. That one misstep could have dire repercussions, and there were two equally unsavory ideas that accompanied the thought. One, that when he went back to 2018 the new reality he'd created would be unrecognizable. Two, that he didn't go directly back to 2018 and had to live through a terrifying new reality of his own creation.

Now he wanted it to all be a dream. He wanted to wake up, alone, in 2018. Whatever pile of drunken shit his life had become then it would be better than this. He'd tried so hard but since he got here, meeting his father for the last time was more than he could handle. He just hoped that Pop hadn't noticed. His father was already freaked out by him turning up on his doorstep black and blue. All this after he'd got a phone call from a cop. This shouldn't be how their last meeting went.

He felt the tears coming, coughed once, and hurried back to the bathroom.

7:11PM

He'd have to go back out there soon. He'd locked himself away here for fifteen minutes. Pop would get suspicious as to what he was doing. Another room that had barely changed since mom had gone - something which added to the hurt he felt at Pop's loneliness.

The sadness of that idea piled on top of the thought of losing Kat. His heart ached. She'd hung up on him the second she'd heard the doubt in his voice. Old Man Time had beaten him on this one. Forced him to choose between saving his relationship with his father, saving his relationship with his girl, or saving the life of his friend. She deserved better than Ray could offer anyway. Whatever had happened with Kat, he was glad he'd stayed with Pop, but looking at the time, he'd have to go back to New York soon, very soon, or he'd miss the meeting with Manny altogether, and he couldn't allow that to happen.

Pop had been taken aback when Ray said the three words that sons and fathers exchange all too infrequently.

Sure, nobody says it. That's what Ray had always told himself. It's the unspoken. It doesn't *need* to be said. It just hangs there, stinking up the conversation, inviting awkwardness in, shutting playful jibing out. That Pop was forced into stunned silence when Ray blurted it out was testament to that.

They'd shared a beer. Despite Ray's illness stopping him from tasting a single drop, it was the best beer he'd ever had. They'd watched the game and joked and laughed more. Sharing stories of Pete's greatness. Now Ray got it. It had taken seventeen years, but the penny had finally dropped. Pop wasn't trying to make him feel like shit. He was trying to inspire him to greater things. It didn't have to be the NFL. He was just sad that Ray had settled for the first thing that life had offered him. Disappointed that he'd never pushed himself.

His big idea had been to come here and confront Pop about how shitty he'd been as a father. How he felt abandoned and alone after Pete died and Mom hit the bottle. How he'd made Ray feel like shit. How he'd pressured him into becoming his dead brother. Pete was always daddy's boy, Ray mom's. But it didn't feel like that now. Pop was alone after Pete died as much as Ray was. In fact Mom too. It should have united them. Instead it tore them apart. Ray was angered by the insignificance of their differences. He felt another sob rise and tried to stifle it. Tried, and failed.

He flushed the toilet to mask the sounds of his crying and stumbled to the sink to run the water. He turned on the faucet and slumped onto the side of the bath, feeling as

GHOSTS OF SEPTEMBER

small and alone now as he had the day Pete died. His sobs seemed to echo from miles away in the cramped bathroom. He peered up through blurry eyes and at the reminders of his old life staring back at him in the mirror. Pop had kept most of the stuff after Mom left. Ray wondered how it must have felt living every day like this. In a museum. Reminders of your wife every time you look at something small, stupid and insignificant like a bathroom rug, or the antique mirrored cabinet she'd chosen hanging over the sink.

His army pension had given him plenty of money. But he hadn't replaced a stick of furniture. Pop had lived all those years surrounded - *haunted* - by the ghosts of his past. It might have comforted Pop, but Ray didn't really think so. And he was certainly no skinflint. He'd just never replaced anything until it was a necessity. Never remarried. He'd kept everything, like time had frozen, so he'd have plenty of money left to leave behind. Leave behind for Ray who'd go on to piss it all up the wall and live life stuck in his own miserable time capsule. Stuck in *that* week. It was only now that Ray saw the sacrifices his father had made for him. He'd never said it, but now Ray saw it.

Pop really loved him. Ray sank to the cold tile of the bathroom floor and sobbed.

There was a gentle knock on the door.

7:13PM

Pop sat alone staring at the TV, but not watching it. It had been a quarter of an hour since Ray went to the bathroom. Looked like he was crying too. A new game had started on TV, but Pop wasn't paying any sort of real attention. The players blurred into one another. The sound too seemed to fade as Pop became lost in his thoughts. It had been nice to see Ray. For the first time since Peter had died, they seemed to be getting along. The chip was missing from his youngest son's shoulder, though it had probably helped that he hadn't spent every few minutes comparing him to his brother.

He'd been looking forward to this meeting all week. Since he accidentally dialed Ray's number on Friday. But since he'd shown up, eye blacked, hand bandaged, Ray had been acting odd. Overly emotional, even for Ray. Peter was the rough and tumble kind, just like him when he was a kid. Raymond was like his mother. But today Ray had looked distant and whenever he'd glanced over, Ray had a glazed expression. Not even watching the game. Like he was a million miles away, on the verge of tears, with the weight of the world pressing down on him. Ray would never open up to him. But that big thing about saying he loved him? It should make you feel good. Since Peter had gone, to say that Ray acted like he hated him would be an overstatement, but there was definitely a wall between them. When Ray said what he said it should have made him feel *good*, but truth be told, it scared him.

It was the one thing that went unspoken between fathers and sons. The fact was, the longer the afternoon had gone on, even from before Ray said that he loved him, he had the feeling that Ray was saying goodbye. That was

GHOSTS OF SEPTEMBER

something he couldn't accept. He'd already lost one son to suicide.

The toilet flushed and snapped Pop from his contemplation. He rose to his feet and limped as silently as he could down the passage toward the toilet, dragging that fucking right leg behind him. The leg that reminded him every few minutes of the attack that had killed half of his team and left him alive. Alive and guilty. It wasn't his fault. He'd been lucky. Lucky that he'd been too hungover to drive. Lucky that he'd won the coin toss that allowed him to switch seats with his best friend. Not so lucky is when a roadside device blows up the truck in front of you in the convoy. When part of that truck flies through the windscreen and kills the guy sitting next to you who'd only driven because they'd flipped for it. He'd drunk too much the night before and a friend had done him a favor. A favor for which he was now dead.

The sound of running water came from the bathroom but it did little to mask the sound of sobbing. He moved closer to the bathroom. Ray was in some kind of trouble. Big trouble. He'd gotten himself mixed up in something, that was for sure.

He tapped on the door. 'You okay in there, son?'

There was a pause, he thought Ray might have been gathering himself.

'I'll be out in a minute, Pop.'

He'd definitely been crying. He hadn't heard *that* voice since Pete died.

'Okay, son. You want another beer?'

There was another short pause, 'Er, I can't Pop. The car.'

'Right.'

The sound of his adult son crying like that broke his heart. He turned back to the living room to the sound of somebody (from the volume of the crowd cheering he guessed) scoring a TD. He limped back into the living room, feeling as hopeless as a father as he had when the whole family, himself included, spent the weeks after Peter's death crying. If only there were some answers as to why his son was so upset. The way Ray sounded with the big "I love you" thing was how Pete sounded before he killed himself. If only he knew then what he knew now.

Driving like he had, on *that* road, at *those* speeds. No seat belt. It had to be suicide. He put too much pressure on the kid, he saw that now. What with football, and school, and him finding out about the divorce lawyers, and being asked to keep it from his kid brother. It was too much. He'd pushed him too hard. Now he'd done the same to Ray. History repeating itself. If Ray ever found out that his big brother had killed himself it would break him, now he had to find out what was driving his second son the same way.

Pop's eyes fell onto the table beside Ray's armchair. Small and spindly, another choice of Margot's, a half empty beer on top of it, a plain manila folder resting against it.

He seemed very protective of that folder when he came in. Jittery too, stealing a glance over both shoulders as he walked the drive, quickly stepping inside the house; checking the folder was there every two minutes.

GHOSTS OF SEPTEMBER

He picked up the folder.

The sound of running water in the bathroom stopped.

7:15PM

Ray splashed cold water on his face. A knock came at the door.

'You okay in there, son?'

Christ, Pop heard you crying. Pull it together, try to make it sound like it's just the cold.

He said he'd be out soon and that he couldn't have another beer because he was driving. Splashing water on his face gave him a hint of normality, but not enough to lessen the red eyes he'd got from the crying.

The more he thought about what Pop had done, the sacrifices he'd made, the bigger the feeling that he couldn't hide from his own responsibility. When the eleventh came, he had to act. Yes, he'd have to stay away from the Ringleader until then, but when that time did come, he'd have to be prepared to do whatever it took to stop him. That meant killing him if he had to. That meant going to jail, if he had to. Maybe if he killed him and the plot was uncovered, he'd be held up as some kind of hero. He didn't want that. He wasn't a hero. He was a regular guy who had to do what he had to do.

Ray checked his appearance in the mirror of the medicine cabinet his mother had chosen, now not so surprised to see the younger reflection staring back at him, but shocked to see the staring eyes of his older self like a subtle change in the picture of Dorian Gray. He shut off the water and straightened himself out.

As he approached the living room from the hallway, he saw Pop staring into space. Facing the TV but not focused there. He looked old. Older than when he'd left him if that were possible. His complexion had taken on a waxy appearance. Ashen, drawn, shocked. He hadn't even noticed Ray coming back. Ray was worried.

Is this how it had started? Maybe looking like this was a warning of the massive stroke that would strike his old man down in a few months and kill him. Not outright, but it would happen at the worst moment possible, as he took a bath. Another victory for his adversary. Pop would have a stroke and he'd drown. By the time the neighbors figured out anything was wrong, the whole floor of the house would be under two inches of water. Ray felt sick that his own wallowing in self-pity and guilt had meant that he'd never got out to visit Pop, and that he'd died alone. It was fair to say that at this moment in time, more than any other, Ray Madison hated himself.

'You okay Pop?'

There was no answer. Ray stared at his chest, checking for movement. Had it already happened? The stroke had come early and huge. A parting gift from his adversary. Then he saw his father's chest slowly rise and a surge of relief strong enough to buckle his knees came.

'Pop?'

His father looked around, and Ray was struck by the

odd look in his eyes. He couldn't gauge it, but it was far too much like the look he thought he'd seen at Pete's funeral. Pop shook his head and the strangeness left his eyes and they focused.

'I'm just tired. I think I need to lie down.'

That seemed like a lie, or at least the truth wrapped up in one. Ray was going to ask if he wanted water, but Pop spoke first.

'Don't you have a meeting with Manny?'

He didn't even remember telling him about that. 'Well yeah, but I'm worried about you.'

'I'm fine,' he snapped.

Ray was taken aback by the shortness in his voice. 'Pop, if you don't want me to go I can stay a while longer.'

His father sat quietly for a second, his eyes glassy. Pop had heard him crying, and the last time he'd heard him crying was after Pete died. He'd brought back the same feelings for Pop. Ray flushed with anger. Not at himself. At Old Man Time. He was determined that Ray wouldn't repair his relationship with his father. That too much water had passed under that bridge. Things had been going well between them today. Too well, it seemed, and now Ray was going to have to leave with this bad feeling between them.

'I'll be fine Ray. You just go. The money and car keys are on the table.'

The words crushed Ray. He would go. He'd have to go anyway; Manny's life depended on it. But he wasn't going to leave this relationship in the mess it was in.

'I'll get my things.'

Ray collected the bag of meds and the folder, Pop just stared at the TV. He knew that between now and Tuesday, he'd have one last chance to talk to him, when he returned the car. That way he could leave things in a way that meant they wouldn't be at odds when Pop died.

Ray cleared his throat. 'So I'll get going.'

'Yeah, thanks for stopping by.'

Ray nodded. Pop spoke.

'Mind if I don't get up? The leg.'

'Right.' Ray nodded again.

He checked his watch. He really did have to get going. He hugged Pop and left, struck by the emptiness of the embrace. As he closed the door behind him and walked down the drive, he noticed the day was turning to night. The light blue skies of before had a soothing navy hue, and to the everyman, all was right with the world. All was right in a way that it wouldn't seem in a few days. In a few days, when terror would beam through the TV and land in the homes of three hundred million Americans, nothing would seem this "right" again.

To Ray of course, that specter was looming already. As he rounded the corner from his old man's place and walked along to where his car was parked, he didn't bother now to check over his shoulders. Now he cared a little less if he was being followed. Ray got to Pop's car, his ribs aching from the slight exertion of a simple walk from his father's house, unlocked the door, and slid into the driver's seat.

GHOSTS OF SEPTEMBER

His father's world ended a long time ago, and he'd been too selfish to see it. There was the ghost of a chance that he could repair things, to a very limited extent, but now he doubted that Old Man Time would allow it.

7:25PM

All he had done in his life, the one thing he'd got right, was Peter. No, that wasn't true. Before Peter, he'd married Margot. That was the first thing. Done well to land her, too. Emotional, but damn if he wasn't batting numbers well above his average in the looks department. And because of her, they had Peter. He'd had a decent run in the military, before the roadside device that had killed his friend ended his career early; his own sports record was nothing to be ashamed of, but Peter was everything he'd been and more.

Peter was an upgrade on him. Mike Madison mark II. Peter had his physical attributes plus Margot's smarts. Ray was a good kid, but he had too much of his mother in him. Too much of her emotional side. Peter was the one. The quarterback on his way to an NFL career, maybe. No way that kid was going into the military, not if he could help it. Ray was too soft; the military would kill him. Peter could go to college. Like Mike Madison hadn't. But he pushed too hard. Like Margot said he did. Like he *always* did. Gave the kid no room to breathe. Just one thing in a long line of tiny things they argued about. When Margot said she wanted a divorce it didn't surprise him. But it broke Peter. There was more of his mother in Peter than he'd realized. He'd pushed too much, applied too much pressure. All he wanted was for Peter to be better than he was. That, in the end, was what had killed him.

After Peter died, the divorce took a back seat, for a while at least. But the old issues crept back, made worse by Margot's drinking. She'd taken to the bottle not long after the funeral. They both knew they were hanging on until Ray was old enough to make his own way in the world. A friend of a friend got Ray work in a courier company and that was a relief, one less thing to worry about. They left Jersey, toyed with the idea of moving back to the old neighborhood in Queens, but it wasn't the same. Everything changes. For the same money they could get a place here in the peace and quiet. It was good for a short while. Margot had quit the bottle. They argued less. They talked less; truth be told. Then he found his wife was still drinking, just hiding it from him. The old arguments came back, and they split. It wasn't long after Margot left that he got the news of her stomach cancer. He'd told her he wanted to take care of her, and despite the divorce, they'd agreed that she would move back. She was dead within a few months. Ray had hardly visited after that. He was a mother's boy. Margot said he'd pushed Ray away, and, as always, she was right. Now Ray was going the same way as his big brother.

He watched from the window as Ray turned the corner without looking back and hobbled over to his chair. The difference between Ray and Peter was that Ray wasn't happy killing himself. The horror he'd seen in that folder.

GHOSTS OF SEPTEMBER

He wanted to take others with him. He felt nauseated by the idea that he'd go this far. How sick was a mind that could even consider something like that? His mother's irrational side was one thing, but Christ, this? There was no way he could allow it. It would break his heart to do what he was about to do, but his son obviously wasn't playing with a full deck. He had to stop him. He glanced over at the rotary dial telephone, the one which Margot had chosen, and stared at it until outside, the day turned to night.

10:25PM

He tried to put the business with his old man out of his mind for now. One thing at a time. Cocky multitasking had led to the fuck up with Kat, he wasn't about to let that happen again. He would be late for his meeting with Manny, that was for sure, but Manny would wait. His Latino blood meant that he was late for everything anyway. Manny always called Ray racist for saying that and Ray challenged Manny to prove him wrong, which never happened.

Ray didn't want to carry the folder and tickets around with him, so he'd gone back to the motel and stashed them. Tonight, he'd have to go back to his place to sleep. His own bed. For one night it wouldn't be a problem. He hoped. After taking care of business in New York, he'd head back out to the motel, ready for whatever awaited him at Logan Airport. He'd made good time and would arrive at the bar in around an hour. He grabbed his cell and picked out Manny's number and dialed. Manny picked up straight away.

'Where the fuck are you, man? I was just about to leave.'

'Leave? You're there already?'

'You're always busting my balls.'

Of course he's on time tonight.

'Sorry, man. I got held up at Pop's. I'll be there in twenty-five minutes.'

'I can't wait that long. Or did you forget we gotta work in the morning?'

Shit. Manny on time. Giving a fuck about his job. This was not good.

'I need to talk to you…'

A sigh came from the other end of the line.

'It's serious, Manny.'

Like your life depends on it.

Manny sighed again, 'Come on, it's a school night, man. We can't be screwing around…'

'Kat dumped me.' Ray interrupted. 'I could really use the company. And a few beers.'

There was silence. Manny and Kat never got along, now he was supposed to give a fuck they'd broke up?

'Manny?'

'Get here quickly, man. These assholes can't play the jukebox. You wouldn't believe the shit I'm listening to.'

'I love you, man.'

'Fuck you and drive faster.' Ray heard the smile in his friend's voice and cracked a smile of his own.

The call ended and Ray sped up. He had considered

GHOSTS OF SEPTEMBER

keeping exactly to the speed limit. His funds had already dwindled almost to nothing, he needed an injection of cash, not to lose what little he had left in speeding tickets. But he would just avoid those. Bigger fish needed frying.

The closer he got to the meeting with Manny, the more he wondered if he was doing the right thing. Not because of the fear of retribution from Old Man Time, but something else. He thought about the impact the terror attacks had had on him. How they'd transformed him from a naïve twenty-two-year-old who thought that everyone's first instinct was to do good, to a shell-shocked, bitter man, horrified that anyone would want to do something like this to regular everyday people because what? They hated their way of life?

On the days he wasn't beating himself up with guilt over Manny's death, he told himself that maybe when that stolen car sped along that road and killed Manny, that Manny got lucky. He died without the knowledge that the world could be so unfair, so cruel, so brutal. It would kill the part of him that made Manny, Manny. The part that lived in the now. The part that took whatever happened in the past and if he couldn't use it now, to hell with it. The part that would deal with whatever tomorrow threw up when he got to that bridge and not a moment before.

If he did save Manny's life and wasn't able to stop the attack, that would be on his head. Part of Manny would die, that same part of him which had died. That was the defining moment of his life. There was a clear before and after.

Manny would have the same.

'At least he'd have *something*.' Ray said aloud.

He checked his speedometer, checked his mirrors, and pressed the gas pedal to the floor.

10:44PM

The night was dark and foreboding and the streets distinctly empty, but for the distant sound of a bottle smashing. Sounds of laughter and the bass thud of music filtered from the bar. Ray peered through the window, hoping familiar faces would bring some sense of calm. He had to find a way to stop Manny from going to work tomorrow morning and with his constitution, alcohol alone would not be enough. The only thing Manny liked more than beer was sleep. This was not going to be easy.

He shoved the door to the bar open and the sound of *It's My Life* rose. He might live in Jersey, but Manny was no Bon Jovi fan. Ray peered through the darkness and found Manny sitting in the corner, nursing a Bud and looking like he'd lost a twenty and found a nickel. A bunch of students were shooting pool, probably the ones who'd defiled the jukebox. Manny perked up when he saw Ray. Then his face darkened, and he stood up.

'The fuck happened to you?'

'I got here as quick as I could.'

'No. Your face, man.'

Ray reached up and touched the blacked eye he'd forgotten about.

GHOSTS OF SEPTEMBER

'Long story. Lemme get a beer, I'll tell you about it.'

Ray went to the bar, grabbed a Bud, fielding questions about his appearance from Steve the barman, and re-joined Manny at the table.

'Thank Christ you got here. I played some real music, but these assholes played so much crap it still hasn't come on. Can you fucking hear this? This is the best thing they put on all night.'

The bunch of out-of-town students surrounding the pool table were having a great time, at Manny's expense it seemed.

'I didn't know this shit was even on there.' Ray offered sympathetically.

'Well, they found it. They found a *lot*. *My* place will have none of this shit.'

'Thanks for coming, pal.'

'Forget it. What happened to your eye, man?'

'My eye, my ribs. I got jumped, in a bar outside Boston.'

'The fuck were you doing there? I thought you were sick?'

'I am sick. I went up to visit my old man.'

Ray retold his story, careful not to give anything of the plot away, all the while gauging how drunk his friend was. Manny had already started his third beer when Ray arrived. It gave him a good head start but Ray was going to need more. He'd come without a plan. All he knew was that tomorrow, he was going to feel worse than today, and the way

271

his mobility had been limited by the kicking he'd taken, there was no way he'd be able to go to work in place of Manny. As it was, Old Man Time's original 2001 plan stood, which meant that Manny had approximately ten hours to live.

Ray felt dizziness at the mix of cough medicine and beer, but there was no way Manny would let him get away with not drinking. Maybe he could get Manny to take some of his cold meds. That would make it harder for him to wake up in the morning. The way the accident happened, the timing of it, he'd only have to sleep in for an hour. Two, tops. Now all he had to figure out was how to administer it without his friend noticing.

'So what happened with Kat, man?'

'I actually had a good meeting with my old man today.'

Manny didn't push for an answer to his question. Ray continued.

'For the first time since Pete died, we had a conversation. Without disagreeing. We kept to sports, so that made it easier, but still. I realized today I've been too hard on him. He's sacrificed a lot. And he's been through way more shit than I have. I was supposed to meet Kat. It just felt wrong to leave him.'

'Why? You'll have lots of time to meet him. I thought you really liked Kat.'

That was sound logic. How to explain that he knew in a few months his dad would drop dead?

'I dunno. Today, we just had this connection. It felt wrong to leave. Like I was worried I'd break the spell and wouldn't be able to get that moment back. I can't explain it.'

'Listen man, I've been here so long I gotta piss. I broke the seal already.' Manny got up and disappeared to the bathroom.

Monday loomed and Manny was nowhere near drunk enough to sleep in. Manny could go on forever if he wanted to. Ray needed a plan, and fast. The more he tried to think the more his head hurt, and he was so tired he was worried he might fall asleep right there in the booth, however loud Bon Jovi was playing. Manny reappeared and Ray stood before he got back to the table.

'Let's get out of here. The music still sucks.'

Manny shrugged, as the song started to fade.

'Wait.'

The new song started. Mariah Carey singing with some boy band or other. Sounded to Ray like he wasn't the only one going through a breakup tonight.

'Okay. Fuck this,' Manny said.

They waved to Steve the barman and left, the students wailing along to the music as they went. Manny looked like he could call it a night any second. Ray needed to keep things going, until inspiration hit.

'Let's have more drinks.'

'You sure, man? You don't look so hot.'

Ray felt like shit, even if it was his twenty-two-year-old body dealing with the illness, the bruising, and the sickening mixture of cold meds and beer.

'I'm fine. I just don't want to stop yet.'

Manny shrugged an agreement. He'd have known that Ray was upset. What he didn't know was that Ray wasn't upset because he'd had a meeting with his dad, or that the girl he loved dumped him. He was upset because the poor bastard in front of him was sitting on a time bomb and had no idea. That was what weighed heaviest on Ray's mind right now.

Manny smiled, 'Let's go to my place.'

They agreed and set off.

.

MONDAY, SEPTEMBER 10, 2001

12:26AM

MANNY AND RAY SAT IN the front room of Manny's tiny apartment, both slumped into the sunken sofa staring at late night TV. The highlights of the Giants and Broncos game played out. He knew the result before the game ended and it only occurred to Ray now that he could have gambled his way to a bit of extra cash. *Too late now.* He stared into the half glass of Jim Beam that Manny had poured before taking a mouthful. It felt nice to be drinking half decent bourbon after the shit he'd slowly poisoned himself with the past few years. They'd sunk a couple while the game was on and Ray had spent the first half hour whining to Manny about Pop and Kat and just as long after in silence. Now he didn't want to talk.

Manny finished another drink. 'You okay, man? You're really quiet. Even for you.'

Ray snapped from his trance. 'Yeah, I'll be fine. Can I use your bathroom?'

Manny laughed at him for even asking and Ray staggered in and flicked the lights on. It was as dirty as his own place had become in 2018, and Ray felt bad for Manny. Not that Manny gave a fuck, but it was a sorry sight. Back in 2001, he hadn't really noticed too much. The place was dirtier than his, but to his young, idiot self it seemed unimportant. Now his late-thirties sensibilities kicked in and he pitied his friend for living like this.

He peed, toying with the idea of vomiting – the mix of cough syrup and bourbon a dizzying cocktail that his body would be better without. He jabbed his fingers down his throat and flinched as the foul mixture came back up. If he could somehow convince Manny to take a spoonful of the medicine it would help a whole bunch. It would guarantee that he'd miss the start of his shift; if he went to work just with a hangover, it would be more likely that he'd get into an accident. *Christ, Ray. Cough medicine? Is that the best you got?*

This was not going well. He was doing more harm now than he had the first time around. Even if Manny did sleep through his alarm, Tony would call and bust his balls. Manny would wake up, rush to work, and Old Man Time would make sure that the bastards out joyriding were waiting. In his bones, he just knew it. An extra hour asleep

GHOSTS OF SEPTEMBER

wasn't going to be enough. Ray was just about to leave the bathroom when, in his pocket, he felt a buzz.

A text message. His heart filled with hope and beat a little faster. Maybe it wasn't too late for him to fix things with Kat. He opened the message. It was from Manny.

'You fall in?'

Ray's heart sank. Typical Manny. He smiled to himself and typed a reply suggesting that Manny fuck himself and pressed send.

Insufficient credit.

Pay and go. He'd been using the phone and forgot that it wasn't on a contract. He left the bathroom and paced down the hallway, now noting how similar it was to his apartment in 2018.

'Manny, I need to borrow your cell.'

Manny held the phone up without even looking. Ray grabbed it and wrote an apology:

>*Sorry about before. I'd like the chance to explain, but if you don't want to hear it, I understand. I hope you can forgive me. Ray. x*<

He typed Kat's number into the phone and sent.

'I need to get to bed, man. You want to crash here?'

Ray would need to crash somewhere; he'd drunk too much to drive to his motel. He'd need to get there later today; the folder and his flight tickets were stashed there. His plan had been to sleep at his place, in his own bed. It should be okay, for a few hours. Then, he could pick up his car (*Pop's car*) and get what was left of his plan back on track.

Logan.

A shiver passed through him.

'Could I? I'll leave early, I sleep like shit these days anyway.'

'I'll be up at seven.'

Ray raised his eyebrows. 'You? Up at seven?'

'My alarm goes off at seven, I'll be up at about eight,' Manny smiled.

'I'll be gone before then.' Ray said.

He pulled the cough syrup from his pocket and poured a capful.

'Want some of this? Help you sleep...' Ray said hopefully.

Manny laughed. 'If there's one thing I don't need, it's help sleeping.'

Shit.

Manny reached down to grab his cell from the table.

'Er, you mind if I keep that? Just for now.'

'You waiting for her to reply?'

Ray was surprised.

'Come on, man. Who else are you going to send messages at this hour?'

'I'm that transparent?'

That is why, but there's another reason. I need you to sleep in so—

'It's okay. Keep it for tonight. I can set my other alarm.'

'Other alarm?'

Jesus.

'I got a radio. I like to listen to Howard Stern in the

morning.'

'Me too,' Ray lied.

Manny disappeared into the hallway. 'See you tomorrow.'

Tomorrow.

If Ray hadn't thrown up a few minutes ago, he might have done now.

Manny's head disappeared back into the short hallway and Ray heard a shout, 'Night.'

'Goodnight, Manny.'

Now, Ray had to wait.

1:08AM

Manny was wasted. He'd sunk enough booze to sleep more than six hours. Ray had his phone, which meant that Tony couldn't call him and wake him up. Because he was such a heavy sleeper, Manny would set his radio alarm, so all Ray had to do was wait for Manny to fall asleep and turn the alarm off. His best friend was drunk enough he'd sleep nine, ten hours, if he went undisturbed. Cancel the alarm, that should do it.

It was after 1am now. Which meant it was already Monday. There were just over thirty hours, and all hell would break lose. He thought about the airport. If he had to, he'd kill the Ringleader where he stood. That was a last resort, but if it had to be done, now he felt that he could do it – Christ, he *had* to. If Ray saw him at Logan on the morning of the eleventh, it confirmed his guilt. It wouldn't be killing an innocent man.

He could do it.

Ray's contemplation was broken by a deep, ragged snoring from down the hall. This was it. It was time. He slipped Manny's phone into his pocket; that would be coming with him when he went.

He crept into the hall, leaving the dim lamplight of the living room behind. He tried to step in time with those deep snores. The door to Manny's room was slightly ajar, the darkness inside softly diluted by the green glow of the digital radio alarm. He reached the door, amazed that the hallway hadn't produced a single creak all the way along. He placed his bandaged hand on the door and pushed.

The slice of gentle living room light widened into a wedge big enough to fit a man, revealing clothes scattered about the floor. The edge of the bed was directly in line with the door, but the radio alarm was on the opposite side. He followed the wedge of light into Manny's dark bedroom, all the while timing steps with snores, until he reached the end of the bed. Manny was facing the near wall, a thin sheet draped over his large frame, with the radio alarm behind him. Ray just had to hope he stayed facing that way. He edged along the end of the bed, to the side where the radio alarm glowed.

Manny stirred. Ray froze.

Manny groaned and rolled over. Ray's heart thudded in his chest. Motionless, he waited, afraid to move in case he made a sound, until the silence was again broken by reassuring snores. Ray crouched and crawled to the nightstand. The cool wood floor was hard under his knees, except for where Manny had dropped old socks and shirts. He rounded the corner of the bed, moving in time with the rattling snore until he reached the nightstand. Unsighted, he felt along the back until his hand reached the electrical outlets. There were two plugs, one of which he guessed was for the lamp. To be certain he yanked out both and the blackness that enveloped him was felt rather than seen. He started back along the side of the bed, the only thing keeping darkness at bay now was soft lamp light in the living room. The moment he got to the edge of the bed; a noise split the silence.

A loud vibration. Manny's phone in his pocket.

The vibration rattled off the floor and he stopped dead, frozen in a crawl amongst his friend's dirty laundry, just a few feet from escape. Manny made a murmuring sound and Ray was sure he was going to wake up. His mind raced for a reasonable excuse that would explain his behavior. Of course the only thing that could explain everything was the truth. Manny would never believe a word of it.

The phone vibrated again. The gentle snoring became an abrupt snort. Then, silence. Ray lay flat, hiding pressed against the edge of the bed. He reached down for the phone and it vibrated again. As he placed a hand on it, it stopped. He held his breath. The snoring was replaced by a gentle murmur. Ray expected the gentle drone of snoring to continue, but it didn't. Instead, Manny screamed. The bed jolted. Ray curled himself around the corner of the bed.

Manny shouted into the darkness. 'Ray?'

Ray held his breath. Maybe it was just a bad dream. He wanted to move and reach for the cell phone. If it went off again, Manny was sure to find him. The bed moved again. Bare feet padded into the living room and the delicate glow of light vanished with a click.

Shit.

The darkness was complete. And obvious. Even a Manny this drunk would notice the radio alarm was off. Well, maybe not, but it was too big of a risk.

Then light came back, harsh and bright. Ray ducked back along the far edge of the bed and out of sight. The splash of peeing came from the direction of the bathroom. He darted back to the radio and plugged it back in, soothed by that calming green glow. The alarm was now off. The sound of peeing stopped, and the toilet flushed. The light went off and the only light in the apartment was that gentle green glow.

Now the question was whether to move behind the door. *What if Manny closed it?* If he was going to move it had to be now. Too late. Ray slid himself back further and hid along the far edge of the bed.

Manny shuffled back into the room muttering. Had he noticed the clock? He mumbled about his missing phone. Ray felt the reassuring movement of the bed as Manny lay back down. He lifted his head from the cool floor, aware that if he didn't, he might fall asleep himself *and wouldn't that be a funny thing*? Manny mumbled a little before the comforting purr of snoring again filled the apartment. He hadn't noticed the clock. Maybe this would work.

He timed his exit the same way he'd entered; moving with the snoring that rose and fell with the comforting regularity of a metronome. He was in the hallway. In the clear. He just had to get out of there. He unlocked the door and was about to leave when he had an idea.

What are you waiting for? Get out of here!

'One more thing,' he muttered to himself.

In the darkness of the kitchen he grabbed a knife from the rack, only a few inches long, but enough for what he wanted.

He slipped from the apartment into the stairwell and again he felt sicker. When he was occupying himself, the flu didn't seem so bad - it was only in these more sedate moments he felt the dull headache lurking behind his eyes. The bourbon and cough mix cocktail wasn't entirely to blame for his grogginess. His breathing had a gentle wheeze to it that he hadn't noticed that morning.

He descended the stairs and stepped into the cool New Jersey night, scanning the street for the last piece of the puzzle: Manny's bike. It sat beneath a streetlight twenty or so yards away. Ray headed for it and crouched along the far side. He pulled the short blade from his pocket and eyed the tires.

'Sorry, Manny.'

He hadn't slashed someone's tires for years. Him and Pete, they'd do it for kicks, with Pete's friends when they were bored kids. More of Liam Whitney's bad influence. Kids nowadays, they stayed home their eyes glued to touch screens. He wondered which was better and stuck the knife into the front tire. It was much harder than he remembered. He wiggled it and the satisfying hiss of escaping air bled into the quiet street. As it hissed, Ray moved to the back tire.

If all else failed, and Manny did wake up on time, he'd climb aboard and set off, only getting a few yards before he noticed that some bored neighborhood kids had fucked with his tires. With no phone to call a cab he'd have to go by public transport, get to work and listen to a roasting from Tony for fifteen minutes before he went to work. Maybe get the shittier drops for the rest of the week. The tires weren't a big thing. Tony would make Manny pay for them to be replaced. Manny would have to work late or early to make up for the time lost. Whatever. None of it mattered. He'd be alive.

2:45AM

Ray trudged along the empty streets of Jersey, accompanied by the gentle, salty breeze drifting over the Hudson. He was looking forward to spending the night in his own bed, his own apartment, the version of his apartment that didn't have the cloying gloom and self-pity that would grow there the way moss grows on the dark side of a rock. As he sloped to his apartment, he stared at the message that had buzzed Manny's phone to life a few moments before. His tired eyes scanned the words over and over, wishing he'd never sent a damn message in the first place. It was just supposed to be an alibi for when Manny eventually got his phone back. Now Kat had replied.

'I'm too hurt to think about it now.'

Now? When did she want to think about it? His younger self would have replied immediately, going on the offensive without much thought. That was what he wanted to do now. It might be the best thing. Tomorrow at Logan he'd need his wits about him. The idea that they could patch things up preoccupying him would be worse than the breakup. A couple of blocks from his place and he could already see his bedroom window from here on the street. Being this close to home, maybe it was best to sleep on it and not do anything dumb, just reply in the morning. He read Kat's message once more and pocketed the phone.

'Hey!'

For a second Ray broke stride, before changing his mind. He sped up. The voice echoed again.

'Ray!'

The voice of an old man, gravelly, yet soothing. He turned.

'Charlie?'

'Yeah, it's me.'

He smiled, but he looked like Ray felt. Tired and old. Like the time that had passed since their last meeting wasn't days, but years.

'I didn't think I'd see you again. Truth be told, I was

starting to question if I'd met you at all. Are you okay? You don't look so good.'

'Listen at you talking.'

Ray had forgotten about the black eye. At least the swelling had gone down. His hand didn't really hurt at all these days. He could probably throw the bandage away.

'Got in a fight.'

'Do I want to see the other guy?'

'I'm sure he looks a damn sight better than I do. Got jumped. I think your friend had something to do with it.'

Charlie nodded. 'You've been rocking a few boats out here.'

Ray shrugged. 'Doesn't seem to have made much difference. Girl still left me. Pop and me are on better terms,' he paused, remembering the odd end to their meeting.

'And your friend, whassisname?'

'Manny.'

'Right. That looks like a good plan. That'll probably do it.'

'How do you know?'

Charlie smiled. 'I hear things.' The smile dissolved and his cheerful features darkened, 'Ray, the other guy, he hears things too. He's as pissed as I am pleased. And I ain't gonna lie to you, it scares me.'

Now he was talking to Charlie it was like there was no breeze. Like time had frozen. Charlie didn't look the type to scare easily. Ray felt a chill descend.

'He'll come after you Ray. He knows about your plans.'

GHOSTS OF SEPTEMBER

'Plans?' Ray tried to play it cool, but knew it was pointless. Like the old man was inside his head.

'Logan. And don't get cute. It's too big to stop Ray. He can't let it happen.'

'Neither can I. I missed it last time. I was asleep. In bed with the flu or whatever this fucking virus is. I woke up and it was all over. I see it in my dreams. I watch as those planes tear into those buildings and I feel everything from inside. The fear. The confusion. The panic. Now I'm supposed to sleep again. Let it happen? I can't. And I won't.'

Charlie sighed. 'I know. Just be prepared for anything. Cause that's exactly what that mean ol' bastard will do. Anything. You catch me?'

Ray just nodded. 'Can I ask you something?'

Charlie smiled that broad smile of his. 'So long as I don't have to answer.'

'Are you... real?'

Charlie tipped his head back and laughed.

Ray frowned, like he was being made a fool of. 'Seriously. Who are you?'

Charlie looked at him. 'I'm a friend Ray. That's all. Everybody needs a friend... Let *me* ask *you* a question.'

'Do *I* have to answer?' Ray smiled, but it was tired.

'Where the hell are you going at this time o' night?'

'My place. Need somewhere to crash.'

'That don't sound too smart to me.'

Ray thumbed over his shoulder. 'It's right there. Just for a couple of hours while I sleep the drink off.'

Charlie nodded, 'And which apartment is yours?'

Ray turned and pointed, 'The one on the lef—' He stopped. Something caught his eye. Something passed over the flimsy curtains, he was sure of it. It looked like the silver beam from a flashlight. He turned back to Charlie.

Charlie was gone. The empty street stared back at him. 'Fuck!'

He ducked to the side of the street for better cover and stared up at his apartment window. Somebody was inside. He wanted to know who but wasn't sure how close he could get without being spotted. His street was just a block away, but the building was around the corner, and the garden of the corner house before it obscured any view he might have had of the entrance. He stared up at the bedroom, hoping to catch another glimpse of the flashlight. Then, in the bathroom window, the frosted glass lit for a second with a beam of silver.

His mind raced at what was in the apartment that might incriminate him. He'd picked up all the papers. The timeline. The sketches of the buildings. Hadn't he? The trash. Had he emptied the trash? He wracked his tired brain, thinking if all the plans had come with him. Had he really got everything right first time? No. He was sure he hadn't. But then, he had used those drafts to formulate the final outline. That had gone into the folder. It would had to have done.

Five minutes passed. No movement. No lights. Then, around the corner in his street, a car started. He looked around for a place to hide, in case they came his way. All around was rusted link fence, chest high, but lousy for

GHOSTS OF SEPTEMBER

offering cover. He scrambled over a fence and lay prone in the front yard of the bungalow within. If whoever came this way kept the garden in their peripheral vision, he was fine. If they looked over, he was screwed. The engine sound rose, and the car turned from his street and slowly cruised past. He put his head down and for a second thought he'd been spotted, but the car continued on. He looked up and saw the rear of a police cruiser.

2:54AM

He raised himself up and scaled the rickety fence again, landing in the street adjacent to his own. He was alone, insecure, and uncertain. The only thing he knew for sure was that going back to his apartment was madness. He reached into his pocket to check his stash. There were ninety dollars' worth of crumpled bills. He'd need money for emergencies tomorrow – *today* - the folder at the motel had a few tens in there, but the hundreds and fifties were all long gone. He couldn't afford a hotel; he was going to have to sleep rough.

He trudged back the way he'd just come. Hanging around here felt like the worst in a series of shitty choices. All he longed for was sleep. The only thing heavier than his feet were his eyelids, and his joints felt weak, like he was aging by the minute. The hour was late and to say he had a big day tomorrow was an understatement of epic proportions.

He passed along the vacant emptiness of tree-lined

Chestnut Avenue, with its houses set slightly back off the street up short flights of stairs, and his mind turned to the police at his place. How had they found out? The young hospital cop. Shaw.

Pop said the cop had called him, and his story would have checked out. There must be something else. If it wasn't connected with the cop from the hospital and they'd found him at home, maybe... the motel.

They could find the motel. The folder. It was well hidden, but the room was a finite space. Given enough time, the cops would find it – and all of its secrets. *It depends on what they were looking for, and how desperate they were to find it.* How they had known to look in the first place was a question which would haunt the little sleep he did get tonight.

He entered Newark Avenue, bigger and busier than the tranquil Chestnut, and decided that for tonight, it had the right combination of out of the way obscurity and not-too-distant location for his purposes.

Purpose. Singular. Sleep.

He lay in the doorway of a locksmith and curled up. With nothing to cover himself and nothing for a pillow, he thought it would be a long time before he fell asleep. He had barely finished the thought before it was proven wrong.

8:44AM

The sounds of traffic had slowly filtered into his dreams, until he was awake. Up to this point, his eyes had remained

GHOSTS OF SEPTEMBER

closed. He wanted to hold onto the feeling of sleep, but he was aware of the numbness of his shoulder and the stiffness of his neck: the same feeling he'd had when he'd slept on the floor at Manny's or Andy's after countless parties, only to feel like he hadn't slept at all. He felt the nudge of a shoe in his kidney.

'Hey. Come on. Time to go.'

Ray looked up at an apologetic guy in his mid-forties. The look on his face assertive, but at the same time it seemed that he had more than a little knowledge of what Ray was experiencing. Ray guessed that under the wrong set of circumstances, anybody could end up sleeping rough. He groaned and struggled to his feet, his movements slow and rigid, those of an old man. Forty-something stepped aside as Ray shuffled past.

'You okay, pal?'

Ray just looked at him, not meaning to, but sure the look had come off as belligerent. He knew in the back of his mind that he'd regret giving him a dirty look. The guy was trying to be nice, and Ray wanted to go back and explain to him that he seemed like a decent person, because come this time tomorrow everybody would be longing for that human connection. Anything to get them through the nightmare that unfolded that whole day long in his dreams. Now more than ever he should be nice to people.

In exactly twenty-four hours a baffled office worker – somebody's wife, perhaps somebody's mom – expecting another uneventful day at the office, would look through her window and see something out of place in the distance. A shape distinct and familiar, but out of place nonetheless. After a short time, maybe a few seconds, she'd be able to recognize it as an airplane. A big airplane. Too big to be flying so low. A passenger plane. She'd have seen many as they flew overhead to JFK or La Guardia. But never this low.

She'd turn to a colleague to point out how odd it was, then, with growing, unimaginable horror she'd see that it was flying toward them. Straight at them. Flying straight at them with such speed that there was no time to escape. She'd freeze where she stood, maybe screaming aloud, maybe screaming the empty wheeze of nightmares, and watch as the impossible grew rapidly closer with ominous speed, more rocket than plane. The windows would explode inward, showering the one acre of office space in glass, but that wouldn't register, because behind it was a missile in the form of a 767 which itself would enter and explode in a jet fuel fireball. The woman and her colleague would be dead, as would anyone else unlucky enough to share that office space. The people on the floors above may not realize it straight away but it would soon dawn on them that they were faced with the most unthinkable of decisions. And to those shell-shocked souls unfortunate enough to bear witness in the building beside it, the buildings all around, and in the streets below, the world would never be the same. And it would all happen this time tomorrow. This time tomorrow. That meant something. For a second, he wasn't sure what that was.

GHOSTS OF SEPTEMBER

It meant that it hadn't happened *today*, as he'd feared since he woke up in this nightmare. There was no bewildered feeling of horror, that whatever the fuck was going on couldn't be real. This was a regular day. The last one of those this city would be able to claim for a long time.

He staggered back in the direction of the bar to pick up Pop's car. Tomorrow was fast approaching, and he had to be ready. Go back to the motel. Shower. Sleep. Take some meds. Try to feel human.

Something vibrated in his pocket. Manny's phone.

He pulled the cell from his pocket and stared. Tony calling. As he stood in the street staring at the cell phone of his best friend, two things were confirmed. Firstly, feeling as he did, as he had the first time around, there was no way he could have gone to work. That gave him a lightness inside that he hadn't felt since Manny had died. It wasn't his fault. Secondly, Tony calling meant that Manny hadn't made it to work. He hadn't made it and unless he was on his way there right now, he was still asleep in his bed and wouldn't get there for another hour. At best. Relief swept through his body. The sounds of the street and the polyphonic ringtone faded. He'd done it. He'd saved Manny.

Ray laughed in the middle of the street, and well-to-do office-workers pretended not to notice him. He stood and laughed, and his knees felt weak. His laughter went on until it was replaced with a sob, and finally, his knees gave way. He sank to the floor.

'I did it! You sonofabitch, I fucking did it!'

Pedestrians streamed around him like a river round a rock, and it was Ray's turn to ignore them. He didn't care. He'd done it. He'd set out to do the impossible, certain it was just that, and achieved in the face of all logic and opposition. Where he'd once have given up and failed, he'd persisted and succeeded. The sands of time were slipping at an accelerated rate through the hourglass, but for a moment Ray let them. For a moment, he was happy to. He didn't care. This was his time.

9:20AM

Ray crouched behind a green Toyota across the street from where he'd left Pop's car the night before. He spent five minutes there, just staring. The world whizzed by, nobody paying him any mind, going about the minutia of their lives with a carefree air that some wouldn't regain for months, and others wouldn't regain at all. Further down the street, about fifty yards from Pop's car, a guy sat in a nondescript black sedan, reading a paper. Every now and then, he'd glance up and eyeball Pop's car, before going back to the sports pages.

The cops were on to him, that was for sure. He just didn't know how. They'd been at his place. They'd probably found his rental car outside Joey's, run his details through the system. When they did, they'd wait. Wait for him to come and pick it up. As soon as he got behind the wheel, they'd tail him to wherever and that would be that. Jail.

The guy in the sedan looked more like an accountant

GHOSTS OF SEPTEMBER

than a cop, but that's probably the best guy to choose for undercover work. It made him wonder how the cops had found Pop's car so quickly if it was them. How long had they been onto him? His place, sure. That was his official residence. His car? The rental? Pop's car? They were all connected to him, but they were tiny needles in a pretty fucking huge haystack.

He bent over and hacked a mouthful of phlegm and spat it into the gutter. The amount he was bringing up was growing by the hour it seemed, but the color was the same, bright-green slime that it had been on Saturday afternoon. Each tickly cough sent fingers of pain clawing up the back of his skull, reaching further each time. He delved into his pocket for the cough syrup and took a swig of its sweetness.

The guy in the sedan peered over the top of his paper and stopped. He quickly folded it and for the first time Ray got a look at him. Stern, cold, a look like he didn't enjoy his time being wasted. Then it changed. A smile cracked. Ray turned to Pop's car. The door to the law office behind it had opened and a firm-bodied woman in a dark suit stepped out. Long chestnut hair waved back and forth as she glanced both ways before starting across the road. When Ray looked back the guy had already started his engine.

As they drove past, the driver glanced at Ray. The swept-back black hair had turned wild, long and grey. The crazy eyes below burned into Ray's. Ray fell back and screamed. The car stopped beside him. Ray fought his instincts and looked back at the driver. The man was leaning forward and looking up at the red light. He was just a man. No more.

Ray dusted himself off and dragged himself to his feet and across the road. He moved slowly, still scanning the street for anyone who might be looking for him. The sounds of the traffic and snippets of one-sided phone conversations faded out. The 70s had flares and lava lamps. The 80s, Rubik's Cubes and Hula Hoops. The 90s had Discmans and Gameboys from Sony and Nintendo. This decade, like all those before it, was still finding its feet. Not really sure what would define it. In the end it was to be the cell phone. And terror.

The motel was now his priority. If they hadn't found his car, it meant they hadn't found his room, which meant the folder was safe. The folder was nothing more than a burden now and though he'd felt safe leaving it behind after meeting Pop yesterday, that cheery optimism had long gone, chased away by cops rooting through his apartment by flashlight. Maybe they were looking for something like the folder. He wanted the damned thing gone. The flight tickets could go too. They were a prop. Simply an alibi to get him to the departure lounge. An expensive alibi that in 2001 he didn't really need, seeing as you could go all the way to the gate without a ticket, but it was an alibi his nerves wouldn't have gone without.

The time for keeping up appearances was done, now was the time to act. He scanned the street one last time, and deciding it was safe, he put the key in the door. Eyes closed, he paused, expecting to hear the barking orders of cops.

GHOSTS OF SEPTEMBER

Hands in the air! Don't move! Step away from the vehicle!

Nothing came. He slid into the driver's seat and sat for a moment, breathless. This was now his default level of paranoia. It was going to eat at him all the way back to the motel, and if, when he got there, his room was wrapped in yellow and black police tape, it might just swallow him whole. He checked the mirrors, pulled out and prepared for the longest four-hour drive of his life.

10:55AM

The roads were surprisingly forgiving. He had to return the car to Pop and pick up the rental. Pop's thinking had been that Ray would get back home, pick up cash, get his shit together and return his car and take a cab back to his own car. It made sense, but of course, it hadn't worked out that way.

This was going to be another long day of shit he didn't have time for. He'd have to go to the motel, pick up the cash and the folder, drop Pop's car off (without spending too much time there), then order a cab to take him back to Joey's for the rental, all in the hope that a guy who tipped him off to be mugged actually went to the trouble of having the tires changed. To say that the last part was a long shot was an understatement. You'd have got better odds on the Giants winning the '08 Superbowl.

Ever since Tony had called Manny's phone, even

though that in itself wasn't a direct confirmation of Manny being alive, he'd been waiting for the reprisal. The cloud had followed him along the I-95 without yielding rain. But there was a storm coming. He couldn't wait any longer. He had to know. The chirp of the phone rang in his ear. Tony always answered fast.

'Cusato Couriers, Anthony speaking.'

'Tony, it's me, Ray.'

'Shit kid, you sound like crap.'

'I don't feel great. I just woke up…'

'That's okay, kid, take the day.'

He hasn't asked about Manny, that's good.

'Listen, Tony, is Manny there? I can't seem to get a hold of him.'

Tony answers in the negative, and that's it. Proof that Manny's alive.

The pause felt like an eternity. It could have been a normal length of pause stretched into eternity by Old Man Time, after all, isn't that what he did best? What it felt like was the length of pause somebody leaves before they announce bad news.

'He came in. Just. Hold on…'

Ray gathered himself. He'd done it. Manny was alive. Relief washed through him and the weight lifted. Ray felt the tears coming.

Tony screamed for Manny to come to the phone and a stream of thoughts rushed at him, what he should say to his friend that he'd been denied the chance to before.

Manny, listen to me. You got a second chance. Don't

GHOSTS OF SEPTEMBER

blow it. Don't blow life like I did. You hear me? You grab life by the throat and don't you let go. Squeeze it for everything you can get. It'll hit back; it always does. But you dust yourself down and run straight at it again. God knows I wish I had. Take that trip to Florida, open that bar. You were born for that. You know it. Listen to those intuitions, they'll take you a long way. Don't be too hard on yourself. You'll fuck things up, we all do. Learn and move on. The world is at your feet, take advantage of that. And surround yourself with good people. You won't realize how much a good friend is worth until he's gone.

You've been a better friend to me than I deserve. You're the best, Manny. I love you, man.

A gasping voice snapped Ray from his thoughts.

'Dude.'

'Manny, listen—'

'Sorry, dude. You won't believe the fucking morning I've had. My power went out, so my alarm didn't go off, and then some piece of shit had slashed my tires—'

'Manny—'

'Sorry dude, I gotta go, Tony is pissed—'

'Wait!'

But the line was already dead.

Manny even being able to take that call should have left Ray elated, but he wasn't. Any sense of relief was short-lived. The idea that he and Manny would be able to take the road trip to Florida like they'd always talked about; that he would get to watch his best friend become a great bar owner; watch him become the man he was supposed to; none of it gave him the joy he expected. In the end it was pure selfishness. Because he wouldn't be around to share in it. Ray Madison was living on borrowed time. The sands that had been slipping through the hourglass for the past week had now almost vanished entirely.

Just like the Ringleader, Ray was on a suicide mission of his own. Old Man Time would want him in place of Manny. An eye for an eye. A life for a life. All's fair in love and war.

He knew where the reprisal would come. Tomorrow morning. He'd try to intervene, and something would go wrong. He'd be killed. Shot by a security guard at the airport. Or worse, arrested. Arrested, blamed, vilified. He'd have to live out the rest of his life as the man held responsible for the worst attack on American soil since Pearl Harbor. The penalty for treason was death.

11:25AM

Ray's thoughts had drifted back to the plan. There was no real reason to think the motel had been found, but even so, he would change motels, and then he could sleep. Save what little energy he had for Logan. Once safely tucked away in the motel, he could call Pop and make sure things between them were okay. Make sure that the last words they shared weren't words of hatred, or anger, or blame. Maybe he would call Kat. Apologize for how he'd treated her. Maybe she'd accept, maybe she wouldn't. If he died it

GHOSTS OF SEPTEMBER

wouldn't matter. All he could do was his best and hope it was enough.

He thought about Kat, and how naïve his ideas of rekindling what they had shared really were. It seemed ridiculous now. The clock was ticking too fast. The best he could hope for was for her not to hate him. And that would be fine. It would be *enough*.

The dashboard clock flicked to 11:27am. In twenty-four hours it would all be over, one way or the other. He was a couple of hours from the motel and making good time. The headache was manageable much to his surprise. He'd convinced himself that it would be unbearable and that he'd have to stop for a break in his journey somewhere about now.

Ever since he'd left New York a cloud had followed him and only now was he sure what it was. The idea that he'd never see New York City ever again. How he'd never enjoy looking at the Manhattan skyline, scarred and bereft as it would be without the Twin Towers. The sight of yellow cabs rushing the latest fare to wherever. The sounds of the city. The near constant distant howl of sirens. The buzz and chatter from the crowded sidewalks. The smells of fried onions as you passed the hot dog vendors. The blast of hot air in the subway. The everyday shit that you never thought about, took for granted. That was what he'd miss. The soul of the city. The feel of the city. Other cities had those things, sure. But in New York it felt different. Better somehow. Now he'd never feel it again. Old Man Time was going to steal all those things.

That's all Time was. A fucking thief, plain and simple. He stole the innocence of youth. The dignity of the elderly. Your prime. Your life. He took them one second, one grain of sand at a time, and all you could do was watch. Time squeezed every second from the good times, and made the worst ones drag out. He ensured the good times, the victories, the celebrations, were fleeting; he made sure the bad times were lasting. And there were always more of the bad times. The times of boredom, of guilt, of regret. Then he stretched seconds out into minutes, minutes to hours until you'd lost months, years, the *best* years, until there was nothing left.

Now he wished it was all over. That he was back in his crummy apartment, watching the plaster falling from the walls with a bottle of cheap bourbon for company. Now he found he didn't care. He wondered if this was how death row inmates felt near the end. That realization that his best years were behind him. Gone. A memory. That's what he was now. This was a death sentence. Soon he'd be eating his last meal.

When he looked down at the speedometer, the needle was creeping along like a second hand in slow motion. His eyes drifted to the traffic oncoming in the opposite lane. All it would take is for him to drag the wheel to the left, and it would all be over. At this speed, it wouldn't even take a truck. A car would do.

No, it wouldn't. That's what you're supposed to think. A car wouldn't do it. It would leave you alive. A vegetable.

GHOSTS OF SEPTEMBER

Worse than dead. Imprisoned in a coma. Then you can live out every second as though it was an hour. But a coma would leave you unaware, and that won't do for Old Man Time. He'd wants you to suffer. Trapped in a coma wouldn't be enough. He'd let you live but leave you trapped in a wheelchair. A prisoner in your own body.

He was never the most athletic, Pop would gladly tell anyone who'd listen that, but the thought of spending the rest of his days in a wheelchair, scared him almost as much as prison. Maybe more. Just like the dreams he'd had before Pete died.

Why are you thinking like this?

Because that's what he wants.

'I didn't ask for any of this!' Ray screamed. 'I didn't want this! You put me here, and now I have to deal with it. I have to deal with it, and you're going to punish me no matter what I fucking choose. You sick bastard.'

His throat burned. Tears fell down his face and blurred his vision. The speedometer needle crept to almost twice the speed limit. Cars blasted their horns as he flashed by. Gasping for air, he eased on the brake. He couldn't quit. That's what he was supposed to do. That's what *he* wanted.

It was the same second he'd had his moment of clarity that the tail of the car started to drift out to the left.

12:16PM

He eased the wheel against the turn trying to regain control.

The cars behind flashed their lights, horns blared. The tail of the car pulled back to the right, but then kept going. Maybe this was it. Maybe this was how it ended. He was going to die here, whether he wanted it or not. Robbed of any chance to make the tiniest difference. He steered against the spin again but overdid it.

This is bad, Ray. This might be it.

To prove the fact, time had slowed to an impossible crawl. He glanced down at the speedometer; he was still doing sixty. The tail of the car span further out until he was sliding sideways. Through his window cars screamed towards him: through the windscreen, the opposite side of the road appeared. If the wheels took now, he'd be stuck in a roll. That would surely end in the opposite lane, *he'd* make sure of it.

But the tires didn't take. The car carried on spinning until he was facing the wrong direction. He yanked the wheel again, correcting so his car didn't deviate from the straight line it was finally on, and looked up, into the eyes of another driver. The driver's face contorted into a caricature mask of fear. Ray had finally come to a rest but was now a sitting duck in the fast lane. His clothes were all stuck to him with cold, clinging sweat. Time regained its natural rhythm and Ray squeezed his eyes shut, the last thing he saw was the other driver yank his wheel sideways. He braced, his body somehow numb and tense simultaneously, preparing for impact. The moan of the other car's horn grew louder. Louder until it screamed past Ray's window.

Ray opened his eyes. The other car was gone. Ray fired

GHOSTS OF SEPTEMBER

the engine again and pulled Pop's car around and straight into the shoulder. All he could smell was the burning rubber of tires. The traffic slowly went past him, it seemed every driver blasting the horn at his idiocy. His chest rose and fell as he gasped for air. One thing was clear. He wasn't ready to die.

1:37PM

Two miles from the motel, Ray drew his car to a stop at the side of the road. Every now and then a car swooshed by, bringing with it a sense of danger. He was firmly on Old Man Time's radar now, and it wouldn't take much for one of these cars to lose control as he had himself hours before. Skid on the road and take him out once and for all. Game over. But it was a risk he had to take. The cops showing up at his place last night meant they might be looking for him. The hidden lot of the motel that had been a benefit before, was now a disadvantage. He pulled around that corner and the cops were waiting, that was that. No way out. On foot he'd have a better chance to assess the situation and turn and run if it was a trap. The trunk slammed and he set off, jerry can in hand. A prop would be useful in this situation. A guy walking along the side of the road here stands out: some poor sap who ran out of juice gets a glance, maybe sympathy, or derision, and everyone moves on. Walking from here was wasting time, but it was a few minutes he could spare against the finality of jail.

MARC W SHAKO

Jail. That's where this walk could end. Don't worry, Ray. They might just shoot ya.

The motel appeared on the horizon and his heart rate quickened. From here, everything looked normal. And normal was good. No unusual activity. Quiet. Plenty of time for the old geezer to watch his game shows. He paused at the entrance to the lot. There were no cars sitting by the road. No strangers in sight. He drew a deep breath and went.

As he rounded the corner, he stumbled. He was short of breath, not just from the walk. His mind prepared to see yellow and black tape; black and white cars. The near accident on the highway had brought into sharp focus how much he wanted to complete his mission. The cops stopping and catching him now, before he had any chance to act, was a fate worse than death. That was his biggest fear now: being robbed of the chance to make a difference.

Aside from the silver Mazda that had been here since he checked in, the lot was as empty as he'd seen it. No cops. Nobody at all, in fact. He slammed the motel room door behind him and slid the chain lock into place. He snatched the curtains closed *Did I open them?* and eyed the lock. One good kick and that thing would fold quicker than Manny holding a 7-2 off-suit. There wasn't much he could do about that now. He pulled the bed away from the wall and eyed the rip in the fabric lining in the back of the headboard. For an awful moment he felt around, and his hand couldn't find the folder and his Guantanamo future flashed before him, until his fingertips broke the spell. He snatched the folder from its hiding spot and threw it onto the bed. The damn

GHOSTS OF SEPTEMBER

thing was a curse. He had to get rid of it. Just as soon as he'd removed the tickets. And taken a shower.

He hadn't showered for two days and his own smell had become noticeable, and that was factoring in his blocked flu-ridden nose tuning out his own musk. Showering wasn't just a luxury; he'd need to freshen up if he was going to blend into society.

He sat on the bed, grabbed the frayed end of the ribbon tying the folder shut and pulled. The last hundred dollars of his savings sat there, pathetic - a heap of crumpled tens he'd forgotten he had which somehow made it this far into the adventure. Beneath the cash was a sketch of the wounded towers. The detail of the sketch seemed more realistic now. The lines more definite. Thank God he'd be elsewhere when it all went down. The reality of it weighed on him, he had to stop this. Nausea bloomed in his gut, but it wasn't the pressure of the task that caused him to feel sick. There was something wrong. Here.

'No.'

He scrambled through the loose pages scrawled with notes. Notes of a diabolical plan written in his own hand. Last time he'd looked in the folder, the flight tickets were on top of the notes, he was certain. Dizziness hit as one by one, Ray watched the pages float to the grubby motel room floor like autumn leaves, each time hoping that the next falling page would reveal his tickets. He dropped to the floor, lifting papers, sure that he'd simply missed them.

'No no no no no.'

He jumped back to his feet and to the headboard. Maybe they'd fallen out. Slipped out of the folder and into the lining behind. He ripped at the fabric of the headboard, tearing, pulling in an explosion of dust, motes floating in the crack of light cutting through the gap in the curtains. There was nothing there. He pulled up a sleeve and checked his watch. Nine minutes after two. He didn't have time for this.

He scanned the room, now aware of a throb of pain in his finger, blood marking the back of the headboard. But everything looked to be in the same place he'd left it. *Looked to be...* What if they'd been, and seen his sign-in in the register at reception?

'You should have changed motels,' he said in a low hoarse voice.

The young cop from the hospital knew he was here. He said outright that he didn't trust Ray. What if he'd come back, found the folder, taken his tickets? What if he'd wired the room and they were listening to him right now? Ray sat on the bed, and the tightness in his chest took hold.

2:09PM

The police cruiser turned off the I-95 and into the parking lot of the Bluebird Motel, and inside, the older of two patrol cops got that tingle in his balls.

'I've got a feeling about this one.'

He drew around back and slant parked in the lot, blocking in a silver Mazda. The two of them got out and headed

GHOSTS OF SEPTEMBER

into the reception where an old guy was watching game shows way too loud in the back. He didn't even stir when the cops walked in.

The older cop turned to his young colleague. 'The Zodiac killer could walk in here in a Michael Myers mask and this guy wouldn't notice.'

The young cop went to ring the reception bell and the old cop grabbed his arm. He pointed to the register.

'Let's look first. He doesn't know shit from chocolate sauce, don't interact unless you have to.'

He slid a finger down the register, stopped and tapped twice.

The young cop cocked his head and read under his breath. 'Ray Kennedy, you think that's him?'

The cop pointed to the license number. 'That's a match for the car found at Logan.'

He dinged the bell and waited for the grumbling old timer to shuffle from his creature comforts and confronted him with the signing in book.

'This man. Checked in a few days ago. You remember him?'

The old timer cocked his head in the same way the young cop had. 'Yup.'

'And he's in room 1?'

'Nope. Eleven.'

'You're certain?'

'Yup. He put the wrong number.'

The young cop piped up, 'How can you be sure?'

The old timer looked up and smiled, 'Because room one is two o' them lesbians. Good lookin' ones too.'

'Any chance you're mixed up about that?' the young cop said.

The old geezer stared at him for a second. 'Nope.'

The older cop spoke again. 'And that's room eleven you say.'

'Hundred percent.'

The older cop nodded and grabbed his partner's shoulder and they stepped outside.

'You think he deliberately screwed the register up to throw us off?'

He tried to sound calm, but these young kids were so damn hot-headed. 'Take it easy, will ya, huh? It's just a car. It don't mean shit if the guy ain't here.'

'We should radio it in, though, right? Maybe we'll get a reward.'

'The fuck are you talking about, Mahoney? A reward? Doing your damned job. *That's* the reward.'

He picked up his radio and with a voice that belied the tingle of excitement, calmly asked, 'Dispatch, this is car Mike Alpha one-nineteen, we have a report on that dark green Chevy Lumina, license JAS 414 at the Bluebird Motel off the I-90. That's the car with the APB from Logan, correct? Please confirm. Over.'

There was that silence, that same silence a speeder would give waiting for the results of his breath test, even the kid knew to shut the fuck up on this one.

'Copy that. That's the one.'

GHOSTS OF SEPTEMBER

There was a pause. The kid looked at him. 'Well at least ask for back up. We don't even know what this fucker's done.'

It was only two and he was already tired of the kid. That's all it was these days - Instant question? Instant answer. Instant soup, instant coffee, instant everything. Now this kid wants an instant career. No long haul these days. Nobody's got the stomach for it. They want it all yesterday or it's boring. Twenty fucking years he'd been doing this. Twenty next year, anyways. The kid did have a point though. The top brass did seem to want this guy pretty bad but didn't want to share why. Governmental thing. Always was. Strange the Feds weren't dealing with it. Probably just wanted the donkey work doing for them. Most likely it was important. Maybe there was a reward. He'd have to split it with the kid of course…

'We'll radio it in after. We don't got anything yet.'

He picked up the radio, 'We'll just take a closer look. Stand by.'

The radio coughed. 'Standing by.'

Their heels clipped off the pot-holed tarmac as they crossed the lot. For all he knew, whoever was in room 11 had seen them and was preparing an escape. There was no time to waste. They crept past the rooms, one by one.

'You ready for some real action, Mahoney?' He smiled and drew his weapon.

'We're supposed…'

'Keep your fucking voice down.' He barked. 'Walls are

thinner than paper.'

'We're supposed to bring him in alive.'

'And we will. You want to go in there with more than your dick in your hand, kid. Keep quiet, listen.'

They drew up to room eleven. The older cop placed an ear to the room door. After a second, he stood aside and gestured for the young cop to listen for himself. After a few seconds the young cop smiled.

'Shower?'

He nodded and whispered, 'Give that door a good hard kick, and… you remember training, don't you?'

The young cop nodded. The old cop regarded his partner for a second and was hit with a twinge of jealousy. Whole life ahead of him. A collar like this? Whoever the fucking guy in the shower is, this lucky bastard's getting a leg up the ladder.

'Okay. So you know what to say. Let's do it.'

The young cop stepped back, raised a leg and kicked. The world seemed to fade out, like there was nothing here. No I-95, no traffic, no motel, no reception, no old timer glued to Wheel of Fortune. Just two cops, and a dumb-ass not smart enough to break the law in somebody else's car in a motel room in the middle of nowhere. They rushed in guns drawn to the sound of running water. The older cop led the way to the bathroom door, shouting 'Police!' before kicking it in. The bathroom was more like a steam room, with a cool draught blowing from behind the shower curtain.

'Freeze! Come out with your hands up.'

GHOSTS OF SEPTEMBER

They waited.

Nothing.

The young cop started, 'Come out with—'

The old cop snatched the curtain away. Steam was pouring through the hole in the frosted bathroom window.

2:27PM

Ray sprinted along the shoulder clutching the folder, heading for Pop's car. It was a couple of minutes away, and he knew now that his chances were 50/50. A coin flip. The cops turn left from the motel lot and he's screwed. He'd been on the bed, gripped by an oncoming panic attack when he'd seen the cops. He knew there and then if they caught him it was all over. That was when he'd fought with everything he had to escape the clutches of the panic attack. He'd turned on the shower and used the jerry can to smash the bathroom window and left it behind. Along with his fingerprints. He wouldn't be able to explain why he was running but couldn't justify to his rational mind any reason not to do so. All he could hope is that the cops he saw pulling into the lot at the motel went to chase him and picked the wrong direction.

Pop's car was a couple of hundred yards ahead. Energy drained from his legs the closer he got. The car was a hundred yards away when the faint wail of sirens rose behind him. The cops were coming. *50/50*. Turn right out of the lot and he's free. For now. But if those cops turned left…

He made it to Pop's car and slammed the door behind him, his chest heaving. How had they got so close to him so quickly? He fired the engine up and set off for Pop's. The journey would take an hour. It should take longer, but now there was no point sticking to the rules of the road. Time was too precious. He didn't have a second to waste, it was all or nothing.

He wondered where the heat had come from. Maybe the cop from the hospital had investigated him and found the trail of the plane tickets and managed to piece the rest together. But the tickets. Why had he taken the tickets and left the rest of the notes? The notes were more incriminating than the tickets alone. Why take the tickets at all? It would be much easier to just wait for him at Logan. Let him think everything's going to plan, then strike. The act of him walking into the airport with tickets for the flight and what was in the folder would be enough to make an arrest. Now they didn't have much at all.

Ray wracked his brains all the way to Pop's place. Scenery passed by unnoticed as he tried to figure out how this had all started, and every time he came back to the cop from the hospital. If he'd had the balls to kill the Ringleader there and then at Joey's, this would all be over. There was no way they could trace it back to him. The guy would be dead, and Ray would have left the bar before the cops got anywhere near the place, checked out of the motel, and gone back to New York. That would have been that. If anyone did question what he was doing in the area, Pop could have been his alibi. He and Pop didn't always see eye to eye, but he'd have backed him up on this, especially if Ray told him what this fucker had planned. Christ, he'd have been a hero. Something for Pop to finally be proud of. Even if Pop would talk him into calling the authorities.

He called Pop from Manny's cell to let him know he was on his way. No answer.

He'd been driving on autopilot, not sure of where he was exactly. He looked for a landmark, or a road sign: something to give him a clue about how far it was to Pop's place. He spotted the roadside memorial of Samuel Knight, a ten-year-old kid killed in 1812 when a "cartwheel rolled over his head". Which meant he was at Ellington. 20 minutes from Pop's. He checked his watch and floored the gas. He just had to hope the cops weren't waiting.

3:53PM

The closer Ray got to Pop's place, the more knotted his stomach became. He'd tried calling twice more, again to no avail. Now he was almost here, he was ready to leave. To just turn around and go. He didn't want to risk staying in one place for too long, he had to keep moving. Getting arrested outside Pop's would be the shitty cherry on top on the shitty frosting of a really shitty cake. The ultimate indignity.

'Hey Mike, I saw your screw-up kid getting arrested outside your house.'

'Raymond? What did he fuck up this time?'

'Could be almost anything. Gee, Mike, you must be real sour that God took the good kid.'

He'd return the car, give back the money Pop had loaned him, ask him to call a cab, and drink as much tea as he could until the cab arrived. Then he'd go and pick up the rental (or jack something, if rat-boy hadn't got the tires changed) and burn this fucking folder.

'Why haven't you already done that, Raymond?' he said to himself, voice raised, sounding more like Pop than he'd ever know.

Christ. Shitty decision making like this was going to see him in jail. He can't burn it here. It would look odd. Unless…

Unless he did it at Pop's. He could explain what was going on. Why he was acting weird and so emotional yesterday. Destroy the biggest threat to his freedom and get credit for doing something worthwhile from Pop. At least he could get back to the rental with the weight of stonewall evidence off his shoulders. He allowed himself a little smile. Perhaps he was going to get away with this after all.

He turned the corner into Pop's neighborhood. This was a quiet place, the only noises here were if one of the neighbors decided to mow his lawn, or birdsong. A million miles from the concrete jungle and just for a second, peace was what Ray longed for. An end to the constant hum of traffic, and beeping of horns, and screaming sirens. Maybe it wasn't the lack of noise that was suddenly so attractive. It was the lack of people. Everyone seemed a threat. Maybe it would be better to stay here. Especially after he told Pop what was going on.

The idea of sharing his secret was liberating. He hadn't carried it for long, but the weight of it was crushing. Criminals hide their secrets for years. The weight of those lies. It was suddenly crystal clear why people eventually cracked. Everyone has a breaking point. The burden gets so great that at some point they *want* to say it. That was the point he was at.

Tell Pop everything. This doesn't have to be bad.

Outside Pop's house he killed the engine. For a second, he gathered himself, all the while scanning the house for movement, but there was none. He made sure he took his phone (and that fucking folder) from the car and got out. He crossed to the front door and knocked, suddenly excited about seeing Pop for the first time since Pete had died. There was no answer, so he knocked again, louder and longer. Nothing stirred inside. He cupped his hands to the living room window. Through the voile-curtain he could make out the silhouettes of the furniture, but Pop was nowhere in sight. He went back to the front door and knocked again.

The anticipation of meeting Pop fizzled. Of course he wouldn't be allowed a moment of glory. He still needed to get to Joey's, although now he held no fancy ideas about the tires being fixed. The car was probably trashed. If it wasn't, he'd burn the thing out himself. Along with the folder. He stepped across the front of Pop's place and into the next garden. As he did the memory of the baseball going through

Mr. Zalewski's window popped into his head (although that was back in Hanover). The slow-mo image of that ball slipping from his hand and heading straight for the window, just beyond Pete's diving grasp. The feeling of rising dread as it did so.

The feeling of dread rose now. He glanced back over his shoulder and stopped. He thought he saw the voile curtain twitch. He stared at it, before deciding it was a trick of the light and turning back, followed by the feeling of being watched.

Sure, they found your place. It wouldn't take much more work to find Pop.

He banged on the neighbor's door and glanced again at Pop's window. Again he thought he saw movement.

'Yes?'

Ray turned, shocked. An old man was waiting patiently at his door.

'Hi. I'm Mike's son.'

He glanced back at Pop's window. If something had been there it was gone.

'Ray? I didn't recognize you. You been fighting?'

He reached up to his black eye, 'I got beat up. I need a favor.'

The neighbor smiled and Ray felt somebody walk over his grave. From somewhere, he felt eyes on him. The net was closing in.

3:58PM

GHOSTS OF SEPTEMBER

Pop stared at his phone. He didn't want a cell phone, not only because he didn't *need* one, but because he knew that it would become a bind at some point, that he'd become a slave to it. He had a landline portable set-up that he could walk around the house with, and it had a caller display window on it, and in that window, the number of Ray's best friend Manny had blinked. He'd called three times. Ray used Manny's phone whenever he'd run out of money on his own cell. He pulled the voile curtain aside and checked outside again and watched as his car pulled around the corner.

He knew that in less than a minute, Ray was going to stop outside his house. What he didn't know was how much Ray knew. He quickly replaced the curtain and stepped back and out of sight. He waited there, pressed against the back wall, for a minute.

When the knocking on the door came, it wasn't frantic, just a regular is-anybody-home knock. It didn't come with shouting. Which meant he didn't know. Not yet. He tried to ignore the knocking, the same way he had when the police came knocking last night. Ray knocked again. They hadn't caught him yet. At least that was something. More than anything he wanted to answer the door. To answer the door and apologize, overwhelmed by the feeling that he'd once again failed as a parent.

The light changed and the room darkened, and he knew that Ray was peering through the window to see if he was home.

Step out into the room. He'll see you and you'll have to *answer the door. Then you can talk to him. Apologize to him. Tell him how much he means to you. Tell him you* love *him.*

But he didn't step out. He stayed there, pressed against the wall until the light changed again and a weary sigh of relief escaped. The strength had evaporated from his legs, but inside he wanted to run to the door and shout to him that he was there. He could listen to the abuse about what a shitty father he'd been and apologize and try to make things right.

He took a half-step into the room, but when the banging on the front door came once more, he stepped quickly back. It was another minute before he moved again. He hoped Ray would come back to the window, that the light would change, and that Ray would spot him. Force him to come out of hiding and answer the door. But none of those things happened. He crept away from the wall and into the room, moving like a one-night stand leaving a lover and edged that way to the window, peeking out from behind the safety of the voile curtain. All he could do was watch as his son knocked at old Bob Newman's house next door. He wanted to call out but said nothing. Then Ray stepped into the house and was gone.

He slumped to the floor by the window and cried.

4:07PM

'The police? What, here?'

GHOSTS OF SEPTEMBER

Ray's mouth had instantly dried and the moisture had migrated to his palms. He stared slack-jawed at Mr. Newman as he carried in two cups of tea from the kitchen.

'Gee, Ray, I didn't mean to worry you.'

'No it's fine. I mean, I'm glad you said something.'

He stared at the floor and saw the bare thread where the carpet had worn almost through. The room had had an eerie silence to it since Mr. Newman had turned off the TV, and Ray didn't like it one bit, although now it would be easier to hear the cops. He glanced out of the window into the empty street and found it of little comfort. They'd been here, at Pop's. What if they'd said something? He felt a new feeling inside. A feeling like he was unravelling. He wanted to get out of here.

'They were here last night. Oh, late. They didn't stay long.'

'Did he speak to them? Did he say what it was about?'

'I didn't ask. It's just, you know, not a lot happens here, so if the police show up...' he trailed off. There was an awkward silence. 'Your taxicab will be here in about fifteen minutes.'

Ray took the tea and nodded. 'Thanks.'

The neighbor exhaled a groan and lowered himself into his armchair. He had about ten years on Pop, not that you could tell by looking.

'Do you know where he might be now?'

'I couldn't say. He can't be far; his car is still there. He'll probably be back soon, you should wait.'

Ray didn't tell him he'd just returned the car, and instead shook his head. 'I don't have time. I'll try calling him again later.' Ray cleared his throat. 'I need another favor…'

The neighbor looked up. He didn't show any emotion like Ray was asking too much, even though Ray was starting to feel that way. Now that the opportunity of seeing Pop had gone, all he really wanted was to get the fuck out of here and on the move again.

'I borrowed a couple hundred bucks from Pop yesterday, and I'd like to give it back, but I don't know when I'll be around next.'

The kindness fell away from the neighbor's face for a second, like he expected Ray to pay the money back for him. He grabbed the money he'd prepared from his back pocket and laid it on the glass topped coffee table next to Pop's car keys.

'Would you mind? If it's a problem… It's just that, like I said…'

'It's fine, its fine,' said the neighbor, in a perish-the-thought tone.

'Thanks for this. The tea, calling the cab. I appreciate it.'

'No problem. Anything I can do. Mike's a good friend.' He stopped. 'He talks about you a lot.'

Ray doubted that. Or that Pop had anything good to say if it was true.

'You still living in New York?'

Okay, maybe some of it was true.

'I live in Jersey.'

GHOSTS OF SEPTEMBER

'I'm from Brooklyn, myself.'

Ray smiled. 'Heard the accent.'

The neighbor nodded, 'You can take the boy outta New York…' He paused, toying with what he wanted to say.

Ray sipped the tea. It was hot and sweet, comforting like a warm bed. God he missed sleep.

'Are you okay, kid?'

Ray looked up, surprised. 'I'm fine. Why? The bruises?'

'Well, there is that…'

'I got beat up. Went to the wrong place at the wrong time.'

'You just, er, seemed awful worried when I mentioned the police.'

There was another silence. Ray slurped his tea. It had cooled enough for him to drink a mouthful. It felt like it had healing powers.

'Why don't you turn yourself in?'

Ray felt his own gaze harden, 'Because I didn't do anything wrong. Are you sure my old man didn't say anything?'

'I'm just putting two and two together. The police show up, and then you show up looking, well, frankly, like hell.' The old guy had a good poker face if he wasn't on the level.

'I promise you it's not how it looks.'

The old guy nodded. 'I believe you kid.'

There was a honk from outside and Ray stood, peering out of the window. The taxi had arrived. The neighbor stood and looked out.

'That's you.'

Ray nodded. 'That's me.'

Thank Christ.

The old timer picked up the wad of bills Ray had laid on the table to repay Pop. 'You should take this. It looks like you need it more than your old man does.'

Ray shook his head. 'I gotta settle my debts.'

'He'd want you to have it. Listen take it, I'll pay him. You'll owe me. Whenever you have it.'

'That's very kind of you, but I can't. Thanks for the tea.'

'I understand. No problem with the tea. You take it easy.'

Ray nodded. 'I'll try.'

They shook hands and Ray left. He glanced at Pop's on the way to the cab. There was no sign of life. The closer Ray got to the cab the more it felt like the cops were going to jump out, just as he got to freedom. He told the driver where they were going.

If he'd taken one last look back at the window as he wanted to, he'd have seen Pop for one last time.

5:33PM

Ray perched on a stool in the dim light of Joey's bar, and while he was facing the mirrors behind the bar, his body was pointed at the entrance. The place was lit by an orange glow, like poor streetlights. And it was silent: no jukebox

GHOSTS OF SEPTEMBER

blaring, no pool balls clacking, no customers laughing. No customers at all, in fact. Just the smell of stale beer poorly masked with cleaning products to hint that the customers had ever been there. Even as a former (or was that future?) alcoholic, he'd never been in a bar before it opened.

When he'd got there, everything was okay. No police. No thugs. Rental car sitting on four fresh tires. It was all a little too good. It was also a relief that he didn't need to steal a car for himself, the less attention he attracted, the better. Corey, the Ratso Rizzo barman appeared just after he'd arrived, looking pleased with himself. Looking like he was actually pleased to see Ray.

'You got time for a beer?' Corey asked.

The dim glow was kinder to his features than the bright daylight from the other day. Ray couldn't recall which day that was. Corey was an okay guy, just one who'd made shitty decisions which forced him into making increasingly shittier ones.

'Gotta hit the road.'

Corey had got the tires replaced as promised. Ray had the taxi driver wait while he checked if Corey was good to his word and was pleasantly surprised with the result. The car looked tip top. No scratches, no broken windows. Not that he could ever trust Corey after the beating he'd received, but the swelling had almost gone and now just light bruising remained.

'Can I take these?' Ray picked up a book of matches, *Joey's* written in pink or red (it was hard to tell in the orange glow) on what looked like a white background.

'That's what they're there for.'

Ray stood and offered a hand and Corey nervously took it.

'Why did you do it?'

Corey's face dropped.

Ray clarified to ease Corey's discomfort. 'Fix the tires.'

'Felt bad about the other night.'

Ray nodded, 'Life's too short, Corey. Make your choices better.'

'I'm trying.'

Corey nodded and withdrew his hand, placing it with the other behind his back. Ray turned and left, not certain that Corey wasn't pulling a gun or a baseball bat from behind the bar. Ray paused, then pushed the door open.

The car park was still empty and for the first time all week, the sky looked angry. He gazed at the folder in his hand, before turning attention to the book of matches in the other.

'Time's up.'

He strode around the back of the bar to where he found Corey the other day. Stacks of bottle crates loaded with empties created a cityscape in a small enclosure surrounded by a high wooden fence. Ray pushed the rough wooden door and it swung open easily. In the corner there was a drum with holes drilled, green at the bottom, black and scorched at the top. He peered into it and saw remains of charred old snack boxes: no recycling here in 2001.

He stuffed the folder under an arm while he struck a

match. Fire took hold of the match, and then took hold of the folder. He watched as the corner burned, fire eating the pages the same way the past stole his future memories. The papers smoked and glowed orange, until the whole thing was alight. He watched it all go. Every link between him and the attacks turning to ash at the bottom of the drum. The plans, the drawings, the timeline, even the scribbled note with take-off times and flight numbers. Everything except the tickets. Wherever they were, they had his name on.

For whatever reason, the tickets were taken, and the folder was left. That still didn't make any sense. The cash had been untouched. They didn't even try to make it look like a robbery. The cops would usually ransack the place, turn the place upside down, take other things of value. The hypnotic dance of flame pulled him further in to the trance, and the more he thought the less it made sense that the cops did this. He'd bought the tickets and stashed them in the folder. Then came here, to Joey's, and got mugged. The cop took him back to the motel, asking too many questions, and the tickets were there then because the cop pulled him up on the different name he'd given. Next day, feeling paranoid about the nosey cop he'd checked the folder, and happy that everything was there, he took it to Pop's and left most of the cash behind. After Pop's he was feeling less paranoid and decided it was better not to carry the folder around and stashed it again, putting the cash back inside. Then when he came back, the tickets were gone. But why would someone only take the tickets?

The tickets were there when he'd stashed the folder again after visiting Pop. When he'd put the cash back in. Weren't they? The flame in the bottom of the drum came into sharp focus. Had he seen them after visiting Pop? He checked before stashing them. Always.

Not yesterday. You were too happy after visiting Pop and not having an argument, remember? Before you were feeling paranoid, so you were checking every two minutes. After the visit you felt stupid for expecting the worst. You didn't check. And didn't he want to get rid of you quickly?

'It can't be.' A sour taste hit the back of his tongue.

The last time he laid eyes on the tickets was right before he visited Pop. It could only have been him. Which meant that it was his father who'd called the cops. That was how they'd found his place so quickly.

His gut turned and heaved, and the contents of his stomach emptied beside the smoldering drum. A waft of smoke stung his eyes as he leaned there, dry heaving uncontrollably. The yard swirled and blurred and he held out a hand to steady himself as he lurched into the lot, his faltering steps marked by the scrape of pebbles and shattered glass. He fumbled the keys from his pocket and jabbed at the lock which moved just before he could spear it. Finally he fell into the seat, slamming the door behind him. His opened palms beat against the leather of the steering wheel over and over and another wave of nausea rose in his throat.

He opened the door and leaned out, but nothing came between the gasps of air he swallowed. He slammed the door again and stared. Stared at the main road beside the

GHOSTS OF SEPTEMBER

lot, expecting police cars to fill the scene at any second.

But they didn't. It was just a parking lot. Empty and darkening in the fading light of day beneath the leaden sky.

6:26PM

As he listened to the phone ringing, he wondered exactly what he was going to say. The sun slowly sank towards the horizon and now the red neon of Joey's sign flickered and fizzed out, with the sky flashing its own neon lightning show behind it. There was a time, probably even as recently as the beginning of this week, that he would avoid any hint of confrontation. Now he wanted answers. His own father had called the police and told them that he was... He couldn't finish the thought.

He wasn't sure exactly what it was he wanted from Pop, but he knew what he didn't want. An apology. He didn't want an apology because deep down, he wasn't prepared to believe it was true. There was no way his own father could have done this. There had to be some kind of mistake.

Finally Pop picked up. There was a deathly silence on the line. Both men too afraid to speak: the silence saying more than any words could. It meant it was true. His thumb moved to the red button to end the call, when Pop spoke.

'Ray.'

The voice was tinny in the speaker and he couldn't be sure, but it sounded like Pop was crying.

He put the phone back to his ear. 'Tell me why.'

More silence followed and now Ray was afraid that Pop would end the call. That everything that had to be said would go unspoken and there was to be no closure. Was that how this was to end? Their relationship suspended forever in limbo?

Pop sounded confused, '*I* should tell *you* why? Tell you what?'

'Pop. You took the tickets I had. I know it was you.'

'Of course I took them. Christ, what did you think?! That I would let you carry out that fucking abomination I saw?'

Ray frowned, 'Carry out? *Carry out?* I was going to *stop* it, Pop.'

'What?' A single word, but it trailed off like it had been dropped down an elevator shaft.

'If you looked at the rest of the folder, you'd have seen that there's a team of guys going to do that. I was going to *stop* them. Christ Dad. Why do you always think the fuckin worst of me?'

'I only told the cops the flight time, the flight number and hijack plans. I never told them anything else.'

Was that true? How had they been onto him so quickly? Before he could phrase the questions properly Pop spoke again.

'How were you going to stop them?'

Ray didn't want to explain he didn't really have a plan for that.

'That's not something for you to do Ray, you'll—'

GHOSTS OF SEPTEMBER

'Screw it up?' he snapped.

'Ray you're a courier for crying out loud. That's a job for the police. The FBI.'

'*I* had to do it. Myself.'

'Why?'

'How do I explain that I know so much? They'll never believe me. I'll go to jail.'

'How come you *do* know so much?'

'There you are again. Believing the worst.'

Pop sighed that way he always did when he was exasperated.

'Raymond. I don't care how you know. All I know is, you explain yourself to the proper authorities, tell your side, you hand over that folder—'

'The folder's gone, Pop.'

'Gone? Get it back.'

'I can't, Pop. I burned it.'

'Why did you do that? They'll put you in prison.'

Ray couldn't believe what he was hearing. 'You aren't worried about me. You're worried I'll end up in jail and it'll be *your* fault. You're worried that you ratted your kid to the cops and he's innocent. And you pushed me away and you'll die alone.'

The words came before he realized.

'Shit. I'm sorry Pop. I didn't mean that.' Ray felt sick. He thought he heard a sniffle. 'Pop. I'm sorry.'

'No I'm sorry, Ray. You're right. I saw what I saw and thought the worst.'

'You don't have to say anything. I don't know what I'd have thought if I saw that.'

'No I do have to say something. I saw what I saw and put two and two together and I screwed up. I was scared. The idea of losing both my kids to su—'

The world fell away. Sounds faded.

'Say that again.'

'Flying a plane into a building like that. It's suicide. And I couldn't bear the thought of losing you that way.'

Ray's mind went back. Back beyond the beginning of this week. Beyond the weird dreams of Pop and Pete visiting him even though in 2018 they were both dead. Back before the funeral and the empty look that Pop had given him. To the late summer afternoon. The buzzing flies and smell of cut grass and Pete looking sad even though it was a happy time and his big brother crouching before him, and it was only now that Ray noticed the whiff of booze on Pete's breath. He dangled his car keys in front of his face 'I want you to have something.' And he removed the keyring. The keyring Ray had never lost sight of since that day. The only link of anything physical that remained from Pete. Pete the golden boy who could do no wrong. He placed it in Ray's fifteen-year-old hand "I hope it gives you more luck than it has me." Ray looked down in his hand now and saw the rabbit's foot keyring.

'That's not what you said. You said *both* sons.' There was dead noise from the other end of the line. 'Pop, did Pete kill himself?'

He thought of what Pete had said and how it never

GHOSTS OF SEPTEMBER

made any sense to him. He'd dreamed of that moment and not heard Pete's words. Not smelled the booze on his breath. He'd heard his mother shout that he should drive carefully. And as Pete turned away, he thought that he saw Pete crying, but put that down to his brain fucking with him.

'Pop? He wasn't going to celebrate his exam results, was he?'

It was all starting to make sense. Pete died in a car accident, but he never went anywhere without his seatbelt, and he was an excellent driver. He died on a road that he'd driven a hundred times before.

'Ray. I'm sorry. Your brother took his own life.'

Pete? Surely not.

'Why would he do that?'

A deep haltering breath came from the other end of the line. 'Your brother was supposed to be going to visit his friends and celebrate his exam results. The results that were going to get him into college. We all watched him drive away and around twenty minutes later I went up to his room to drop off a gift I'd bought for him. A new set of football protectors. On the bed I saw his results. He'd failed. He failed the exams and he'd written that he was sorry on the bottom of the first page. I ran downstairs to follow him, but that's when the police called, and your mother answered and...'

'How could you? All my life you put me down and let me live in his shadow and made me feel like shit. And it's a fucking lie. You and all your bullshit. You told the cops that I'm going to hijack a plane.'

'Please Ray, I told you, I didn't tell them your name.'

'They fucking found me pretty quickly Pop.'

'Ray wait.'

He didn't wait. He ended the call and fired the car into life. The car screamed from the lot and roared headlong towards the black clouds and lightening. Towards New York.

9:47PM

The storm roared over New York City, and angry clouds hung in the sky, barricading the wedge of moon. The drive back had passed slowly, his thoughts his only companion. The decision not to get a new motel had been easy enough. He could have paid extra to the owner to not ask questions, or just use a fake name, but that wouldn't matter so much - if they wanted to find him, they would, after all, they'd found his place. If getting a motel was a bad idea, driving this rental was idiotic. As soon as he hit New York, he'd ditch it in some random place in the city. The drive back had made him nervous enough. He'd spent half of the journey checking his mirrors, looking over his shoulder. Looking backwards. Now his journey was coming to an end.

The idea of going to Logan was well and truly off the table now; the cops would definitely be waiting for him there. He'd be finished if they got their hands on him and that would happen before he set foot in the terminal building. The good news was, now that the cops were looking out for someone trying to hijack Flight 11, it would make

GHOSTS OF SEPTEMBER

life harder for the real terrorists. Surely that would be enough.

The other thought he'd had about Pop calling the cops was that it could actually work in his favor. He was going to be nowhere near Logan. If he had a solid alibi, then nobody would blame him for perpetrating the attack.

Was Pop telling the truth about not giving his name to the cops? How did they find him so fast? Pop had only given the flight number and take off time, or so he said. But the same night there were cops at his place. If Pop had called the emergency services, they would have had his number on record. He mentions a flight, and someone with the same surname appears on the flight manifest... It wouldn't take Columbo to put that together.

Now he wanted to go to the police himself. He wanted out of this whole thing. If he did go to the cops, they'd arrest him for sure. He could call them. Tell them to watch out for the hijackers. That would be two calls about one flight. They'd have to take that seriously. It would clear his name too. They'd catch the real guys - they wouldn't need Ray. The real terrorists didn't know who he was, so they couldn't finger him for the crime.

A siren, up close and obnoxious, quickened his pulse. He glanced in the mirror to see a police car driving through the intersection behind. This car had bad juju. He pulled over to the curb and got out. No need to pay for a parking ticket. He wasn't coming back. Nice knowing you. He was close enough to the hipster bar where Kat worked to hot foot it from here.

As he trailed through Manhattan he missed the anonymity of his courier uniform. He missed being one of society's invisibles, as bad as it was that such a thing existed. He had his doubts about how good an idea it was to visit Kat. She'd be pissed that he *wasn't* invisible. A wry smile touched his mouth.

She had every right to hate him. She had every right to be angry. But still, she might forgive him.

Take pity on you, you mean.

She was always angry with him, that much he could handle. Eventually she'd calm down and then he'd be able to talk to her. Convince her that he could change. That was the sad part. He'd done that so often in the past that he'd changed her. Worn her down until there was nothing recognizable left of the woman he fell in love with. He hated himself for it. The irony hadn't escaped him that the person he was now *could* change. Maybe he was already different. The man he was a week ago was a quitter. Now he was someone worthy of her, or at least starting to be.

He ambled through the downpour along Broadway towards Dino's, past the crowds, who all seemed to be multiples of two. Couples all the way along, mocking his loneliness. He stood in the median across from the bar and froze, peering from behind a tree. Inside was all dim lighting and hipsters, drinking cocktails and fancy foreign beers in oddly shaped glasses. At the table closest to the window, the coolest looking couple were ordering drinks from the prettiest waitress. She smiled as she took their order.

GHOSTS OF SEPTEMBER

She looked more beautiful than he could remember seeing her. The smile gentle, her eyes different somehow. They shared a joke, and she turned away from the table. And as she did her mask slipped and the smile faded, and Ray saw that the look in her eyes was sadness. Sadness that he'd caused. Suddenly, standing in the street and staring into the bar, he was a little boy again, looking at his neighbor's broken window. And just as that feeling of guilt swallowed him whole, she looked up. Straight into his eyes. But she didn't smile.

They stood there for a moment, just staring, expressionless. Ray wanted to apologize, but from there all he could do was smile, and he was too afraid to do that, certain that the gesture would go unreturned.

Movement caught his eye close to the door and unsettled him, like an animal sensing a predator. He could only watch, frozen, as two police officers entered the bar. Kat's eyes had followed his, and she turned to see them to. Gripped by panic, he looked back at her, watching her watching the cops as they spoke to a colleague. When the colleague pointed at Kat, she turned back to Ray. Even though he was standing in darkness, across a road with crowds of people passing between them, he knew that she could see his fear. And it became clear in that moment, that if she was done with him, she would tell the police. The cops drew closer, making their way toward her through the crowds, and Ray had no idea what she was going to do.

MARC W SHAKO
10:01PM

Ray crouched behind the bushes and peered over the top. Every few minutes, lightning lit up the skies, highlighting his position, exposing him. The taller of the two cops showed a photograph to Kat, and she tilted her head to an angle to examine it. He held his breath. She nodded her head and he waited for her to turn to the window - to point out where he was standing - *hiding*. He'd run and maybe they'd catch him, maybe they wouldn't. Now, after all that had gone on in the last few days, part of him felt it would be a relief if it was all over. Even if she did rat him out, who could blame her? His eyes came back into focus and he saw her shrug. The cop asked her another question. This time she shook her head. The second cop pressed her, but now the head shake was more pronounced.

The cops thanked her and turned away. She waited until they had left before looking back at Ray. He saw her from the corner of his eye, but waited himself, until the cops were out of sight. The second they left, so he left the refuge of the bushes and stood at the curb, waiting for a gap in the traffic. She hadn't told the police he was there. That meant there was a chance. She might see the change in him, which meant she might forgive him. He dashed across the road, the petrichor smell of fresh rain filling the air.

It was replaced with cologne and cigarette smoke as he entered the bar. Chatter drifted above an old blues track that he didn't recognize, and his eyes met Kat's. She stood at the entrance to the kitchen. If Ray was hoping for a clue as to

GHOSTS OF SEPTEMBER

her feelings, he was out of luck. Undeterred he weaved through the crowds but by the time he'd reached the kitchen entrance, she was gone, like an elusive dream. Hands in pockets, he entered the kitchen, hit by a wall of heat in the darkness from the cooling equipment. He stroked the soft fur of the rabbit's foot as a hapless fly crackled in the blue neon of the insect killer.

That was when he saw the look in her eyes. It wasn't sadness, or even anger. It was much worse than that. A wounded look of disappointment. The possibility that she would forgive seemed a little farther away. Old Man Time and this fucking predicament he had woken into... If he could explain what was going on, it might buy him time.

'What the hell happened to you?'

'Kat I'm sorry. I was at Pop's.'

'Jesus, I knew you two didn't see eye to eye but...'

'Oh no, I mean... The bruises are from a fight. I mean I cancelled because I was with Pop. I hadn't seen him for such a long time, and for the first time in ages we weren't fighting. I felt guilty.'

'It's okay.'

He let go of the rabbit's foot altogether. 'It is?'

Hope bloomed in him. She was about to forgive him. Forgive him and say that she loved him, and it wasn't important. She could tell that he'd changed. She could see that he was a man who'd fight for her. That she knew how important it was for him to bond with his father. Even though she didn't know that he was going to die.

'You thought it was more important.'

'Yes... I mean no.'

She laughed, but it was joyless and bitter. 'You always manage to find something more important than us. Than me.'

'That's not true.'

He felt himself falling.

'Isn't it?' A tear fell down her cheek.

Her eyes burned now. He preferred the inflamed anger to the empty disappointment, but whatever it was in her eyes now, it wasn't love. It was over.

From the noise of the bar, a man entered. Handsome. Cool. In control. A little older than Kat. He was dressed in the black shirt of management, as opposed to the black and white of staff. 'Kat? We could use you out here.'

'Just give me a minute.'

He nodded, glancing at Ray before he left.

Just tell her.

But she spoke before he did, and he was gripped by that falling feeling of terror. Unable to predict what was coming.

'I don't want to give up on you, Ray. I want to give you a chance.'

There it was. Hope. 'Yes. I won't let you down again. I can be the person you need.'

'I need to know that you can put me first Ray.'

The moment she said it, he shrank. How can he promise he'll be there? Tomorrow was the end of the fucking world. He makes a promise he can't keep now; she turns her

GHOSTS OF SEPTEMBER

back on him forever.

'Ray. Can you do that?'

He shifted awkwardly. He lowered his shoulders and angled his face to see her better, 'Kat, it's really complicated...'

She stepped back, tipped her head towards the ceiling, and barked another bitter laugh. 'I should have known.'

The look in her eyes killed him. She was crushed, but looking at her, it was his heart that broke.

The boss re-entered. 'Kat.'

'I'll be right out.'

That was it. The moment the flame was snuffed out. Despite the thick heat in the kitchen, the temperature dropped. Ray caught the concern in the boss's eye and Ray watched Kat's future unfold like he was watching an out-of-body experience. The way she left Ray and started with the manager. The way he gets her pregnant and then leaves her because the other girl he's seeing on the side is pregnant too. By then Kat will be a single mother with bills to pay and no time for anything, let alone something resembling a music career. He wanted to tell Kat, but it would sound like bitterness and just push her further away. Closer to him.

'You know what the worst thing is? I love you. You know that? I love you, Ray. And now I have to walk away.'

'Kat please.'

She wiped the tears from her face and composed herself. 'I gotta go back to work.'

'Wait.'

But she was already gone. She stopped at the door. 'Goodbye Ray.'

10:39PM

Tired, broken, and desperate, Ray headed through the storm to West Village. He was going to Horatio Street. To Andy's house. Andy's place was the venue for their Friday night poker games, and Ray welcomed the familiarity, God knew that he'd been lost and alone for far too long this week. Worse than that, after the phone call with Pop and the breakup with Kat, it all seemed to be for nothing.

Manny. That's the silver lining. It was more than worth it for that alone.

He hadn't been able to convince Kat to see beyond his shortcomings, despite now being the kind of person she deserved. The uncertainty of what was coming meant that he couldn't bring himself to make yet another promise that he'd be unable to keep. It was a matter of time before the cops caught up to him, and she deserved better than to have her relationship ended like that.

Pop had called the cops on him. It hurt him to think that he had so little trust, but at the same time, looking at it from Pop's point of view (something that, if he'd been able to do years ago would have saved a lot of grief), he could see how he'd connected the dots and come back with that picture.

Yes, the only plus point out of all of this was Manny. He'd be pissed at Ray for almost costing him his job, but

GHOSTS OF SEPTEMBER

they'd get over that quickly enough. He was safe, alive, that was the main thing.

Ray trudged to Andy's place, and hoped that Andy rather than Tina answered the door. The sympathy from her was more than he could handle. He rang the buzzer and waited. It wasn't long before Andy replied and buzzed him in.

Ray made his way upstairs and knocked on Andy's door.

He was wearing the Iron Maiden shirt from his desert dream. 'Holy Hell, Ray, you look like shit. Come in, come in.' He stepped aside and held the door back.

Ray instinctively kicked off his shoes as Andy closed the door behind him.

'What the hell happened to you?'

'You got a beer, Andy?'

'Sure, come on.'

They moved to the kitchen and Ray sat at the dining table, home of Friday Night Poker. Andy went to the fridge and grabbed two bottles of Miller.

'You get in a fight, dude?'

Ray twisted the cap off the bottle and drank half of it in one go. 'It's been a hell of a week. I got jumped. Mugged.'

Andy lowered the bottle before it reached his mouth. 'Jesus.'

'And I broke up with Kat.'

'When?'

'Just now. It's for the best. She needs somebody she

can count on, like how you and Tina are, you know?'

Andy shrugged, 'Shit, I'm sorry, dude. I thought you two would last…' He trailed off.

'What can you do?'

'The spare room's made up. Tina's at her sister's place, so it's just us here, but I got work in the morning.'

'It's fine, I wasn't expecting beers and fireworks.' Ray swigged the rest of the beer down. 'Thanks for this, means a lot.'

Andy was up and at the fridge getting Ray another beer. Ray didn't argue.

'Hey, come on. Don't mention it.'

He returned, sat down and slid the beer across. There was a moment's silence, but Ray just enjoyed it. The atmosphere in Andy's place was always relaxing. Tina and him had a nice home here.

'You can stay as long as you need, you know that.'

Ray was sure Andy's mind was on the time Tina had kicked him out over a huge misunderstanding with a text message from Sam (who turned out to be a guy) and he'd crashed at Ray's for three nights while they sorted things out.

'I gotta ask though, Ray. And don't get me wrong, you're welcome here for as long as you need, but… Why can't you go home?'

Ray thought of a lie. The shit he'd been through this week was nothing he'd easily be able to explain to anyone. But he didn't want to lie. He was tired of it.

'Cops.'

GHOSTS OF SEPTEMBER

'Cops?' Andy leaned back in his chair, shocked. 'What's going on?'

Ray thought about how much to tell him. Neither Andy nor Tina worked at the WTC, and as far as Ray knew, none of their family did either. If he did tell him, Andy would want to call the cops. He'd already broken the "no instigating interactions" rule. He remembered his "Butterfly list" of shit he wasn't supposed to do and wondered where exactly in the past week he'd forgotten about it. Not long after he'd got back into 2001 he guessed. But not instigating interactions was small fry. Telling the whole horrific truth was the big enchilada.

Ray could feel his voice breaking, 'I'm in some big trouble, man.'

Andy shifted uneasily in his chair.

'Don't worry, no one knows I'm here. The cops won't come here.'

'What's going on, Ray?'

Ray took a deep, halting breath. 'What would you do if you knew that something bad was going to happen?'

Andy was silent, but Ray could see the cogs turning, working overtime behind the vacant eyes.

'How bad?'

'Fucking really bad. Like, awful.'

'Like what? A murder? An accident?'

'Right, something like an accident.'

'Fuck I don't know, dude. What kind of accident?'

'I don't know. Let's say a plane crash.'

Andy thought for a second. 'How much do you know? You know the details? Flight number and all that shit?'

Ray nodded, but as he did, he became acutely aware of the fact that in his mind, where the information should be, there was a gap. Like redacted words in a government document.

'Then I'd call the airline. Tell them everything. Then they could, you know,' he paused searching for the right word and quickly found it, 'ground the flight.'

Ray didn't say anything, just stared at the bottle as he turned it quickly in his fingers.

'Wait a minute, if it's an accident,' he paused again and Ray looked up, but Andy was looking away, thinking, 'how do you know it's gonna happen?'

Don't tell him, Ray. Shut the fuck up.

It was a burden too much for himself to bear, passing that burden on to Andy didn't make him brave, it made him a coward. And if Andy called it in, Ray was sure that crazy ol' Chuck Manson would make *him* pay for it. Andy was smarter than Ray had given him credit for. Just because the guy didn't say much, didn't mean he had nothing to say. Andy's poker skills should have hinted at how smart he was. Ray was the idiot here.

'Unless it's a hijacking or something like that…' Andy said.

'It's really bad and the cops are under the impression that I'm connected to it and I'm fucking not.'

'Well you have to tell the airline. What can the cops do if you stop it from happening?'

GHOSTS OF SEPTEMBER

Ray searched his mind for the flight numbers again. The gap was a black hole and the harder he thought, the blacker it got. This wasn't like the headaches he'd had earlier in the week when he was trying to remember the details; this was much worse. It felt bad, like a concussion, but there hadn't been any trauma. No injuries, bumps, scrapes, nothing. It was like time had slipped again and he knew nothing. And it scared him.

Why did you burn the fucking folder?

'I need to write a letter.'

'Will it get there in time?'

Ray replied firmly. 'Yes.'

But the letter wasn't for the airline. There was a mailbox outside, he could mail the thing himself. Andy would never see the envelope, the address. It would get Andy off his back. Then he could do what he really needed to and that was sleep.

Andy got up and disappeared and Ray heard drawers opening and closing somewhere behind him. He reappeared and dropped the writing materials on the table in front of Ray.

'Want another beer?'

Ray nodded.

'Think I need one.'

11:54PM

Andy sat with Ray as he wrote the letter. Ray was pretty

sure that Andy wasn't trying to peek at what he'd written and when Ray sealed the envelope and stuck on the stamp, Andy seemed relieved. Ray made his excuses and went outside to post the letter, before returning upstairs to finish his beer.

'One more?'

Ray shook his head. He was tired of beer. The cold brought down the fever he had but the buzz wasn't much with his headache and besides, with the flu he had it tasted like shit anyway.

'Can I take a shower?'

Andy nodded. 'There's a towel in your room.'

'Thanks again, buddy.'

Andy smiled. Ray left for the spare room. He knew where it was, and after a few beers he went there on autopilot anyway. It was nice to get out of his clothes; he'd been wearing them for days and they smelled like it. He crossed the hallway to the bathroom thinking about what Andy had said about reporting "it". He closed the door and turned on the shower, letting clouds of steam fill the room. If he was going to report it, he'd need as much information as possible, so it couldn't be written off as some sick prank. He dropped his towel and stepped into the stream of hot water. It soaked his hair and pounded his aching body and it felt refreshing and revitalizing. Another few minutes and he'd feel halfway human again. Maybe even enough to find an answer.

As he showered, he tried to fill the void in his mind where the information on the flights hid. It was like an image in his mind, distant and blurry, and the more he thought, the further away the image seemed. His headache returned, harsh and blinding. He doubled over; his eyes scrunched shut. The sound of the water rose and thundered, amplified by the acoustic echo. He reached out a steadying hand and it made contact with the tile, and it shocked him, icy cold to the touch. He opened his eyes a crack, searching for the faucet to shut off the water and saw that the spiraling water that vanished into the endless black of the plughole was tainted red with blood.

He stumbled from the tub to the floor, and as he set his foot down, it slipped. For a second, he was suspended in mid-air as his thoughts turned to the man on the bus from his dream, falling, clothes billowing out behind him, until he came crashing to the floor. The impact was on the bruised ribs he'd got from Joey's. A sharp pain sliced at him and snatched his breath away. There was a pounding on the door.

'Ray? You okay in there?'

Ray drew in a breath, trying to steady it as best he could. 'Yeah I'm fine. I just slipped getting out.'

There was a brief pause from the other side of the door. 'Might help if you shut the water off before you got out.'

Ray breathed in again. A staggering, halting breath scarred with pain. 'Right.' He raised himself up and shut off the water.

'If you're sure you're okay, I'm gonna turn in, dude.'

'I'm fine. Thanks. Night, dude.'

MARC W SHAKO

Ray scrambled to the toilet and threw the lid back. He stared into the water; smell of pine freshness masking Christ knew what stinging his nostrils. Out in the hallway, Andy's door closed, and he released a stream of vomit into the bowl. Hot liquid spewed into the bowl and Ray stared for a moment before retching again. Acidic bile tumbled into the beer colored water. Blood dripped from his nose as he retched again, but this time nothing came. He wiped his nose on toilet paper and flushed. More paper mopped up the bloody mess by the bathtub that had gushed from his nose. He threw it into the john and waited for the cistern to refill as he wrapped the towel around his shivering shoulders. He opened the door and peered out, making sure the coast was clear before staggering back across the hall and into the darkness of the spare bedroom. He collapsed onto the bed and dragged the sheets over his trembling body, and before he knew it, he was gripped by a dark, haunting sleep.

Heat. Not the natural heat from the desert sun. This was artificial. It had a smell too. Acrid. Chemical. This was in an office and he was sitting on the floor; on thin and itchy carpet tiles, backed up against a desk. He rolled up his shirt sleeves and loosened his tie. *cornflower blue.* In front of him clear skies and high-rises of different shapes and sizes stretched for miles. And the river. News helicopters buzzed around outside like worker bees. But those were all in the distance. Up close was another building, tall. Maybe taller even than the one he was in.

Or exactly the same size.

GHOSTS OF SEPTEMBER

In the ceiling, some of the tiles were displaced, revealing black and red wiring behind them through the smoke. The sprinklers weren't working, despite the black smoke hanging, threatening, by the ceiling. It was just like his dreams from when he was a kid. From before when Pete died. But there was no wheelchair. He tried to move his legs and found to his surprise that they moved easily. The temperature rose as he stood and noticed the area behind him was shrouded in darkness.

The windows there were blacker than night, concealed by dense smoke, much thicker than that which clung to the ceiling above. It was outside; black and billowing constantly by the windows.

Suddenly, somebody rushed by him, pushing a desk. A man not in suit and tie but dressed something more like a vagrant. Burgundy outsized trousers swooshing together below a beige corduroy jacket as the legs pumped headlong for the windows. Then the desk hit, and the sound of a cool breeze followed breaking glass. The man turned back.

'Charlie?'

He smiled, 'Who the hell else did you expect?'

Ray stepped closer. 'What's going on, Charlie?'

The lights came on behind Charlie to illuminate the darkness but flickered ominously.

'What does it look like, Ray? If you had to guess.'

'The end.'

Charlie nodded. '"The end."' He sat on one of the desks and took off his sunglasses. His eyes weren't the usual dead milky white, but deep brown and alive. 'How do you feel?'

Ray shrugged. Charlie reached into the inside pocket of the jacket and removed an hourglass. The small kind you'd use to time a soft-boiled egg. He sat it on the desk and the white sands trickled into a pile in the bottom half.

'You can see?' Ray asked.

'Always can, in my dreams. Don't change the subject. You must know how you feel. Scared? Sad? Angry?'

'*Your* dream?'

'Oh Ray-mond? The question. How do you feel?'

Ray answered without thinking, 'Resigned. Bereft.'

'Resigned to what?'

Ray sat on a desk facing Charlie and watched as the black smoke drifted endlessly past the windows.

'Resigned to failure. That's why I feel empty. I did my best and it wasn't enough.'

'You were facing a tough enemy,' Charlie said, as if to explain.

Ray looked at Charlie, 'The old man with the crazy hair. That's Father Time, isn't it?'

Charlie looked at him and for the first time Ray noticed he wasn't smiling, 'If you'd been around as long as he had, you'd be a little cuckoo, too.'

'If he's Time, then who are you?'

'I'm just a friend, Ray. Nothing more.'

A loud explosion ripped through the building somewhere below, and the floor shuddered. For a reason Ray didn't know, he looked straight at the hourglass. Half of the sand was gone, the grains which had accumulated in the

GHOSTS OF SEPTEMBER

bottom half were black.

'Is this it?'

'Almost.'

'Will I see them again? Kat, Manny, and Pop?'

'I don't have the answers, Ray.'

Ray looked at the sands trickling endlessly, less than a third remained. Less than one minute.

Charlie peered up from the timer, 'How would you feel?'

'How would I feel what, Charlie?'

'How would you feel if you were to die right now?'

'I told you, resigned and empty.'

Charlie shook his head. 'That's how you felt a minute ago. Now you know you're going to die; I want to know how you feel. Any regrets?'

'Some. Too few to mention, like the man says.'

'No biggies? With Kat or Pop?'

'No. It is what it is.'

That's what he believed. He'd done what he could. He'd shared a beer with Pop. Shared an afternoon without arguing or feeling belittled and inferior. Shared real love. And with Kat he'd shared the truth. There were no secrets. He'd failed, but it was his best, and he'd be able to look at himself in the mirror.

'You believe all that?' Charlie asked.

Ray frowned, 'Shouldn't I?'

Charlie leaned forward and looked Ray straight in the eye. 'If you feel fine with your failure, why are you so damned angry?'

Ray looked down and saw that his hands were trembling. He balled them into fists. It was a fire in him that rose from his core and exploded.

'Because those things are not why I'm here. Those things were tests. For this.' He spread his arms to present the burning building around them. 'I passed the mid-terms. And failed the big one.'

Charlie stood and moved around the desk into the flickering lights of the dark half. Ray got up and followed. Ray wanted to catch up, but his legs were heavy. Too heavy and Charlie was already at the broken window. He held out his hand and the egg-timer was almost entirely black now, a few grains sinking into the bottom half like a pinch of salt. Another savage explosion swayed the building and half of the few remaining grains disappeared.

'That what you think? That you're here to stop *this*?' Charlie held out his arms.

'I don't know. I'm confused. Frustrated. It's too much to ask. Too big.'

Before Ray could explain, he was standing beside Charlie at the window. The smoke was still rushing past, a blanket of choking blackness that parted momentarily when the wind blew revealing a sea of specks - blue flashing lights on the ground.

Charlie turned to him and shouted over the winds, 'How did you fail?'

Ray shouted back, 'I'm not going to be at the airport, Charlie. Christ, I don't even know for sure which damned

GHOSTS OF SEPTEMBER

airport I'm supposed to be at. And I don't even know what good it would have done. Andy said that after the attacks, some of the hijackers were found alive.'

'So?'

'So?! I don't know if I'm trying to stop the right people,' he said, words choked with frustration.

'Think about it. So what if Andy's right? Did the attack still happen? What does it change? I'm not talking about the grand scheme of things, I'm talking about for you, Raymond Madison, here and now.'

Ray nodded.

'What if Andy is wrong? You ask yourself that?'

'If he's wrong? That sick maniac and all his little terrorist buddies are going to get on that plane. And that will be that.'

'Ray, Manny is alive. You saved him. You're right. All this,' Charlie again gestured at the surroundings as the tower groaned, fighting against its own inevitable demise. 'It's too much for one man to stop. You came here and made a difference. With Manny. Now you have a choice. You can wake up back in 2018, or you can stay. Here.'

'Can I stop it?' Ray asked.

His heart hurt and all he wanted to hear from Charlie was "Yes", but he knew it couldn't be.

'You're asking the wrong question Raymondo. You got to ask yourself if you can live with it.'

Charlie held Ray's hand and stepped into the void. In slow motion, Ray reached for the frame, but felt the cold metal slip against his fingers as he fell into the black cloud. He looked at Charlie, surrounded by black.

'What if I fail?' Ray shouted.

He shouted against the rushing air, 'We only fail when we give up, Ray.'

Ray looked down at the shiny black shoes that were half camouflaged against the cloud and watched as they burst free into the sky. He looked back for Charlie, but he was gone. He was alone. Falling. The sound of wind rushing by grew louder as he fell, faster and faster until he was tumbling towards the ground at terminal velocity. The ground that rushed up to meet him - the fire engines no longer looked like toys and the people no longer like ants: there were no more insignificant specks, now they had faces; faces that held expressions of terror, and as he looked at them they watched him helplessly as he fell and the ground rushed upward and as he got closer and closer he could hear the screams of the crowds and then he could see the cracks in the pavement—

Ray jolted awake, aware in some darkened corner of his mind that today was very important, yet for a strange second, he couldn't recall why. Charlie's words about going back to 2018 echoed through his mind and he glanced at the room around him. For the life of him he didn't recognize where or when it was. Then, slowly, surely, reality crept into him; its cold fingers scraping at some unseen part inside. Today was the day.

It was Tuesday. It was September 11th.

TUESDAY, SEPTEMBER 11, 2001

8:12AM

IT WAS THE SPARE ROOM at Andy's. He zeroed in on the radio alarm. Old Man Time had one last joke for him. Keep him asleep long enough to hinder his interference at the Towers, but not quite long enough that he'd have the luxury of sleeping through the awaiting horror.

All Ray could hope was that miles away, at some international airport he'd once known but had since forgotten, a team of terrorists intent on hijacking passenger jets had tried to board their targeted flights and the FBI had intercepted them, based on the limited information that his father had given to the police. That's all he *could* hope. But he didn't. Hoping was pointless. Like the man said, wish in one hand and shit in the other, see which fills up first. He knew that someway, somehow, the Ringleader and his cronies had slipped through the cracks in security, just like they had the first time, and were currently on course for New York. Manhattan, to be precise.

For the first time this week he was truly afraid. The last few days he'd been busy putting out fires, dealing with the smaller issues that had plagued him the first time around. This was different. He could feel the cold hand of death upon his shoulder. Every time he closed his eyes, even to blink, he saw the flashing pink neon of his dream: *Time Can Not Save You.* All week he'd spent making plans, and

GHOSTS OF SEPTEMBER

keeping, or at least trying to keep the appointments he'd made. Now he was afraid to even think of planning anything, for fear of jinxing the impossible chance he had of a future.

He stepped into his clothes and bolted for the front door. He snatched the handle and yanked the door open, and then he stopped dead. He stood a couple of feet outside Andy's front door and looked up. He tilted his head downward to take in the street around him. It seemed like the last of many cruel jokes, that this morning, a day that would be remembered by anyone old enough to live through it, was the most beautiful that he could remember.

For that split second, he wasn't a man out of time. Not some anachronism fighting the impossible fight to stop the tide of terror drawing in. For that second, he got to experience that morning not as somebody with advanced warning of nightmares immeasurable, but as a human being. An ordinary citizen. A New Yorker. The black smudges of cloud which had dominated the sky yesterday had vanished, leaving a hopeful, clear blue. The smell of the rain excited his nostrils, and in that one second the sound of birds singing had the crystal clarity of a bell.

Then, as quickly as it had come, it was gone. The crushing weight of expectation and doom pressed down on him again, and once again, he feared for his life. But now there was no thought of quitting. This morning he would go toe-to-toe with an opponent undefeated. Nobody beats time. He glanced at his watch. The only way to reach the

Towers now was to drive.

He glanced up and down the sun-drenched street, cars lined either side all the way along. He marched down the street looking for one model in particular. A Toyota Camry. This was one of the easiest to steal. The easiest to hot wire into life. He'd done it once before with Pete.

I'll see you soon, brother.

Now it was time to do it again.

8:16AM

The scooter trundled along the streets of Hell's Kitchen. 9th Avenue lit in bright, early morning sunshine. Soon he'd switch over to 7th, that would get him to where he was going. Today he felt better about things. Why not? It was a beautiful day. Last night's storm had really cleared the air. He loved New York City on days like this. The cloudless sky made him feel like he was being given a clean slate. A fresh start. Draw a line under yesterday and move on. The fire escapes here reminded him of the Led Zeppelin *Physical Graffiti* album cover (even though that building was in Greenwich Village) and he loved the way the sun projected them against the buildings. The storm had brought a freshness to the air that had smiles on faces, and at the crossing on West 50th street a girl smiled at him. Beautiful. Slim, blonde. Going wherever she was going without a care in the world, taking his mind with her, even if it was just for a few seconds. It wasn't just his feeling.

Yesterday was a nightmare. Ray had almost cost him

his job. He'd taken his phone; he was pretty sure he'd fucked around with the radio alarm (God knows why). And because shitty luck came in threes, some piece of shit had slashed his tires. The way it seemed Ray had been fucking with him, the crazy idea entered his head that it was Ray who'd slashed his tires! Today shone an entirely different light on the matter.

Whatever Ray had done he was sure he'd had good reason to do so. He'd visit his place later, pick up his cell, and they'd no doubt have a good laugh about it. Ray did crazy shit sometimes after he'd been drinking. Christ knew he'd been acting fucking weird all week.

Credit to Tony, he'd taken it all pretty well, all things considered. Maybe he hadn't kicked his ass to the curb because they were fucking way short of numbers. Maybe he was feeling generous. Manny smiled. Tony did the usual: five minutes of screaming until he was hoarse, telling everyone in earshot what a worthless bastard you were, then after saying that the driver in question couldn't be trusted, he'd give him "one last try" to redeem himself by working extra hours. That was it. He even let the driver choose when the extra hours were going to be. He barked loud, but his bite was more of a friendly nibble.

Whenever Manny got extra hours, he always took them ASAP. Some of the others, like Ray, put it off for as long as possible. Manny didn't see the point. He liked to get it over with. So as usual, he'd taken his hit first thing, and because fortune favors the brave, he'd got lucky.

Not everyone thought so. There were two things most of the other guys hated. One was going to the top floors of buildings, because it wasted too much time. Manny loved the views and the different perspectives you got on the world's most famous skyline. The other thing they hated was Manhattan. Because at any time of day, even on a bike, it put more minutes on the clock. Manny fucking loved Manhattan. To him Manhattan *was* New York. And more than that, there was one address in Manhattan that he placed above all the others; *that* was his slice of good fortune - that was where he was heading right now. To the top of the North Tower of the World Trade Center.

8:28AM

Ray raced along the empty streets of uptown Manhattan; eyes glued to the road save for the cursory glance at the dashboard clock. He was heading for Greenwich Street, it was going to be tight, but if he gunned it, he could reach the towers before disaster. His plan was a simple one: to set off the fire alarm. Perhaps it would be enough to clear the floors above the strike zone. After the plane hits nobody would need convincing that exiting the building was a good idea, it would be hard to find somebody who'd want to stay in the tower.

He glanced again at the clock. He hoped to God that the tip-off of trouble on the flight had set off a chain reaction that currently had the skies above the US in a state of lockdown. He hoped that one arrest had led to another until

GHOSTS OF SEPTEMBER

every single flight was grounded for safety's sake. There would be complaints from the passengers, there always were. The story they'd receive from the flight attendants would be a cover, probably a baffling one at that - something that would serve only to infuriate them further. If only they knew. He leaned forward in his seat glancing up into that now infamous clear blue morning, a sky that offered hope, rather than veiling the nightmare it yielded in reality. There were no planes that he could see, but that would only be coincidence.

He was about fifteen blocks from the towers, which grew from the roofs up ahead. Only now they didn't look strong, impervious, immovable. They had a look of fragility. Of knowing. Like a tree that felt the vibrations of a nearby chainsaw. As if they were alive and had been forewarned of disaster.

Ray was on Greenwich Street when suddenly, from somewhere behind, the sound of screaming sirens rose. Ray glanced instinctively down at his feet, eyeing the specks of broken glass that glistened in the foot well like diamonds. He sped up. The window he'd broken to steal this jalopy was totally out. The cops couldn't see if it had been broken or was just rolled down. Besides, it was too late now to stop. They could chase him all the way to the towers. When that plane struck, they'd have different priorities pretty fucking quickly. There they could help. He'd lead them there like some Pied Piper from a fairy tale, only this time, they in turn would lead others to their safety.

MARC W SHAKO

The sirens screamed ever louder. Ray glanced in his mirrors, and his eyes fixed on the NYPD car trailing him along a street that would soon be filled with horrified civilians fleeing disaster like extras in a monster movie. His mind toyed with excuses he could use to delay them until tragedy inevitably struck. Then, as he was watching the police car in his mirror, it turned, hard and left, disappearing down some nondescript side street. The wailing shrank away and pulsed more slowly. Ray afforded himself a little smile and turned back to the road.

What happened next came in slow motion, like his brain wanted him to save this memory for posterity. As his feet jammed down on the brake and clutch, he pushed himself back into his seat and felt the blood draining from his face and it tingled, bracing itself for the incoming impact. The rider of the motorcycle in front reached out a pitiful arm, as if to stop the onrush of crushing metallic death. There was a low screaming; the wail of tires on asphalt slowed to a crawl. The hood made contact with the bike forcing it from beneath the rider and the rider himself up onto and then over the windshield, smashing it into a spider-web as he went.

Ray screamed as time reverted itself to its breathless full pace. The car slid to a stop as Ray grimaced into the mirror, just in time to see the driver thud onto the asphalt and sickly bounce before coming to a stop. The stench of burnt rubber filled his nostrils and the engine hissed steam into the morning as New York City faded back in around him. His eyes turned to the mirror and there he saw the

GHOSTS OF SEPTEMBER

forlorn rider and his bike.

Only it wasn't a bike.

It was a scooter.

Ray had screamed not because he feared for his own safety, but for two different reasons. The first, as soon as he hit the courier and watched him bounce over the cracked windshield and onto the waiting city street, he knew he was as good as dead. The second reason, he knew that the motorcycle courier he'd struck was his best friend.

Ray sat motionless for what could have only been a few seconds, but it felt like hours. The hissing sound of leaking fluid onto the hot engine faded into cough-like spurts as his heart pounded against his ribcage, pleading for exit. He eyed Manny's broken body lying limp in the street behind him. It felt like a nightmare, like watching a bad decision unravel before your eyes. The way his hand had arranged itself looked unreal; index finger curled as if frozen mid-beckoning. He wanted to get out, but just sat frozen, staring into his mirror. He wanted it to be someone else. Anybody. But he stared at the clothes. Recognized the uniform. The same as his own back at home. It could have been any of the guys, but for the gold ring on that curled index finger. That was Manny's. Passed along from his old man. He stared at the ring, at the curled finger, and it moved. He was sure of it. He leaped from the seat and ran on shaky legs to the side of his best friend.

He sank beside him. 'Manny. Manny say something.'

Manny's face was unharmed inside the protection of

the helmet, but there was a growing amount of blood. Ray could see no cuts on his face, as the horror dawned on him. There was no twitch. Only wishful thinking. He'd been spared for one day, only to have that one day be the lousiest day he could imagine. Ray felt hot tears streaming down his face.

'Ray?'

He looked up. Manny's eyes were open halfway, on heavy lids. He blinked slowly.

'Manny! Jesus, you scared the shit outta me. Don't try to move, I'm going to call an ambulance.' He scrambled for his phone.

Manny coughed and blood rolled slowly along his cheek. 'No.'

'I'm calling. Don't move.'

'What the fuck happened?' The words were stuttered, on jagged breaths.

'Manny. Listen to me.' He dialed 911 and hit call. 'Manny, I have to tell you.'

Manny shook his head. The movement was almost imperceptible. He coughed more blood. 'Ray, it's okay. It's okay. I'm glad you're here. My friend.'

Ray listened to Manny while the phone rang on endlessly into his ear. 'Come on, answer you son of a bitch!'

Ray looked up from his friend's shattered body and surveyed the streets. He'd never seen New York so empty.

'Somebody. Please anybody, help me.' His screams broke off into sobs.

'Ray, stop. It's okay. I'm glad you're here. You too

GHOSTS OF SEPTEMBER

Pete.'

'Pete?'

Ray dropped the phone. Manny had never met Pete. He'd only seen the photos of him and Ray together that took pride of place in Ray's apartment. But Ray looked around, expecting to see his dead brother standing right there, where Manny's glazed eyes were directed.

'No Manny, Pete's not here.'

Manny nodded, and squeezed Ray's hand. Ray had been so taken aback by the moment he didn't even recall taking Manny's hand. Manny's eyes narrowed, as if struggling to concentrate.

'He's right there, Ray. He says...' Manny coughed again; this time thick ropes of red spilled down his cheek. 'He says...'

A car horn sounded in the distance drowning his words.

'What does he say? Manny?'

Manny smiled. His eyes moved from where he could see Ray's dead brother and fixed on Ray's face. Then the life in them faded.

'Oh, no. Manny no. I'm sorry Manny. I'm so sorry.'

The eyes came into focus. And then faded out.

A deep sob rose in his throat and he let it overtake him. New York City faded from around until there was just him and his friend. He felt a squeeze on his hand. He looked up to see Manny's mouth moving, whispering words into the ether. Ray moved his head closer to Manny's. His ear was as close as it could be, but there were no words. He leaned away and regarded Manny through his tears. He felt his friend's hand squeeze his own and for the briefest of moments, Manny's eyes came back into focus on Ray and he smiled. That Manny smile. Then it was gone. Manny was dead.

8:40AM

The New York morning faded back in around him. He kneeled on the floor beside Manny and was hit with a sense of shock. Not at what had happened; the odds were stacked against him and he was playing with loaded dice. No, the shock came from how he felt. What had just happened was no coincidence. It was a gift. From Old Man Time. One for the road. The first time this happened, and Manny was killed, he was overcome with guilt. Now he felt no guilt. Now he was certain that what had just happened was ordained. Plotted from the beginning. He'd been one step behind at all times. There had been no warnings. Nothing direct. This was cold. Underhanded. His fists had balled into solid masses of bone, his fingernails cutting into the flesh.

Now he was supposed to give in. To stop. You've been warned, son. These are the stakes. You can't win. Give up, go home.

He screamed again, planting his fists firmly onto the cool morning asphalt. He lifted a knee from the hard floor, then rose from the road. This was personal. It didn't matter to him now if he died. All that mattered now was getting to those towers. Even if he saved only one life. One in place of Manny. An eye for an eye. Even if he lost his own doing it. That was all he wanted. And God Himself couldn't stop him.

'Are you okay?'

'What happened?'

'Did you see who did it?'

He ignored the questions from the small crowd that had formed from nowhere around him and Manny and forced his way through back to the car.

'Hey, where are you going?'

He grabbed the handle of the driver's door and yanked it open.

'Hey, you can't drive that.'

The owner of the voice was an officious little man in a suit.

'That car was involved in—'

As far as Ray knew, because he would never truly remember the moment, the man never finished his sentence. That was as far as he got when, overhead, the screaming engines of a passenger plane roared past.

All heads in the street, Ray's included, angled upwards and followed the source of those sounds as they thundered overhead. Of course, Ray was the only one who knew the final destination of this plane travelling at impossible speeds. He knew what it meant, what it brought.

MARC W SHAKO

This plane cleaved the timeline of modern day into distinct parts. Before and after. Before the plane was hope. Life. Freedom. Trailing in its wake were shock. Mistrust. Death.

The true moment of epiphany had already taken place when control of American Airlines Flight 11 was wrested from the pilot and put into the hands of sadistic madmen. For most, the moment of epiphany would come later, when the second plane hit and what was seen as a nasty accident mutated into something infinitely more sinister. But for those watching in the street that morning, that plane was it. And at 8:45 in the morning on Tuesday, September 11, 2001, that plane sailed into the North Tower of the World Trade Center and exploded into an orange fireball which rose above the building itself. Nothing would ever be the same.

He stared as the bright orange fireball expanded against the clear blue and slowly darkened black. A plume of dark grey spilled upward into the sky as debris rained into the street below, and Ray heard faint gasps and screams seep into the reality behind him. He froze, feeling the same helplessness he did in his dreams. The numbness that subdued his anger. Shock working as anesthetic. His hand trembled on the cold metal of the door handle as he turned to the officious man whose face he would see when he dreamed of this moment, whenever he thought of Manny, whenever he recalled the moment that he decided to fight instead of give up. Already the New York morning was filling with sirens as he spoke.

GHOSTS OF SEPTEMBER

'I'm sorry. I have to go.'

In a split second the man stared at Ray's face, assessing the lines, the depth of thought in his eyes, and a dawning broke on his face. He took a step back, never breaking Ray's gaze, and just nodded. Ray nodded too, and as the wail of sirens swelled, he slid into the seat of the car he'd stolen what felt like a lifetime ago.

He turned the key in the ignition and the battered car coughed immediately to life. Ray imagined it not starting, but of course, Old Man Time didn't want him to miss the main event. He wanted Ray to experience the horror firsthand.

He squinted through the splintered glass of the windshield and floored the gas. In his peripheral vision it was difficult not to notice the dozens of people who'd gravitated into clumps, discussing the shock, exchanging the few details they had. Ray was surprised now that at the time, many thought this could be an accident. Hitting the tower instead of the open sky that encompassed it. Perhaps it was a sign of the times. Applying 2018 skepticism to a 2001 problem. Since then, we don't just fear the worst, we expect it. We seek it out. Even when the opposite seems so much more likely. A mirror to the past. The worst did happen. Nobody wanted to believe that it could have been deliberate. A horrible accident. Nothing more. Ray wasn't from that time. He knew the worst. He expected it. It was coming.

And he was going to fight it.

MARC W SHAKO
8:48AM

As he drew closer to the Trade Center, the papers that fluttered down from the cloud now surrounded him in increasing number, a ticker tape parade for the fallen. The sirens grew louder. Not just close, but in the brief moments of silence between the rise and fall of those nearby, he heard the distant, closing in from all quarters of the city. The roads were also filling. With emergency vehicles, with first responders, with office workers and employees, some of whom had just seen their offices blown into the clear blue. But it wasn't just the physical. As he got closer the sense of confusion, of shock, of panic, they grew too.

Ray got two blocks from what was no longer the World Trade Center, but Ground Zero, and pulled over to the sidewalk. Adrenalin had taken over. As he left the car, he barely felt the effects of the illness that had spared him this nightmare the first time around. He sprinted along Greenwich street against the flow of those wanting to put as much distance between themselves and this horror, or past those who wanted answers. Every fiber of his being knew he was running the wrong way. Every fiber of his being screamed at him to follow the crowds and run. Run as fast as he could in the opposite direction. For the first time in his life, Ray didn't listen.

8:50AM

Ray burst into the plaza, legs and lungs struggling to keep

GHOSTS OF SEPTEMBER

up with him, and he didn't recognize the scene awaiting him. The usual bustle had been replaced with static as papers continued to flutter and see-saw around him, the motionless crowds there staring up at the wounded North Tower as it bled black into the otherwise immaculate sky. Ray smelled burning and wondered if it was real or imagined. As he passed the clumps of people the sounds of crying and questioning rose and fell.

The North Tower belched dark smoke out continuously as Ray stared: coughed it out just as the emergency workers would breathe it in over the next days, weeks. A group of firefighters nearby also stared. Ray saw maybe twenty floors ablaze. The firefighters saw twenty acres of fire, ninety stories up. They were questioning logistics, how they could even get up there. Their frustration was palpable. Ray glanced at his watch. He had around an hour and a half until the North Tower was gone. Until both towers were gone. Anyone above that black gash in the side of the building was already dead. Anyone below was probably making his or her way downstairs. There was little he could do.

He switched his focus to the South Tower.

There were people upstairs in there who still had a chance. Ray still had a chance. He had maybe fifteen minutes. It was nothing. In the grand scheme, it was a blink. Yet it was all he had. He *had* to make it work.

Ray paused in the lobby, just for a second. An eerie calm had settled in, despite the alarm sounding, perhaps aided by the soothing female voice echoing from the PA:

'Building 2 is secure: Return to your office.'

Ray stood agog as a heavy-set security guard ushered those trying to leave back upstairs. The guard's size and appearance, bald head and beard, gave him a mean look, but still some remonstrated to different degrees, forcing their way past. With a wide area to manage and only his voice and arms to stop the crowd, to walk around him and out into the street to safety was easy, yet, to Ray's astonishment, most calmly followed his instruction; amazing what the sight of a uniform and the authority it represents can achieve.

Ray's eyes followed those turned away from safety, as if guided to do so. By who? *Charlie.* One short woman being led by a taller male colleague glanced back at her only means of escape. She was no different from anyone else here. Grey skirt suit. Glasses. Her bookish features clouded with confusion, and, as Ray watched, the most extraordinary thing happened. Her face changed. As if being lit by a faulty light fitting, it flickered. It flickered between two images, just as the faces had in his dream. In flashes her face was replaced by an X-ray image of itself and then back again. Ray shook his head, trying to shake reality back into it. It was no good.

Ray sprinted to the guard. 'Wait!'

The toe of his shoe caught the floor and stuck, he lost his footing and was heading to a railing designed to separate the elevators from the main part of the lobby. He threw out his arms to stop himself as he fell, instinctively shutting his eyes. He landed hard and scrambled back to his feet as quickly as possible, ignoring the pain in his right wrist.

Some of those around them stopped. Ray was facing the wrong direction to notice if the small woman was one of them.

'What the hell are you doing? These people need to get out of here!'

The guard frowned, pissed that Ray had challenged his authority. Ray saw a man doing his best to deal with a circus, and somewhere behind those eyes, was fear.

'Please calm down, sir. The last thing we need is a panic on our hands.'

'A panic? Did you see what fucking happened out there? A passenger plane hit that building.' Ray turned when he heard the gasps behind him. 'Everyone has to get out of here, right now!'

The people trudging back towards the lifts stopped, turned and started making their way back towards Ray. The soothing female voice again oozed from the PA system, telling everyone that this building was safe.

He turned to the guard, 'Is this message being played through the whole building?'

The guard was trying to stop the crowds, 'Please, everyone remain calm.'

'Hey! Is this message—'

'Yes!' The guard scowled at Ray.

'These people go back upstairs, they're dead. Turn it off.'

'What?'

The crowds were streaming past them now. Among them the short woman. She glanced back at Ray and looked as if she wanted to smile but didn't. She exited the building with the rest of the crowd.

'How do you turn it off?'

'You don't.' The guard finally stopped trying to talk around Ray and focused on him. 'Listen, when this place was bombed in ninety-three, people were crushed trying to get out. Not only that, they leave here, go out into the plaza and what? Get in the way of the firefighters.' His tone was short. He sighed and reset himself, calmer. 'Listen, we know what we're doing. Let us do it.'

'You can't send people back upstairs. You're going to kill them. Another plane is coming.'

'What?'

'A plane hit the other tower. A big one. Another plane is coming and it's coming here.'

The guard's mouth dropped open. 'You're sure?'

Ray nodded. 'In…' he glanced at his watch, his wrist aching as he turned it. The glass on the watch was cracked, it had broken. It stopped at nine minutes to nine. 'Shit. Please let them go.'

Without another word Ray turned and ran to the elevators.

The guard shouted after him. 'Where are you going?'

Ray shouted back without looking. 'To get them out.'

He jabbed at the elevator button repeatedly. He had no idea how long it was going to be before the next plane came rocketing into the belly of this building. Behind him there was a *ping*! as another elevator arrived.

He turned to see the guard standing before it. The doors slid open to reveal around fifty people who all began to pour from the car. The guard raised his arms to stop them. Again they stopped.

'Everyone listen to me...'

Ray felt his heartrate rise, thudding blood through his ears. This guy was going to turn them back. He was going to get them all killed.

The guard shouted. 'Listen! Everyone get out of the building and stay out of the plaza. Take the other exits to the street. Let the firefighters do their job.'

Ray felt a surge of relief. The elevator emptied and the guard held the door open for Ray. He gestured him inside with his head.

Ray shook his hand on the way past. 'Thank you.'

The guard nodded, 'No problem.'

Ray pressed the button for the Sky Lobby, as high as he could go, the guard stared as the door closed. Suddenly the guard's face flickered dull grey, shocked with bright white by the bones of his face. Ray grabbed the closing door and opened it again.

'Listen. That plane hits, this building is coming down. The other one too.'

The guard shook his head. 'Not this building, mister. They designed it to take a hit from a plane like that.'

'You gotta believe me. It's coming down. After that plane hits, you got forty-five minutes to get outta here.' Ray rounded down to allow for his addled memory.

'If another plane hits, I'll go.' The guard said, locking eyes with Ray.

Ray nodded. He let the doors close. As they did, the guard's face flickered.

8:55AM

The elevator car sailed unhindered to the Sky Lobby. There were a few loitering there waiting to go down. Chatting. Speculating. Laughing. Not realizing the magnitude of the situation. *Their* situation. Soon they would. Ray raced for the next set of elevators that would take him onward and upward. A young man in a blue suit was waiting for a car with a pretty woman. They too chatted, like this was any other day. Most days they'd be right. Not today.

Ray interrupted their conversation. 'What time is it?'

The man ignored Ray completely. The woman made a face of disgust.

Ray grabbed the man to face him and shouted, 'I said what's the fucking time.'

The woman yelped a half-scream, pitifully imagining that this was the worst thing that could happen to her today. The man was bigger than Ray, but the color drained from his face. He reached for his wrist and glanced at his watch.

'Five minutes to nine.'

'Fuck!' The elevators now worked against him. There were none here. They were all on their way up to the higher floors, on the way to save those above, or carrying others

GHOSTS OF SEPTEMBER

down, to their safety. To freedom. He let go of the man and headed for the plain grey door marked Stairway B. Halfway through, he stopped and looked back at them. 'Get the fuck out of here. There's another plane coming.'

They stared at him.

'I said GO!'

They nodded and called the lift as Ray let the door close behind him and bolted upstairs. He knew that the plane approaching would hit the tower somewhere around where he was in a few minutes. It left him time to check one floor. Maybe two. Anyone further above the strike zone was as good as dead. After that he could go down through the rest of the building clearing it out before moving on to Tower 1. If he didn't act fast, he'd be one of those stuck above the strike zone. He'd told himself that saving one in place of Manny would make it worthwhile. While he'd saved the small woman and the others in the lobby, it didn't feel anywhere near enough.

He reached the top of the stairs and grabbed the door handle. He pulled. Nothing. It was locked. He rattled it back and forth, the sounds of his struggle echoing in the empty stairwell, but nothing happened. He didn't have time to waste. He bolted and went up the next flight of stairs. At the top there was another plain door. Echoes fell down the stairwell as he pounded against it. There was no response. He'd come all this way for nothing. He thumped again, feeling that same helplessness from his nightmares. He couldn't wait. He'd have to go, or risk not being able to help those below the strike zone. That was the one thing he couldn't take. He felt the weight now of Manny's death. He banged a frustrated fist on the door, and it opened.

'Yeah?'

A man, about forty years old, handsome and confident was leaning through the door, the PA system blithely playing the safety message behind him. Suddenly, his face flickered that dull grey and bright white.

'Thank God there's someone here.'

The man's brow dropped. 'What's going on?' his voice sounded like a commercial announcer.

Ray pushed his way into the office.

'Hey! You can't come in here!'

He entered a plain looking office, desks, computers, filing cabinets. One just like any other here, on any floor. In the office, a group of six people peering up through the window or chatting. All older than this twenty-two-year-old version of him, his eyes were drawn to a woman, and a guy in a wheelchair. The guy in the chair's cherubic face flickered that broken X-ray grey and re-emerged from the cloud. Ray looked at him for a second longer than the guy was comfortable with. He broke his stare and turned to the handsome man behind him.

'What are you all still doing here?'

The guy raised a finger to the ceiling, attracting Ray's attention to the comforting safety message.

Building 2 is secure: Remain in your office.

He'd heard stories about sailors being killed by siren song. This was the closest he'd ever hear to one.

GHOSTS OF SEPTEMBER

'Where's everyone else?'

The guy in the wheelchair replied. 'They didn't get here yet. Or they left. Who are you?'

'You have to get out of here.' Ray said, trying to maintain his composure. 'All of you.'

'What's going on?' The woman asked over his shoulder.

Ray turned. 'You see what's going on out there?'

'My husband called, there was a bomb in Tower 1?'

Ray shook his head, 'Not a bomb. A plane. A hijacked passenger plane. And another plane is coming. It's heading right here. Right now.'

The woman put one hand over her mouth and laid the other on the desk beside her to steady herself.

'Bullshit!' The man said, walking around Ray to face him. 'You can't know that.'

Ray surveyed the faces of the others, the people he was charged with saving, each one flickering in time, as if there was a faulty fluorescent light overhead. He settled on the guy in the wheelchair.

He crouched beside him. 'What's your name?'

'What?'

'I'm Ray, what's your name?'

'It's Steve.'

'Listen to me, Steve. A hijacked plane crashed into the building next door. There are three more in the sky at the moment. If one of those planes hits this building below where we are now, we're stuck. Then we gotta choose burning to death or jumping out of one of the fucking windows. The others. They can stay. If we do survive and the elevators break down, they walk. They take the stairs. You don't. I'm going now. Will you come with me?'

Steve looked pale, clammy. He turned to the handsome guy, who Ray felt had somehow pressured them into staying put, though they were all old enough to have been around in '93, maybe they had bad memories from that day. 'Tom, Ray here is going downstairs. I'm going with him.'

Tom had been standing close enough to hear every word that Ray had said, they all had. The suave, confident facade had gone. He just nodded. Ray saw that the lined forehead had a thin layer of sweat. Tom was scared.

The woman shouted. 'Maybe we should all go.'

'We *should* all go,' Tom said.

Ray stood beside Steve. 'Can you lead us to the elevators, Steve?'

Steve set off without hesitation, 'Let's go.'

Ray and the others filed behind him, Tom last. They made it through the corridors and out into the elevator hall. Ray called the elevator and turned back. 'We all here?'

There were muttered responses and sideways glances and rudimentary headcounts. Ray studied the six of them. The woman had the look of a schoolteacher about her, someone the others might listen to, if it came to the crunch. Steve looked dead ahead, occasionally peering up at Tom from his position in the wheelchair. There was a black guy with a red tie clutching a big bottle of water, like most of the others, rings of sweat were forming under the arms of his grey shirt. Like the other two men, a thin man, and a shorter, overweight guy who was out of breath just moving to the elevators, he didn't say much. One thing was clear, they all looked up to Tom.

'What time is it, Tom?'

They had formed a line in the hallway, each covering a few elevators a piece and the shout came back from Tom, 'It's nine.'

Ray didn't want to ask if he'd set his watch correctly. Tom looked like the kind of guy who set his watch fast so he'd never be late for appointments, but he couldn't be sure. He didn't want to know if they had more or less time in reality than Tom's timepiece was letting on. All he wanted was an elevator to come down and get them out of here. What he did know was that the gaps in his memory had filled. A final gift from Old Man Time. Information that would only serve to add pressure. The official record stated that at two minutes past nine, less than twenty minutes after the first plane hit, Flight 175 would smash into the Sky Lobby. Which meant that if Tom's watch was correct, they had less than two minutes.

There was silence but for that soothing female voice that radiated from the PA system. Ray felt guilt and shame for his feelings of self-preservation. He knew that sometime in the next few minutes anyone on the floors above where they stood was dead. They would live out the final hour of their lives in fear, waiting for the smoke and flames to take them. That or choose to step into the void from a window.

The image of the man from his dream, the man on the bus - the falling man, popped into his head and he wondered if he'd already taken the decision.

'Ray!'

It was Steve's voice.

'The elevator.'

Ray ran along the hall to where Steve waited, all the way hoping that when the doors parted, the elevator would be full of people waiting to be carried to safety. He stood beside Steve and watched as the doors opened. When they slid back to reveal an empty car, Ray could have cried.

Ray held the door open and the others poured in. He got in last and let the doors close. The elevator would take them down two floors to the Sky Lobby where they'd switch for one that could carry them to the ground floor. To safety. All Ray could do was hope that they'd get there before screaming engines and metal and fire smashed through the side of the building, bringing Hell with it. Every few seconds, the flickering of the others' faces would come, and Ray knew they weren't safe.

'Time? Tom?'

'About a minute after you last asked.'

'What's the fucking time? This isn't a joke.'

Tom cleared his throat, and without a modicum of smugness said, 'It's nine oh one.'

The doors opened to the Sky Lobby and an old man in a dark suit was waiting to go up.

'Call the elevator down,' Ray shouted to the others. As they burst from their car hitting as many elevator buttons as

GHOSTS OF SEPTEMBER

they could, Ray grabbed the man. His face was one of comic shock.

'Where are you going?'

'To work. Take your hands off me.'

'You can't go up there, sir. Have you seen what's happened to the other building?'

'I haven't missed a day's work in twenty-seven years.'

The race to the ground floor was on. This guy was going up. He'd surely die. Their group were one elevator ride from safety, but the elevators were taking their sweet time.

He shouted to the others, 'You guys should take the stairs now, while you can. And go fast.'

'No.'

Ray turned.

It was Tom. 'I'm staying with Steve.'

'Me too' The woman agreed.

The others nodded. All the while their faces flickering.

Ray turned back and the old timer had got into the elevator car, the doors were sliding closed.

Ray grabbed at the doors and the man hit him with his briefcase. The doors slid closed, and Ray jabbed at the button, but could only watch as the elevator ascended. There was nothing he could do.

From behind him came a *ping!* and he scrambled across the Sky Lobby and towards the elevator car, the black guy holding the door. He glanced out of the windows placed between the solid steel beams and saw that papers were still fluttering past outside like giant confetti. And through them, off in the distance as he took in the view out towards Liberty Island, he thought he saw something else. He jumped into the elevator car and hoped he was wrong.

They set off for the ground floor, with the knowledge that these elevators covered around ten floors a second, and then Ray noticed that Steve was smiling. The woman too. Tom laughed. The others followed. Ray didn't. All he could think about was the old man who hadn't missed a day's work in twenty-seven years. Ray's heart was heavy that he couldn't save him and wondered who was waiting for him back home. Today, he wouldn't return.

Above the relieved laughter Ray was sure he heard it. It was impossible through all that steel and concrete, but he was sure all the same. The high-pitched roar of two Rolls-Royce engines pushed beyond the absolute limits of their capabilities. The Rolls-Royce engines of United Airlines Flight 175.

9:02AM

The laughter inside the elevator car stopped as quickly as it had started. The sound of rolling thunder passed into the building and it swayed like a fighter rocked by a body blow. The elevator car jerked to a stop as the building swayed towards the Hudson River and amid the screams and cries of terror, Ray thought it might not stop. The image of the entire tower falling like a felled tree flashed into Ray's mind, as the lights inside the elevator car flickered. And as they did, the dull grey and bright white flashed onto the faces of

GHOSTS OF SEPTEMBER

those in the car. Just as it seemed the tower wouldn't recover from the blow, it righted itself and leaned back into place. The smell of burned aviation fuel filled the car; Ray heard nothing now but a high-pitched whistling that drowned the screams that silently fell from the mouths of those with him. Those trapped with him.

All he'd wanted was to be able to help clear the building. Now that was gone. He'd sit in this elevator car, and watch as slowly, minute by minute, it filled with acrid black smoke and they would die by degrees, and, if they were lucky, they'd do it before the South Tower gave way and crumbled into the streets below. Manny was gone, and perhaps he'd saved the ones who were heading back up to their offices in his place. Perhaps they'd have come back down anyway. Maybe they worked below the strike zone.

Ray stood, ringing ears muffling the voices of those around him, and tried to prize the doors of the elevator apart. Straining every sinew he screamed out with exertion and frustration. He heard muffled shouting behind him, then felt a tap on his shoulder.

He turned. It was Tom.

There was a resignation in his eyes where confidence lived a few minutes earlier. The transformation scared Ray. Through muffled hearing, he heard, 'The doors have restrictors. They'll never open. They need to be prized apart with a crowbar or something.'

He scanned the inside of the elevator car. The others sat crumpled in the corners. They'd all removed their suit jackets and sat in shirt sleeves. The small, out of shape guy rolled his sleeves up. The tall thin man looked impossibly gaunt now, and was trying to make a cell phone call, though his hearing must have been as shot as everyone else's. The strong looking black man drank from a large bottle of water and offered it to the others. The woman and Steve held hands. Out of all of them, Steve looked the calmest. He was comforting her, and Ray thought that out of all of them, if that were him, he'd be the most terrified. Even if they did get out of here, he was the only one who wouldn't be able to make it downstairs alone. The flickering light reflected in the chrome of his chair made it appear almost ethereal.

Ray approached Steve. He crouched before him. 'Steve. Can you hear me okay?'

Steve nodded. 'Just about.'

Ray paused, unsure of how to phrase his next statement, then just barked it out as plain as he could. 'I need your chair.'

'What?'

Ray said nothing and watched as Steve quickly worked out what he was getting at.

Steve nodded. 'Okay.'

Ray turned, 'Tom, gimme a hand here.'

He started to lift Steve from his chair; Tom quickly maneuvered around the other side to help. Steve threw his arms around their shoulders and they lifted. Steve was almost dead weight, easily two hundred pounds and Ray wondered what they would do if they ever got out of this elevator. The idea of leaving him behind so that he could save the others flashed in his mind and sickness welled in the pit of his stomach.

They sat him beside the woman, who was glazed over in shock, unable to process what was happening to them, and probably contemplating the same as everyone else in the elevator; the same as those trapped on the floors above the strike zones in both towers - that this could be the day she died. She and the others didn't know what he did. They thought death might come through smoke inhalation. They didn't know that in about one hour, they would be crushed in a mangled elevator car in the midst of a six-story pile of debris where Tower 2 once stood. Ray had to keep that to himself. Now they were frightened, but they were calm.

Ray looked at Steve again, 'I want to break your chair, to open the doors.'

Steve just nodded.

Tom spun around, 'What? That's not at all necessary. Let's just wait here for the firefighters, I'm sure they're on their way.'

'And if they're not?'

'What? Of course they're coming.'

Ray took a deep breath. 'Tom, listen. They probably are coming. They probably are. But we shouldn't wait. There's a lot of fire up there. All that fuel—'

Tom raised his voice, 'The fuel is gone. Burned up.'

'And it set about fifteen floors on fire when it did. They have a lot to deal with. I'm just saying if we can help ourselves, we should.'

The others sat around them, watching. Tom weighed the options. It wasn't long before his shoulders sank. 'You're right.'

'Good. Lady, what's your name?'

The woman looked up. 'Susan.'

'Susan can you try dialing 911? In fact anyone with a signal. Try 911. Tell them what's going on.'

He glanced at the LCD window over the elevator buttons, but it flashed random numbers, the wires fried inside.

'Did anyone see what floor we were on when...' he trailed off.

The out of shape guy said, 'It was below sixty, for sure.'

Others nodded their heads.

'Okay good. Between sixty and fifty. That's a start.' Ray turned to the black man who sat, one hand holding the top of his water bottle, 'What's your name?'

'It's James.'

'James you and me are the biggest guys in here, you wanna help me smash this chair up?'

'Sure.' He stood. Then glanced at Steve. 'Sorry, Steve.'

Steve shrugged and offered a forgiving smile. 'Don't worry, James.'

They stomped on the chrome frame of the chair for five minutes as the others tried to contact the outside world. The gaunt guy finally got a signal and got through to 911, only to hear a recorded message about call volume. He called his wife and asked her to keep trying emergency services. He passed his phone amongst the others so they could get word

GHOSTS OF SEPTEMBER

out to their families, asking each in turn to tell whoever they spoke to to call 911. Ray sensed that the seriousness of their situation hadn't fully dawned, but the creeping feeling that this was growing graver by the minute built within them.

Tom subbed in for Ray or James to help smash Steve's chair which was better put together than Ray had hoped.

'I'll get the cheaper model next time.' Steve said, wan smile touching the corners of his mouth.

The frame finally gave way and James worked a part of it back and forth until it snapped off. The end was ragged teeth that you could use to cut through wood, if you set your mind to it. James laid it on the floor and smashed his heel onto the end, flattening it into a wedge. He picked it up and offered it to Ray.

'Here.'

Ray took the slim end and rammed it into the thin gap between the doors. This felt good. He just hoped that when it opened, they'd see another set of doors and not a blank wall.

'What time is it?'

'It's ten after nine, not that it matters,' Tom replied.

Ray couldn't mention the ticking clock that hung over them and just nodded. He also wasn't sure if Tom's watch was right.

'Everyone have the same time?'

There were mutterings around, and Ray noticed now that his hearing had come back completely.

'I make it almost nine fifteen,' the pudgy guy said.

Ray's heart sank.

'Same,' said James.

Ray couldn't worry about it now.

'Okay guys, when this opens, grab a door a piece and pull.'

Tom and James silently moved into position and Ray worked the broken chrome into the gap. Tom and James hooked their fingers into the space and pulled. Ray turned and grabbed the smaller front wheels of the chair which had come loose, ready to stuff them into place to hold the doors open. Tom and James groaned with the effort and the doors moved.

'Help us!' Ray shouted, dropping the wheels and grabbing Tom's door. The pudgy guy moved fast, aiding James. He must have been strong too because that door slid back easily. Ray and Tom held their door and Susan was ready with the wheel to jam it open. She did and they all stood back. The front wheels held, and the doors stayed in position. Everyone's gaze shifted between the others in the elevator, and the blank stone wall which now faced them.

Ray had been proud of his ingenuity. He wasn't usually an ideas man. Pete was also blessed with the brains in the family. He'd got them this far, this *close* to escape, and failed. Old Man Time never gave up. He was relentless. Everything Ray had tried this past week; he'd had an answer for. He was being toyed with. He'd always turned his back on challenges. Now he was rushing into them headlong - with the exact same results. The lights in the elevator flickered again, and when they did, Ray once more saw the Xrayed outlines of the other's faces.

'Why did you bring me here?!'

The others backed away, shocked.

'What's the fucking point?'

He slammed both fists against the concrete and bowed his head. He felt the tears coming and did nothing to fight it this time. But from his misery, he heard something.

'Do that again.'

Ray heard James but wasn't sure who he was talking to. He didn't care. He'd been the punchline to an elaborate joke for the past week. He didn't want to talk to anyone.

'Ray. Do that again.'

Ray looked up and felt the tired redness of his eyes as he did. He stared blankly. James placed a large hand on Ray's chest and gently ushered him away. He stood facing the wall, where Ray was standing a moment before, then he turned to Ray.

'Listen.'

He raised his fists over his head as Ray had done and brought them both down on the wall. Where there should have been a slap, came an empty boom. Short, but there all the same.

Tom smiled. 'Sheet rock?'

James nodded. 'It's plaster board. That's all.'

There was relieved laughter around the car.

Ray gestured to Susan, 'Pass me the water.'

She handed him the bottle and he poured a small patch that expanded slowly outward. 'Hand me that,' he said pointing to the stick of chrome from Steve's chair. The gaunt guy handed the cold metal to Ray, and he started to scrape.

9:22AM

Tendrils of smoke snaked around the ceiling of the elevator car as Ray and James scraped at the wet patch of plaster board using parts of Steve's smashed wheelchair. There was a crater in the wall now, not so deep, about the size of an orange, though through the smoke it was hard to tell. About five minutes ago the lights had flickered then finally gone out, and the car was now lit only by dim emergency lighting. The darkness hadn't stopped Ray seeing the X-rays which spelled doom for him and the people he was trapped with.

The gaunt guy had reclaimed his cell phone "To preserve the battery". Not that it mattered. All the cell networks had gone down at some point. That was the last time he spoke, and it was more than the surprisingly strong pudgy guy had said since they'd been in here.

Ray knew the Fire Department were here. They'd had to split themselves between the two buildings in the past half hour, but they were here. Climbing up, bringing relief to those lucky enough to set eyes on them. Climbing up, when they should have been climbing down. Past the point where they would safely be able to get back down in time to save themselves. Any attempt at extinguishing the fires was futile. They were too high. Too big. Ray threw another glance at James's wristwatch as he scraped the crater into the sheet rock.

Susan sat closest to Steve, but the conversation was thin - questions of "Do you think they're coming?" or "Do they even know we're here?" met in the affirmative and followed by silence. The flickering X-ray faces told Ray otherwise. He could still see it happening in his peripheral vision every couple of minutes or so, in spite of actively trying not to. Tom switched in for Ray and he sat for a breather next to Steve.

Susan leaned forward around Steve and looked at Ray. 'I don't mean to sound ungrateful, but I have to ask...'

Ray turned his head to look and gestured that he was listening with a raise of his eyebrows, before quickly looking away. He didn't need to see what her bone structure looked like again.

'How did you know?'

Ray was taken aback. He'd been so busy trying to plan their escape that he hadn't had time to think of a story. An excuse. At the wall, Tom and James had stopped scraping. The two silent members of their company had also turned to look.

'How could you know?' asked Tom, his tone accusatory.

How the fuck was he supposed to answer that? I had a dream? He'd have to do better than that. They demanded better. They *deserved* better.

'Nobody knew,' Tom said. 'The building didn't know.

They were sending us back to our desks.'

'He *saved* us, Tom.' Susan said.

'Maybe he helped set this thing up. And now he feels guilty.' Tom was looming above him.

The air in the car was thick and warm and doing nothing to improve anyone's mood. Ray still had no answers, and his silence could easily be mistaken for guilt. He also didn't want to look up and see the X-ray nightmare he'd been actively avoiding for the past ten minutes.

'Say something,' Tom shouted.

The stout guy finally spoke. 'Does it matter?'

Tom turned on him, 'Of course it matters, Greg! Jesus Christ.'

'He saved us!'

'Maybe it was him trying to kill us!'

'It wasn't like that,' Ray said, barely speaking above a murmur. He glanced at James's watch again. They didn't have time for this. 'I can't explain. I just… I just knew.'

'How? How did you just know?'

'Leave it, Tom.' James now.

Tom was in no mood to "leave" anything. 'And what's going on with the time?'

The question hung there. Ray had stopped asking, not wanting to alert the others to its importance.

'Ray? You kept asking what time it was. Before the plane hit. Like you knew *when* it was going to happen. Then we got stuck in here. And we're in here. Stuck. So the time doesn't matter anymore, but you asked anyway. And I keep seeing you looking at James's watch, so I know it's still important. What the hell is going on here?'

'I know what's happening because I've seen it before.'

'Like in a dream?' Greg asked.

Tom turned and gave him a shitty look for interrupting.

'No. Like I lived it before. Like the worst déjà vu you ever had. I saw this happen, and it was the worst thing, and it changed everything that came after it. And people fought over it. Friends. Families. Because it was too horrible to just accept. And wars were fought because of it. And people died. Thousands of people. People who had fucking nothing to do with it.' The car was silent, rapt. The tears had come again. Tom didn't look angry anymore. He looked scared. They all did. 'And more people are going to die because of it. Today. This ain't over.'

Steve looked at him, and for the first time today, he looked frightened. 'What do you mean, it's not finished?'

As Ray answered, he tried to look at everyone in the car with him. They all had to get the message. 'No-one is coming to save us. You have to understand. If we don't get out of here, ourselves, we're dead.'

Tom looked at him and looked like he wanted to say something. James tapped him on the shoulder.

'Let's get to work. I just want to get the fuck out of here.'

Without waiting for a response he turned and carried on scraping at the wall. Tom stared a second longer, before turning back to the job at hand.

Ray bowed his head. He just wanted to help. It looked

like he'd failed. Kat didn't hate him, but he'd never see her again. He was relieved they'd spoken and set things straight. That was something he supposed. Pop and him had cleared the air. That was a long time coming. You let something fester like they had and pretty soon, it's too late to operate. Gangrene sets in and that's that. But Manny was dead. That was the one thing he'd wanted to fix and couldn't. He began to cry and felt Steve's hand on his shoulder. He peered up to see Steve's smashed wheelchair, and the thickening smoke clinging to the ceiling. Maybe that's what that whole dream had been after all.

'Faster…'

It was James.

'Come on…' Tom replied.

'Yes. We're through!' James said, voice touched by laughter. The depth and warmth in it reminded him of Charlie.

Ray looked up to see a hole in the wall the size of a grapefruit. James pushed Tom aside and lay on his back. He drew his knees back to his chin and kicked hard. He planted both feet against the wall, and it shook, a long crack snaking from the hole. He drew his feet back again. This time a chunk of plaster board the size of a sheet of paper, like those that spilled from the gash in the buildings outside, fell into the space the other side and a gust of cool air flooded in.

'Yes!' The gaunt man shouted as a burst of clapping and cheering rose and lingered for a moment before falling away.

'Fresh air.' Tom said and drew in a deep breath.

GHOSTS OF SEPTEMBER

James laughed, 'Not quite.'

Ray leaned to see what was on the other side and laughed himself. They all did. They were peering into the bright white of a men's room.

'We're out of here.'

James looked back at Ray, smiling. As he did, his face flickered.

9:31AM

James climbed into the coolness of the men's room and went straight for the faucets.

'Off,' he reported.

Tom was next through. They pulled Steve through and waited for the others. Ray watched as each one embraced the others after climbing into the relative safety of the bathroom. Ray was last out.

Whichever floor they were on, the smoke had reached, here it clung to the ceiling as it had in the elevator, but there was much less of it. The group exchanged hugs, thinking they were home and hosed. Ray knew otherwise, and as Tom was hugging Susan, he glanced at Ray. His face changed. He saw that there was more to be done. He broke the hug and gestured at Steve. Ray and Tom bent and raised Steve up and propped him between them.

'Let's get out of here.'

They went out into the hallway and Ray noted the sign on the wall. Floor 56. The tall man spoke.

'It takes fifty minutes to get from the top to the bottom using the stairs.'

As he said it, he looked at Ray, trying to gauge his reaction to see if they had enough time. It was at least half an hour, plus they had to carry Steve. It wasn't enough. Then, among the flickering lights and smoke, someone shouted.

'Hey!'

A young firefighter jogged across to them from somewhere unseen.

He smiled. 'There *is* someone up here. I haven't seen anyone for fifteen minutes.'

The sight of the fresh-faced firefighter seemed to have a calming influence on the group.

'You hurt?' the firefighter asked Steve.

'Disabled,' Steve replied.

He pointed to an elevator at the end of the hall.

'I would never say this normally but the fire's all above here... That elevator... It still works. It's that or you'll have to take the stairs. Stairwell C.'

The others had seen Ray's face and were already moving to the elevator. James took Ray's place at Steve's side and led him away. Ray looked at the firefighter and wondered if he had any family. Kids. A wife. A brother.

'What about you?'

'I'm going up.'

'You shouldn't. You should come with us.'

The firefighter shook his head.

'Let's go, Ray!' Tom shouted from behind.

The firefighter shrugged. 'We can't go. Got a job to

GHOSTS OF SEPTEMBER

do.'

'We?'

'My crew. They're upstairs. Clearing the building. Not sure what we can do with the fires, but we'll try something.'

He gestured to the backpack of equipment he was carrying. Just looking at it Ray guessed it weighed a hundred pounds. Ray thought of the rest of this guy's crew. They were already dead. This guy had a chance.

'You're sure I can't convince you to come with us?'

He smiled. 'Can't leave my boys.'

As he did Ray saw the young face flicker and he quickly squeezed his eyes closed.

'Ray!'

Ray opened his eyes. 'Coming.'

He held out a hand for the young firefighter. He shook it. 'What's your name?'

'Joey.'

Ray smiled as genuinely as circumstance would allow. 'New York's finest. We're all proud of you guys.'

'Go. Take care.'

Ray nodded and turned to the elevator.

The doors closed behind Ray and the car descended in silence. The journey was short, but from the confines of the elevator they heard a huge explosion. It rang out and, in the car, glances were silently exchanged, eyes questioning: Is this it? The elevator shuddered, then stopped. Ray almost threw up at the thought of being trapped again. There was no time for a second escape. But as the sound of the explosion faded, the doors opened, and they were faced with the hallway of the forty-fourth floor. They had around twenty-five minutes. They might make this yet.

All seemed well. It was eerie, as if the chaos of the day wasn't happening at all, like it was some strange dream.

'Jesus. I've never seen it so quiet,' said Tom, propping Steve up between himself and James.

Nobody answered, they just nodded their heads as they left the car. Without a word they headed for Stairwell C. It was already crowded with those who ignored the message "stay at your desk". Ray was last in and felt the difference not just in the cold of the concrete, but in the mood of those attempting escape alongside him. As their shoes echoed in the stairwell there seemed to be an unspoken resolution amongst them all. That today wasn't going to end here for them. That they would do what New Yorkers always did. Get on with it. Fight for what was theirs, and God help anyone who tried to stop them.

'We'll take turns with Steve,' Ray said.

But nobody answered. To them it was clear. Obvious. They were going to get out of here as they came in – as a group, as one. Ray felt time pressing upon him, he glanced at his broken watch, but knew that even if it did work, knowing would do nothing to help him, or any of them for that matter. He thought about asking Tom but held his tongue and traipsed down towards escape with the others.

He saw that Tom was struggling with the dead weight of Steve, but he refused to complain. Ray waited until they reached the next landing and tapped Tom out. James looked

GHOSTS OF SEPTEMBER

as if he might have another flight or two in him, but no more. Steve weighed much less now than he expected. He seemed to weigh more upstairs, strange what urgency can do. That said, he doubted he could carry him much farther than James would. He'd almost forgotten about his illness. The fever had broken in the night. He supposed that's where the heat had come from in the dream, but the headaches had been with him all morning, though he'd noticed those only intermittently. Now he felt a chill despite his shirt clinging to him.

James swapped out, and two floors later, the gaunt guy took over from him, and that's how it was. Silent. Hoping. Willing themselves and one another to take that next step. They reached the twentieth floor and somewhere above another large explosion rang out, but nobody mentioned it. There were a few instinctive flinches, but nothing more. They carried on.

Ray caught a glimpse of Tom's watch. They had made good time. Ray guessed they had another fifteen minutes or so. That would have been fine, but he'd also noticed that they'd visibly slowed.

James asked to take an extended rest, and in that time they had only made it, four guys alternately carrying Steve in twos, down eight floors. Every part of him ached. Last time around he'd only had the energy to lie in bed and it amazed him at the resilience his body had shown. He felt a sadness at the proceeding years he'd wasted, feeling he could do nothing. He glanced at the floor number to see how close, or far away, they were. Twelve floors to go and nobody knew how much time they had. Ray could only remember that the South Tower had lasted around an hour before it lay in the streets below as debris and dust.

'What time is it?' he asked the others.

Tom replied. 'Nine forty-eight.'

There was a pause as people gathered breath.

'How long do we have?' Tom asked.

'Ten minutes. Maybe fifteen,' Ray replied.

There was another second of silence. Nobody wanted to look upstairs at the long trail of souls descending.

'Leave me.'

Everyone turned to Steve. It was the first thing he'd said since they'd left the men's room upstairs; Ray knew that he'd been thinking it ever since.

'No way, Steve,' Susan replied; her face drawn into the scowl that Ray imagined she scolded her kids with.

'Not a prayer, buddy.'

Everyone spoke except the gaunt guy whose name Ray couldn't remember. Ray knew his silence wasn't an indication of disinterest, instead Ray saw that he was ready to throw the towel in himself. If the others had all said they were okay with leaving Steve behind, he'd have volunteered to stay behind too.

James walked over to Steve, 'Let's go.'

He bent down, and with strength that Ray could only dream of, he raised Steve over his shoulder like a firefighter would. Like Pete used to do to him when they were screwing around in the yard together.

GHOSTS OF SEPTEMBER

Without a word James set off. The others followed in silence. But now they were faster, and Ray imagined that the gaunt guy had got a boost watching the show of strength. James carried Steve in that fireman's lift down to four almost as if he wasn't carrying anything. He reached another concrete landing and paused. Ray tapped his shoulder.

'Come on.'

He waved signaling he could take over. James just nodded. They transferred Steve over to Ray's shoulder, but this time Ray felt the weight. This was a more efficient way of carrying someone, but the walk down had taken a lot out of him.

Another explosion rocked the tower. This one close. By now the floor numbers were single digit.

'This thing's getting ready to come down,' Tom whispered, his tone flat.

They sped up and Ray counted the floors off as they went. They reached the bottom and Greg, the small guy, opened the door.

'Jesus wept,' Susan said in a low voice.

They stepped into the lobby. It was chaos itself. Unrecognizable to the one that Ray had left behind just over an hour ago. Large chunks of marble were missing from the walls and the thick windows that led to the street and the plaza were blown out. There were small numbers of people, mostly firefighters trying to coordinate rescues, marching through the lobby.

Ray knew there was no time to stand around, they had to get out of here, and fast. Suddenly, Ray heard a voice he recognized.

'Hey! You came back!'

It was the security guard.

Ray looked at him amid the shouts and squawks from walkie-talkies and explosions. 'You gotta get this guy to an ambulance. He can't walk.'

He nodded, taking Steve from him.

Ray turned to the others, 'Go with this guy. Susan, ride in the ambulance with Steve.'

She nodded; they all knew that the only chance for Steve to survive this was by ambulance.

'James, big guy.' They shook hands. 'When the guard gets Steve out, drag him the fuck away from here or he's dead.'

James nodded.

The group waved quick goodbyes, but Tom stopped. 'What about you?'

Ray watched over Tom's shoulder as the others ran to freedom. A part of him wanted to run too. Go with them and put as much distance between himself and this nightmare as possible. But he knew that was never going to happen; not now. In his mind, he'd always be here and all the distance in the world wouldn't change that. Besides, Charlie was right; if he left now, he wouldn't be able to live with it.

Tom unstrapped his watch. 'Here, take this.'

'Whoa, no I can't.'

'I've seen how you keep checking. Take it.' He put it

GHOSTS OF SEPTEMBER

on Ray's wrist beside his cracked watch. A thousand-dollar timepiece. He hugged him for a second.

'Thank you, Tom. Now get as far from here as you can. Run.'

'Are you sure?' Tom's eyes were filled with tears.

'I gotta go. Please, Tom. Get going.'

'Thank you, Ray.'

Tom nodded and turned, sprinting to catch the others. Ray turned too. To the North Tower.

9:57AM

The lobby in Tower 1 looked the same as in the South Tower. Dust, shattered glass and fallen marble strewn. Ray jogged towards the group of firefighters inspecting blueprints, trying all they could to figure a way out of this nightmare, when he heard a sound. A new sound. Something he hadn't heard before, and the expression on the face of the young firefighter told that it was new to him too. It was a loud bang, not an explosion, but rather the sound of a heavy impact. And then he remembered it wasn't a new sound. He'd heard it before, in his dream. The falling man on the bus. Ray couldn't get the image of Rocky Balboa using a side of beef as a punching bag out of his head. The sound the same but amplified a thousand times. As the knowledge of what he'd heard dawned on Ray, so it did the firefighter. Ray watched as a black cloud of horror crossed the young firefighter's face, and in his eyes, Ray saw the same notion pass into his mind.

This is madness. We shouldn't be here.

Then Ray's mind went to the most natural place it could. The jumper. The falling man from his dream. He had no way of knowing if it was the sound of the impact of the poor soul who'd stepped into the abyss or something else, but through the dust and the dirt and the chaos, his eyes saw something his mind couldn't believe.

It was the woman from his dream, filing from one of the stairwells. She moved in slow motion, that long mane of flowing hair golden, unmistakable. Ray held his breath, waiting for the man in horn-rimmed glasses to appear behind her, but he did not.

Ray was bounding up the short rise of stairs towards the bank of now defunct elevators that served only as a signpost to the stairwells. Towards the dozens of people filing out from the door marked "Stairwell B".

A burly firefighter grabbed Ray's arm, his grip strong, intense black eyes scrutinizing his face. The notion that this was going to be the longest day written in the lines on his forehead. The longest day if he got through it. Today had thrown up something that even New York City firefighters hadn't seen, and that was something that scared Ray anew.

'The hell are you going?'

'I have to speak to that woman.' Ray pointed to where the woman had been a moment ago.

Now there was nobody but grey and blue suits filing endlessly to the exit. He wondered now if he'd seen her at all. If it was just Old Charlie Manson fucking with him.

GHOSTS OF SEPTEMBER

That awful sound had triggered an illusion. His eyes searched desperately through the throngs of people, but she was gone.

'Hey!'

Ray turned back to the firefighter. 'Please, let go.'

'You shouldn't go back up there.'

Ray stared at the firefighter. Maybe he had seen the woman, maybe he hadn't. The chances of him getting out of here alive grew slimmer by the second, but he had to know. He had to try to find the man from his dream. The falling man. He had to know if he was alive.

'I have to,' Ray said. 'My friend. Please.'

The firefighter released the grip on Ray's arm. He gestured with his head. 'Go.'

Ray nodded and ran to the door marked "Stairwell B" and he prepared himself to climb.

9:59AM

Ray had reached as far up as the second floor when it started. Office workers filed past him, some bloodied, some marked, all sweating, all scared, but not one of them put themselves above the others. They were streaming silently down, down and out thinking the nightmare was over when, from the direction of the South Tower, an intense rumbling started. The noise grew louder by the second. Ray ran up more stairs, like an animal running to high ground, and some followed him. The noise swelled and echoed and the stairwell they were in suddenly seemed weaker: no longer impervious to harm, now vulnerable. Some screamed, thinking that the building above them was coming down. Ray smelled it before he felt it. The sound was deafening and a hot wind gushed into the stairwell, carrying with it dust and debris. Ray stared down as clouds of thick dust chased him up the stairs. Finally the rumbling stopped but that cloud came and came. Threatening. Surging.

He remembered the footage of the tsunami that would devastate Thailand and Indonesia in the coming years, and how the dirty water rose and kept rushing into a hotel lobby. Now he felt that same fear as the cloud enveloped him, hot and dry. Visibility dropped to zero and the air was filling with moans and cries and screams; the realization that the nightmare was not over. Ray knew better than anyone that it was only just beginning, that it would continue to unfold: minutes of new horror when the other planes crashed; hours of a rising body count; days of dashed hope as the tiny numbers of potential survivors dwindled; weeks upon weeks of clean up, waiting for the inferno in the footprints of the fallen giants to die down; months of frustrating inquests with little or nothing to dowse the rage or quench the thirst for vengeance; years of untold suffering as the War on Terror swept the Middle East and the brave first responders endured untold damage to their respiratory systems.

All thanks to you know who.

For minutes nobody moved and the cloud thinned out around Ray. The people around him looked as if they'd been at a volcanic eruption. Nearer the bottom of the stairs they were completely grey with dust. Dust that didn't just come from the South Tower, but everything that was in the tower too. The same toxic dust that was still killing people in 2018. The first responders who'd gone to Ground Zero that same day to do what they could to help their fellow citizens, breathing dust that would kill them slowly, over time.

'What the hell *was* that?' A voice shouted from below.

There were some murmurings until a voice came back. 'I think it was Tower 2.'

'It was Tower 2.' Ray confirmed; his voice low, not even sure if anyone heard him. He looked around him at the others and shouted. 'Everybody get the hell out of here and as far away from here as you can.'

His words were unnecessary, as he looked down and saw those fleeing the tower doing so with renewed energy, but still holding the decorum that had fascinated him before. Even when faced with what was now obvious death, nobody pushed. There was no panic. Urgency and encouragement was what Ray heard.

He glanced at the watch Tom had placed on his wrist less than ten minutes ago. If his memory was correct, he had just under a half hour to do this. Going up would be slower than coming down but coming down he'd have less energy. It didn't matter. His concern now was to find a needle in a haystack. To find a man who was likely in a different place entirely. If he were to find him, it probably meant finding a man who had already decided that choking on toxic black smoke was better than falling hundreds of feet to your death. He was seeking a man who in all probability was already dead. That was his job now. So, as hundreds trekked down the stairs of the stricken North Tower, Ray Madison went up.

10:14AM

The monotonous grey concrete and echo of his heavy steps were the only company he had now. Every now and then, the silence would be punctuated by an explosion somewhere overhead. Sometimes far away. Sometimes close. In the minutes since the South Tower had collapsed, and taken with it the iconic Manhattan skyline, Ray had fewer and fewer people for company. The train of survivors became a smattering. Now each cold, identical concrete floor provided him with a sense of déjà vu he hadn't felt since the beginning of the week.

Ray had stopped looking at the floor numbers. To do so was pointless. He'd even stopped checking Tom's watch. He figured that he was fast approaching the point of no return. He could turn back now, and he would have time to get out. Just. Then he'd be racing a hellish pyroclastic cloud to the nearest place that represented shelter. Just a couple of days ago that idea would have been enough to send him into a panic. The idea of continuing upstairs would have had him teetering on the verge of unconsciousness. But he didn't want to give up. He wanted to find the man from his dream, even though he was probably already dead. If he

GHOSTS OF SEPTEMBER

hadn't jumped already, he would be preparing to do so now. Sizing up the two equally awful options as the choking black smoke thickened around him. He'd have a bird's eye view on something nobody had seen for years. He'd be looking down on a New York City without one of the Twin Towers.

Ray recalled the footage shot right after the first collapse; that was the reality unfolding outside. The building had exploded into a fine powder, and that powder now covered most of lower Manhattan. Ash covered people - grey and disoriented, or in some kind of shocked jubilation at cheating death - would be staggering through a scene akin to the End of Days. And cheated death they had. The cars that surrounded where the South Tower once stood were mangled, burnt-out, twisted skeletons of vehicles. Those shells of vehicles and dust and never-ending flutter of papers made Manhattan look post-apocalyptic. Alien. Unreal.

Ray's legs were leaden. He about turned from his ascent and sat at the top of the flight of stairs he'd just conquered. His shirt clung to him with sweat. In some sort of sick irony, he no longer felt the effects of the virus that had gripped him in the past few days. He decided to look at the watch Tom had given him. Not to check the time; just because. Maybe to make himself feel connected to someone. Maybe to admire it. Despite the wilderness decade plus that followed this horror show, the time where he'd been glued to the couch in his apartment with only bourbon for company, he'd never felt so lonely as he did right now. This was his reward. He'd taken on Old Man Time, and this is what he'd got. In the end, this is what everyone got.

He wondered if Tom, James and the others had escaped the collapse. When he closed his eyes, he could see them running in slow motion into the Plaza, Steve raising a hand of farewell from his fireman's lift over the fat security guard's shoulder. Thinking back to their departure, the X-ray flash that had haunted him all morning was absent. That provided a little comfort.

He wondered if by some miracle his cell phone now had a signal. To hear his father's voice now, or Kat's voice, that would give him the closest thing he could ask for to comfort. Then he wouldn't feel he was dying alone. But of course it wasn't his phone. It was Manny's. Even if there was no signal, even if he was unable to speak to anyone, that would be all the connection he'd need. He reached to his pants pocket. Then the other. Then his shirt. Somewhere in the frantic morning he'd lost it.

He looked again at Tom's watch. It had survived without a scratch. The brown leather strap looked new, certainly newer than the watch itself. The silvery surface with gold Roman numerals was a classic, and Ray wondered if this was maybe some hand-me-down with some sentimental value. He undid the strap to see if the back was inscribed. He liked the weight of the watch in his hand as he turned it over. The back was plain, but for the maker's mark.

Ray started to cry. His sniffs echoed through the empty stairwell. Then he was aroused from his contemplation by a sound he'd grown used to the past fifteen minutes or so.

GHOSTS OF SEPTEMBER

Another sound masking itself behind his sniffling. From the staircase overhead, he heard the shuffling of feet.

'Hello?'

Ray jumped up and ran to the handrail. He craned his head up the floors above. A hand was gripping the handrail two floors up.

'Hello?' the man shouted in return.

When the face of the man leaned over, Ray almost fainted. On a morning where nothing made a damned bit of sense, this should have felt the same. But it didn't. Ray heard the man speed up as he himself bound up the stairs to meet the other survivor. And when he saw Ray, he should have been shocked too. But he wasn't. It was as if he'd been expecting to see Ray.

They laughed for a second and then hugged, again, briefly.

The man with the horn-rimmed glasses and cornflower blue tie who Ray had first seen in a dream held out a hand and smiled. 'Pete.'

Ray shook the hand. 'Ray. Pete is my brother's name.'

Pete looked down and Ray's eyes followed. The left leg of his pants was torn and the leg beneath was streaked with dried blood.

'Need a hand?' Ray asked.

Pete nodded. Ray glimpsed at his own right hand. He saw Tom's watch and checked the time. It would be close. Maybe they could make it. Maybe not. They'd try. He put the watch against his leg and fastened the brown leather strap. He turned it over to inspect it and as he did, he caught sight of his own reflection. Just in time to see it flicker grey and white.

10:25AM

With Ray clutching Pete to his side they were making good time. They had made it as far as the twentieth floor. Not quite good enough.

'It's gone isn't it?' Pete said in a flat tone. 'The South Tower.'

Ray nodded.

'This tower will probably collapse too.'

'I think so,' Ray answered.

They descended as quickly as Pete's leg would allow; even if Pete had been working with two healthy legs, their escape bid would still have ended in failure.

'What happened? To your leg?'

Pete didn't answer for a few seconds, and Ray thought the answer was a mystery even to him.

'I should have been freaked out to see you where I did, but I wasn't. To tell you the truth, I expected it. Sure there was a moment when I thought I wasn't going to see anyone. Building 2 went, and I figured it wouldn't be too long before the same thing happened here. That's when I started heading down.'

Another explosion reverberated through the stairwell from somewhere above as if to punctuate like a warning shot.

GHOSTS OF SEPTEMBER

They turned another corner and Ray thought how much Pete weighed like Steve when he carried him with James. Ray glanced at Pete's face. Frowning behind those glasses. Pete used a finger to poke them back up the bridge of his nose.

'It sounds crazy now, but...' he paused again. 'For the past two weeks, I've been having *dreams*. More like nightmares. Like I haven't had since I was a kid. I was up in the Windows, you know, the restaurant on the top floor. And I was there with my colleagues, we were supposed to have a breakfast meeting up there, and you were there.'

'Me?'

'Yup. I can't tell you how freaked out I was to run into you in the lobby on Friday.'

Friday. It was a lifetime ago.

'Anyway, we're in the Windows and we'd just be having breakfast, my colleagues and I, and you'd come in, and I didn't know you from Adam, and you were shouting crazily: "Get out, you have to get out." And I didn't listen. I'd call a waiter and have them throw you out. And you'd go then there was... an explosion. And that was it. That was when I'd wake up. But that's not the weirdest part...'

A shiver of cold slithered up his back. They'd got as far as twelve and Ray was scared at what Pete was going to say next. He thought about how much he'd like a beer right now.

'Ever since last Friday when we bumped into each other in the lobby...' he tailed off. 'Ever since last Friday, the dreams *stopped*. I didn't have a single one since. But when we bumped into each other in the lobby, something happened. I had a… *vision*.'

Ray glanced across at Pete. He was pasty, pallid.

'I know, it sounds nuts. I'm the most rational guy you'll ever meet. And if somebody else told me this I'd think they were ready for the crazy house. I saw the whole thing as if it were a movie. I saw what *caused* the explosion. We were discussing the next phase of the project, and behind Jack, he's the project manager, I saw this shape in the sky… and pretty quickly I knew what it was. It seemed so odd that a passenger plane would be so low. And I felt this, like pins and needles in my face, like the blood drained, and Jack asked me if I felt okay. And I just pointed, and the others, there's like twelve of us all in, they all look and a discussion starts at why he's flying so low and what he's doing there and all the while he's getting bigger and closer and Jack just says, "Oh Christ". He doesn't shout it or anything like that. He just says it like he heard the Yanks lost, you know? And then I see the front of the plane and it disappears below the line of the window and we hear the explosion, and next thing, there's this time jump and I'm outside. I'm falling. Falling, tumbling. Terrified. The wind's rushing past my ears, and I'm falling faster and faster and… And I look down and I see you. Just standing there. And just before I hit the ground, that's when I snap out of it.

Ray wanted to say that he'd seen Pete in a dream too, but kept it to himself, for now. He knew Pete had more to say.

GHOSTS OF SEPTEMBER

'That's *still* not the weirdest part. You ever go up there? The Windows on the World restaurant?'

'Never.'

Ray thought that it was odd, living in New York City for so long and not going up, but he guessed that it was more for the out-of-towners.

'Oh man. It's the best view of the city. Was the best. It's huge. Jack just calls, makes a breakfast reservation, they assign a table. It's never the same one twice. Well, maybe, but what I'm trying to say is where you sit is potluck. So this morning, I bump into a couple of guys in the lobby and we ride up together. And it's such a nice day out that I forget about the dreams and whatever the hell happened to me last Friday and we're talking about the storm last night. And... and we get into the place and the table booked for us is the one from the dream. The same one from the vision. And the meeting starts and that's when I notice that everyone is sitting in the same seats. *Exactly* the same seats. Have you ever had déjà vu?'

'Sure.' Ray answered simply.

'So I got déjà vu so bad I felt sick to my stomach. And I'm still not thinking about you or the dream, just this fuckin' déjà vu. Jack tells me I look awful. I made my excuses and left. I didn't take the elevator. Again, not because of the dream. I thought I was gonna vomit and it was too claustrophobic, so I took the stairs. I got down to 88, and that's when it happened. And my leg...'

He fell silent and stopped walking. Ray wanted to tell

him that they didn't have time to stop, that they were only eight floors from the bottom and that they should carry on, but he knew that even if they ran down now, they wouldn't have time to get out. He looked back at Pete and saw that he was sobbing. Ray placed a hand on his shoulder and Pete grabbed him into a hug.

'I didn't tell them. I didn't tell them, and I left them. I left them and I tried to call them after, and nobody answered. They're all dead. They're all dead and it's my fault.'

'How could you know?' Ray said. Unsure of what else to say, he repeated the same.

Ray had no idea how long they stood there. He felt that while Pete sobbed onto his shoulder, they might have got down four flights. Maybe less. Pete had got control of the sobs that had threatened to overcome him completely.

'Come on,' Ray said. 'Let's get moving.'

Pete nodded and they set off.

Ray knew first-hand what survivor's guilt felt like. He had to get this guy to think about something positive. There was no way they could get out but if Pete was going to die, Ray wasn't going to let it be with guilt weighing on his heart.

'I've had dreams too.'

'You have?' Pete sounded confused, but not surprised.

'Yeah. About you. About this.' He gestured up at the tower with his head, not sure if Pete was looking. 'Had a vision myself. When we bumped into each other in the lobby.'

'What happened?' Pete asked. 'In the vision.'

GHOSTS OF SEPTEMBER

'I bump into you. Like I did upstairs. And your knee's all messed up. And...'

Ray stopped. They were on six. Minutes from escape, yet just as close to death.

'Tell me, Ray. Please. What happened?'

'We're here and, we don't get out. The building. It collapses. And it's loud and it's scary. And we're still inside. But it's the strangest thing. We don't get out, but... we don't die. It's like a miracle. I don't know how it happens, but you save my life.'

Ray didn't know where it came from. A complete fabrication. He didn't feel a scrap of guilt for lying to Pete like that. Maybe he should have. But for the last few moments they were alive, Pete was unafraid. And when the inevitable came, he wouldn't be scared then either. Not as scared. He'd lied, but he'd given him hope. For that he felt no guilt.

They stepped down onto the fifth floor and Ray knew that the final few sands of time were slipping through the hourglass, stolen by Old Man Time. With his lie, Ray had given Pete something that he wouldn't be able to steal, and for that small victory, he was grateful.

'You married, Pete?'

'Yeah.' He smiled. 'Got a kid on the way too.'

'That's great.' A wave of nausea passed over him. Pete must have felt it, too.

'You okay?'

'Yeah, sure,' he smiled. 'Just tired. Boy or girl?'

They were almost at four.

'A boy.' He smiled again. 'Marie wants a girl.'

He wanted to say more, but as his foot planted on the step, the vision of a solitary grain of sand circling a smooth glass bowl appeared. It swirled beautifully around towards the bottom of the bowl almost like it was dancing. Ray noticed in the bottom of the bowl, there was a hole and the grain of sand neared it like a ball on a roulette wheel, round and round until it fell. When it did a huge explosion rang out that stopped him in his tracks. This explosion didn't just echo. It continued. Endlessly rumbling towards them, crushing concrete rushing towards them like a wave. Pulverizing, indefatigable, indiscriminate. Rushing down. The two men held each other, and Ray wanted to say something, but no words came.

The deafening rumble drew ever closer and darkness descended and through the noise and dust and panic and fear an image came to him. Nebulous, hazy. It was Pop, smiling. Proud.

Then it was gone.

And then there was silence.

Then there was nothing.

AFTERMATH

HE REMEMBERED A LOT. MORE than he had a right to. That thick smell of dust. The darkness. The odd feeling of no pain, like he was suspended in liquid. Then the feeling subsided and there was still no pain, but discomfort. His body was in an awkward position, and he could hear voices. Distant voices, and heavy machinery, and cutting tools. And there was a feeling of warmth from somewhere below. He only knew it was below by the tears that ran up his forehead when he cried. The sounds all came from above. He was alone. The voices belonged to other people, not Pete.

Time had no meaning here. It was hard to say if it was night or day. And then in the distance, through the sirens and shouting and noise of machinery he heard another sound: The sound of a dog barking. It echoed like the dog was in the cave from his desert dream *Time Can Not Save You*. The sound came again, and he didn't know if it was real, or a dream, or something else. All he knew was that he had to get the attention of that dog, but when he tried to speak, no words came. He wanted to scream with everything he had, but just like in his dreams, he was powerless. The harder he tried, the more difficult it became to make a noise.

He tried to open his eyes. That too, was too big a request. So he lay there in the darkness, suspended upside down, unable to do anything. All he could do was taste that dust. Dry and foul. Feel the texture in his mouth, like sand. That was all he could do. Taste the dust and hear. Hear the machinery. Hear the voices. Hear the sirens. Hear the dog as it got farther away. Then all of the sounds were farther away. Growing more and more quiet by the second. Then all he could hear was Tom's watch as the second hand ticked in a steady circle to mark the passage of time. And then, after a while, that faded too. Until there was nothing.

Slowly the sounds faded back. Not the same sounds. Different, but familiar. Cars going by somewhere outside. Then the color came back. Deep and red and bright. And the feeling that he was lying down. Horizontally, not suspended upside down in some bizarre pose. All of these things were familiar, but the feeling.

The deep red broke and bright light came in, harsh and unyielding, causing him to close his eyes once again. But the glimpse he'd got, however brief, was enough to know where he was. He recognized the lines, the angles, the shades. There was one thing he'd caught sight of, in the corner of his eye. He hoped that when he reopened his eyes, that it would be gone. But he knew that wasn't going to happen.

8:25AM

Ray opened his eyes to see what he'd glimpsed moments before. His old bedroom, not quite as it was. The lines were the same. The angles and corners as they had been, but it was different. Now it was bright as it had been in 2001. The décor and furniture had all been updated from the old. The object he'd seen but didn't want to acknowledge sat by his bed like some hungry vulture, but he still ignored it. He closed his eyes again. He wasn't ready to see it, to accept it.

At least now he knew where he was: more importantly, he knew *when* he was. That was a feeling he liked. No déjà vu, no foreboding. Just being.

WEDNESDAY, SEPTEMBER 12, 2018

MOST OF ALL HE KNEW it was time to look at (and accept) the one thing he could no longer avoid. He opened his eyes. To the left of his bed, exactly where he'd left it the night before, was a wheelchair. *His* wheelchair. Not like the one Steve used. It was a new model. Electric. With a heavy heart he peered down the bed at the empty space where his feet should be.

He surveyed his room, not surprised by the relative comfort in which he now lived (though *old* Ray would ask where the hell all the money came from). What did surprise him was how the past seventeen years all came back to him in a flood of memories. He remembered hearing the noise of Ground Zero.

The smell. That taste. Somewhere in his memory, amid the machine noise of cutting steel and the faint beep of reversing machinery, he remembered the barking of a dog, loud and urgent. And a voice talking to the dog *What have you found boy?* Then a series of voices *Is he alive?*, and tones of growing disbelief *He can't be*, then jubilation *He is! He's alive!*

If ever there was a noise that summed up humanity, that was it. That noise was something he'd never forget.

The rest came in snatches of memory, like a highlight reel. He remembered waking to find that it all hadn't been a dream. Being pulled from the rubble of the collapse in darkness. The sounds and smells of metalwork as workers cut what remained of the towers by glaring floodlight. The doctor telling him that it was a miracle that he'd survived. That in the crush of the collapse he'd been unfortunate to have his legs squeezed between two steel beams, and that by the time they found him, saving them was not an option. That the chance of blood poisoning was so great that it was his legs or his life. He recalled the moment the doctor told him – warned him – he'd still feel them from time to time. Sometimes pain. Sometimes itching. But that they were gone, and that he was sorry. He remembered feeling afraid and that it was all very real, and that Manny was dead. The sickening guilt and stinging tears as Tony came to the hospital and tearfully confirmed the news.

He remembered all of those things. He also remembered sitting in the wheelchair, *his* wheelchair, by the side of his father's grave as they lowered the coffin into the ground. He recalled the regret that they never had the time to reconcile before he died. His father died exactly as he had the first time. Three months to the day after the attacks,

GHOSTS OF SEPTEMBER

a stroke which hit while he was taking a bath. Topping up the water as it struck. By the time they found him he'd been dead for two days, the house floor covered in two inches of water.

One thing had changed. He remembered sitting in his wheelchair as Kat came to visit him. She said she would be leaving New York and heading for Minnesota because that's where her new fiancé was from. That they'd be marrying in the fall and that she wouldn't be coming to see him again. For her it was too painful. She'd started to see her boss from the restaurant, but they'd split when he became too controlling. He wanted her to give up on singing. Her new guy was a musician. He hoped that he'd had something to do with that. When he closed his eyes he could see as she walked away for the last time, not stopping to look back, head bowed, shoulders trembling. And he remembered that it was months before he washed the lipstick from the coffee cup that she'd drunk from that day. And that he'd cried while doing it.

Hard as he tried, he could barely remember any other life. Those drunk years he'd originally spent in the aftermath of the attacks were faint. Like a ghost. The years that the bottle had stolen were gone like they'd never existed. Every now and then, if he did come into contact with his old life, he'd get that strange feeling of déjà vu. He saw his old sponsor once, when they bumped into one another at the supermarket. They both apologized and went their separate ways, both touched by that odd feeling that they'd been there before. Neither man looked back.

With the grace of someone who'd been doing it for years, he deftly maneuvered himself into his chair and steered out into the hallway. He flicked the light switch, and the light came on straight away. As he entered the living room he was compelled to go to the window. The one that faced Manhattan. He pulled the curtain aside and looked at the jagged skyline.

Cutting from it, One World Trade Center. Standing tall, and alone, and Ray thought it was testament to New Yorkers' ability to carry on; to keep moving forward, whatever adversity they faced.

He heard a voice. The voice in the back of his mind that often called him and told him to drink. Now it was a whisper. He ignored it and went to the dresser. The same dresser from where, seventeen years before, he'd pulled the notepad. The folder. Now it wasn't cluttered. Now it was regimented. Organized.

Just as before he was looking at a folder. A folder and a small metal container. A square New York Yankees tin with flaking paint and a removable lid. The one that Pete had given him. Maybe Pete used it to hold his stash. Ray smiled to himself as he reached down and pulled them from the drawer. He placed them in his lap and wheeled over to the dining table.

He lifted the lid from the tin and there was a satisfying *whoop* of sucking air giving way as it popped open. He stared inside for a moment. There was no feeling of pride, no sorrow, no *anything* much to speak of. That wasn't true.

GHOSTS OF SEPTEMBER

There was a *little* pride. He shook the contents of the tin into his hand and then, one by one, he placed the colored discs onto the table in order.

The designs were all similar, a triangle set in the disc, and in the triangle the time you'd managed to not fall off the wagon and into the doghouse. There were seven white chips, representing one day sober, and of course representing the six times he'd fallen off the wagon. Four silvers to show one month without the booze. Three dark gold, showing 2 months. Two reds showing three months. Two yellows. Those were for six months. A hockey season. Two greens for nine months, and twelve blues for a year. He'd already reached a year when Kat visited him to say that she'd visit no more. That's when he'd had to start from scratch. He got a special one for ten years. And the last one was special, too. His favorite. It was black with a silver triangle, and in the silver triangle a black circle. In the circle were gold Roman numerals. An 'X' and two 'I's. When he was thinking he liked to play with that coin and roll it over the back of his knuckles like a magician. In that sense the coin had replaced the balding rabbit's foot he'd rub when he was thinking. Rolling the coin across his knuckles was a trick Manny used to do with a poker chip. It was one he now did on Friday nights at Andy's poker games.

He pulled the folder over the top of the coins and stared at the red ribbon carefully tied into a bow. This folder was the same style as the one from 2001, only that one was battered, the corners curled which had made it easier for him to set on fire. This folder was pristine. He pulled the ribbon. He lifted the front of the folder open to reveal the contents. Two small newspaper clippings, and a white envelope.

He carefully lifted the first of the two newspaper clippings, from the Wednesday evening paper, September twelfth, and read the headline:

Miracle survivors pulled from the wreckage

Seventeen hours after the collapse of the North Tower, it is reported that first responders with the aid of sniffer dogs found two men alive in what has become known as the 'pile'.

One of the survivors had to undergo a double leg amputation and is in a critical condition in an undisclosed hospital.

"It's incredible that we're finding anyone, really," said a New York City firefighter who wished to remain anonymous.

On the men surviving the collapse he said: "I think it has something to do with where they were in the buildings when they came down. [The first responders] have been sharing stories, to keep up morale, and the [survivors] we were able to speak to, except for one guy, were all somewhere around the fourth floor. Those above fell too far and those below... well."

This brings the reported total of survivors pulled from Ground Zero to ten. The search continues but the task is becoming more difficult and less fruitful by the minute.

GHOSTS OF SEPTEMBER

Ray set the article back down before picking up the other. Ray could tell from the font that this clipping was from a different newspaper, though he couldn't see which.

Mystery man saves group of office workers

The strange stories from that day continue to reach us, but this one is weirder than most. An anonymous source tells how he and a group of colleagues were saved from the South Tower of the World Trade Center last Tuesday by a man with **advanced knowledge** of the events.

The mystery man claimed to have **foreseen** the catastrophe in a dream. The source would only say that his office was **above** where the plane hit and that the man had convinced them to leave moments before disaster struck.

"It was spooky. None of us realized at the time, I don't think. We were too shaken at what was happening. But when I look back now, I get the chills."

Asked if he thought the man was in on the plans he replied, "Oh no. Not this man. He's a hero. I hope he'll get to see this somehow because we owe him our lives and I'd like to thank him."

When asked for a name for the mysterious hero, all our source would reveal is that he called himself 'Ray'.

Do you know Ray? Are you Ray? If you have any information that could lead to...

Ray wondered who it was that had given the interview. It didn't sound like James and he was certain it wasn't Tom. It could have been the short guy, Steve, or the tall guy whose name he never got. His money was on the tall guy. He set the article down and picked up the letter. It was slightly worn at the corners, like a much-loved book. He turned the envelope over and instantly recognized the handwriting. It was his own, written with all the carelessness of his younger self. It was the letter he'd written to himself at Andy's. He raised the flap and pulled out the letter. He was sad. A little.

He opened the letter to see more of the scruffy writing. A page long letter.

Dear Ray,

I'm writing this to you from Andy's place in the middle of the mother of all storms. It's Monday night, the tenth, and it's late. I should be in bed, I'm sick and I'm tired.

I need you to know something very important. I said something to Pop earlier, and I shouldn't have. I was angry, and now it's too soon to smooth it over. Time heals all wounds, but you need to apologize. I realize now that he didn't mean to make it so hard, all he wanted was what's best, but he just pushed too hard. I

GHOSTS OF SEPTEMBER

see that now.

Losing Pete hit him as hard as anyone, harder than me even. After his leg, he couldn't do a lot, and he was frustrated. And he lived through Pete. Pete was the all action hero. And when Pete died, a part of Pop died too. Just like part of me died. We all missed Pete.

Things with Kat are a mess, but they can be salvaged, I think. Maybe give her time, and just check how she's doing every now and then. All you can do is be there for her (and hope she feels strongly enough to give you (me. Whatever) a second chance)

The good news is Manny is alive! I managed to save him. I just hope it was the right thing. I mean, obviously, it WAS the right thing, but there are strange consequences to our actions.

Which is why I'm writing this letter. This week has pushed me more than I thought I could take. And every time I push back, like saving Manny, then it digs in and pushes back twice as hard. I feel like I'm pissing into a HURRICANE. My point is, things are going to go wrong at some point. I don't know how, but when they *do, they're gonna hit HARD. I'm just tired of taking shit. I did it my whole life and I can't do it no more. Just be ready is all I'm saying. And please, remember, whatever happens:*

IT'S NOT YOUR FAULT

That's all. If I'm right, chances are you'll never even see this, but if you do, just remember what I said. I'm sorry to put on you the shit for what I'm doing and what I'm about to do. For the first time it just feels wrong not to push back.

Be kind to yourself, Raymondo.

P.S. If you're still around in 2008 and you have some spare cash, (and if you can bring yourself to do it) put it ALL on the Giants to win the Superbowl. They won first time around, maybe we'll be lucky!

He had been able to bring himself to back the Giants and they had won. He saved five bucks a week until the start of the 2007 season and placed the whole seventeen hundred dollars on the New York Giants. He got odds of 30-1. He picked up just short of fifty-three grand.

All's fair in love and war.

He folded the letter and slipped it back into the

GHOSTS OF SEPTEMBER

envelope, before it got wet with tears. He put everything back in the folder, placed the coins back into the battered Yankees tin and placed it in his lap before he wheeled over to the drawer. He pulled it open and was surprised to see that he'd missed one item. He reached in and took out a watch with a brown leather strap. He turned it over in his hand, enjoying the weight, and saw the smashed face. The idea of getting it repaired entered his head again, and once more he banished the thought. It didn't have to work. He stared at the face, hands frozen at ten thirty on the eleventh of the month, and realized the ticking he'd heard from underneath the pile must have been all in his head.

Behind him, the door buzzer went off, buzzed again, then fell silent. He placed the watch, the folder and the tin into the drawer, slid it shut and maneuvered himself to the door. Just before he reached it, it buzzed long and angry.

He pressed the button for the intercom, 'Hello?'

'Come downstairs,' said the voice. Warm and throaty.

He wasn't expecting anyone, but that voice— without knowing why, Ray found himself saying, 'Okay.'

9:05AM

He grabbed his keys and went out into the hallway. The cold concrete and echoes the same. His brain imagined the flickering lights and thin smoke clinging to the ceiling, but he pushed the thought aside and rolled over to the elevator and hit the button. It arrived and he wheeled himself inside, stomach tightening oh-so-slightly as the doors drew together before him. He hit the button for the ground floor, his mind's eye seeing the smoke as he imagined it always would, and the elevator rattled downward.

He thought of Tom and Susan and James and the others. The short, stocky guy who looked out of shape but was strong, and the gaunt guy who said very little, but who Ray thought might be the kind to write to a tabloid newspaper, just because he found it difficult to share his thoughts verbally. He recalled the growing sense of panic as his arm-hair prickled, just like it always did, then he felt the relief of the cool air as James kicked the dry-wall through.

Then he was at the ground floor. And then he was outside in the fresh air and gentle warmth of the day. And that's when he saw it. A dark green car. *His* car. His 1991 Chevrolet Lumina Z34. And from his left he heard a familiar laugh. One he hadn't heard for about seventeen years. When he turned his head he smiled.

'Charlie?'

Charlie beamed his warm smile. 'Damn right. Like my new wheels?'

Ray laughed hard and loud. 'Yeah. I do. I really do.'

Charlie stood and walked over and held out a hand. Ray took it gladly. They shook hands and laughed for a minute non-stop. Ray noticed Charlie looked around sixty something years old. Like he hadn't aged a single day.

'Wanna ride?' Charlie cocked his head at an angle as he asked.

Ray laughed, 'You're *blind*, Charlie!'

GHOSTS OF SEPTEMBER

'Shhh! I won't tell nobody if you don't.'

They laughed again and went to the car without a word. Charlie helped Ray into the passenger seat and Ray was shocked at how strong he was. He closed Ray's door before taking the chair into the lobby of Ray's building. Ray was going to ask if the chair would be okay there, but he already knew the answer, and by the time Charlie opened his door, the problem of the wheelchair was already forgotten.

Charlie strapped himself in, looked at Ray with those milky eyes over the top of his dark sunglasses, and said, 'Ready?' with that smile of his.

Ray just laughed and Charlie fired the engine into life, and it sounded like new.

'Where are we going?' Ray asked.

'You'll see when we get there.' Charlie said before pulling out.

He drove quickly and carefully through the streets of Jersey. The day was mild; puffy clouds marked the blue skies, and he felt *good*.

'How long you been dry now?' Charlie asked.

'Twelve years, nine months and two days.'

'Nice.' Charlie smiled. 'You still go to the meetings?'

'I'm a sponsor now.'

Charlie grinned. 'My man.'

'And once a year I go to collect the coin, give my speech. It's a big help to the others. I know I wouldn't have gotten this far without that.'

Charlie was nodding, 'Good. Good.'

MARC W SHAKO

They travelled in silence for a few minutes, Ray watching New York pass by his windows. Charlie turned into the Holland Tunnel and they headed for Manhattan. His recollections of that day were in his mind, but they were somewhere in back, distant and faded. A new ghost of a memory in place of the others. They would always be there. Ray new it was important to acknowledge them, but not let them overtake him.

'I need you to do something for me,' Charlie said.

'Okay,' Ray said, not afraid of the favor, no matter how big.

'When are your meetings?'

'I usually go Thursdays.'

'Is there one tomorrow?'

'Sure. I mean, I guess...'

'So tomorrow I want you to go to the meeting.'

Ray nodded.

'I want you to go to the meeting, you don't have to speak, but there's someone I'd like you to meet. He's one of the sponsors. Small guy, kinda puny looking with these little hands. Bald. When you lay eyes on him, you'll know who I mean.'

'I think I know who you mean.'

'You bumped into him once at a supermarket, years ago.'

Ray shouted, '*That's* where I know him from.'

'You ever talk to him?' Charlie asked.

'Not really.'

'He ain't nothing to see, but I'd like you to talk to him.

GHOSTS OF SEPTEMBER

His name's Joel.' He paused for a smile. 'I think you'll become good friends.'

The fancy boutiques and cast-iron architecture of Soho passed by outside, tall and imposing. For a second, he got the rush like he used to. This place was alive, and he could feel it as they passed between the buildings. Ray looked at them and smiled, he felt right at home.

'Can you do that for me, Ray?'

Ray nodded. 'Sure.'

Ray wanted to ask how he knew all of this. He wanted to ask a lot of questions. Like who Charlie really was. But he didn't ask. He knew he'd get some cryptic half-answer and a smile.

The idea brought him no anger.

The rest of the journey passed in silence. Well over an hour, but never awkward. He spent most of the journey enjoying the scenery, whenever he did glance at Charlie, he had that contented little smile on his face. The ornate lofts and stores of NoHo changed for the New York University buildings of Kips Bay. They were entering the leafy suburbs of Long Island when Charlie finally spoke.

'Almost there.'

The houses were low, single story, with green lawns out front. The street was relatively empty, it being mid-morning of mid-week. One lawn had a middle-aged guy throwing a baseball with a kid in his late teens. Ray rolled the window down as they passed, and their laughter blew into the car and Ray smiled.

MARC W SHAKO

Four doors down, Charlie pulled to a stop.

'This is it?'

Charlie smiled. 'This is it.'

He got out of the car and took something from the trunk. He arrived alongside the door and Ray saw it was a collapsible wheelchair. Charlie deftly unfolded it to its pre-collapsed shape and opened Ray's door. The rich laughter from the father and son wafted along the street and again it made Ray feel good. Charlie helped Ray into the chair that looked a lot like the model Steve used, all those years ago.

Charlie interrupted his thoughts. 'Just before we do this, I know you've got some questions, so I'm gonna let you ask one.'

Ray looked up and grinned. 'Just one?'

Charlie smiled too. 'Just the one. So pick good.'

He knew he'd never get a straight answer to the question of who Charlie was, but then again, deep down, he thought he already knew the answer to that one. Charlie nodded gently, almost imperceptibly, then held out his arms, 'Well, is you gonna ask or is you ain't?'

Ray smiled, 'Gimme a minute.' Then he felt the smile fade a little, and Charlie's expression mirrored his own. 'I got one.'

Charlie nodded.

'I'm not going to see you again, am I?'

Charlie frowned, 'Damn, Ray, I said ask good.'

Ray shrugged.

'You already know the answer to that question, don't you?'

GHOSTS OF SEPTEMBER

Birds sang around them, and somewhere in the distance a dog barked, a big dog but friendly, something like a Labrador, and Ray knew without looking that it belonged to the father and son.

'I'm not going to see you again. Because I don't need you anymore.'

Charlie smiled a mouth full of perfect teeth and nodded. He held out his hand and Ray shook it.

'I'll always be with you, Ray. But you already knew that.'

'Goodbye, Charlie.'

'Goodbye, Raymondo.'

He strolled around the car and climbed in.

'Charlie! Wait!'

Charlie looked across and peered over the top of his glasses. Ray shouted through the open window.

'What the hell am I doing here?'

Charlie cocked his thumb over his shoulder back in the direction of the father and son playing in the garden. Ray swiveled his head down the street and saw that the family had indeed been joined by a big golden Labrador.

'Have a nice day, Ray. It's going to be a good one.'

Ray watched as Charlie disappeared down the street in his old car. The car turned the corner and out of sight and Ray waved all the while, but Charlie never looked back. He spun round in the direction of the laughter and wheeled himself along the street and as he got closer, the butterflies fluttered wildly in his stomach, and at first, he just sat there.

MARC W SHAKO

Sat looking at the man in the horn-rimmed glasses and thinking that he would never recognize him, so engrossed was he in the chat with his son. Eventually he did glance over and his eyes met Ray's. He stopped still. His son's talk tailed off into nothing.

'Dad?' he shouted, but the man just stared at Ray.

His mouth had dropped open. In the corner of his eye, Ray saw the kid turn. Ray smiled and the man's eyes filled with tears.

Finally the man said, 'Ray? Ray is it you?'

He'd already started across the lawn towards him before he'd finished. His eyes were full of tears, but he was grinning broadly. Ray held out a hand.

'Hey, Pete.'

Pete ignored the hand and gave him a hug. And Ray knew, just like Charlie said, it was going to be a good day.

The End

Thanks for reading!

Reviews are gold for authors!
If you enjoyed *Ghosts of September*, please rate and review at Amazon.com!

To stay abreast of the latest developments with future book releases, and my blog of all things unexplained, find me at the following:

My website:
www.marcwshako.com

My Facebook page:
www.facebook.com/marcwshako/

Follow me on Twitter at…
www.twitter.com/MarcWShako

THE DEATH OF LASZLO BREYER

MARC W. SHAKO

THE DEATH OF LASZLO BREYER

A JACK TALBOT THRILLER

A FULL MOON. AN EMPTY GRAVE.
A SERIAL KILLER HUNGRY FOR REVENGE...

"Pure spine-chilling brilliance from start to end!"

"One of those books that you pick up and cannot put down."

Former detective Jack Talbot stands accused. The grave of Laszlo Breyer, his dead wife's killer, has been robbed.

His former colleague would love nothing more than to pin the crime on Jack. And his alibi of being too drunk to remember is helping nobody.

Then a dead body turns up, with the dead killer's MO. Torn to pieces as if by a wild animal. All on the night of a full moon.

If Jack's not the killer, then he's surely on the copycat's hitlist. And he'll need all his cunning and determination as he treads the fine line between suspect and detective to catch the killer… before the next full moon.

"One of the most … gripping stories I've ever read." Isabel Fuentes Guerra, author of *The Island of the Dolls*.

THE DEATH OF LASZLO BREYER
A JACK TALBOT THRILLER
Available now at Amazon

THE WILDE DIARIES

A ROCK LEGEND, A OUIJA BOARD, A DEAL WITH THE DEVIL...

"A belter of a novel... a skilled weaving of the words"

"I couldn't stop until the last page."

Struggling writer Joel Brewer is spurred to investigate his friend's untimely suicide, but something more sinister is afoot. The only clue he has for help is a mysterious box...

His friend's fate is somehow tied to the mysterious death of rock star Lucas Wilde some 40 years earlier, who, according to legend, sold his soul for success. The answer to what really happened lies in the box in the form of Lucas Wilde's diaries.

Desperate for an answer to his writer's block, Lucas played with a Ouija board. From that point on, the rock star's dreams were haunted by the sinister presence of a dark shadowy figure many refer to as the "Hat Man". A man who could make all of Lucas Wilde's problems disappear with a simple handshake... well... for a price...

THE PRICE OF FAME IS HIGHER THAN YOU THINK

For more information visit:
www.marcwshako.com

SPECIAL THANKS

To Jojo, for your unswerving support.
Thank you for making everything worthwhile.

To Mum and Dad.
Your support means the world and more.

To Katie Smith, Isabel Fuentes Guerra, and special mention to Kayleigh Robertshaw and Forever Ewa. You've been a huge help with your feedback (and corrections!), thanks for everything!

And to YOU, dear reader. Thanks for buying this book! I hope you enjoyed it.

WWW.MARCWSHAKO.COM

ABOUT THE AUTHOR

MARC W. SHAKO is a horror/thriller novelist, screenwriter, and aficionado of all things paranormal, from Yorkshire, England. When not reading or writing about the undead, hauntings, modern-day wolf-men and UFOs, Marc can be found watching football, playing the guitar with various degrees of success, or engrossed in his latest addiction – binge-listening to podcasts.

WWW.MARCWSHAKO.COM

Printed in Great Britain
by Amazon